BEING
SOMEONE

BEING SOMEONE

a novel by Ann MacLeod

spinsters book company

SAN FRANCISCO

First edition.
10-9-8-7-6-5-4-3-2-1

Spinsters Book Company
P.O. Box 410687
San Francisco, CA 94141

This is a work of fiction. Any similarity to persons living or dead
is a coincidence.

Grateful acknowledgment is made to Alix Dobkin for permission
to use two lines from her song "View from Gay Head," from
Lavender Jane Loves Women (WWWA001), distributed by
Ladyslipper Music, Durham, North Carolina.

Cover art by Tanya Joyce
Cover and text design by Pamela Wilson Design Studio
Copy editing by Ann Morse
Production by: Jennifer Bennett   Linda Catalano
                 Aron Morgan   Linda Moschell
                 Pamela Ai Lin To   Jennifer Worley
Typeset by Joan Meyers in ITC Bookman

Printed in the U.S.A. on acid-free paper

Library of Congress Cataloging-in-Publication Data

MacLeod, Ann, 1940-
      Being someone : a novel / by Ann MacLeod. — 1st ed.
          p.   cm.
      ISBN 0-933216-86-6 : $9.95
      I. Title
PS3563.A31864B4   1991
813'.54—dc20
                                        91-21475
                                        CIP

Acknowledgments

My gratitude to the women who gave of their time and energy to help this book along: Mab Maher, Charlotte, Rosemary Warden, Maxine Gerber, and especially Nisa Donnelly for her generous editing of an earlier draft. Thanks to my mother and sister for their support and affection, and to Shirley Hecht and Philip Brooks for their wise counsel. Sherry Thomas was an excellent editor and Joan Meyers a fine production manager—they were a pleasure to work with. And my heartfelt thanks to my most enthusiastic and constant helpmate, Karen.

For Carol Sanders, my wise and witty feminist friend.

Ellen Harmon, the new fourth-grade school teacher, arrived in the New England town of Bowles in August 1974, not knowing a soul. The woman who rented her a room, Mrs. Banks, reported to her bridge club that her new guest had brought only a few possessions with her, was recently divorced from an insurance man in Buffalo, New York, and, although basically a bright, considerate girl, had a difficult, moody side. Certain men in town were not impressed by Ellen Harmon. She'd responded to their initial interested glances not with warmth or coyness but with stony looks. These unflinching stares, added to her height and flat-chestedness, canceled any attractiveness she might have had for them and they dismissed her as "a cold fish."

As for the fourth-graders, generally they liked her: she knew some riddles, had a big smile, dark fluffy hair, fair skin, and was "like a movie star." Still, now and then, when they were all talking at once and she looked wild, raising her hands to her head and pressing hard against her temples, they exchanged frightened glances: was she going to go crazy right before their eyes?

To Janey Kowalski, the town librarian, Ellen might as well have ridden into town on a plumed horse, she was that welcome. Here at last, Janey thought, was a smart, exciting, independent woman who seemed to be looking for something other than a man. Almost as soon as their eyes met, Janey felt attracted, but not before she'd had time to reel back to her girlhood. She remembered once on a trip out West with her mother and sisters when she'd looked out the car window and seen a face like Ellen's: a girl, twenty or so, turning from a mailbox, no letters in her hand, her eyes desperate. On that damp, cloudy day, Janey had been glad she and her family were going somewhere. She would have liked her mother to pick up that girl and take her to Hollywood or the place of her dreams.

Seeing those restless eyes above Ellen's animated smile, Janey had felt the same way: that she wanted to carry Ellen off and make her happy. It had been as certain a feeling as she'd had in her life. It was why, as the days passed and they became friends, she laughed appreciatively at all of Ellen's jokes, funny or not, and listened attentively to Ellen's feminist theories, full of words like "patriarchy," "misogyny," "macho pig," and "jerk."

"I'm on a flight from niceness," Ellen said one day as she sat beside Janey on the marble steps of the little library building, watching the maples in the front yard drop their red and orange leaves.

Janey smiled. She'd propped the door open so she could hear if either of her two regulars, bent over their newspapers, needed anything. "You came to the wrong place then," she told her new friend, taking in Ellen's delicate profile and the large, flaring turquoise skirt that drooped over the teacher's long, outstretched legs like the wings of an exotic bird. "We're all pretty nice here in Bowles."

"Too nice, if you ask me," Ellen said. "You're one of the nicest people I know. But don't tell me you honestly like smiling at everyone, being thoughtful and considerate, listening to every Tom, Dick, and Harry who wanders into the library spout off about his precious ideas!"

"I like listening to *you,*" Janey teased. To hear this long-legged, elegant, honey-voiced woman talk on about the new ideas of the women's movement, radical ideas like this questioning of niceness; to feel the excitement of these ideas and at the same time yearn to embrace Ellen, to kiss her long and deep, to drink her all up: her idealistic dreams, her words, her tongue, her small breasts that rose and fell as she talked, her urgent gaze—Janey melted with desire, her eyes alight, captivated.

Ellen bloomed under this fervent attention. In the middle of her monologue on the conditioning of the sexes, she switched topics suddenly, without knowing why. "Lesbianism is interesting, philosophically. It's the ultimate feminist act."

Janey blanched. She had had two important lesbian relationships in her thirty-six years but had never spoken the word aloud.

Ellen went on, "Back in Buffalo, women are actually 'learning' to be lesbians. They say it takes two years, starting from scratch."

Janey glanced around anxiously. No one was in sight, although at any minute someone might turn in from the street or, worse, appear suddenly out of the library door behind them.

"Keep your voice down," Janey warned.

Ellen chastised her friend, "There's nothing wrong with homosexuality. I—" She stopped. Up to now she'd thought of Janey as a pleasant, rounded, koala bear sort of friend who wore old-fashioned, lace-trimmed blouses and pleated skirts and was a potential convert to the feminist movement. The thought that Janey might be much further along the path of independence from men than Ellen was, that Janey herself might be a lesbian—Ellen was temporarily speechless. The woman beside her loomed suddenly larger, wiser, more mysterious, a powerful, shrouded figure coming up through a vault from the depths of the earth. This new Janey seemed to reverberate like a gong.

Ellen blushed. "Well, actually..." As she awkwardly resettled herself on the stone stoop, her hand touched Janey's. "Oh!" she cried, shocked by the current between them.

"So," Janey said, in an effort to get the conversation under control again, "it's possible that I'm *too* nice. Was that the point you were making?"

"I guess so." Now Ellen looked at her, Janey seemed to radiate some kind of direct sexual vibration. In fact, it was quite strong. And very agreeable. And hopeful somehow. She liked Janey enormously. Impulsively, Ellen leaned toward her friend, lowered her voice, blushed, and suggested, "Maybe we could go for a walk this—"

At that moment Don Miles, a large, jovial man who was the engineer at Public Works, came striding up the front path through the red-orange blaze of sugar maples. "Hello there, girls!" he boomed. "Aren't we both looking pretty today!"

Like a shot, Janey, without so much as a glance at Ellen, jumped up and asked charmingly in her husky voice, "Hello, Don. What can I do for you?"

Ellen, left hanging in mid-sentence, sat where she was, frowned, and snapped at him, "We're women, not girls."

"Yes, ma'am, little lady. If you say so." He chuckled and climbed the steps to join Janey. "I need to look at some of those water table figures again."

They disappeared inside. Ellen sat brooding, her elbows on her knees, her chin on her knuckles. She hardly felt the evening autumn chill descend; in fact she felt hot.

"Little lady..." she muttered. "What a pig." Again and again she saw Janey jumping up, smiling at the engineer, and trotting after him. "She's certainly no lesbian...! And I thought she was special," Ellen reproached herself. She felt embarrassed to have glorified Janey. "She is rather ordinary, can't really think for herself, like a child actually."

"What *am* I doing in this backward place?" she went on to wonder.

The door swung open and Janey stepped out. "Ellen, he's going to need me for a while," she said apologetically.

Ellen stood up. " 'Bye then."

"See you tomorrow?"

"Maybe not. I have some things to do."

"The day after, then? We'll plan that walk?"

"Actually," Ellen explained, "I have to think about whether I really want to stay on in Bowles." She spoke confidentially but coolly. "I took this job because it was the first decent thing that came up. But actually I'd be happier with something bigger."

"Bigger?" Janey let the door, which she'd been holding open, swing shut behind her. Her heart sank. She'd been upset at Ellen's rudeness to Don Miles and had been smiling hard at him to make up for it. Now she forgot all about him. Her hopes of a romance with Ellen, which had flooded up as she dug out water table charts and graphs, drained away. She saw now: Ellen had not meant anything intimate earlier—she'd just been thinking aloud. In truth she was like the wild bird she resembled, flitting here and

4

there, searching for something: something bigger than Bowles, someone bigger than Janey. "If that's what you want..." she managed to get out.

Ellen sighed. She felt very disappointed with Janey, who seemed at the moment so undefined and passive, so like an ordinary "little lady," that Ellen wanted nothing more to do with her.

All the way home Ellen felt troubled by the hurt she'd seen in Janey's eyes. "I can't help it if you're just an ordinary girl librarian," she told an imaginary Janey. When she reached the safety of her rented room, she tossed her class work aside and threw herself down on the bed to brood.

The organdy curtains at the windows seemed to sag, the little desk and hooked rugs were lost in the dimness. Her thoughts tumbled over one another. "Janey's your average small-town woman," she thought, "not worth very much. No, how *could* I think so coldly! Janey's really quite mature and wise to put up with me. It's me who's not worth very much."

She tossed on the quilted bedspread. It was hard, this business of respecting women after so many years of despising them. She remembered her first visit to the women's consciousness-raising group back in Buffalo. To the seven women there she'd described herself as "too tall," "too selfish," "too stupid," "too serious." She was "too competitive," "too jealous," "too sensitive." She was "neurotic" (her husband's analysis).

The other women had spoken of themselves. One was "too aggressive," one was "too dependent," one's nose was "too big," another was "too fat," another "too thin," one "thought too much," another "talked too much." At the end of an hour, the woman who "smoked too much," suggested they were all "too self-hating." They had laughed and felt a burst of energy; they swore they would not think so little of themselves again.

Every Wednesday night after that, Ellen had returned from the group with a little less for her husband, a little more for herself, until one night as they sat on the couch watching TV she'd interrupted the evening news to confront him: she wanted a divorce. "That damned pussy-power," he'd said in his hurt and anger. If she had doubted her decision before, that phrase cinched it.

5

Leaving him had changed some things: she made her own decisions now. Still, every night she went to sleep lonely, every morning she woke to a moment of panic. She longed for something, she was not sure what. She wanted most desperately to *be* someone, someone other than the dissatisfied, anxious person she was. She wanted to be someone who spent her days in profound discussion, not spelling bees and multiplication tables. She wanted to be the someone life had meant her to be, the someone the women's movement assured her she could be, given a chance.

Ellen felt a surge of hope and excitement. Yes, to be what she could be, to take her place as a real human being in the world, with a fitting amount of attention coming her way—how she yearned for that. She could almost sense it when her mind stood on tiptoe: a feeling of specialness, of being chosen.

For a moment this afternoon she'd thought Janey Kowalski shared that specialness. But no...Janey was ordinary. Ellen turned on the bed restlessly. Ordinary, she told herself. The worst fate in the world: *ordinary...*

She frowned. Ordinary or not, that moment when their hands had touched had verged on the exquisite. In the dimness of her room, she examined her hand. It was too dark to see much, but she imagined all its molecules on the move.

Ellen lay, staring at her hand. After another few minutes, she switched on the overhead light, went out into the hall, looked up Janey's number, and wrote it down in the notebook Mrs. Banks kept beside the phone. As she dialed, her face broke into a smile. "Hi, Janey? I was such a pill earlier. Can you see your way to forgive me?"

The next Sunday, a day that smelled sweetly, moldily, of autumn, the two women struggled up a small, winding mountain path, Janey's black and white cattle dog Ida crashing through the brush nearby, her nose to the ground. Sunlight streamed down through thin, white-trunked birches and delicate, dark green pines. Drops of water sparkled on the tips of pine needles. Partway up the mountain Janey stopped and turned to Ellen, who was panting from the unaccustomed effort of the climb. "Look, the colors on this tree trunk."

They gazed at the soft, snowy-white and black peelings of bark, the velvety, pink inner skin of the birch. "That tree's how I think of you, Ellen. Pale, and delicate, and strong."

Ellen struggled to catch her breath. She felt weak and hot, looking into Janey's serious, mysterious eyes. She wanted to touch Janey's plump lips, stroke her soft, pink cheek, but her usual courage deserted her. "I'm not strong," she said finally, her voice like a croak in the silence. "I can hardly make it up this hill."

"Want to rest?" Janey asked. She pulled her red sweater off over her head. Underneath she wore a thin white shirt open at the collar. Her throat was tanned and shining with sweat. Her breasts were large.

"No, no. I'm okay," Ellen said nervously. As they continued up, she remarked, "Mrs. Banks says you're engaged to a man in England. That's not true, is it?"

Janey laughed shortly. "Don't tell Mrs. Banks, but no, you're right, it's not true."

"I didn't think so."

Janey swung up the path, the daypack bulging with their lunch hanging from her shoulders. "It's easier if people think there's a man around somewhere," she explained, tripping on a root and catching herself.

"They leave you alone."

"Right." After a moment, Janey said suddenly, "I never liked men. In the sense of marrying one of them." Her decisive tone said something big was coming.

Ellen's heart beat faster. She wiped the sweat off her forehead with the back of her hand. "You were smart."

"Bert's okay, the man I work with," Janey went on. "But men being romantic always made me laugh. They were never addressing me. It was like they were talking to someone in a movie. Or a comic book."

"You never fell in love with a man."

"No." Janey hesitated, cleared her throat. "That 'ultimate feminist act' you were talking about the other day?"

"Yes?"

"Well, I've committed it. I've always been with girls."

"Janey!" Ellen exclaimed. "I'm so glad."

Janey rushed on up the path as if she hadn't heard. "No one else knows. I hope it doesn't offend you."

"Of course not." Ellen's heart raced. She stumbled, hurried after Janey. "It pleases me," she called, out-of-breath.

Janey turned questioningly. "But you're not...?"

Ellen blushed. "No, but..."

"Where's Ida? That dog! Ida!" Janey called unnecessarily. Ida was rustling nearby. Both women bent to pet the dog as she came rushing up. When their eyes met, Ellen saw her own excitement reflected in Janey's. Their hands touched in Ida's fur and pulled back tingling.

"It's not far now," Janey said. She too seemed breathless as she turned to lead the way.

"Deviled eggs...tomatoes...corn muffins...and look, a little port wine...and apple pie." Janey laid her offerings on a flat rock surrounded on three sides by juniper shrubs and blueberry bushes. From their spot, they could see a small valley rise to meet a nearby hill, rich with copper and gold and the watery orange of sugar maples, and beyond that, the clear blue horizon.

Ellen was keenly aware of the food, the sprigs of parsley on the deviled eggs, the crisp air, the cold rock beneath her. She was pleased by the view: the far horizon and the nearby glow of the hills. But mostly it was Janey who delighted her; something tremendously exciting about the line where Janey's thigh squeezed against her calf as she crouched over the food, so that once Ellen noticed that meeting of flesh against flesh, she could not take her eyes away.

Their hands brushed as Janey sat down next to her. They glanced at each other. There was something giving up about Janey's deep-set brown eyes now, as if she were delivering herself away. It was a wonderful look, very loving, and yet it was a terrible look, so expectant.

Ellen swallowed, wet her lips.

Janey moved toward her, their hot mouths touched, trembled against each other. Drenching pleasure. A hand gentle on Ellen's cheek, her neck.

Ellen kissed this woman longingly. She kissed a new life, a new hope. She kissed Janey, who was Janey, and she kissed every woman she'd ever known and loved without knowing it.

When Janey drew away finally, there were tears in both their eyes.

They sat holding hands, looking around in a dazed way. "I never could have imagined it would be so sweet." Ellen felt a dreamy peacefulness and comfort, sitting there on the cold rock.

"I never knew this spot could be so beautiful."

"And look at the food. Isn't it gorgeous!"

"Can I feed you some? Here, have a bite." Before Ellen's mouth Janey held a plump yellow muffin. Ellen took a large bite, felt the sweet corn-flavored cake dissolve in her mouth. From the corner of her eye she saw the dog sniffing the deviled eggs.

"Your dog..."

"Oh, Ida-Shmida, you bad beast." Janey laughed as she handed Ida an egg and then waved her away. "Don't you know this is a wonderful day?"

"A wonderful, wonderful day!" Ellen rejoiced.

Two nights later, Ellen, invited for dinner at Janey's, walked the ten pleasant, tree-lined blocks to her friend's house just after dark. She had debated what to bring and ended up carrying her briefcase full of school work, fresh underwear, and a toothbrush.

She had bathed carefully. Sitting in the Banks' claw-footed bathtub, the floor of the tub under her slightly gritty with age, her knees bent and pointed as she shaved her legs, her shoulders and chest chilly, she had felt gangly and knobby and unattractive. She imagined Janey disappointed. Ellen wished for plumper breasts, fatter calves, and rounder arms. "I never thought I could get so excited over simple skin and bones," her husband had once said. Even now, no matter how religiously she used the word "woman," Ellen secretly remained a "girl" in her mind because she lacked generous womanly parts.

Between narrow, dark green shutters, the old windows of Janey's small white house were lit up dimly through heavy shades. Near the front door moths flitted in the yellow light of the outside lamp. A honeysuckle vine—leafless now—climbed around the lamp and a tangle of dusky bittersweet hung heavily along the right side of the house. Framed in one window was Ida, who had wedged herself under a shade and stood looking out, her front paws on the windowsill. The dark air smelled of wood smoke.

Ellen paused, shifted her briefcase from one hand to another. Ida was eyeing her eagerly. Ellen took a deep breath and knocked at the door.

Inside, the house was warm and pleasant, although not exactly to Ellen's taste: there was a large maple cabinet whose doors must conceal a huge television and the two reclining chairs to either side of the fireplace looked clunky and crowded. Janey seemed uncomfortable and kept bumping into her own furniture. "Would you rather have macaroni and cheese, or spaghetti? Or a steak?" Janey asked. Ellen wondered if she had prepared all three.

"Spaghetti," Ellen chose and sat in the breakfast nook buttering garlic bread as Janey boiled pasta, the steam billowing up from the metal pot to the old wooden ceiling. During dinner, which they ate formally in the dining room, Ellen dropped orange spaghetti sauce down the front of her white blouse while Janey knocked the salad off the table.

"Why don't we just do it?" Ellen asked at one point as they sat looking awkwardly at each other.

Janey flushed. This wonderful teacher she'd been dreaming of had kissed her earlier in the evening, a hard, thrusting kiss that felt as if Ellen had sent a robot in her place while she herself sat in some corner a million miles away shaking with terror. There'd been no warm feeling at all in the kiss; Janey had felt repulsed. That this *it* that Ellen wanted to do might be more of the same was alarming. "Maybe not tonight," she suggested.

"Oh." Ellen slumped, felt ready to cry. "You don't want to. Is it because I'm too thin?"

"Oh, no," Janey protested. "It's nothing like that. It's because you seem so scared."

"I'm not scared," Ellen declared. "I just want to get it over with!"

She laughed and Janey smiled.

Janey told her, "It might start us off on the wrong foot."

"But we will start off sometime, won't we?"

"Of course we'll start off."

They sat in silence. Ellen pronounced gloomily, "I don't see when."

"It could happen anytime."

"But how?"

"Oh." Janey blushed. "I don't know. I suppose we'll be looking at each other sometime. You know."

Ellen ogled her, her lids lowered. "Like this?"

Janey laughed nervously. "No, not exactly."

Ellen sighed. Her face fell.

Janey reached across the table. Her fingers stroked Ellen's cheek softly, moved to trace the line of Ellen's chin, touch her neck.

Ellen grew still, her eyelids fluttered down; she became lost in the pleasure of Janey's tender touch.

After a moment, Janey's hand retreated.

Ellen opened her eyes. "Why did you stop?" she asked awkwardly.

Janey was smiling at her. "I just felt...well, I've learned it's better if, uh, you know..."

"What?"

"If it's more like a conversation," Janey blurted out. "You know, you touching me too."

"Oh, I'm not used to that," Ellen said. "I'm used to just lying there."

They smiled, laughed a little; suddenly they were almost drowsy with relief, as if they'd been pulled from a world of sharp, jagged corners into one of soft, round curves.

Ellen stood up, dragged her chair around the table to be closer to Janey. Her fingers reached up to touch Janey's lips, feel their fullness. They closed their eyes and, joined only at that delicate spot where Ellen's finger tips touched Janey's lips, soared away together into some dreamy, exquisite place.

An hour later, Ellen was wildly ecstatic. She lay on her back across Janey's mahogany bed. In their ardor, Janey had unbuttoned Ellen's blouse and eased her rust-colored skirt up around her waist. Her chest was heaving and her flushed hands were gripping folds of the thick, creamy bedspread. She had felt Janey's soft, full mouth kiss her lips, her neck, her whole body—her whole being—and then all her moist, hidden places. Janey's soft, insistent tongue stroked her so delicately, so gently, that she had clutched the bedspread tight in her fists and cried out in pleasure.

Janey, afraid a neighbor or passer-by might hear, reached awkwardly to the head of the bed and grabbed a pillow. This she tossed over Ellen's face. There was a strange, silent, questioning moment during which they both acted as if nothing had happened. Then Ellen shifted the pillow slightly so she could breathe and Janey devoted herself even more dedicatedly to her new lover's pleasure.

Whether it was the pillow or just the newness of it all, Ellen shortly gave up and pulled Janey to her.

"But I've never been so excited," she told Janey as they crawled between the clean sheets. "I just couldn't go over the edge. It's so perfectly just what I want. But I'm sorry. I don't know..."

"We're going to be fine," Janey assured her. "Just wait a few days, you'll see."

They shifted and rearranged themselves. Ellen's fingers brushed against Janey's bare thigh; a tickle of hair against her hand surprised her. Such a wealth of emotion and confused images that tickle generated in Ellen: her mother saying no, her little naked sister in the bath, her mother's bushy triangle, the final moment of a striptease she'd once seen in London, forgotten elements of her own sexual fantasies—breasts, thighs, buttocks. For a moment her feelings ran hot and cold. She felt Janey's breath on her neck, she saw Janey's unknown face and sniffed her own shocking, punk scent on Janey's cheeks. Who was this woman with the deep-set, hooded eyes, the plump, partly-open lips, the hot, red tongue, the fleshy, muscular legs and something rough and unknown about her? Ellen felt the beginnings of panic.

"I'm very happy just lying here." Janey's familiar voice reassured her. "I'm dead tired," Janey went on.

"I bet."

They smiled at each other. Janey's eyes were quiet and tender. "Really I am."

Ellen nodded, feeling better. After a minute, she moved her hand tentatively to Janey's breast, feeling the tip go taut as she touched it. Janey's flesh was deliciously soft and smooth. They lay almost still as Ellen stroked that wondrously soft circle of Janey's breast, closer and closer to the dark center. Janey's eyes closed and her breath came faster, but she didn't move.

Ellen swallowed. She felt weak and unsure. "I..." she began, but Janey brought a hand up to Ellen's lips, drew her finger along them.

"Just relax," Ellen told herself. To be so intimate and so ignorant at the same time. She wanted to squeeze Janey to her and bite her hard, but that didn't seem right. Her hand brushed lightly against Janey's nipple, which stiffened and melted and stiffened again. Ellen was losing her own excitement in worry over what to do when she felt Janey tremble under her hand.

"S'okay, Ellen," Janey muttered breathlessly and with that Ellen finally reached down with care over Janey's belly and, fumbling gently, not knowing what the future held for her, bravely left the world of convention and moved her hand between Janey's strong, trembling legs.

The next morning Ellen danced down Janey's narrow wood stairs like an awkward, impassioned ballerina while Janey followed, beaming and trying to keep Ida from tripping them both. As Janey cracked eggs for breakfast and Ellen scrubbed the tomato sauce out of her blouse, Janey suggested, "If anyone asks why you stayed over last night, why not say you're taking some medication that makes you sleepy?"

Ellen raised her eyebrows. "Best medication *I* ever took." They laughed. Through the old glass window, the green grass and yellow poplars were bright under a cloudy sky.

Janey went to the refrigerator, stood looking in. "Anyway, shall we use that excuse, 'some medication that makes you sleepy?' We should have our stories straight."

Ellen hesitated. "Why do we need a story?"

"In case anyone asks."

"No one I know will ask."

"Come on, Ellen. What about Mrs. Banks? And you never know who else'll be curious. This is a very small town."

Ellen was silent, holding her blouse under a trickle of hot water. She wore an old red flannel shirt of Janey's. The steam wafted up to her pink cheeks and dark, wavy hair.

"Ellen?" Janey persisted.

Ellen looked up at her in surprise. "You're really so worried about someone finding out?"

Janey tried to keep her voice calm. She no longer remembered why she'd opened the refrigerator and she closed it. "Is it hard for you to tell a fib? Do you want to think of another excuse?"

"It's not that. Why lie about it at all?"

"Well, we certainly can't tell the truth."

Ellen frowned and bent over her blouse again, scrubbing determinedly.

Janey leaned against the counter, steadying herself against a dawning suspicion. What if Ellen were to insist on freely discussing last night's "ultimate feminist act," as she'd called it? Janey's life in Bowles would be ruined.

"You're right, probably no one will ask," she persevered. "But just in case."

More silence.

"For my sake," Janey added desperately. The eggs sat untended in their blue bowl.

"Since you're so scared about it," Ellen answered, "I'll lie if it's necessary. But how about making it a headache?"

Janey gave a huge inner sigh of relief. "A headache's fine."

Over breakfast, they tried to repair their estrangement. Janey smiled widely but felt jittery. Ellen kept tapping her fork on the placemat nervously. Eventually, while clearing the table, they bumped into each other and this jostling and touching seemed to straighten them out. They laughed, they kissed, and something about kissing while still holding dirty dishes pleased them. They felt graceful and competent and themselves again.

Janey thought wildly, "I love her, whatever she does," and also, less wildly, "She'll just *have* to learn to be discreet."

Ellen thought, "I love her being so determined, even if she's wrong."

Janey dropped Ellen off near Bowles Grammar School at quarter to nine. Ellen did not try, as she wanted, to kiss Janey good-bye. Instead, they simply looked at each other, Ellen jumped out of the car, said brightly, "See you later," and Janey smiled and drove off. Ellen watched Janey's blue VW bug go tootling off under the dark, shadowy oaks. The sky was grey and cloudy, and yet there was a brightness everywhere, colored leaves on the ground, the warm damp scent of fall. Ellen hummed absently, "You've Brought a New Kind of Love to Me." She bent to pick up one extraordinarily beautiful yellow leaf; she would save it for Janey, give it to her that night. She spotted another, also exceptionally beautiful; she would take that, too. And a third...and a fourth. Every leaf, every stone, every blade of grass was beautiful today.

The school lay slightly below her: a low brick building with a sloping, grey shingle roof, large, unnaturally round shrubs to either side of its open doors, and a host of crisscrossing paths worn in the grass. To the left of the school, children shouted as they swarmed over the playground equipment; they swung and hung and flipped and slid. In the nearby woods, girls earnestly played "house," sweeping the earth with twigs, and behind the school, boys hit balls across a playing field. Normally the idea that in five minutes all these loud, physical little beings would be squirming into chairs would have made Ellen sigh at the amount of energy she must summon up, but today she smiled benevolently over the scene before she headed down toward the school. There were no shouts of "faggot," a common enough insult among the boys, to dampen her spirits. Her breasts, hips, thighs, belly—all her thin, flat parts—felt different this morning: bigger, lusher, and full of life. She felt she might burst out of her clothes, and as she passed two fellow teachers in the formal entryway of the school, she imagined her body reaching out and sliding smoothly across theirs.

Her classroom was large with tall windows down one wall, children's art down another. In response to the warning bell, the fourth grade charged in upon her.

"Okay, okay," she cried. "What's all this foolishness?" She had a warm, physical sense of them. She would have liked to reach out and pull their small, excited bodies to her.

The children could tell their tall, sometimes demanding teacher was in a good mood: she wasn't at all fussy about the multiplication tables. After they'd whizzed through them, she suggested they make collages for a while: most of them loved paste. She went from desk to desk as they called her, "Miz Harmon, Miz Harmon!" Amid the sharp smell of paste, the sawing of scissors, the buzz of their talk, she strode up and down the aisles happily.

During a lull, she went to the window, struggled with it, flung it open. The breeze ruffled her dark hair, her rust-colored skirt, the papers on her desk. Standing there with the coolness on her cheeks, she shivered with something between pleasure and fear. She reeled at the thought of Janey. Everything that was happening between them seemed suddenly swallowed up by a blinding light and at the same time so huge, so close, so definitely her own choice that she felt hardly big enough to contain it. She felt as if she might explode with the excitement and newness of it.

At recess, she hurried to the small, cramped teacher's lounge with its smell of coffee grounds and cigarette smoke. On the old maroon upholstered couch, a new friend, third-grade teacher Laurie Bachlund, alternately yawned and drank chicken bouillon from a china mug: she was trying to give up coffee. Her round, wide-mouthed face brightened as Ellen burst in.

"You look happy. What's up?" Laurie asked, her small eyes crinkling. She wore a crisply ironed blue and white dress with a wide, red patent leather belt and black flats. "Richard play hooky today?" Laurie had more than once remarked how glad she had been to pass this particular bad boy up to fourth.

"No, he's here." Although Ellen had rushed to see Laurie, she felt tongue-tied. She searched her mind for something to say, but all she could find was Janey and Janey had so impressed on Ellen her fears of discovery that it was impossible to mention her. "How's Bob?" she asked finally.

Laurie laughed. "I told you about his habit of leaving his clothes around for me to pick up? Last night I let him have it. 'When I married you,' I said, 'I thought we were two equal human beings getting together, not a master signing on a slave.' "

"Wow! Good for you. What'd he say?"

" 'Let 'em lie there. Who's asking you to pick 'em up?' I could kill that guy." Laurie chuckled, took a drink from her mug, made a face of distaste. "But what's a girl to do?"

Ellen volunteered, "Carl picked up his clothes all right, but he never would clean the john. He told me, 'A man doesn't really like to clean the john.' "

"And a girl does?" Laurie hooted. They laughed together. Ellen felt strange. She liked being Laurie's confidante, their conversation was as friendly and lively as usual. Still, to talk of men's underwear while Ellen was falling in love?

"You can't live with 'em and you can't live without 'em." Laurie ran a hand over her short, blond permanent, playing with a tight curl.

"Maybe you can," Ellen said.

Laurie laughed. "No way."

"But really," Ellen persisted.

"Well, if you're going to be serious, of course I know what you mean." Laurie put her mug down, crossed her legs and clasped her hands around her knee. "I admire you for living on your own. It's important for a girl—a woman—to learn to stand on her own two feet. But you'll see. You'll meet someone and fall in love again."

Ellen imagined taking hold of Laurie's small, plump hands and saying, "But I *am* falling in love, Laurie. With Janey Kowalski." She imagined Laurie regarding her with dark, heartfelt eyes, crying, "Oh, Ellen, how terrific," and, "When did you first realize you loved her?" and, "I've always thought Janey was one of the finest people I know." Or, better yet, "I've felt attracted to women too."

But no, Laurie was asking, "Why don't you come to the show tonight with Bob and me? It's that *Sound of Music.*"

"I'd like to," Ellen answered, "but I'm going over to Janey Kowalski's."

"Oh, Janey, yes, well..." Laurie's round face clouded and then brightened. "Bring her along!" she urged. "I'd like to get to know Janey better."

Ellen hesitated.

"Don't worry about Bob. The more women the better as far as he's concerned."

"Thanks anyway, but..."

Laurie regarded her with some concern. "Ellen, stop me if I'm putting my foot in my mouth, but..."

Ellen looked worriedly at her.

Laurie plunged on. "I know Janey's a nice girl. I'm sure she's warm-hearted and I know you're lonely. But don't do anything you'll regret later. There'll be a man that'll come along, a good man."

There was a silence while Ellen absorbed this statement. Her heart shriveled. "I don't want 'a good man,' " she finally said, her voice faint.

Laurie flinched as if she saw the enormous gulf that had opened between them. "Ellen, I'm sorry, I was only—you know me, always putting my foot in my big mouth."

Ellen didn't smile. She glanced at her watch, said, "I should check my mail," and left the lounge. Behind her the door closed with an abrupt click.

Her throat ached as she walked down the hall. "Ignorant woman," she muttered defiantly. "What does she know? Who is she to give me advice and such stupid advice. She'd never have the nerve to leave *her* husband. How could I have thought we had anything in common? How *could* I?"

Swallowing, trying to stay calm, she automatically checked her empty mail box in the front office and returned down the busy hall to her classroom, hardly aware of the children and teachers around her. Her dark hair flew out from her pale, upset face.

"Who are you to criticize Janey?" she accused Laurie in her mind. "She's worth a hundred of you. Talking behind her back—no wonder she has to lie to you."

She opened the top drawer of her desk and looked at the yellow leaves she'd saved for Janey. They seemed pathetic suddenly and she threw them in the wastebasket, then reached down, plucked them out again and pressed them to her heart.

The bell rang; recess was over. Ellen pulled herself together. All her lightheartedness was gone. The children, sensing she might snap at them, read aloud in rushed, earnest voices. They read about a family—father, mother, boy, and girl—who, while travelling through South America, learned about the climate, geography, and exports. Occasionally the two children of the story grew bored, but the father thought of some clever joke to interest them again. The mother never said a word.

Ellen stopped the reading halfway through. "Do you notice that this mother never talks?" she asked the class. "Are your mothers like this? What's wrong with this mother? What's wrong with this *book*?" and she snapped it shut.

The children were surprised. They shut their own books willingly and waited. Outside it had started to rain and the drops pattered against the windows.

"We'll do science," Ellen announced. "Take out your science books."

As the day wore on, her anger at Laurie cooled. After all, Laurie wasn't a mean person, she was probably as natural and kind a person as Janey. So what was happening? Why was Ellen, when she should be celebrating, instead entering this shadowy, whispery, angry, frightened world? What if, because of those terrible moments this morning, her camaraderie with Laurie was lost forever!

They did not see each other for the rest of the day, but as Ellen left the school that rainy afternoon, trying to keep a stack of fourth-grade essays on "My Favorite Animal," her lesson plan, and her yellow leaves from getting wet, she heard Laurie call behind her, "Good-bye Ellen. Have a good evening." Laurie was leaning out a window of her third-grade classroom, a newspaper over her head.

Ellen was touched. "You too," she called feelingly.

"See?" she told an imaginary Janey as she trudged past the clean white houses, dripping red trees, and wet lawns of the town. "Laurie's accepted it. It's okay, Janey." She felt lighter, happier suddenly. "It's going to be okay." Ellen turned her face up into the rain, feeling it wash over her eyes and cheeks, and trickle down her neck.

When she got home, drenched, Mrs. Banks fussed over her. "Where were you last night, dear? I worried so."

"I'm sorry. I should have called you. I stayed over at Janey Kowalski's." Ellen glanced at Mrs. Banks, who busied herself adjusting Ellen's wet skirt on the drying rack in the spotless kitchen. "I may be staying there quite often in the future, so you shouldn't worry if I'm not here."

There was a short pause and then Mrs. Banks said, in a more distant tone, "That's fine, dear. Now you run along and have a nice, hot bath."

"Okay. And thanks, Mrs. Banks."

As she padded upstairs, Ellen continued her conversation with an imaginary Janey. "See, Janey? She didn't need to know why I stayed over. There was no need at all to make an excuse. No need at all."

After dropping Ellen off at school that morning, Janey had driven straight home. By the time she arrived, she had already imagined her years with Ellen right through the moment when one of them died of old age and the other hovered over her deathbed. She cleaned up the house, tried in vain to nap, studied some seed and bulb catalogs, and at quarter to two crackled into her poncho and swung off through the rain for her afternoon shift at the library. She arrived with her hips swinging more than usual and strands of hair sprung from her ponytail floating around her quiet face; she was whistling "Night and Day."

Her co-worker Bert looked up from his desk. A man of seventy, he worked two afternoons a week as well as every other weekend. Five years ago, he had retired from his engineering job at a Chicago utility and returned to Bowles to take care of his younger sister Maude, who was dying of cancer. He treated Maude, in her irritable, painful state, with all the tenderness he had not shown her as a boy.

"Here, look at these, Bert," Janey said, laying the seed catalogs in front of him. "See what you think." They often talked gardens together.

He smoothed his ragged, wrinkled hand over the bulging tomato on the cover. "Janey, Maude's worse." His long, tanned, old-man's face looked tired.

She sat down, regarded him compassionately. "Oh, Bert, I'm so sorry."

"The pain's going down her side."

Janey sighed. "Is there anything I can do?"

"Could you work this weekend for me?"

She paused only a split second. In that second, dozens of plans she and Ellen had concocted were summarily canceled. "Of course."

"Thanks, Janey. I'll take a look at these catalogs."

"Good, yes." Janey began going through the stack of mail. She stared at the first piece, a mailing from Planned Parenthood, suggesting a library display on contraception. Bowles would never go for that. She tossed it away, picked up another, sat looking off into space. It had just occurred to her that Mrs. Banks, Ellen's landlady, had recently offered, in Bert's presence, to take care of Maude whenever she could; she was a retired R.N.

"Bert, what about Mrs. Banks?"

"Who's that?"

"You know, Mrs. Banks. On Oak Street. The nice, grey-haired woman who was in here the other day and offered to watch Maude when you weren't able."

Bert shook his head and bent over the catalog. "She couldn't lift Maude."

"She's a retired nurse. Maybe she knows how."

"No, I don't think so." He pointed out one of Janey's selections. "Why are you ordering the package? You could get three dozen daffodils and two dozen tulips for less."

"I don't know, Bert," she said, with a trace of irritation.

He looked at her in surprise.

"Well, change it then," she urged him. "Go ahead, change it."

"Right." He executed the change in his neat hand with an air of satisfaction while Janey attacked the mail again. Only her feet pressing the floor under the desk betrayed her dismay.

This, then, was Ellen and Janey's first day as lovers out in the world. When they described it to each other at five that night, they at first skipped over the unpleasant parts. "I missed you. I got hardly anything done," Janey whispered feelingly and Ellen, handing her the yellow leaves on the steps of the library, agreed, "I kept remembering last night and this morning. God knows whether those kids learned a thing today." This was exactly what each woman wanted to hear: that all day she had been alive not only in the troubling way of ordinary life but in the heart and mind of her lover. As they walked back to Janey's over the shining streets—it had stopped raining and the air was fresh with ozone—Janey took a stick and rescued the occasional earthworm stranded on the sidewalk. "There you go, boy." The women's shoulders touched occasionally and when their eyes met, their gaze held.

"I feel terrible about it but I have to work this weekend," Janey told Ellen. She had found a popular psychology book which had suggested this approach when you have to give someone bad news: let the other person know how much you hate to do it before you bop them on the head.

"Oh, Janey." Ellen's disappointment showed. "I was so looking forward to it."

"I know." They smiled at each other ruefully.

"I thought Bert worked this weekend," Ellen said.

"His sister's worse and he has to stay home with her."

"Couldn't he get someone else? Didn't you tell him you have plans?"

"Ellen, she's *dying!*"

They walked through the darkness in silence for a minute.

"But doesn't he know you have your own life? Does he think you're free to cover for him just any time?"

Janey felt angry for a moment and dropped the earthworm she'd been saving onto a nearby lawn. "Don't blame Bert."

Ellen's temper rose too. "Well, pardon me for breathing. Who should I blame? Not his dying sister surely, she can't help it. Should I blame you?"

"Don't blame anyone."

Ellen sighed. They walked along the glistening street. Rain drops plunked from the trees into someone's tin rain gutter.

"I so wish we could tell people about us," Ellen pleaded in a low voice. "Then I bet he wouldn't have asked you."

Upset, Janey grabbed Ellen's arm and stopped them right where they were on the sidewalk. "Do me a favor and don't talk that way," she urged.

A car turned onto the street, its headlights reaching toward them through the twilight. Janey dropped Ellen's arm and started walking again.

Ellen let out an exasperated noise. "You'd think we were criminals."

"If you haven't the sense to worry about yourself, worry about me." Janey hardly noticed the earthworms about her now. Her harsh whisper had a defensive, righteous tone to it. Ellen's talk about criminals, that was exactly how she was beginning to feel, as if Ellen were leading her into some police spotlight where they would both be summarily executed.

"You know, some people already know you're a lesbian and nothing terrible has happened," Ellen said suddenly.

"They do *not* know." Janey quickened her pace. "Will you be quiet!" she burst out.

"There's no need to be so upset, Janey." Ellen hurried alongside.

Janey's heart was pounding. She saw her garage ahead, its white paint flickering through the trees. She resisted the urge to break into a run.

"I'll make us a cup of tea, shall I?" Ellen asked.

"Yes, okay." Janey could not calm down. The word "lesbian" hung in the air. She felt the eyes of the neighbors upon her.

Here was the path, the stoop, the door. She pushed it open, crossed to the stairs. "I'll just go up a minute," she said, already climbing, gripping the banister tightly. "No, no," she reassured Ellen, who was saying something below.

In the bedroom, Janey sank down in the white rocker, closed her eyes, hugged herself across her chest, breathed deep. She must pull herself together. This was not the end of the world, even if it had felt for a moment like her skin was being ripped off.

Ida sat on the braided rug, watching with worried, black eyes.

"I'm okay, Ida." Janey laid her hand on the dog's warm head. Her breathing slowed.

Footsteps came slowly up the stairs. Ellen peered into the bedroom. She was carrying a tray with a teapot and two mugs. "Janey?" she asked softly.

"Did you tell someone, Ellen?"

"No, Janey, no. I didn't."

"Who knows?"

"Laurie Bachlund."

"Who else?"

"Nobody that I know of."

"What did she say?"

Ellen came into the bedroom and set the tray down on the dresser. "She just let me know that she thought you were a lesbian. That was all."

"And you didn't contradict her?"

Ellen looked startled. "Of course not. It never occurred to me."

"You could be fired, Ellen, if they found out about you and me."

"I'm not worried at all."

They regarded each other. Ellen's innocence astounded Janey; Janey's paranoia confounded Ellen.

"Don't you realize," Janey asked her school-teacher lover, "that what we are, that what happened last night right here in this bed, that how we feel about each other, is looked on with fear and loathing by most people?" She kept her eyes on Ellen's. "Fear and loathing? Like, like—" Janey tried to think of something suitably awful, "like someone fucking a baby?"

Ellen drew back. "You're exaggerating, Janey. Some people may not like it, but that's just because they don't know about it."

"No, it's down deep, it's like recoiling from a person who's deformed. No matter what they may say, once they know, they don't want us around."

Ellen sat down on the edge of the bed. "Did you have a bad experience in the past?" she asked solemnly.

Janey sighed impatiently. "No. I haven't been fired, if that's what you mean. No one has spit on me. My family hasn't disowned me. But that's because I've been careful. Other people have had those things happen. The world isn't ready for us to be open, Ellen. People like Laurie—they wonder, but they don't really *know*. They don't even *want* to know. And it's much easier for you and me if they don't."

"Times are changing. Gay people are standing up for themselves. You can't want to live in darkness all your life."

"Ellen—" Janey's voice rose.

"No, I know you're more experienced than me. Maybe I am naive. But, Janey," Ellen went to kneel by Janey, take her large, competent hands in hers. "I hate the idea of being afraid and having to hide. It sounds so bleak."

"It just goes with the territory."

"I—"

"It's not really being afraid and hiding, it's being private," Janey explained. "It's being sensitive to other people's hang-ups. You're not in this alone, you know. I'll help." She felt some hope; Ellen's hands were gentle on hers. "Pretty soon you won't even think about it. It'll become second nature."

"Oh, Janey, take lessons in being afraid?" Ellen looked up at her new lover sadly. "Do you really want me to do that?"

Janey turned her hands to hold Ellen's, sent all the loving energy she could muster into Ellen's arms and breasts and heart. "I want us to be happy together, that's all."

Ellen smiled, fell silent, and laid her head resignedly in Janey's lap.

During the first months of their love affair, the fact that Janey wanted to tell the public nothing and Ellen wanted to tell it everything was secondary to their continued delight in each other. The two friends spent so much time together that one day Mrs. Banks said to Ellen, "Now if you want to board with your friend, that's all right with me. I'll miss you, Ellen, but you're at her place most of the time anyway, aren't you? You should really be paying her your rent."

"I suppose I should," Ellen agreed. She had not found it necessary to use any of the excuses Janey dreamt up to explain their behavior to the town. Everyone except Mrs. Banks steered clear of the subject of Janey. To Laurie, Ellen regularly mentioned Janey's name: "Janey and I did this, Janey and I did that." Laurie nodded; the conversation proceeded. Still, Laurie never brought Janey's name up herself.

Janey had often suggested that Ellen move in. Not only for their own sakes, but because in the eyes of the town Ellen's becoming a boarder made more sense than her constant visits. But Ellen had qualms. She believed she loved Janey; she certainly liked being with her. But sometimes moving into that little house, eternally blinded by shades, seemed not a step forward into the world but a leap away from it. Gradually it had become more clear: Janey was genuinely happy with her garden, her work, her dog, and her privacy. Ellen wanted something more. She did not know what exactly, but she could sense it when her mind stretched.

Janey could not have been more respectful or admiring. She continued her courtship, making pot after pot of Ellen's favorite spaghetti, changing her appearance to suit her lover, praising Ellen's intellect, and becoming exquisitely sensitive to Ellen's body. Ellen grew softer and more tender through this attention. Only occasionally did she lash out like she had the afternoon the town engineer had called her "little lady." Her sense that she might be too "special" for ordinary Janey grew dim. She found herself yielding to the pleasure of this warm woman's love.

Then she returned home to Buffalo for Thanksgiving.

Ellen's father met her at the Buffalo airport on a cold Wednesday afternoon. A balding, distinguished-looking man with a grey mustache and sensitive, full lips, he pulled her to him warmly. "How's my princess?"

"Fine, Dad." Her voice sounded smaller, younger than she'd intended. When she hugged him, childhood tears welled in her closed eyes: for his grey wool coat, his familiar, wintry smell, his deep male voice saying, "How's my princess," for the old desire, impossible now, to climb into his arms.

"The girls are waiting for you. They've been at it for hours."

"I'll bet." They exchanged a smile. "The girls" were Ellen's mother and younger sister Patsy who were busy preparing for Thanksgiving dinner. They were both skilled cooks and accomplished hostesses; Ellen envied them this. Still, how pleasant it was to imagine, just for a moment, that her father saw her as a person of a different, higher order than those "girls."

She had always wanted him to see her as special. When she was four he'd taken a teaching job in upstate New York and for two years they'd lived on the shores of a lake on a rambling old estate with its own dock and green rowboat. While her sister was still a baby, home in her mother's arms, Ellen's father would occasionally row Ellen over the quiet water, the muscles in his arms flexing and relaxing as he pulled at the oars. "Alaska, please," she'd announce and he'd answer cheerfully, "Yes, princess." They'd head north toward Alaska, toward a scene she'd seen in a picture book, where the snow and ice stretched and shimmered for miles into the calm, pinkish distance. Sometimes they'd stop at the town pier and he'd carry Ellen on his strong shoulders to Murray's Drugs where they'd get cold chocolate ice cream sodas. Then they'd be back in the boat, heading north again. Such a fine achy feeling it had been, imagining them leaving her mother and new baby sister forever.

She smiled at him now as they headed down the escalator to the airport garage. He insisted on carrying her bag, waved her ahead of him through doorways.

"What's up at school?" she asked him. He was principal of a suburban grammar school, the same school Ellen had attended almost twenty years before. He had been her eighth-grade teacher. She remembered wanting to please him, feeling devastated when she was not the first with her hand up, when she gave a wrong answer.

"More politics." He sighed.

On the road, the bright sun shone down on winter slush and sheets of ice that crackled over shallow puddles to either side of the highway. They sped toward home.

"What kind of politics?"

"Some women are trying to get Jack Kelsey fired. He's coming for dinner tomorrow, by the way."

Ellen remembered Jack Kelsey. Tall, handsome, appealing, with a look that seemed to reach into your soul, he'd arrived as fifth-grade teacher just in time for Ellen and her sister, along with half the grammar school, to fall in love with him. Every Valentine's Day, he'd handed each girl from the fifth grade up a fresh red rose. Ellen remembered her heart beating faster as she had glanced into Mr. Kelsey's clear, warm, blue eyes. Her roses, as well as her sister's, were still pressed between waxed paper somewhere. "What's he done now?"

Her father glanced at her reproachfully.

"I mean," said Ellen, "why does anyone want him out?" The last time she'd known Jack Kelsey to be in trouble was fourteen years earlier when a student, with the support of her widowed mother, complained that Kelsey had put his hand under the girl's skirt after school. Nothing had come of it. The verdict: it was a case of wishful thinking—the (unattractive) student had imagined the whole thing and duped her own (hysterical) mother. At the time, Ellen had believed that version of the story. Now she wondered. The idea that Jack might be using little girls for his own pleasure, could such a terrible thing be true?

"Jack's always been too attractive to the female of the species for his own good," Ellen's father said drily. "One of our teachers—a new one, you don't know her—has gotten to one of our lady board members." His tone changed to one of bitter sarcasm. "The two of them form a formidable block in one sense—they must weigh about four hundred pounds between them."

Ellen shifted uncomfortably.

"What do they say he did?"

" 'Misuse of the teacher-student relationship,' I believe, are the exact words. Your mother's quite upset about it."

Ellen, too, felt upset. On the one hand, her memories of him were affectionate. In fact, often when she felt particularly drawn to one of her students she was reminded of the pleasure of her old feelings for Jack. She remembered him as her first small crush. "Do you think he'll lose his job?"

"There'll be a hearing next week. To tell you the truth, I'm afraid he may not come through this one okay." Her father suddenly slapped a hand against the steering wheel. "Damned women," he said angrily. They were both silent as he swept off the freeway toward home.

Ellen's mother and younger sister Patsy came laughing out of the floury kitchen to greet her. Ellen's mother was tall with an erect bearing, salt-and-pepper hair and thin lips. She hugged Ellen warmly: the family custom was to hug only at greetings and good-byes, so these hugs were always powerful events.

"We would have come to the airport to meet you but thought you'd rather have supper ready when you got home. Crepes with powdered sugar and orange juice!"

"Wonderful!" As children, this had been Ellen and Patsy's favorite supper. Ellen turned to embrace her sister. Patsy was a natural beauty: light brown curls, friendly eyes, a slow sweet smile. "Where's Tom?"

"He'll be here tomorrow," Patsy answered. Her husband Tom was a building contractor, a quiet, solid man who adored her.

At that moment Patsy's sons Eric, five, and Mike, three, thundered down the stairs and hurled themselves at Ellen's legs. "Aunt Ellen, will you wrestle with us?"

"Sure I will. After dinner."

"You shouldn't get them over-excited," Ellen's mother warned. "Eric, why don't you go get your certificate to show Aunt Ellen?" She turned to Ellen. "He's won an art prize."

"And then come right back. Supper's ready," Patsy called after the two boys.

At supper, as Ellen savored the sweet, familiar flavor of crepe and orange juice, the talk and activity revolved around Patsy's sons. They used "too much sugar," "squirmed," should "sit up straight," were "good boys." An argument: did Eric have "real talent" or was it too soon to tell? She learned in an aside from her mother: "Eric is the smart, artistic one; Mike's a little slow." They both had "Patsy's eyes." Eric had his father's build. Eric was to star in the kindergarten play. Over the course of the meal, Ellen grew subdued. The boys and their mother Patsy were everything to her parents. At one time, before her sister had come along, Ellen had had the same kind of attention Eric was getting now. But it had all vanished when Patsy arrived; it was as if her parents in their excitement over Patsy had accidentally dropped Ellen and she'd been falling through space ever since.

When the boys finished their supper and were back upstairs playing, her mother suddenly turned to her. "Ellen, dear, I've been meaning to tell you something. We've had some sad news."

Ellen glanced at her sister Patsy. For one dark, jealous moment she hoped that this sad news had something to do with her sister's happy life. "What is it?"

"Great Aunt Doris died."

Ellen absorbed this sudden announcement. She had not thought of Great Aunt Doris for years, except for ritualistic Christmas cards. But one of the few times Ellen's family had visited Doris, the older woman had sat Ellen down for a talk. They were in Doris' comfortable living room, sitting at a card table left from a canasta game the night before. Ellen, twelve at the time, was awed by this stern, handsome woman who, her great-nieces knew, had been "the first female Certified Public Accountant hired by the Bank of Idaho."

"Your sister Patsy is a very pretty and engaging girl," Great Aunt Doris had told Ellen. "She reminds me of my sister, your grandmother."

"Yes, she's very pretty." Ellen had dutifully nodded.

"I expect she gets a good deal of attention."

Ellen nodded again, feeling the sad truth of this.

"I remember. It's a hard life being sister to a very pretty girl. Even if you're pretty enough yourself. But there're other things to life. Remember that."

Ellen bit her lip. Although she had somehow known that Patsy was the prettier, and thus the more valuable one, it hurt to have this fact confirmed by an adult.

"There's the life of the mind. The mind can be a wonderful friend to you."

Ellen had gazed at her great aunt through a haze of tears.

"Oh, now dear," her aunt had said awkwardly. "Don't start crying on me."

Ellen sniffled, barely got control of herself, nodded.

"That's better." Her aunt patted her hand. "Stiff upper lip. It's hard, very hard. I learned early on that I didn't fit exactly right into this world. Do you know what I mean?"

Ellen stared at her, confused. "I guess so."

"Well, I suspect you do. And if you do, remember. Other people have felt the same way."

Ellen nodded.

"You're not alone. So chin up." And her aunt had sat up straight and tilted her strong, manly chin.

During the ensuing years of seeing people's eyes skim over her to alight with pleasure on Patsy, Ellen had remembered this peculiar conversation with her aunt. She considered Great Aunt Doris to be her particular friend. Now she felt a rush of sadness. "Have they had the funeral yet? I'd like to go if I can get off."

"Ellen, it was two weeks ago. I'm sorry, I didn't realize you'd care so much. Patsy and I sent a wreath. The card mentioned all of us." Her mother nodded reassuringly.

Ellen felt a familiar constricted feeling. "I wish you'd at least told me!"

"I'm sorry, dear. It happened so fast."

Ellen felt wounded and then defensive, but when she saw Patsy smiling at her fondly, as if none of this mattered, she sighed.

"Grandma sent us some photos," Patsy said. "And a grey sweater of Great Aunt Doris' that'll be perfect on you."

While Patsy and her mother calmed the boys down at bedtime—Ellen had wrestled with them for ten minutes and the three had reached such a pitch of excitement Mike's face had gotten bright red and he'd started coughing —Ellen wandered around downstairs. On the tea wagon were the photos Patsy had mentioned. Ellen picked them up.

She recoiled in surprise. Each photo of Aunt Doris had been tampered with. Mustaches had been drawn on every one.

Ellen heard Patsy's step on the stairs; her sister came to stand beside her.

"Jesus!" Patsy breathed. "When did he do that?" It was clearly five-year-old Eric's work, the penciled-in hairs distinct and fine.

"All of them," Ellen murmured.

Their mother had just come in from the kitchen. Ellen was about to show her, but Patsy looked up, said brightly, "I want to look at that sweater again, Mom," and whisked her mother out of the room.

Ellen stood wondering what to do. She herself had always chosen confession over connivance, but her sister's ways were different. Patsy protected her sons as she had always successfully protected herself against her parents' interference and judgment. Ellen laid the photos back on the tea wagon, stood there uneasily, then stuffed them in her pocket, found a pencil with an eraser in a drawer in the kitchen, and went into the downstairs john. She tried erasing one pencil mustache from a picture in which her aunt, at about age fifty, looked solemnly out at the camera, her dark hair pulled severely off her face, her dark eyes unblinking, her strong jaw set.

The eraser smeared the photo. Ellen sat on the toilet seat staring at it, at her aunt's stern face with the little straight pencil lines under the nose and the smudge across the mouth. Her aunt's face remained unflinching, as if she were ignoring this desecration. With the mustache she looked more than ever like a man.

"Poor Aunt Doris," Ellen whispered to her. "I wish Janey could have met you and we could have all talked."

She pressed the photo to her chest before she returned it to her pocket. The others she held for a moment, undecided. Her mother would be looking for them on the tea wagon. And that's where Ellen put them, wedged under a cup and saucer, ready to be found and avenged.

By two the next afternoon the house was filled with the smell of roasting turkey. The dining room table, fitted out with all its leaves, was covered with a starched white linen tablecloth. At each place setting, the best china, trimmed in gold, was surrounded by silver plate, crystal goblets of various sizes, and rose glass salad plates. In the center were two crayoned pictures of turkeys (signed by Eric) propped up against an assortment of gourds and squashes. Only Ellen was downstairs, delegated to watch the food in the kitchen while the others dressed.

The doorbell rang. Ellen opened the door to Jack Kelsey, his breath frosty in the clear November sunshine. Twenty years ago he had seemed very grown-up to her, but now she saw there was something boyish, an eager innocence, in his wide-set eyes, his half-smile. His dark, wavy hair had a little grey; he was about fifty now, she decided. He smiled at her, reaching out both hands. "Hello, Ellen."

She hesitated a fraction of a second, then took his hands and drew him in. "Hello, Jack. The others'll be down in a minute. They left me in charge of the food although, God knows, that may have been a mistake. I'm no cook."

"Neither am I," he agreed.

They smiled together. Ellen went to the bottom of the stairs, called up, "Jack's here!"

"That's all right. I'll just sit here. You do what you have to in the kitchen." He sat on the edge of a chair, adjusting his trouser legs as he did. Ellen's eyes strayed to his crotch and bounced away in embarrassment. She imagined his penis, small, curled in a nest of hair, and packed away in his underpants. At the moment all she could think was: is there something off about him sexually? He'd been reduced to that question.

There was the click of high heels and a familiar voice. "Ellen! You should have offered Jack a drink! Hello, Jack!" It was her mother on the stairs behind her.

"Curiosity," Jack said later at dinner, as he sprinkled pepper on his mashed potatoes. "That's the most important quality I can instill in my students. That's what I aim for."

"Honesty," Ellen's father declared. "Time and again, I come back to it. It's the honest people in the world who make it worth living in."

"Yes, I agree with George," Ellen's mother added. "Honesty. If you can be honest with yourself, that's the important thing."

"What do you think, Patsy?" her father said. "You're bringing up the next generation. What's the main thing you try to teach them?"

"There's so much." She looked across at her husband. "A sense of humor?"

Tired, kind-eyed, he shrugged. "Tolerance?"

"Ellen, you're in this business, what about you?"

"Self-esteem."

"Most of my students had a bit too much of that," her father said. "I'd still say honesty."

" 'If you tell the truth, you won't be punished,' " Ellen intoned, remembering this lesson from her childhood.

"Yes. And that was a good rule," her mother said. "More people should have learned it. I've been sitting here thinking about those women who are after Jack. I can't understand it. To just get up there and lie like fishes!" She looked unusually stirred up in her bright green wool dress. "Did you hear about this, Ellen?"

"A little."

"I can't think why they should make up such awful things."

"Let's not talk about it now, Alice," her husband said.

"No, of course not. What an awful subject, really. Now, Ellen dear, tell us about your school. I don't suppose there're any perverts there."

The room was silent for an awkward moment and then everyone broke into small talk, protecting their guest from this terrible word.

Immediately after dinner Jack and Tom took the boys out for a walk while the rest of the family moved into the living room with its dark red sofas, beige carpeting, and large, upholstered chairs covered in pink, floral wreaths on grey.

"Remember the red roses Jack used to give us, Ellen?" Patsy reminisced. "I found them packed away in one of our old photo albums. They were dry and dusty as old butterfly wings."

"That reminds me," Ellen's mother said. "While I remember, Ellen, will you look at those snaps of Aunt Doris and see if there're any you'd like to have?"

"Uh, I already looked through them," Ellen said.

"Did you find some you liked?"

"I took one."

"Let me see which one, dear."

"Uh..." Ellen reached her hand toward her pocket.

"She packed it already, Mom," Patsy put in quickly.

"Mmmm," Ellen's mother stood up and went through the archway into the dining room. "Where are those..."

Ellen and her sister exchanged a look.

In a moment Ellen's mother was back. "Look at these, Patsy! How could he!" She stood in the archway with the pictures spread out in her hands. "Poor Aunt Doris. Has he no respect? You knew about this, didn't you? Both of you." She shot disgusted looks at each daughter, turned, and walked out.

"What is it?" Ellen's father asked.

"Eric drew mustaches on Aunt Doris' photos," Patsy said.

Ellen's father smiled, shook his head, said unconvincingly, "That's terrible."

"Actually," Patsy told her father in a low voice. "It was quite a good job. He must have remembered from that time he saw her." She was obviously proud of her son.

Ellen watched as her sister and father exchanged a smile. She thought it was awful that they could laugh at Aunt Doris, shameful. They were no better than children themselves, snickering at the hair above an old woman's lip.

But she longed to be part of their camaraderie, to share their secret smile. She pulled the picture with the smudged mustache from her sweater pocket. "I have one of the pictures here."

As she'd known they would, Patsy and her father came to stand on either side of her to look down at the picture. She felt the comfort of their shoulders touching hers, a warm family feeling, standing there between them. The righteous anger in her vanished; she smiled in pleasure.

"Oh, my," her father said. "Poor Aunt Doris." He laughed in a stifled way. "Now, let's be serious, girls."

"I'm not laughing," Ellen said, but she still smiled.

"What a tough old bird," Ellen's father said.

"Poor old maid!" Patsy said. "Well, she *did* have a mustache."

Ellen stared at Aunt Doris, who was watching her steadily through the smudge. She suddenly jerked the picture and herself away from her father and sister's warm embrace. "So she had a mustache!" she cried. "Is there anything wrong with that?"

"Now, don't go getting excited, Ellen." Her father looked at her, puzzled. "A person can't say anything to you these days."

And Patsy told her placatingly, "I'm sure, with all the pictures Mom and I have, we can find some other snaps of Doris. You can have one of those, Ellen, if you want."

Ellen had come home determined to tell the family about her new life as a lesbian. She wanted to start with her sister and she waited that night for an opportunity. The two of them sat in the bedroom they'd once shared, each cross-legged on her old twin bed, going through their school yearbooks.

"Isn't Mom naive about Jack?" Patsy said. Her eyes were bright and amused as she leafed through the pictures of herself as queen of this and that dance. Her stockinged legs were brown and smooth against the white chenille bedspread.

"You think he may be guilty?"

"Not of anything terrible. But didn't he used to, you know, kind of hug you?"

"No." Ellen had been looking proudly at the yearbook that showed her winning the Fourier Prize "for excellence in mathematics." She felt an attack of a familiar, anxious envy. "He hugged you?"

"It was just horsing around."

"But that's awful."

"It wasn't really awful." Patsy paused, considering. "Now that you ask, I guess it did make me feel a little weird."

"And you never told anyone?" It always amazed Ellen how her sister could hide the truth so easily.

"Just my friends. No one else would have believed me anyway."

"Patsy, you should speak up now. He shouldn't be allowed to do that sort of thing."

"Oh, I suppose I should." Patsy wriggled her shoulders. "But it was innocent enough, I guess. Anyway, I like Jack."

"But what if he were doing that to Eric or Mike?"

Patsy frowned. "I'd *hate* that. A man with a boy?"

"I...I meant, any teacher taking advantage of any child—it's just not right. Jack may have really done what people are saying."

"But Ellen, wouldn't you hate a world where a teacher couldn't show affection for a child without being accused? I would." Patsy looked appealingly at her sister.

"Yes, but—"

At that moment, Patsy was called to the phone: her husband calling to say he'd gotten home safely. She did not return for an hour and by that time Ellen had sunk into depression. There was no opportunity to tell Patsy about Janey. Besides, Ellen no longer had the heart for confession. Janey would seem, well, pathetic, next to Patsy's husband Tom and all the other men who'd fallen at Patsy's feet.

As Ellen lay in bed that night, she found herself wishing that Jack had tried to hug her too. "Ellen," she reproached herself, "don't be ridiculous. You would have wanted to be molested just because your sister was?" She tried to think of Janey, but in her parents' house Janey had shrunk until she was as small as Ellen herself.

Janey sped through her house with a carpet sweeper and rag, dusting each familiar room, stooping to pick up black fluffs of dog hair that stuck to the rugs. She paused at the doorway to what she still thought of as "Angie's room," the room her last lover had left when she was promoted out of Bowles to a bank in Boston. Whereas Janey thought it looked cozy, she knew Ellen would find it too cluttered. She maneuvered one of the two small stuffed green chairs through the doorway into the hall. She'd store it out of the way, at least until Ellen had seen the new desk.

"You know who's coming back today? You know why I'm going to all this trouble?" she asked Ida, who kept threatening to trip her as she hauled the chair downstairs, through the kitchen, and down the narrow steps to the cellar where she plunked it down with a thud. "Our favorite person, that's who. She's coming back."

Ida sniffed behind the old washing machine.

Janey had wanted Ellen to stay so the two of them could have Thanksgiving together, but Ellen had been determined to go home to Buffalo. For Janey, Bowles was home; she wrote her mother regularly but hadn't been back to Harrison for three years. Anyway, holidays in her family had never been celebrated in the usual way. Her father had died when Janey was a baby, leaving her mother to manage the small family travel agency. Holidays were always hectic and so, instead of Janey's mother cooking, the family had gone out for Christmas or Thanksgiving dinner to some restaurant whose owner gave them coupons. There, Janey's mother had three scotch and waters while her daughters felt her drifting away. Now the other daughters drank too and a family gathering inevitably ended up with somebody in tears. Janey preferred not to go.

What was Ellen's family like? "A really beautiful sister," Ellen had said. Janey had been curious to see and, sure enough, she was beautiful in a photo, but not nearly as interesting-looking as Ellen. And Ellen's father—it must be hard to have a school principal as a father. Ellen's mother? She didn't talk about her mother much.

Ellen had said she was planning to tell her family about Janey. A mistake, Janey had argued, but Ellen had insisted her relatives would be sympathetic. Janey couldn't imagine bringing the subject up with her own family. She'd had a dear straight friend at library school, Beverly, to whom she'd once confided her crush on their shyly competent cataloging professor. Things were never the same with Beverly again. She'd begun to seem uncomfortable with Janey and had stopped talking about boys. To Janey's mind, homosexuality was too big a revelation for a relationship to bear.

When she was little, her mother used to troop her and her sisters out to do the "Beans Song" for the tourists:

> Beans, beans, the musical fruit,
> The more you eat, the more you toot,
> The more you toot, the better you feel,
> So eat your beans for every meal.

The tourists laughed and signed up for her mother's personalized tours of Harrison. "Do you know what that song means?" they'd asked Janey.

"Yes," Janey would reply, thinking of angels eating dishes of green beans and playing little trumpets. She hadn't known it was a song about farting until years later.

That's what coming out was: you might convince yourself it was a song about angels, but the people who heard you knew it was a song about farting.

Janey walked alongside the cool, tall, dark-haired woman who had emerged from the plane wearing a false smile and an impatient look.

"So you just stayed home?" Ellen asked.

"Yes. But I was busy."

"I thought you said you'd drive up to see your friends."

"I know. But I ended up staying home."

Ellen sighed. Her elegant face in this mood looked pinched and mean.

Janey didn't understand why Ellen was so upset. "And your visit went fine?" she asked.

"Yes. Well, a few things happened. My old teacher that I liked turned out to be a child molester."

Janey let out a nervous laugh.

Ellen shot her a dark glance. "I don't find it funny." They had reached the car and Ellen swung her bag into the back seat and climbed in. "Then an aunt I liked died and no one told me about it. My nephew drew mustaches on pictures of her."

Janey laughed again, and again it was the wrong thing to do. Ellen shot her a disgusted glance.

"You've got your funny galoshes on," Ellen remarked as Janey drove out of the airport parking lot.

"Yes, I do have my funny galoshes on," Janey agreed. "And my funny coat and funny hat too." This was certainly different from the homecoming she'd imagined. At this point they should have been dying to get their hands on each other. The snowy road blurred through the tears that came unbidden into her eyes. The windshield wipers slammed back and forth across the glass. "Have you got your period?" she finally asked.

"No, I don't have my period. I'm just irritable. I wish you hadn't just stayed home while I was away."

"Why not, for Christ's sake?"

"Why didn't your friends ask you over?" Ellen rubbed at the steamy windshield. "To just stay home on Thanksgiving? It's as if you don't have anywhere to go."

"Don't be silly," Janey said, but she felt heavy-hearted. Ellen *wanted* to hurt her, she could feel it.

They continued in silence.

"I didn't mean anything bad," Ellen said finally. She patted Janey's knee through the green wool coat.

"You could have fooled me," Janey said. She took a deep breath and focused on her driving.

When she saw the desk, Ellen smiled, but Janey heard dismay in her voice. "It's so big!" Ellen shook her head. "It's a wonderful big desk for you, but not for me!"

"No, it's for you."

"You shouldn't give me such an expensive present. It's not right."

"It wasn't expensive."

Ellen ran a hand over the silky, corn-colored oak. "It's in such good condition!"

"It needs another coat of polyurethane."

"Oh, no, not polyurethane. It's fine as it is."

"So you like it?"

"It's beautiful wood."

Janey watched her. "I refinished it."

"You?"

"It had been painted. It was a real wreck."

"You did it while I was away?"

Janey nodded.

Ellen let out a breath, flushed. "It's a big job."

"Yes. I figured you needed a good place to work."

"Janey," Ellen said. "It's a wonderful gift. But I mean it. It's too much, too big. We hardly know each other."

Janey started to argue, but Ellen simply repeated herself. "Look in the drawers," Janey urged. "There's paper and..." She felt panicky. What was going on? "What the hell did your family do to you?" she burst out. "What do you mean, 'We hardly know each other'?"

"It's true. I've been thinking about it," Ellen said hotly. "You're a lesbian, okay, but maybe I'm not. I just don't think I am." She bristled.

Janey glowered at her. "You are one hell of a bitch."

"You think just because you spend day and night sanding some enormous desk for me I'm supposed to move in."

"That's not why I did it."

"Oh, yes it is. You lose one girl, find another. Easy come, easy go. You're like a flycatcher waiting for a fly to fly by. And I'm the fly."

"Ellen!" Janey was flabbergasted.

"You don't understand me at all."

"You don't understand *me* at all."

"Yes, I do. You're scared to death to be who you are," Ellen accused. "And you want me to be scared with you!"

"What's that got to do with anything?"

"So you admit it."

"I don't admit anything. And where do you come off saying I pounced on you? It wasn't me that got us into bed the first time."

Ellen glared at her. "I didn't know at the time I was going to have a pillow stuffed in my mouth!"

Janey was furious. "I didn't stuff any goddamn pillow in your mouth. And stop needling me. What's eating you, anyhow? Did you tell your wonderful parents about us and they gave you a hard time, huh?"

"No, I didn't tell them," Ellen said in a low, tight voice. "The opportunity didn't come up."

"It's not so easy, is it?" Janey taunted her.

"No."

Janey breathed deep a few times to calm down. She sensed that the fight was going out of Ellen.

"It'd be easier if I had you as a good example," Ellen said bitterly.

"Well, you don't."

Ellen moved the desk drawer in and out, in and out. Janey stood at the window watching the snow fall.

"Why's it so important to tell them, anyway?" Janey asked. "If they're like my mother or Angie's folks, they'd just be upset."

Ellen rubbed her forehead tiredly. "I don't know." She sank down at the desk, looked up at Janey. Her eyes had lost their hardness. "It just is."

Janey felt drained too. The horrible things they'd just said to each other had lost their detail, but she still felt battered.

Ellen's eyes looked pained. Nervously she tapped the point of a sharpened pencil on the surface of the desk.

"Be careful of that desk," Janey said. She turned back to the window. Snow lay in soft bundles on the big fir tree behind the house. "Did you want to stay for dinner?" she asked. "I made a spinach quiche."

"That sounds good," Ellen said. Her voice was subdued, like a sorry child's.

As she tore lettuce for salad at the sink, Janey's mind was blank. Her body ached, she wanted to cry but couldn't. Thoughts of breaking up came and went without much force. After a while she heard Ellen come down the stairs, through the living room, and into the kitchen behind her. Janey glanced at her. Ellen looked pale and haggard and her eyes were red.

"I feel awful," Ellen said tiredly.

"Me, too."

"I'm sorry I said those terrible things to you."

"Me, too."

"Can I have a hug?" Ellen appealed to her with outstretched arms and unhappy eyes.

"Oh, honey." Janey crossed the kitchen and took her lover in her arms.

That night Ellen and Janey lay exhausted together on the mahogany bed listening to Judy Collins records. Janey's arm was around Ellen, Ellen's dark head was on Janey's shoulder. Watching her lover's profile, smelling her smell, feeling Janey's warm, forgiving arm, Ellen loved her uncritically. She yearned toward her, knew that of all things in life, this, the feeling of loving, was the most precious. How she'd been that afternoon—suspicious and angry and mean—she longed never to feel that way again. She patted Janey's soft, flattened breast through her nightgown; she sent her love to Janey through her hand; her insides swam with reassurance and pleasure. This now was how she really was and wanted forever to stay: safe and warm and thankful and in love.

Their fight had "cleared the air," Ellen said later, and Janey agreed, for even though terrible things had been said (Janey never really forgot Ellen's "flycatcher" remark), the fact that they'd lived through it and still loved each other was reassuring: what storms couldn't they survive?

In the wake of their fight, they treated each other gently and avoided arguments. Making love, pressed sweating and motionless together on the mahogany bed, their eyelids fluttering; or Janey kissing between the tiny moles on Ellen's smooth white stomach; or Ellen tenderly cupping Janey's breasts in her hands; or both of them moving hard and hot against each other—then they felt in love and gave themselves over to passion.

But sometimes, even as she was physically in thrall to her, Ellen felt Janey was wrong for her: too frightened, too secretive, too homebound. Janey, too, had her doubts. Occasionally her dream of living happily ever after with Ellen seemed just that: a dream. That look of discontent she'd first noticed in Ellen's eyes was still there. When they were at their closest, their warmest, Ellen might suddenly act restless and distant, as if being with Janey stifled her.

Although it hurt, Janey canceled the order for the ruby ring she'd intended to give Ellen for Christmas; she'd sent away for it before their Thanksgiving fight. Instead she gave her a plain black turtleneck that Ellen had once remarked on at the shopping center. Ellen's present to Janey was a green wool cardigan from the same store. They opened their presents Christmas morning next to the tree they'd decorated with shiny balls, feathery birds, and popcorn strings. Ida loved her rawhide bone and two squeaky toys; the two women played tug-of-war and hide-and-seek with her. They roasted a small turkey and made mashed potatoes and gravy, but to Ellen their Christmas dinner felt small and lonely. "I wish we could rent a wonderful family for Christmas," she said.

"We *are* a wonderful family." Janey picked up a long, sharp knife and cut into the mince pie she'd baked.

"Not in the eyes of the world. We're just two spinsters."

Janey shrugged. "That's fine by me."

"No, I want *everything*," Ellen cried, as Janey heaped whipped cream on their slices of pie. "I want a big family, I want everyone to know about us and love us! I want people streaming in the doors, anxious to be with us. I want to be famous and wonderful and accomplished and have you be the same and Ida too, Ida the most talked-about dog in the world!" She tousled Ida's head.

Janey laughed, infected by Ellen's excited dreaming. "And when we get tired of all the attention, we'll just snap our fingers and all the guests will depart, leaving us alone together, just the three of us."

"Just the three of us," Ellen echoed, "Janey, Ellen, and Ida. Alone in our own famous family."

Janey nodded, but she wondered about her lover. This was not the first time Ellen had mentioned wanting to be "famous." Being "popular," "successful," having "done something": these were all commonplace desires of Ellen's. She explained them as part of her feminism: she was building herself into the "someone" the man's world had not let her be. She would no longer be the "good girl" society wanted.

"But I like you the way you are," Janey often said as she struggled to calm down Ellen's ambitions. "Do you want to change your job?"

"I don't know. I want to achieve something, you know?" Ellen replied. "I want to be respected by a lot of people. I think I have it in me, Janey. I think I do."

Janey did not argue. She was impressed by Ellen's quick mind, strong ideals, and stores of energy. Janey had always assumed she herself was lucky to have a good job. Not so, Ellen: she complained regularly. Her students could memorize but didn't understand, she must go over and over the same things, the textbooks were out-of-date and sexist, already the girls were starting to act stupid to impress the boys, and the male teachers were paid more than the female.

Janey's way was to slide over situations she assumed she couldn't do anything about, but Ellen had brought feminism and its discontents into the house. Much of what they read and discussed Janey felt skeptical about. No amount of argument could convince her that a new world would evolve in her lifetime where women and men were equal and alike. But some of it got through. She was particularly interested in a study which had compared the evaluations of a certain article when printed with a male author's name and the evaluations of the same article printed with a female author's name.

"The subject group found the male one 'cogent, thorough and well-thought-out,' " she told Ellen. "A similar group found the female one 'scattered and weak.' " Janey felt a thrill of outrage. "And it was exactly the same article!"

In late February, Ellen received a message in her box at school which read, "I would like to talk to you about sexism in fourth-grade reading texts." The note gave a phone number and times to call and was signed with a graceful flourish: "Audrey Stokes."

Ellen was at the same time pleased and intimidated. Audrey Stokes was the mother of a new student, the quick and lonely Carmella, recently arrived from Boston. Audrey herself came with a history that had quickly spread through Bowles. She was the daughter of the Stokes investment family of Boston, had married an up-and-coming lawyer, and become one of those wealthy women who sat on boards of charitable organizations.

Through connections, she had been appointed as the first woman to sit on the Central Region's Energy Commission, which made policy decisions concerning light and power for Boston and the surrounding area. But (so the story went), instead of behaving sensibly she had, just like a woman, taken a public stand against nuclear power, even weeping in front of reporters at a hearing. Her performance embarrassed her husband and fellow board members but caused a sensation in the press. When the Commission decided not to recommend the construction of any nuclear plants, calling them "economically unfeasible," the press speculated that one reason must have been the strong public sympathy for Audrey's "I'm frightened" speech. She could have become a politician, people thought, but instead she retreated from public life, divorced her husband, and moved to the country "to write." Sam Miller, the park ranger, was courting her now, but secretly nobody thought it could work because of the class differences.

Nervously, Ellen phoned the famous Audrey, whose voice was clear and high and friendly. "My daughter Carmella thought you probably shared her dislike of that sexist geography textbook," Audrey said.

"It's awful," Ellen agreed. "But they just bought it two years ago. It's supposed to be the latest thing."

Audrey hooted. "The latest thing! Perhaps you and I can see about replacing 'the latest thing.' " She sounded as if this was just a matter of the two of them deciding and whatever they wanted would be done.

Ellen agreed eagerly and they arranged to meet for lunch the Saturday after next. This would give each of them time to scout around for alternative texts. When Ellen hung up, she cradled the receiver gently, as if she'd been talking to a queen.

That night, as they fixed dinner together, Janey listened to Ellen's enthusiasm for Audrey with the troubled feelings of any possessive lover. "She's definitely straight," Janey said, partly to reassure herself.

"Oh, Janey!" Ellen stopped in the middle of setting the table, silverware in hand, her dark hair tightly wavy from her latest permanent. "This doesn't have anything to do with that! Do you have to see everything in terms of sex? I admire the woman. She stood up for what was right! And she's a feminist."

"I admire her too," Janey agreed, but she felt wary. "She's so attractive and rich, though. You know what I mean?"

"She's no different from us, Janey," Ellen answered doubtfully. They stood picturing Audrey, whom they'd seen in town occasionally, a small, exquisite person with a royal bearing and perfect smile.

On the appointed day, Ellen met Audrey at the Colonial Inn. Audrey was wearing a dark green turtleneck sweater and beige wool pants that looked tailor-made. She was gracious and friendly, with a direct way of talking and an easy laugh. They spoke briefly of Carmella: a very intelligent student, Ellen assured her mother. "She's always been so shy," Audrey said worriedly. "Do the other children like her?"

"Oh, certainly they like her," Ellen said with too much enthusiasm; she hated lying. Carmella, with her expensive clothes and correct answers spoken in a timid voice, had yet to be embraced by the majority of the fourth-graders. Ellen imagined she had been like Carmella at nine.

"I'm relieved to hear that." The two women sat silent for a moment. Then Audrey went on in a different tone, "I've found a book I'm quite pleased with. Tell me what you think." She pulled a colorful text from her canvas bag and handed it across their sandwiches. It was one Ellen had asked Janey to request through inter-library loan, but it had not yet arrived. Ellen leafed through it. Like the current text, it used an entertaining style but the central characters were two meticulously equal children, boy and girl, who travelled all over the world with their faithful dog, noting exports, capital cities, and major rivers. The girl was portrayed in action.

"Not once standing with her hands behind her back," Audrey pointed out. "I'd be willing to donate the money to buy thirty of these," she volunteered.

"That's a very generous offer," Ellen said. "Let me talk to the principal, Harold Briggs, first. He's a forward-looking man."

That night, as Ellen was extolling Audrey's virtues to Janey, Janey interrupted, "Shall I cancel that book request I made then?"

"No...yes...I don't know. Don't you want to hear what else happened? We had some other good ideas, Janey. Like starting a women's consciousness-raising group in Bowles. And putting an end to these antiquarian customs of yours, like the 'Father-Son Deer Hunt' and the 'Family Day' in July."

"They're not *my* customs."

Ellen laughed. She was riding high. "I know, sweetheart. I mean Bowles' customs."

Janey frowned. She supposed she should be happy over this outspoken feminist, Audrey; she should welcome the appearance of someone who might be destined to change women's lives in Bowles. But what Janey really wanted was to work in the garden with Ellen, to hike in the hills, to make love, and listen to music. She didn't really want her life changed. She wondered if Ellen ever felt as enthusiastic over her, Janey, as she did over this woman whose major claim to fame was that she'd cried in public.

By now Ellen had moved most of her clothes and other belongings to Janey's, though she was not officially living there. Her school work was done at the big oak desk; almost every night she spent next to Janey in the mahogany bed.

"How would you feel about having a consciousness-raising group meet here at our place?" Ellen asked one evening after she'd talked to Audrey on the phone.

Janey was paying bills at the kitchen table. She smiled. "Our place?"

Ellen was embarrassed. "I can't believe I said that. Your place, of course."

"Interesting slip of the tongue." Since their Thanksgiving fight Janey had refrained from mentioning Ellen's moving in.

They sat silent.

"Do you need the rent?" Ellen asked finally. "I *am* practically living here."

"I could use the rent." Janey sat, holding her breath.

"And you'd like me to come?" Ellen asked in a small voice that didn't sound at all like her usual one.

"Of course," Janey assured her. "Of course I would. You know I would."

They gazed at each other with a kind of tearful hopefulness. "And you think it would work out?" Ellen asked. "I'm not too moody for you? You wouldn't be my *owner?* You wouldn't be mad if I let the water run too long or put a nail in the wall?"

"Do I get mad at you now?"

"Well, now, I'm just a *guest.* You have to be nice to me."

They both laughed.

"Well, I am practically living here," Ellen repeated. "I guess I should be paying rent."

"I guess so..." Janey beamed.

The next day Ellen gave Mrs. Banks notice. "Well, of course, dear," said Mrs. Banks sadly. She had not had the kind of closeness with Ellen she'd hoped for, nor even seen much of her young tenant since she'd become companion to Janey Kowalski. Together they went upstairs and surveyed Ellen's room, which looked almost as it had when Ellen moved in: the small, rosewood desk with its ancient pen and ink stand gathering dust, the colorful patchwork quilt on the bed, the tall, wavy mirror, the quietly drooping organdy curtains. Mrs. Banks felt the loss; she wondered whether anyone would ever again sleep in this, her husband's old room, while she was alive. Boarders were hard to come by. Simultaneously both women noticed a spot on the pink and grey hooked rug. Ellen bent to it, ready to apologize, but it was only a broken piece of leaf. She picked it up and they smiled fondly at each other.

"I'll miss you," Mrs. Banks said.

"And I'll miss you," Ellen answered warmly, feeling her affection for this woman at the moment of leaving her. The room, too, seemed suddenly precious. Perhaps, Ellen thought, she was indeed making a terrible mistake, her reservations about life with Janey were valid ones, she belonged alone in this small rented place, and she would always regret leaving.

But once she'd loaded her bags into her old Ford and driven over to Janey's, the feeling of nostalgia changed to excitement. Although nothing much changed in the externals of their lives, the two women settled in with each other differently; they cherished each other in their new commitment. And, instead of feeling "caught," as she'd feared, Ellen felt freer in "their" house than she had when it had been Janey's alone.

As Janey began to speak up about the articles she was reading on lesbian rights and feminism, the two women's conversations became more balanced. No longer did Ellen do most of the talking and Janey most of the listening. The house rang with fiery discussion. What could never have happened six months before happened now. The first Bowles Women's Consciousness-Raising Group was conceived. Its first meeting was scheduled to take place at the house of Janey Kowalski and Ellen Harmon, and a call for members, typed up and carried to the newspaper office by Janey, was published in the final March edition of the *Clarion,* Bowles' weekly paper.

In early April, on a cold, starlit night, Janey raised the shades in her living room just in time to welcome the first ten members of Bowles' Women's Consciousness-Raising Group. In addition to Janey, Ellen, Laurie Bachlund, and Audrey, there was Olivia, a calm-faced woman who lived in a neighboring commune and practiced free love; Linda, a tired young mother of twins; Gladys, the retired fourth-grade teacher who'd once held Ellen's job; Claire, the doctor's wife and a friend of Audrey's; two friends of Claire's eager to meet Audrey; Janice, a secretary at the bank; and Nancy, who described herself matter-of-factly as a bored housewife.

Going around the room each woman spoke her thoughts on the topic: "What does it mean to me to be a woman?" Audrey, a wave of dark hair falling over her large, appealing eyes, described the moment in Boston she was famous for: "the time when I was most a woman, both to the world and to myself."

"I didn't intend to speak out that night," she told them, brushing her hair back. "As a junior board member I was honored to be chairing a public hearing. Especially one on such an important topic as the proposed construction of a nuclear power plant. I was covering my nervousness by acting clipped and chilly, trying to impress those important men with just how rational and objective I could be. But I grew dismayed at the arguments for the plant. And even those who were opposed seemed to use the wrong reasons, economic reasons: decreased real estate values, traffic congestion, and so forth. The people who I knew wouldn't want the plant—mothers like myself with children—had not shown up, probably didn't even know the hearing was taking place.

"An hour into the hearing I was suddenly moved to speak out. I had the floor, an engineer had just finished his advocacy. 'As a board member I would like to say a few words,' I began. And then words I hadn't ever prepared or thought through spilled from my mouth as if someone or something was speaking through me. Until that moment I had never faced my real horror of nuclear power. I trembled as I spoke and could stop neither the words nor the trembling. I described not a cataclysm but a series of small mistaken steps from which no recovery was possible. I saw a world of helpless humans, a red ring around the sun. I saw tiny changes in tiny molecules, infinitesimal shifts of balance. I saw the atom as if it were the earth. I saw it exploding into a million tiny pieces that whirled off into space. The vision was so clear, so final...

"When I finished there was dead silence. And then the harsh sound of someone sobbing bitterly. I realized it was myself crying into the microphone. At that point—I don't know how long I'd stood there—I excused myself and returned to my seat. Another member of the board leaned over to say he would take over my duties as chair, for it was clear I was no longer 'rational.' The next day the *Boston Globe* carried the story on the front page. Phrases like 'women's emotionality' and 'a woman's soft heart' were used to explain what had happened. My husband warned that whether the plant was built or not—and it wasn't, you know—I'd made a tactical mistake in speaking up as I had. 'You've lost any power you might have had on that board,' he said. He was right in that respect, but he was wrong to think I had any choice about speaking up. I had no choice. The feelings came surging out of me.

"Later I thought: they were right. The tears, the intuition of horror, the feelings of fear were not only mine, they were 'me'...me as a woman. The voice that I'd been told 'over-reacts,' the voice I'd almost lost, the voice that I now know as my woman's voice was restored to me that night."

Every woman in the group was moved by this account. Until then, each of them had seen Audrey as a cool, confident princess from another world. They had not been able to identify with her. But, as Ellen told Janey that night, "Even as I envied her, tried to scorn her for crying and acting weak, I loved her, was inspired by her, longed and yearned to let that voice of righteousness and truth well up from my own heart."

Janey, too, felt a thrilling sense of hope and power when she thought of Audrey's story. It seemed to throw over everything she'd learned about concealing her feelings. But, as she told Ellen, Audrey's situation was unusual.

After all, if they all let go with their deepest, hidden feelings, the bored housewife might burn her house down, the communal woman might stab the guru who ran her place, and the woman with twins, who hadn't wanted them, might turn out to strangle them one day. For Janey, the truth of one's deepest emotions seemed cataclysmic.

At first, the town reacted to the formation of the women's group with a variety of mild feelings. Some knew nothing about it, some found it amusing and expected it not to last, and some felt irritated at this annoying evidence of change. Ellen Harmon, the new school teacher, and Audrey Stokes, that Boston woman, were known as the instigators of it. That Bowles' own Janey Kowalski was hosting it was not surprising, given her liking her roommate so much. It was thoughtlessly assumed that the women spent their meetings talking about men.

One night, during an angry exchange in a very expensive bedroom, the doctor accused his wife of "joining a group of lesbians." She was outraged; that anyone in Bowles was a lesbian had never occurred to her, particularly any of the nice women in her group. However the next meeting she was unable to attend; also, the one after that. And the one after that. Eventually the others did not expect her.

Ellen and Janey were excited by this small community of women who every Tuesday night either ended up in communal tears over someone's story of sadness and injustice or broke out in smiles over another's tale of assertion or success.

"So, when are we going to tell them?" Ellen asked Janey one night as they got ready for bed. She had just come out of the bath and was holding a towel around her pink body as she searched in the dresser for a clean nightgown. The room was lit by the warm glow of a small lamp with a rosy parchment shade.

"Tell them what?" Janey had been stretched out, her arms behind her head, relaxed, and enjoying watching Ellen. Now she frowned.

Ellen pulled on a blue-flowered flannel nightgown and jumped into bed beside her lover. "That we're lesbians."

"There's no need to tell them that," Janey protested. "Why do you want to tell them that?"

Ellen raised herself on one elbow, fiddled around absently with the button on Janey's pajamas. "The main topic of this group is women, isn't it?"

Janey nodded.

"And in particular, accepting and loving ourselves and other women, isn't it?"

"I don't know about that," Janey said.

"Yes, it is," Ellen insisted. "And you and I love each other. Of all people we're the ones who know most about loving women to the nth degree. And we can't breathe a word of it."

Janey sat up straight and assumed the worried, set look that Ellen had learned meant there was no reasoning with her. "There's no need. The group's doing fine."

Ellen lay back and sighed, "You are so afraid."

Janey hated this accusation. She reproached Ellen, "You thought Audrey was the cat's meow for being afraid. Why can't I be?"

"Audrey's afraid of nuclear power, of the end of humankind, the end of the earth. You're afraid of—I don't know what—embarrassment."

"More than that," Janey cried. Ellen's being so hard always hurt. She stared down at her. "You read all these pamphlets, Ellen, and they get you off. These new ideas about coming out of the closet are for people in cities, people who march and write petitions, that sort of thing. They're not for small-town librarians and school teachers."

Ellen rubbed her forehead tiredly. "Can we just tell Audrey, then? I need to tell someone."

"Why?"

Ellen looked at her, distraught. "I just do!"

Janey twisted as if caught. "I don't see why."

Thus began a series of similar arguments. Nothing was resolved until June when they finally agreed: Janey would accompany Ellen to New York to watch the annual gay rights march. As Janey said, "There's sure to be someone there you can tell *anything* to."

It was a beautiful June day in New York, a day of partly cloudy skies, hot sun, and cool breezes. Ellen and Janey, wearing visors and sunglasses and carrying daypacks, emerged from Grand Central Station to stand beneath the surrounding skyscrapers and study their map. After conferring, they glanced around and then proceeded west to catch a subway downtown.

Twenty minutes later they emerged again into the daylight and once more headed west. Directly ahead of them three men walked with their muscled arms around one another. In her thirty-six years, Janey had known only a couple of gay men. Occasionally one turned up as a character on TV and a pamphlet Ellen had sent away for recently included photos of men laughing and raising their fists in past demonstrations. Still, these men ahead seemed so...physical. One of their hands lay familiarly on another's blue-jeaned rear end.

Janey adjusted her dark glasses. After she'd agreed to come, she'd started to have fantasies of disaster.

"What if some person who hates homosexuals throws a bomb?" she'd asked Ellen the previous week.

"That has never happened in any of the Gay Day parades."

"There haven't been that many. Or—you know New York, all the crazy people there—there might be a sniper."

"That's never happened either." But Ellen had frowned as she turned back to the papers she was grading. A little later she'd asked, "Why do you have to think of the worst thing that could happen all the time?"

"I'm just afraid."

Instead of arguing, Ellen had pulled her close, kissed her, and they had floated upstairs and away into sex. Early the next morning Janey had waked from a dream in which Ellen and a tough-looking woman were vanishing down a street that was all decked out for a colorful carnival. Janey had never felt so abandoned. She sat up so she could look down at Ellen who lay curled up with her back to Janey. She gazed at the curve of Ellen's pale cheek, the translucent skin, the dark, dark eyelashes, the hand nearby guarding her face as she slept. Janey reached over, touched Ellen's soft cheek tenderly.

The next morning she reminded Ellen, "We're only going to watch, right? Not march. And we're going to stay together."

"Right."

So here they were, watching. Reggae music, fresh from Jamaica in 1975, blared out from a portable radio set in the open second-story window of an old brick apartment building on Tenth Street. Onlookers were already lining up on the sides of Seventh Avenue. Janey looked them over suspiciously: curious gawkers, most of them. Here and there in the middle of the street gay men and women dressed in T-shirts and jeans headed downtown toward the area where the parade was forming. Their voices were animated; they acted important. Janey felt a mixture of embarrassment and pride.

"Look, Audrey should see that." Ellen motioned to five young women in flannel shirts, talking excitedly. One of them held a sign: LESBIANS AGAINST NUCLEAR POWER.

Janey stared at them as they moved down the street. They looked the same age as some of the high school students who came into the Bowles library worrying about what they were going to wear to the basketball game.

She tried to calm down, shifted her weight from one leg to another.

Beside her, Ellen too jiggled restlessly. Ellen looked good: she wore jeans and a blousy red shirt and she had put some rouge on her cheeks that set off her dark hair and eyes. Janey noticed a red-headed woman in a lavender pantsuit eyeing them. Janey rubbed her back with both hands so that her breasts stuck out, glanced over her shoulder at the woman, and smiled a half-smile. This flirting seemed automatic; she did it without thinking.

"Isn't it exciting?" Ellen said as she looked around. Janey had to agree.

This world was divided into two groups, she noticed. There were the silent, gawking onlookers: they tended not to know one another, stared at everyone, looked away if you met their eyes. They gave her the creeps. Then there were the gay marchers and supporters. Many of them seemed acquainted and, when they were around, the air vibrated with shouts of greeting and laughter, the banging of drums. A man walked by with pink stripes painted over his practically naked body and pink ribbons streaming behind him. One piece brushed Janey's arm and, without knowing she was going to, she caught hold of it. He felt the pull, turned, smiled, said, "Wrong sex, honey." She let it go, felt herself blush.

Ellen's hand reached to take hers. Out of habit she dropped it, but not before she'd noted that Ellen's palm was cool and clammy; it felt better to know no matter how easygoing Ellen acted about all this, she was nervous too.

"When's it going to start?" Janey bobbed in time to the music. If she'd just landed from Mars, she might even enjoy this moment: the laughter, the costumes—there was a man in a fairy costume with gossamer wings, swooping around on roller skates—two tall women, very striking, with old-fashioned hairdos. She had never seen women like that; they spoke with exaggerated gestures.

"I think they're men," Ellen muttered.

They *were* men. Janey did all she could not to stare at them, more interesting in their unfemaleness than any real women could be at first sight.

A burly man across the way surprised her. He fell into step with the two men/women, his arm around one of them. All three went off together, laughing.

"Weird," someone behind Janey said.

"Weird yourself," Janey said in a low voice only Ellen could hear.

They waited. In the distance they could hear a band. The crowd shifted, consolidated and strained to see down Seventh Avenue. Two policemen rode by on shiny brown horses. They moved slowly, not interfering with anyone.

Janey no longer felt so worried. She offered Ellen a drink of water from her canteen and took one herself. The weather was perfect: clouds drifted across the hot sun occasionally, sending shadows over the city; a faint, cool breeze blew over the people in their expectant hush.

There was a dull roar in the distance: the parade had begun. Janey stood on tiptoe, craning to see. The sound of the band grew louder. Coming toward them was a mass of people, far away still, faceless, but inching forward.

Janey's heart beat unreasonably fast. As strange as if she had been marching herself, that was how she felt.

The first thing she saw was the banner—in big purple letters: NEW YORK GAY DAY PARADE 1975. Eight people led the parade, their arms around one another's waists. The two on the ends held up the poles of the swaying banner. Their faces were growing clearer. Most of them were smiling; they looked happy. Janey stared: four young women and four men, wearing ordinary jeans. So vulnerable and brave they looked. Her throat ached for them.

As they came nearer one of the young women met Janey's eyes and smiled right at her. The woman had blond bangs straight across her forehead. Janey smiled back. "Join us!" the young woman called to her.

Janey shook her head and felt herself blush, but the woman had already moved past. Roiling, pulsing, noisy, and proud, the parade passed by: groups with signs—GAY ACTIVIST ALLIANCE, GAY SWITCHBOARD, PARENTS OF GAYS, HARTFORD GAYS; floats made of flowers with men and women dancing, drinking beer and waving; bands—baton twirlers, drummers, and horn players. "OUT OF THE CLOSETS AND INTO THE STREETS!" the marchers shouted. And over and over Janey and Ellen heard the call, "JOIN US!"

"Let's march," Ellen said at one point excitedly but Janey shook her head no.

"I don't want my picture on the front page of the paper tomorrow." There were people everywhere taking photographs. To actually step into the street! Impossible.

And yet...she could almost feel herself tipping forward, an excitement deep in her gut, tears in her eyes. To *do it*, just to *do it*. Like marching to war, her arms around the shoulders of other women, their voices raised together.

"JOIN US, JOIN US..." The cries continued. And then another chant starting up, as the marchers stopped for a moment and people on the sidelines watched curiously. "HO! HO! HO-MO-SEXUAL. THE RU-LING CLASS IS IN-EFFECTUAL."

There were only a few feet between Janey and the chanting marchers: a slap-happy group of gay men waving banners advertising their bar, a place called Hard Rock. The man in pink ribbons was one of them; she could hear his bass voice. He looked her way and she smiled. Looking right at her, he waved his hand like a baton toward the sideliners. "HO! HO! HO-MO-SEXUAL."

She heard Ellen's tentative voice take up the chant. "...THE RU-LING CLASS IS IN-EFFECTUAL." A few others from the crowd were joining in. Janey half-opened her mouth, closed it; he waved gaily, his pink ribbons flying wildly, his hairy near-naked body swinging in time to the chant.

An exhibitionist, she thought. But she liked his nerve. What colossal nerve. "Come on, everybody. You can do it," he yelled. "Let me hear it. HO! HO! HO-MO-SEXUAL."

And she let him hear it. "THE RU-LING CLASS IS IN-EF-FECTUAL!" Her voice rang out loud and strong. She could feel Ellen beside her gain confidence, she could feel Ellen's hand squeeze hers; their hands clutched each other's as if they'd never come apart. How the man with the pink ribbons rejoiced and jumped from foot to foot as they chanted. All Janey's pent-up emotion came out in those strong sounds. The cry spread down the parade until the whole world seemed full of it. For a moment Janey had lungs like a tiger, felt as strong as a tiger among thousands of tigers, roared fiercely; then the cry died away, the parade moved on, and the pink-ribboned man was gone.

She and Ellen stayed in their spot till the last float had passed, a lily pond with a big green frog made of men doing the hula. Making their way back to the subway, Ellen and Janey swung their hands gently together, singing in low voices, "Ho, ho, homosexual. The ruling class is ineffectual."

Near Sixth Avenue, Janey noticed a man in a business suit looking at them. She dropped Ellen's hand. "Damn straights," she muttered.

Ellen laughed happily. "Why, I've never heard you say such a thing before, Janey."

Driving back to Bowles, they were soft on each other, they were sweet to each other. They rode in silence most of the time, holding hands. They stopped for dinner half-way home, fell into bed exhausted as soon as they walked in the door. Somewhere along that ride it was understood, neither of them remembered just how: the hopeful, idealistic fire of the march had ignited the door to Janey's closet. Perhaps they could tell Audrey, after all.

While Janey was still under the spell of the march, Ellen lost no time in asking Audrey and her daughter for dinner. "Tomorrow?" Audrey asked in surprise; it was her first dinner invitation from Ellen and Janey, and she seemed to sense the urgency behind it.

"Yes, of course, how lovely. We'd love to come. What shall we bring?"

The next night Ellen and Janey, dressed in pale summer blouses and slacks, welcomed Audrey and Carmella to their white-covered card table in the garden. Janey's rose bushes were covered with soft blooms: dark reds, tender pinks, and pure whites. The sweet fragrance of honeysuckle wafted over the bed of violets and mixed with the stinging odor of mosquito repellent, which the women had just sprayed over the table.

Janey felt weak and mildly depressed as she smiled gamely at Audrey in her white lace halter top and upswept hair. Carmella, in pink shorts and a little sleeveless blouse, looked equally nervous and unsure. Ellen was sweeping Janey headlong into who knows what. Those few moments of fervor at the march had so excited them both that now Janey could not even mention her worries without Ellen shaking her fist encouragingly and intoning, "Ho, ho, ho-mo-sexual." The strange thing was, it seemed to work.

That same thrill and arrogance that had pulsed through her in New York could seize Janey now when she remembered.

She and Ellen had rehearsed the evening earlier and she now began her part. "Will you help me fix the dinner?" she asked Carmella in the slowed-down voice that was part command which she used with children at the library. This simple request had been much discussed: if Audrey should object to the revelation she was about to hear, wouldn't she be upset that her daughter was out of sight and in Janey's clutches? "Ridiculous," Ellen had responded to this fear of Janey's, but her own worries seemed just as ridiculous to Janey: was it non-feminist to ask a little girl to cook?

The shy little girl looked at her mother, who smilingly urged her, "Go on, dear."

"Do you help your mother cook at home?" Janey asked as they walked in together.

"Some." Carmella spoke in a small voice.

Janey's heart reached out to this timid soul. "Can you help me shell some peas?" They sat in the breakfast nook with a pile of green peas in front of them, dropping the peas into a saucepan and the pods into a paper bag. Janey popped a pea into her mouth; Carmella did the same. "Here, open your mouth and I'll see if I can throw one in," Janey suggested. They played for a moment, laughing, and then Janey stiffened at a stray thought. What if Audrey came in to see her daughter's little pink mouth open and Janey concentrating on it, even if only to throw a little green pea in? Wasn't there something wrong with this game, something that showed Janey's perverted nature? She stood up nervously and went to the window.

Outside, past the roses and in front of the poplars and fir, Ellen's face was toward her; she was talking excitedly, animatedly to Audrey. Janey stared at Audrey's back, trying to deduce her reaction. She seemed normal; her hand reached back to tuck a strand of hair into a comb. Now Ellen was smiling; Audrey might be smiling too. Audrey was gesturing, her hand in the air in a fanciful motion.

Janey turned to find Carmella looking inquiringly at her. "We'll make a salad," Janey announced.

They had torn all the lettuce and were mixing the salad dressing when Ellen and Audrey appeared at the screen door. "Hey, you two," Audrey said. "It smells good in here."

As Carmella scooted to welcome her mother, Janey glanced nervously at Audrey. Their eyes met and Audrey gave her a radiant smile. "I'm so happy for you," she said.

Janey flushed. "Thank you." She could feel Audrey's nervousness on top of her own; they were both Ellen's willing victims, in a sense. "We've just been making salad," Janey explained.

Carmella asked, "Why are you happy for her, Mummy?"

"Because she's..." Audrey stood behind her daughter, laid her hands on Carmella's shoulders. "Well...I just am," she said lamely. Carmella seemed to accept this but Audrey, suddenly inspired, went on, "Remember Christine and Leona, how we always liked visiting their place and called it the 'women's house'?"

"I don't remember."

"Of course you do, dear. Well, this house is another women's house. That's why I'm happy."

"No, I really don't remember," Carmella repeated.

"Yes, well, in any case, Carmella..." Audrey brought her palms together in a soft, dismissive clap and appealed to Janey. "Now, what can I do to help?"

Every summer the town of Bowles joined with other towns in the county to sponsor Family Day, a day of picnicking and games for their citizens. The highlight was the father-son, three-legged race, but there was also a mother-daughter bake sale and a fund-raising booth for the Chamber of Commerce informally known as "Dunk the Spinster." Local single women were encouraged to sit over a big tub of water on a board rigged to a target. When a customer's ball hit the target, splash, in she went!

"I've never heard of anything more barbaric," Ellen told Janey.

"Some girls get a kick out of it."

"You never did it, did you?"

"Once or twice. You should try it."

"Are you kidding? I'm not letting anyone treat me like that."

Ellen, willing or not, was enmeshed in preparations for this day. As a newcomer, she had been asked to teach summer school for the fourth- and fifth-graders. The sessions met weekday mornings during July and August and centered on drawing, games, and special activities that were outside the usual order of things: sessions on how to care for your pet, for instance, and how to make shoes out of tree bark. The summer school children were responsible for painting the large mural which was the backdrop for Family Day, and every day some child brought to Ellen a drawing of a classical nature: father, mother, and one to six children under a sunny sky. "Very nice, very nice, very nice," she encouraged them dutifully. To one little girl, she added, "Why don't you draw a picture of your own family now, of you and your mom together?"

The girl considered, her hand behind her head feeling her ponytail. "Do I have to?"

"No, of course not. I'll put this one up, shall I?"

"Oh, yes." Shirley watched eagerly as Ellen pinned her picture into its place on the mural plan.

"Are you awake?" Ellen whispered. Beside her, Janey lay curled on her side, a motionless lump under the bedclothes. Ellen squinted through the darkness at the small face of the alarm clock: four-ten. She'd been awake for over an hour. She turned over with a loud sigh, rocking the bed.

An idea had seized her, invaded with as much force as another personality or a voice from God. It was this: she must introduce to her summer school class her family—Janey, their dog Ida, and herself.

"Janey?"

"Yeah?" Sleepiness talking.

"Sorry to wake you."

"Bad dream?" Janey mumbled.

"No. I got this idea. You know this Family Day business? Well, couldn't we teach the kids about real families, different kinds of families, by introducing ourselves? Our family? You, me, and Ida?"

Silence.

"Janey?"

Janey flicked on the light. She was wide awake now. "I don't see the point of it, Ellen. They already know we live together. You're not thinking of telling those kids about us, I hope. Some of them aren't even ten yet."

"Not the sex part but—"

Janey's voice took on a real note of alarm. "Just because Audrey didn't have a fit when you told her doesn't mean you can tell ten-year-olds!"

"It's the way I'd like to teach, with real people speaking from their hearts."

"Audrey Stokes is probably the most progressive person in town!"

Ellen got out of bed and paced around the room excitedly. "We wouldn't say anything about sex or anything like that. Just that we love each other, and that we live together with our dog, and what we do. You know—to give them the idea there're all kinds of families."

"It's a crazy idea. Even in the big cities, a teacher can be fired for being gay. When you've calmed down, you'll see what I mean."

"You're thinking in old ways—homosexual, lesbian, all that, the old stereotypes. That's what I want to fight. This is about family, about love. That's my idea. To reach the children. That's where we have to start. Before their ideas are fixed." Ellen was fired with conviction.

"Ellen, you're not thinking straight. You know some people would hate us if they knew what we were! Even if you call us a family, they're going to know what you're saying. And they're not going to like their kids being exposed to it!" Janey cried, rising up on her elbow. "We're happy here. Our life's been fine. People are nice to us." Her face was agitated in the pink light from the bedside lamp.

"I'll say that I'm a long-term boarder here. A few of their homes include boarders. There's nothing upsetting about saying I board here, that we eat together, that we care about each other and that we're a family...You don't have to look so alarmed."

Janey's face was worried and flushed; her thumb rubbed nervously at the place over her heart.

"Maybe it's a good idea, but for some other teacher to do, not you." Janey spoke earnestly. "We're too vulnerable. We have too much to hide."

"But we've got to start somewhere," Ellen said patiently, sitting down on Janey's side of the bed and taking her clammy hand. "I know it's a good idea, I can feel it. Will you at least think about it? I can't do it without you, sweetheart."

"Oh, Ellen," Janey groaned.

Ellen felt that the voice that had spoken to her in the night was the same one that had spoken to Audrey on the podium; the need for the family lesson seemed as compelling and inevitable as the dangers of nuclear power. During the next few days, she beamed a steady stream of impassioned energy on Janey. To every one of Janey's objections, Ellen had an answer. Not that these answers impressed Janey— she hardly listened to them, so misguided did Ellen seem to her—but the strength of Ellen's conviction began to tell.

Without any idea of participating, Janey thought a good deal about Ellen's obsession. It struck her that the only thing in her own life that she felt with equal intensity was love. She saw that when Ellen talked of the family lesson, her voice deepened, her words grew simpler, and in a strange way, despite all her excitement, she grew calmer. Angie had felt devoted to football; because she loved her, Janey had spent hours in front of the TV watching huge men struggle against one another. She'd even begun to like the game. Just so, despite her fears, the idea of giving Ellen what she wanted began to flicker. *This*, the family lesson, was what Ellen yearned for. Not kisses or adoration, not a new desk, not her favorite dishes, but this joining together for an idea, this public acting-out of something Ellen imagined could change the world.

"How long would it take?" she asked the third morning of Ellen's campaign. They were sitting in the breakfast nook eating French toast with cut-up bananas.

"Not more than twenty minutes."

"And there'd be nothing about being lesbians or any of that?"

"Nothing." Ellen regarded Janey as eagerly as Ida at her most hopeful.

"You promise?"

"I promise. Oh, will you do it, Janey?" Ellen beamed.

"I'll think about it." Janey had been about to take her last bite of toast, but saying this she lost her appetite and put down her fork.

Ellen reached over and squeezed her hand, asked, "How about I bring it up at the women's group tonight, see what they think?"

Janey flushed with a strange embarrassment, but she quickly agreed. Imagining others hearing about the family lesson, she saw it again as provocative, inappropriate, and dangerous. The members of the group would likely feel the same way. Hopefully they'd disabuse Ellen of the notion.

But gently. She hated to think how disappointed Ellen would be.

"Why are you looking at me that way?" Ellen asked her. "You look so sad."

Janey shook her head. "I never knew anyone like you."

"You mean anyone as beautiful, wonderful, and wise?" Ellen teased.

That night Ellen explained the plan to the women's group. Contrary to Janey's expectations, its members were hard put not to approve. In fact most of them were deeply moved at this earnest description of two companions in life who each took her share of housework, genuinely listened to each other, loved their pet, and entertained themselves with gardening, hiking, and reading. Those of the women who knew or suspected that Janey and Ellen were gay were particularly careful not to show any disapproval of the plan; they did not want to be thought prejudiced. The words "gay" and "lesbian" were never mentioned.

"I'm delighted you're mentioning the single-parent family," Audrey put in. "It's about time."

"And communal living," the woman from the commune put in. "It's great you're mentioning that—nobody ever does."

Janey, although she sensed things unsaid, couldn't stop smiling at the response from these supportive women. Telling of her days with Ellen and hearing Ellen's own description of their routines pleased her far more than she could have imagined; the goodness of their life together seemed confirmed. She could feel the others' respect. Nancy, whose husband was a constant disappointment, said she envied Janey and Ellen.

After the others had gone, the two women carried the empty glasses, the bowl of leftover buttery popcorn kernels, and the plate of cracker and cheese crumbs back to the kitchen. Janey felt Ellen's eyes on her.

"All right, all right," Janey said.

"You will?" Ellen ran to embrace her.

"All right. But I'm going to be very nervous and jumpy and you better make it fast."

"Oh, Janey." Ellen hugged her wildly and tight, then danced her around the kitchen, banging their elbows against the refrigerator. As they stopped to catch their breath and rub their funny bones, Ellen said excitedly, "You'll see, it'll go fine. It'll be even easier than tonight. Shorter. The kids don't have the attention span our friends do."

The following Monday morning, when the children's faces turned to the door shortly after they'd reconvened from recess, Ellen looked over to see Janey standing in the doorway and seeing her, felt weak for a moment, as if they were two frightened rabbits about to be devoured.

"Hello." Janey nodded to the children nervously. Some of them knew her and chorused, "Hello, Miz Kowalski."

"Come sit down."

Janey sat somewhat awkwardly on a straightback chair Ellen had placed in front of the class. "I feel like an exhibit," she muttered.

"Class, this is my friend Janey Kowalski. You know her from the library where she works. I asked her here today, along with our dog...Where *is* Ida? Didn't she want to come?"

"She said, 'Ida wanna come,' so I didn't bring her."

Janey had pronounced Ida's name so it sounded like "I don't," and the fourth- and fifth-graders laughed.

"Ida is the most stay-at-home dog," Ellen told them. "We ask her, 'Want to go down to the river, Ida?' and she says, 'Ida wanna go.' So we say, 'Well, if you don't want to go to the river, do you just want to go on a short walk?' and she says, 'Ida wanna walk,' so we say, 'Well, if you don't want to go on a walk, do you want a dog biscuit?' and what do you suppose she says?"

"Ida wanna dog biscuit!" the class roared.

Janey joined in with hopeful spirit. "We just have to go against her wishes," she said. "We can't let her starve, so we have to give her a dog biscuit. And she's very good. She eats that dog biscuit in two gulps even though she didn't want it."

"So you didn't bring Ida," Ellen prompted, moving a stack of papers away from the edge of her desk.

Janey stood up and went to the open window. "Ida, come!" And suddenly through the window bounded Ida, narrowly missing Ellen's desk but performing every bit as well as she had in her rehearsals over the weekend.

When the class had settled down and Ida sat relatively quietly beside Janey, Ellen began, "I wanted Janey and Ida to come today because I wanted to talk about a certain word." She caught Janey's involuntary look of alarm and went on hurriedly, "The word is family."

The children, who had perked up at the mystery of this "certain word"—it could have been any of those forbidden words that held so much power—lost interest.

"What does a family do?" Ellen asked. "What do you do with your family? Evelyn?"

"We eat together."

"Good. What else?"

"Screw."

"Richard!"

"Well, they do! My mom and dad screw. All the time!"

The class snickered mightily at this undeniable wit.

"Love is certainly a part of a family. And what else?"

"Divorce."

As they spoke, Ellen wrote their contributions on the blackboard. Ida started moving through the class, collecting pats and caresses.

"Can any group of people call themselves a family?" Ellen asked.

There was a chorus of negative sound.

"Who's in your family, Tommy?"

"My mother, my dad, and my kid sister."

"That's right. That's one kind of family. Today I want to show you there're some other kinds. For example, I want to tell you about my own family. That's why I asked Janey and Ida. They're my family."

The class accepted this with no particular interest. They were more intrigued with Ida, to whom someone had just passed half a peanut butter sandwich which she chewed once and swallowed in a single gulp. She sat smacking her mouth.

"Ida, get back here. We're not sisters. We're not mother and daughter. We're a family the way a man and woman and children are a family."

"Are you homo?" Richard asked.

Silence for only a second. "No, we're not," Janey's voice came.

Ellen heard the words, felt the lie as pressure in her throat. While she stood silent, Janey proceeded on as planned: told how they shopped together, went to the dump together, took Ida to the park. Ida was sitting by Janey again, still working at the peanut butter on the roof of her mouth.

"Ida knows we're going when—"

"No, we *are* homo, we *are* gay," Ellen blurted.

The room fell silent, shifted, held its breath. Even those children who had no idea what "homo" or "gay" meant knew from the urgency in Ellen's voice and Janey's startled look that something important had happened. Ida whimpered.

"You children have got to understand: we're gay and we're just like everyone else. Being gay is okay. You shouldn't call anyone a faggot. That's a gay man and it's an insult. Gay people are no different from your own parents and your parents' friends. We're a family just like you and your folks are." Ellen stood before the class, her eyes bright and fixed, her hands extended in appeal.

The children rustled uncomfortably. Ellen turned to see that Janey had stood up, her face white and stricken; she looked about to walk out.

"Miz Harmon, can gay ladies have babies?"

"Yes, certainly, Shirley."

"They have dogs instead," Richard said.

At that, Janey fled, with Ida trailing after her.

The class giggled, fell silent.

"Richard, you're to stay after school," Ellen said.

"Jumping Jesus," Richard groaned.

"Okay, class," Ellen said. "Take out your reading books. We'll read the story, 'The White Toad.' Carmella, you begin."

The white toad made friends with a black cat, but to Ellen it seemed nobody much cared. Some surface of life had been cracked; she imagined the children's eyes rested on her differently. Feeling those curious eyes, she felt raw and frightened. Remembering Janey's horrified face, her heart shrank. Perhaps, like the nuns who were driven by God to set themselves afire, she thought, she had struck a match herself and was beginning to feel the flames lick at her skin.

As soon as class let out that noon Ellen dismissed Richard and phoned Janey, but there was no answer.

Ellen found her in the garden mixing fertilizer for a new flower bed. Still dressed in her light blue blouse and grey skirt, she had dumped half a bag of peat moss into a garbage pail of manure and was thumping it vigorously with a spade. She was silent, looking at Ellen with hurt, angry eyes.

"It's not as bad as all that," Ellen said.

"Everyone in town must know by now." Janey's voice was dead. "We'll be fired."

"Oh, come on, Janey." Ellen tried to sound confident but Janey's face and words tore at her. "I didn't mean for you to be so upset, but I just *had* to tell them."

"You must be crazy. That's all I can think." The skin around Janey's eyes was red from crying.

"They forgot all about it. I swear to you, none of them treated me a bit different. Maybe with more respect."

"Respect, sure. They'll fire you, Ellen. That's how much respect you'll get. I'll probably be fired too."

"Don't be ridiculous." Ellen kicked at a stone in the rock garden to keep from crying.

"Right this minute, the mothers are telling their daughters, 'Don't you go near that Miss Harmon or that Miss Kowalski. Don't let them touch you.' " Janey worked the brown mixture with a vengeance.

Ellen laughed bitterly. "For the boys, though, the warning's off. You suppose they warned the boys when they thought we were straight?"

"It's not funny!"

"You didn't have to walk out on me. A fine family we seemed."

"You lied to me!"

"I didn't lie. I didn't know I was going to tell them. I just had to!"

"Ellen, you did lie. You swore to me you wouldn't say anything."

"I didn't lie!" Ellen felt wild.

Inside the phone rang and they both started. It was the principal, Harold Briggs. "What's this I hear about you talking up homo-sexuality," he tripped over the word, "in the classroom?" His voice boomed over the line at Ellen, the voice of God. She tried to stay calm but felt her insides start to quake.

"Did someone complain?"

71

"Yes. 'Someone complained,' " he imitated her. "Well, I suppose you have some idealistic reason for all this. I need to know precisely what was said. Did you describe sexual acts?"

"Of course not."

"What words did you use? Homosexuality?"

"No."

"Lesbian?" He snapped out the word, cruelly, it seemed to her, with contempt.

"No. I said 'gay' and I said 'homo' and 'faggot,' " she said, trying to keep her voice steady.

"Why 'faggot'?"

"They call each other that. It's an insult."

"Okay, good. And you said you and what's-her-name were homosexual?"

"Janey."

"Janey. You said the two of you were homosexual?"

A moment where she felt nauseous. "Yes."

"Well, I'll see what I can do."

"Yes," she said again dully.

"You're a good teacher, Ellen. But this was a stupid move. I'm disappointed in you," and with that, he hung up.

Janey had stood watching her during the call. As Ellen laid down the receiver, her hand shaking, Janey ran to her, threw her arms around her, pressed her face against Ellen's cheek. "Oh, honey!" Her cry was heartfelt.

"Janey, what did I do!" They held each other tightly, burying their faces in each other's necks.

"I suggest you issue no retraction and make no promises of any kind." Although Audrey's words were polite, her tone was firm. "I know a lawyer in Boston that will be delighted to take this case if we should reach that point."

Ellen and Janey sat on Audrey's elegant and comfortable couch, watching small, dark-haired Audrey radiate conviction for this cause they'd become. She had dropped work on her nuclear-power book as soon as she'd heard of their troubles and thrown herself into a new role as civil-rights activist.

"I've already arranged for some Boston women I know to form an ad hoc committee to insist the family lesson become part of the standard grammar school curriculum. Their press release will go out tomorrow."

"But I think Ellen should issue a retraction," Janey argued. Someone had suggested that a retraction would reassure the majority of worried parents. "All she has to say is it was a political act and she won't do it again."

Ellen stood up and, sticking her hands in the rear pockets of her jeans, flexed her shoulders importantly. "Janey, I'd really rather not if Audrey thinks it's a bad idea. It's like giving in to them." Ellen and Janey had become the focus of two tiny, fierce groups: Audrey's PAR, People and Rights, and the Rev. William Wilson's CAC, Citizens against Corruption. The groups would be fighting it out at a public school-board meeting scheduled for the following Thursday. The subject was: "Should avowed homosexuals be teaching at Bowles Grammar?"

Janey sat back. "I'm in this too, you know."

"You're not losing your job, Janey." Audrey spoke reassuringly. "I have Bill's promise on that." Bill Townsend was the mayor of Bowles. Although technically not Janey's boss, he was influential with the county administrators who had hired her. During the past two weeks, Audrey, through drawing on her previous connections, had become enough of a town power to be on a first-name basis with the local officials.

"I can absolve Janey of responsibility," Ellen said. She was to make a statement at the school board meeting.

"I don't think so, Ellen. Better we stand firm," Audrey advised.

Ellen sighed. Audrey sometimes acted as if it had not been Ellen and Janey who had given the fated family lesson, but Audrey herself.

"You've sparked public discussion about the issue. That's the important thing," Audrey said.

Ellen and Janey exchanged a glance. Every day they received at least one letter about the family lesson, usually hate mail. Cars slowed down in front of their house. The Friends of the Library were having discussions, closed to Janey, about the issue. A group of teenage boys had taunted her, calling her "Miss Dykeski." Ellen's job was up in the air; a substitute had taken over her summer school class.

Until now Ellen had enjoyed the refuge of Audrey's brown and rose living room. She liked receiving letters there calling her *the hope of the future.* She liked Audrey's vision of her as heroine: "This pale, brave martyr inspiring others like her," Audrey had written to Senator Kennedy the day before in a letter about civil rights.

But *how* pale, Ellen wondered? So pale she had made her declaration to a roomful of captive children rather than mature adults? So pale that it was Audrey rather than Ellen who was making the decisions now? Ellen's words quoted in the newspaper—"want to be ourselves, just like regular folks"—sounded a bit off. It seemed incredible to Ellen that she could ever have been so naive as to think the town would open its arms to her. Now, when she said "hello" to someone, the unspoken words between them were ten times as loud as they used to be. Ellen rubbed a hand over her forehead and tried to focus on the rightness of her stand. Whenever she glanced at Janey, Janey seemed to be looking at her reproachfully.

The door burst open and Nancy from the women's group rushed in with a fresh, brown package. "The leaflets!"

They scrambled to look at them: black and green on white. A photo on the front showed Janey and Ellen laughing as Ida held her plastic mouse. Underneath, "A family..." was printed in dark green script. Inside, the history of the family lesson was broken with photos of a fourth-grader whose parents had been agreeable: "I don't care if Miss Harmon is gay or straight or purple, she's A-okay by me."

"I'll get these out to everyone in town this afternoon," Audrey promised. "Don't worry, we're going to beat these antediluvians." She nodded encouragingly at the women. "Everyone I speak to is with us."

Driving home from Audrey's expensive log cabin, Ellen was determinedly cheerful. "That's heartening—hearing from Audrey that so many people are sympathetic. It's just the way I thought it would be actually. People are kind and decent. They know when something's right."

"Sure," Janey agreed drily. "They know what they *should* think. They know what to say to Audrey. But what they really *do*, that's another story."

Ellen sighed, stepped on the gas, was forced to brake for an old man slowly crossing the street. "I wish this damned thing was over." She turned onto their block. "Oh, God, no!" Something was written on the black tarmac in front of their house.

They stared, hearts sinking: "LEZZIES" in white letters.

"Could be worse," Ellen said as she parked near the garage. "They could have said, 'Lezzies eat pussy.' "

"Oh, Ellen!" Janey slammed out of the car and stormed away. A minute later she was back with a can of dark blue paint, which she proceeded to spray thickly over the letters on the road, stepping back stonily when a car passed. At the second z, Ellen took the can from her and finished the job. Then she tossed the empty can in the trash, clanked down the lid of the garbage can, and the two women tiredly disappeared into the house.

It was later that night. Ellen and Janey lay in bed, doors locked, shades down.

"I can't, I can't." Janey, sobbing, turned from Ellen.

"You can't make love? Or you can't come to the school board meeting?" Ellen asked wearily.

"I can't do anything." *You've ruined my life*, Janey thought.

Ellen was silent. Her hand patted Janey's hip through the covers.

"If you'd only..." Janey began.

"Only what?"

"Why don't you say you're sorry!" she cried.

"To the school board? Are you kidding?"

"To *me*, Ellen. To *me!*"

"To you..." Ellen raised herself to lean over Janey and stroke the tears off her cheek. "But of course I'm sorry, Janey, that you're hurting so bad," she ventured. "I never wanted to hurt you. I was naive. You told me and I didn't listen to you. Of course I'm sorry."

"You're sorry you told the class?"

"Yes, of course, in the sense of hurting you. But—"

"You'd do it again."

A pause. "I had to do it." Ellen tried to explain. "I still think being honest is the best policy...You'll see," she concluded lamely. "It may all turn out for the best."

Janey flounced back. "The best!" she burst out. "You like our life these days? *This* is being part of the town...? I went along with you because...I don't know...I must have been crazy. I wanted to support you, I thought you were a good person. But, Ellen..." She began to cry again, angrily. "I used to belong here. This was my town." The sweetness of the breakfast nook, the smiles of the Johnny-jump-ups, Ida jumping to catch her yellow mouse, the house she'd worked so hard at for so long: all seemed lost.

Ellen was distraught. "What kind of belonging was that anyway? You're making me feel so terrible."

Good, Janey thought miserably. She turned to watch Ellen's pale, tired face soften and crumple, tears begin to run into the pillow.

The mahogany bed, which had held them in its arms through so many nights of passion and talk and argument, now held their tears and grief. Ida padded from one side of the bed to the other, peering anxiously. Outside, the moon cast eerie shadows over the garden.

At seven-twenty Thursday night, it appeared that most of the eighty folding chairs set up in the town hall for the school board hearing on the gay teacher would go empty. By seven-thirty, they were all taken; at the last moment everyone had come. From her place in the front row beside Ellen and Audrey, Janey heard the hum in the wide, low-ceilinged room grow louder and louder until it seemed to be crawling down her neck. Only once since they had sat down had she turned around and that was to scan the crowd for Bert. She hadn't seen him, but out of the swarm of faces Ellie, the friendly checker from Top Foods, had smiled encouragingly.

"Hello, Janey." It was Mayor Townsend, tall, confident, and prosperous-looking, bending from his patriarchal height in the aisle to bestow his blessing. "Nice weather we're having."

"Yes. Yes, it is." Although she had no fondness for him, she smiled widely. According to Audrey he had saved her job.

He greeted Ellen, then Audrey, nodded, and moved on, bestowing his favors on everyone he passed.

On a raised dais at the front of the room the nine school board members were gathering around a long oak table. The buzz of conversation faded as the chair, Ernest Orr, a balding retired school administrator, raised his deep voice to call the meeting to order. "Ladies and gentlemen, please. We are ready to begin."

Janey stared at the seven men and two women on the board. She had a speaking acquaintance with every one of them. Some of the ones she liked best would vote against them, according to Audrey. Audrey had divided the school board members into "dill pickles" and "sweet gherkins." She had obtained detailed knowledge of each member's voting record and personal opinions. Three of the male dill pickles, the "reading, writing, and 'rithmetic" contingent, were very much of the old order and might very well vote against Ellen on principle, Audrey said. The dill pickle woman had sat on a statewide committee dedicated to abolishing pornography: she was also likely to vote for dismissal. The two dill-pickle liberals could be counted on, but the three remaining sweet gherkins were hard to predict. To Janey, fidgeting with the folds in her summer dress, the nine faces blurred and became one unyielding mask. They were not Hester Smith, grey-haired, charming, a regular for the latest thrillers at the library; or William Burroughs, the realtor with the toothy smile who had found Janey her house; they were parts of the official fist of the town, ready to descend and squash her and Ellen like bugs.

After the regular business of the board had droned on for a few minutes and come to an end, the chair called the first speaker on the topic of the evening: the Rev. William Wilson. A strong man with a flushed, angry face, he strode confidently to the microphone. His eyes roamed over the room, rested on Janey and Ellen, turned to the board. Janey looked into her lap.

"Satan comes in many forms."

Janey's heart pounded in fear. She swallowed, reminded herself his words might be powerful but his voice was quite ordinary, too high and strained for oratory.

The audience, previously struck dumb by his fierce appearance, soon resumed their rustling and whispering.

"Satan can come with words of righteousness. He can come disguised as a young woman.

"These homosexuals," he drew the word out, "say they are the same as us!"

He paused for the audience to take in this horror.

"They want to teach our little children!

"They want to button our little children's galoshes, wipe the tears from their little cheeks."

Ellen whispered, "Right." Janey smiled. Audrey scribbled notes.

The Rev. Wilson went on in this vein, gave a last fierce glare around the room, received strong applause from the dozen paranoid-looking men and women who formed his contingent, and stepped down.

Audrey was next. At five-foot-four, she looked small and perfect in a dress the color of a fresh peach. Notes in hand, she slowly repeated William Wilson's words:

" 'These homosexuals say they are the same as us. They want to teach our children. They want to button our children's galoshes, wipe the tears from their little cheeks.' "

She paused, pushing her dark wing of hair back, then burst into a warm smile.

"We have the chance here in Bowles to say, 'Fine. Of course. Thank you.'

"We have the chance to say, 'Yes, we're delighted you love our children and want to teach and guide them.'

"We have the chance," Audrey continued as Janey listened intently, hoping Audrey could sway the people of Bowles as she had the people of Boston, "to honor those among us who have the courage to stand up for what they believe in. No, I should not say 'what they believe in,' but what they *are*. How many of us can really own what we are when it goes against what the world says we should be? How many of us in Ellen Harmon's shoes—and it could have been any of us that stood there that day—would have had her courage? She was inspired with a conviction that what she did was right, that it was the young who must be educated if the old were ever to understand, that it was..."

As Audrey went on, Janey wished she could grab Ellen's hand. According to Audrey, nothing was so brave as what these two noble souls called Ellen and Janey had done; their goodness and courage brought a lump to Janey's own throat.

Audrey concluded, "Members of the board, I would describe the origin of this family lesson we've heard so much about, but I think you'd prefer to hear it from the teacher herself, Ellen Harmon. Ellen?"

Applause, Audrey herself clapping as Ellen mounted the two short steps to the dais. Earlier that week Janey had watched as Ellen tried on different outfits: the navy dress might show sweat under the arms, the red and white one was too bright, the pink one too sweet, the pant suit too manly. She wore a turqoise dress, stockings, low heels. Her face was pale, translucent. A pimple near her lip that had terrorized Ellen—would people think it had something to do with sex?—was invisible.

Janey gazed at her proudly. Used to being in front of a class, Ellen seemed at ease as she nodded her thanks to Audrey and turned to address the board. Janey had heard this speech many times, had timed it, had even written parts of it.

"I grew up very protected," Ellen began. "My parents protected my health with inoculations and fences and bandaids. They also protected my mind and imagination. Certain subjects were never mentioned, certain people were never seen, certain feelings were never recognized. I'm not faulting them. They lived through two world wars and the Depression, their lives often felt out of control, I expect, and they wanted to create a happy home for us. Along with all the unspoken rules in our household, though, was a spoken one, a rule that did not necessarily fit with the unspoken ones. And that rule was: to be honest.

"Now honesty doesn't always make for happiness, sometimes it almost seems the opposite. New things scare us, new feelings scare us. Sometimes we want to deny them. *Often* we want to deny them. As adults, we can all agree to this.

"But there's a certain time in our lives when new things do not necessarily scare us, when we're confronted every day with new things, when we regard new things with curiosity, when we say, without judgment, 'Oh, so this is the way the world is,' and we're not hampered with notions of how it should be, how it's always been, how we need it to be. That time is," Ellen paused, "childhood."

Ellen smiled shyly, appealingly. Janey thought how fine she looked and sounded; anyone, hearing her, must be moved.

"I've been teaching fourth grade for almost ten years. Any teacher can tell you this is one of the hardest grades to teach. Children in fourth grade, nine- and ten-year-olds, are just about to enter the adult world of judgment and opinion. Just about, but not quite. They still retain a certain freshness and openness to what the world has to offer. Isn't this the time to present them with the truth, rather than the illusions we adults like so much? I thought so, anyway. We all know the nuclear family—mom, dad, and the kids—is held forth as the proper kind of family. We see it all the time in books, on TV shows, and in advertisements. But a quarter of my students don't even live with their dad. Two or three others don't live with their mom either. So I thought, shouldn't their families be honored? Should a ten-year-old have to feel bad because he doesn't have the exact family grouping prescribed by our culture?"

A rustle of sympathy. Someone murmured assent.

"As for introducing my own family and acknowledging that I loved them, isn't that exactly what we should be teaching our kids, that it's who you share your life with that matters, not whether it conforms to some picture in a book? I may have been wrong to assume these children could handle the notion of me and Janey loving each other, but I don't think so. It's not the children who are upset with me tonight. In any case, I certainly intended no harm to anyone. Please consider this as you make your decision. Thank you."

There was a moment of silence and then the room broke out in applause. The board chairman thanked Ellen and shook her hand. She turned and made her way off the stage, returning to sit beside Janey, who squeezed Ellen's hand quickly, conscious of the eyes on them.

There followed other speakers: two mothers and a father extolling Ellen's virtues as a teacher, and a mother and father protesting that precisely because of the openness of their children's minds, Ellen should have been more careful. Janey was astonished and touched to see Bert walk nervously to the microphone: "I have known Janey Kowalski for eight years now," he said in his cracked voice. "There's not a finer young woman around unless it be Ellen Harmon, whom I don't know too well yet, but hope to."

By the time a halt was called to the hearing, it was almost ten. As the board conferred in whispers, Audrey bent toward Janey and Ellen, quickly patting each of their hands.

Janey met Ellen's eyes and smiled.

The chair announced that the board was ready to be polled. He stated the proposition again: "Should avowed homosexuals be allowed to teach in Bowles Grammar?" Then he called each member's name.

Two "nays," an "aye," a "nay"—from a man they'd been counting on.

Janey's heart sank. Beside her Audrey was muttering under her breath. An uneasy stir went through the room.

Another "nay," an "aye," a fifth "nay"...

They had lost. Janey wanted to vanish from the room. She sat with her chin resolutely up.

The audience buzzed. The chair banged his gavel, continued the vote over the hum of satisfaction, the bitter notes of indignation. He raised his voice calling for silence, waited in vain, then over the noise announced, "The question, 'Should avowed homosexuals be allowed to teach in Bowles Grammar?' has been answered in the negative. The vote is seven to two. May I have a motion to adjourn?"

Very slowly, carefully, Ellen stood and followed Audrey and Janey through the watchful people and out of the town hall. Everything strong and hopeful in her had vanished. She plummeted into the void.

"We're not defeated yet." Audrey's meaningless words came from miles away. "Don't be discouraged, Ellen. This is only the beginning."

Ellen knew Audrey was waiting for her smile. She moved the corners of her mouth slightly. Here was Audrey's car: open the rear door, climb in, sit down.

"You okay, honey?" Janey had climbed in after her, was taking her hand, holding it.

Don't bother me, Ellen wanted to say. She nodded.

"I should have known better than to trust those liberals," Audrey said sadly from the front seat as she started the car. "They always seem so perfectly understanding."

The town at night passed by the car window: blank-faced houses, oily trees like sticks, lonely lights.

The car was silent. Ellen felt Janey glancing at her, waiting for her to do something. Although she wanted to stay perfectly motionless, she heaved a sigh.

"I'll call that lawyer tomorrow," Audrey said brightly.

"They don't want me," Ellen said flatly after a moment.

"It's not personal, Ellen."

"Janey was right. She said I was crazy to trust this town."

Janey was holding her hand very tightly. Ellen turned to see her face, a white mask.

She roused herself to say, "Don't worry, Janey."

Audrey chattered on. "Cliff can use you down at his office for the rest of the summer, if you need the money." Cliff was the local insurance agent, a great giver to charity and bestower of friendly, too-wet kisses.

"Maybe that would work out," Janey urged Ellen.

"Thanks...but these small towns are so backward. I don't know that I want to work with any of those asses..."

"You took a chance," Audrey reminded her.

Ellen translated this: it was her own fault. Rage welled up in her and she slammed a fist sideways against the car window. It shattered in place.

There was a shocked silence.

Ellen stared at the frizzled cracks that radiated out from the clot where her fist had struck. "I'm sorry. I didn't realize I hit so hard. I'll pay for it." She rubbed her hand. The others were making soothing sounds as if she were a mad dog.

"It's just a job, after all," she said. "I can find something else, start over. I wasn't such a hot teacher."

"We'll get your job back." But Audrey's conviction seemed forced. "Do you want to come to my place for a drink?"

"Let's go home, Ellen," Janey said.

Ellen imagined curling up in bed, passing into oblivion. "Yes, home."

"I'm sorry about the window," she said as they climbed out of Audrey's car in front of Janey's quiet, unlit house. "Tomorrow I'll see about getting it fixed."

"Please." Audrey looked up at her. "I regret I didn't do better for you, Ellen."

"You're about the only good thing in this town." Ellen patted her shoulder good-bye.

That night, Ellen woke around two. Bowles was a silent town; the silence seemed to stretch out to infinity. In Buffalo there had always been noise.

Her chest ached with the pain of rejection. She could still see the faces of the board after the vote: self-important, animated. They had avoided meeting her eyes, and she, theirs.

She and Janey would move, leave Bowles.

But Janey would not want to leave. "Have you done that before?" she had asked, referring to Ellen's violence against the car window. Who would relish staying with a failure with violent tendencies?

Then Ellen would go alone, west to...San Francisco. It was okay to be gay in San Francisco. There'd be other lesbians standing up and speaking out as she had done. Change had to start in the cities in order to filter back here arching into the clouds...but the clouds seemed dull and grey.

She would find a job there. Would they hire her as a teacher? Yes, in San Francisco they would, and then Janey would come too. They'd swim every day, never have snow. Ida could run in the golden wheat fields...or something.

The faltering vision died. She turned, clutched the pillow, tried to escape into sleep. Her mother's face, looking down at her calculatingly: no, this child is no good.

Her mother was right. She *was* a misfit. This thing called Ellen had no value. She fell into emptiness. Her sister had been the special one, Ellen the "other one," the "pale one."

"A pale child." She had always been called that. Something pale about her life. As a child she'd felt excluded; in her dreams she was an outsider, yearning to belong. Now, with this vote today—thrown out of town, ridden out on a rail—proof positive. She was judged and found wanting.

She took a deep breath. Maybe some of the townspeople would get together and insist she come back. A campaign would be mounted by the children: they'd refuse another teacher, make signs by hand, and parade in front of the school. "We want Miz Harmon! We want Miz Harmon!" The members of the board would call to apologize. "We were so ignorant and prejudiced. Please forgive us."

If only that would happen. They must reinstate her. Had she really done something terrible enough to deserve this?

Janey stood at the gleaming white stove boiling an egg for breakfast. Ellen had tossed much of the night and was finally asleep. Outside, the sunlight was sporadic: a heavy bank of clouds hung in the west. The white blossoms of the cosmos waved gently; butterflies fluttered over the garden.

She braced herself against the thought that had haunted her the past few weeks as they organized for the board meeting: Ellen would want to leave Bowles. A cold wind blew over her.

If only Audrey could get Ellen's job back. Or could Ellen find something else she liked to do? Maybe work in the library with Janey. Maybe the mayor could urge the county to find the funds.

It was unthinkable to lose Ellen. Janey's chin trembled. Would Ellen want to move to some city? Go back to Buffalo?

In taking the egg off the stove, Janey dropped the pan. Boiling water spread over the linoleum; the egg cracked and lay steaming. Without cleaning up, she sank into the breakfast nook and buried her face in her hands.

A letter arrived in the mail that afternoon when Ellen was home alone:

Dear Ellen and Janey,

You don't know us. We are lesbians living in River Falls and have read about your case with the grammar school. Would you like to get together? We invite you for an August 10 picnic (see invitation). Good luck at the board meeting.

-Rhea and Sally

Gloomily, Ellen studied this cheerful letter written in green ink on a piece of typing paper. She had an urge to crumple it up and throw it away. No calls had come that morning rescinding the board's decision. Janey had gone to work as usual. Cars drove by in their customary rhythm.

Don't brood. Get out and do something nice for someone. A message from childhood concerning disaster surfaced in her mind.

Only there was no one she wanted to do anything nice for. She picked up the new issue of *Ms. Magazine*, leafed through it: an article on child care, a story about two old women, a column advising how to invest in stocks. She laid it down.

Nothing worse than to be alone without a job in a small town, Ellen mourned, the sparse everyday world proceeding merrily along without you.

Janey smiled as an excited woman in red jeans eyed Ellen admiringly and asked Janey, "That's Ellen Harmon, the teacher?"

"Yes." Around them a dozen women holding paper plates weighted down with cold fried chicken and potato salad chatted with one another or stood awkwardly silent. A heavy rain had fallen all day and the August 10 picnic was taking place in Rhea and Sally's rented bungalow. The living room, chilly and empty-feeling when Janey and Ellen had first entered, had warmed as more women showed up. Across one wall was tacked a homemade, brown-paper banner painted with red letters: "Welcome, Ellen and Janey!" In a corner, an aluminum pail noisily caught most of the drips from a leak in the ceiling.

Since they'd arrived an hour before, neither Ellen nor Janey had been long without an admirer. Whenever Janey glanced at Ellen, she was talking importantly. *Good, she's enjoying herself,* Janey thought. Janey had found the discarded invitation to the party under the living room couch; for a change, she was the one to drag Ellen to something.

Janey had been curious to meet Rhea and Sally. It seemed strange to find that only seventy-five miles from Bowles two women had managed to gather so many lesbians around them. Sally was an artist who had left a good city job illustrating textbooks, wore red wedgie sandals with slacks, and accompanied her nervous laugh with graceful, fluttery motions of her fingers. Rhea was a short, solid real estate broker who told corny jokes and knew all the TV shows. Seeing them together, seeing these other women in couples, gave Janey the same teary feeling she'd had at the gay rights march.

"You must be Janey!" the woman in red exclaimed.

"Yes, I am." She smiled, although their making a fuss over her seemed vaguely off, given her own reluctant part in the family lesson.

The woman introduced herself. She was Judy, an old friend of Rhea's; they used to coach a girl's softball team together. "You two were so brave."

A woman in an un-ironed shirt and denim overalls appeared beside them. "Sure picked yourself a hard way to meet some country dykes."

"Pardon?"

"Her getting fired and all."

Janey smiled. This woman, improbably named Jumper, had a rustic, ruddy face with a small, snub nose and short, sandy hair in wisps. Something about her was immediately likable. In fact, just seeing her made Janey want to smile.

"What's she going to do now?"

"She may get her job back," Janey answered.

"Good luck." Jumper looked unconvinced.

"It's hard finding a job," Judy put in. "Unless you've got a skill like Jumper here. She's an electrician. But she's leaving anyway."

"How come?"

Jumper's eyes crinkled at the outside corners. "Orders from Mars."

"She wants to see California. She's driving out to San Francisco," Judy explained in her loud, excited voice.

"San Francisco?" Ellen spoke up from halfway across the room. She excused herself and came over to ask, "Someone's going to San Francisco?"

Jumper nodded. "Yeah. Want to come?"

Janey saw Ellen's eyes go from Jumper's face to hers, back to Jumper's. Her heart sank and her liking for Jumper cooled.

"No, we don't," Janey said. "Don't ask."

"Did you like that girl, Jumper?" Janey asked as Ellen drove them back down the lonely country road that night, the headlights startling the trees and leaves.

"She's not a girl, she's a woman. Yeah, she was okay."

Janey was silent. Ellen and Jumper had liked talking together, that was obvious. How could anyone help liking Jumper?

Ellen remarked, "I told her about the porch light not working and she said she'd stop by and look at it before she goes."

"Oh." Janey's thumb rubbed at her chest.

"Do you ever think about going?"

"I suppose you mean to San Francisco."

"Yeah."

"I don't think that when something goes wrong, you should just up and leave," Janey said. "That's not my way." She set her jaw as Ellen steered the old Ford through the tall trees. "No, I don't think about going."

It was a pleasant summer night; the day had been hot in Bowles, but the evening was balmy and the sounds of children playing ball in the distance were comforting to Janey as she walked home from the library. This was the first day since the family lesson she'd felt anything like normal. The clutch of panic when a shape appeared at the library door was almost gone. The worst seemed miraculously over. She sang a nonsense song to Ida as she sauntered along: "Ida, the goof ball, she's my moof ball. Ida, the wally, she's my folly." On her own street, the blue paint that covered the word "Lezzies" had flaked away, but so had the white letters of the word itself. The goldenrod and black-eyed Susans across the street were in full bloom and she knew as she came past the garage she'd see her own wild flower garden...But there, blocking her view, was an unfamiliar pickup truck instead.

In the living room, Jumper and Ellen were crouched on the floor looking at a map of the United States.

"Hi, sweetheart. Is the Painted Desert worth going to?" Ellen asked Janey as she came in. Janey had taken a trip out West as a girl.

Janey took a deep breath. She liked Jumper but she would have preferred she stay away, given the circumstances. She concentrated on Ellen's question, dimly remembering pastel rocks. "Yes, if you like hot and dry."

"I like hot and dry." Jumper nodded. "The parts that aren't too prickly."

"When are you leaving on your trip?"

"Soon." Jumper considered. "A few days."

"Why don't we go with her, Janey?" Ellen pleaded. "She has room. Audrey could watch the house. We could even take Ida. I'm never going to find another job here."

Janey stood, her hands on her hips. "Ellen, I *do* have a job, remember? And you haven't even looked for a job in Springfield yet. That's not such a terrible commute. Besides, this house needs a paint job before the winter and I want to be here for it. I don't have any desire to run off and try to start over in some city just because you lost your job."

"San Francisco's not just any city. It's—"

Jumper interrupted. "I'll be getting back home now."

Ellen turned to her. "You'll stop by again before you leave?"

"Better not," Jumper drawled. "I'll stay in touch. Send you postcards. I fixed your light, Janey."

Janey collected herself. "Thanks, Jumper." She felt warmer now that Jumper was leaving and pressed her hand as they stood by the pickup. "You have a good trip now. Hope you come back East."

"Jumper, you write now." Ellen looked wistful. "I wish I were you."

"No, you don't. You've got a family," and Jumper backed up the pickup, straightened out, and was gone.

"He doesn't need me, Janey." Ellen threw her dusty dress into the wicker clothes hamper in the bedroom. She'd been to see Audrey's friend Cliff Burns that afternoon. "There's not one paper in that office he's willing for anyone else to touch."

Janey sat on the bed, her chin in her hands. "Maybe you could help out down at the library. I've been wanting to do an inventory."

"Work for you?"

"Why not?"

"It's nice of you to ask but it just doesn't..." Ellen sighed.

Janey pushed her feet into the floor. "Ellen," she said warningly. "I won't go to San Francisco."

Ida looked worriedly between the two of them.

Janey continued, "San Francisco's all I hear about. If you want to go, go by yourself."

Silence. Ellen stood stock-still for an instant, then continued buttoning her shirt.

"I didn't mean it. I don't want you to go, Ellen." Janey went to her lover, took her hands pleadingly. "Don't give up, honey. We'll make a life for ourselves here. As a family, like you want." She tried to pull her close. "I'm getting used to people knowing. It's not as bad as I thought. And I'm sure you can find a job, hon."

Ellen pulled back and tucked her shirt into her jeans. "You're frightened of leaving here, aren't you? That's what it is."

"I'm not frightened," Janey said hotly. "You're the one who's frightened."

They glared at each other.

"There's nothing for me here," Ellen argued, her voice growing high. "I'll never really be comfortable in this town again. You don't really think I'll ever get my job back, do you?"

"You might. Audrey—"

"You know this kind of thing takes years. I'm supposed to hang around meanwhile, having everyone put up with me? Getting bitter and sour? When I think of San Francisco, all my worries vanish. I feel excited, Janey, like we felt at the march. I feel like a bird escaped from a cage. I feel like San Francisco's the promised land." She stared at her lover hopefully. "Please come with me, Janey. Just to look. You could take your vacation days; you could try it out just for a month or so."

At the sight of Ellen pleading, Janey wavered. The last weeks had been one argument after another. Ellen was always so intense, even desperate, in her determination to move on that Janey wondered why she didn't just go with her. It was on the tip of her tongue to agree when Ellen once more urged, "Don't be frightened."

Janey hardened. "Where do you come off telling me not to be frightened after the mess you've made of our lives?" she burst out. "And don't try your tears on me. I told you, I'm not frightened. I just don't want to go to some new place at this point. I'm trying to rebuild my life here. Why don't you try listening to me for a change?"

"Jumper left half an hour ago, Ellen." Sally's voice was sympathetic over the phone. "Can you beat that?"

"She's headed down here to catch the interstate?"

"I imagine so. She was headed for New York City."

"Oh my God. Thanks, Sally." Ellen hung up the wall phone and stood near the breakfast nook gnawing on her thumbnail, her eyes bright. "She just left."

"Well, that decides it," Janey said with obvious relief as she scrubbed dried egg from their breakfast forks. "Now we can have some breathing space."

"We could still go."

"Ellen!"

"I could intercept her at the toll plaza." Ellen raced down the cellar stairs, grabbed a suitcase, raced back up, took the stairs to the bedroom three at a time, and started throwing her clothes in the bag.

Janey ran after her, arrived in the bedroom doorway breathless and alarmed, her eyes wide. "You're not serious!"

"I'll go meet her and get her to stop by here. Jumper won't mind. You can call Audrey and arrange about taking care of the house. You can be all packed when we arrive. That way we won't delay her much at all."

"Ellen, *Ellen!*" Janey shouted, grabbing Ellen's arm in her strong hand and holding it angrily. *"I do not want to go to California!"*

Ellen sighed; her eyes blazed. "You said to call Jumper and see when she was leaving."

"I agreed you could call her. That doesn't mean I want to go."

They eyed each other wildly.

Ellen wrenched her arm away. "I'll go myself then." She ran into the bathroom, grabbing anything she could find in the medicine cabinet.

Janey's hand flew to her forehead. "You can't just suddenly leave!"

"I'll only stay a few weeks." Ellen stopped and faced Janey. They stood in the old-fashioned, wall-papered hall, their eyes frantic. "I've got to go," Ellen said. "I just have to."

"Oh, Ellen," Janey moaned. "Oh, go, then." She slumped into a chair. "You always do what you want," she said in a dead voice.

"Come with me then," Ellen cried in exasperation. She snapped the suitcase shut, checked her purse. "Shall we come back here and pick you up, sweetheart?"

"Don't be silly." As far as Janey was concerned, Ellen might already be as far off as California, she seemed so unaware of reality: Janey's job, Audrey and the attorney, the house, the garden, the painters coming tomorrow, the women's group.

"If you don't want to go, then can you arrange to have my car picked up? I'll leave it at the entrance to the turnpike, near the bus stop."

Janey remained silent, still slumped in the chair. Looking down at the floor, she saw Ellen's feet in socks and sneakers standing in front of her.

"Come on, sweetheart, don't be so glum," Ellen coaxed. "This isn't the end of the world. It's just a chance I can't refuse. It's an adventure. Maybe I won't connect with Jumper. Maybe I'll chicken out and be back in two days. Then you can say, 'I told you so.' " She laughed nervously.

Silence. Janey stared at Ellen's frayed laces. She was on the verge of giving in, so destitute she felt.

"'Bye then, sweetheart." Ellen leaned over and kissed the top of her head. "I'll call."

Janey heard her go downstairs, Ida after her, heard Ellen banging around, saying good-bye to Ida, heard the front door open.

"Janey?" Ellen's voice came up the stairs.

"What?" Janey called belligerently.

"I love you."

Janey said nothing. In a moment the front door was slammed shut. Ellen's car started up. Janey held her breath, listening. The engine revved, then settled into a steady hum. Ida came clicking up the stairs to rest her head on Janey's knees. Janey's hand held Ida's soft ear tightly as she sat immobile, listening to the sound of the engine grow fainter until there seemed no sound in the world at all but the roar of Ellen's absence.

Ellen stood at the side of the road near her Ford, watching the direction from which Jumper should come, concentrating on making the pickup materialize. She was determined not to think about Janey; if she did she might change her mind. Fate had put Jumper and this trip to San Francisco in Ellen's path for a reason—she knew it. This trip was one of those chances life offered that she was compelled to take.

She tried to focus on Jumper. In her mind's eye she conjured up a low, shack-like place over at Stone Creek with weeds and car parts lying around. Jumper's cabin perhaps; Ellen had never seen it. She imagined Jumper's farewell. Jumper would emerge from the shack, swing her bags into the back of the pickup, climb in with hardly a backward look, and drive off. Down that leafy country road she'd come, her overalls hitched over her shoulders, her good-humored face calm, her shoulders relaxed. Down past the bridge, the sawmill, the old park road, through Quarrytown...

Ellen looked at her watch. An hour since Jumper had left. This one little meeting of two people, two specks in God's eye, was all she asked.

She was conscious of the weight of her bag and lowered it to the grass.

"Ellen! Your car break down? Need some help?" A fellow teacher, a sweet-faced woman with an English accent, was just coming off the turnpike.

"No, no, Connie. Just meeting someone!" She waved, self-conscious about the suitcase beside her. God, make Jumper come. In another minute Ellen was going to realize how what she was doing could not be done. Janey's cries would reach her, she would look up to see Audrey's disappointed eyes.

You can't run away, Ellen.

I'm not running away! I'm going to something new, some place I have to go. I'm going to the promised land.

Another city is going to solve your problems?

Let me alone. Let me out. *Jumper!*

The pickup had just come into sight. Ellen waved wildly. "Jumper! Come save me!"

The light-blue truck came slowly closer, pulling over to the side of the road. Jumper looked curiously out at her. "What have we here?"

"We have a very confused woman who has to go to California."

"Right now?"

"Right now. Can I come?"

Jumper frowned. "You're serious?"

"Yes."

Jumper reached across to open the door of the pickup. Ellen threw her suitcase in back and scrambled into the cab. They made the turn toward the toll booth.

"Oh, thank God you came." Ellen sighed and sank back in the seat. She felt infinitely grateful to Jumper: for showing up, for welcoming her, for not mentioning Janey. "I don't know if this is the worst thing or the best thing I ever did."

Jumper reached into a bag at her side and, pulling out an apple, held it out to Ellen. "Whyn't you have something to eat? You look awfully pale."

"Yes...thanks." But Ellen just held the apple, smooth and cool, against her cheek. It reminded her of Janey. She closed her eyes, bit her lip, and waited, pressing the apple hard against her face, while Jumper drove up to the booth, paid the toll, and accelerated onto the on-ramp.

"You're sure you want to do this," Jumper asked again after a minute.

"No."

"Shall I take you back?"

"The next exit's not for twenty miles, is it?"

"No."

Ellen took a deep breath. "Let's see how I feel then."

Late that afternoon, the phone rang once, twice. "It's Ellen!" Janey thought excitedly. "She's changed her mind!" She jumped from the bed where she'd been lying listlessly and grabbed the receiver. "Yes?"

"Janey, hi." It was Audrey.

Janey's breath caught in grave disappointment. "Oh... hi, Audrey."

"Is this inconvenient? Shall I call back?"

"Yes, well...yes, better call back," Janey's voice broke.

"Janey, are you okay?"

"Oh, Audrey..."

"What is it?" Audrey's voice was gentle.

"Ellen left me to go to San Francisco with this other woman!" Janey wailed. Sobs shook her. She could not believe what had happened. Nor could she believe that she had just blurted it out to Audrey. She tried to collect herself. "I shouldn't..."

"Janey. Shall I come over?"

"No, no." Janey slowed her breathing. "No, I'll be okay." She tried to laugh. "She's not left for good. There isn't really another woman. I shouldn't be making such a fuss. No, I'm fine. Fine."

After Audrey hung up, Janey paced. She was embarrassed at having been so raw with Audrey. Anger shook her. Her thoughts whirled. What a sly pair they were—she hated them both. Jumper had lured Ellen away; Ellen had gone willingly. Fixing her light!

Janey switched the porch light on and off. Indeed it was fixed. She walked into the garden, bent to touch the little, cheerful faces of the Johnny-jump-ups. "Oh, you're so unfeeling," she told them sadly. "Don't you know life is hard?" She sank down into the cool, damp grass and curled up near the border. She wanted to sink into the earth and never come back.

After she'd lain there for a while, feeling bereft, another spirit took hold of her. "What, am I supposed to lie here catching pneumonia over her?" she said aloud to Ida. She scrambled up. The painters were due tomorrow and she hadn't disengaged the honeysuckle from the house: she was hoping to save the old vine by gently bagging it in plastic. Swiftly she rounded up her tools and set to work. She felt a surge of power and confidence as she inserted herself between the house and the vine and began to haul its tendriled bushiness away from the wall. It was as if Ellen no longer mattered to her, nor ever had.

"I'm fine," she told Ida excitedly later as she got ready for bed. "I can't believe how good I feel." This feeling stayed with her halfway through the night. It was five in the morning when she woke, her heart beating wildly as she encountered the emptiness beside her in the bed.

"Janey?"

"Ellen! Where are you?"

"New York City. Are you okay? I'm having a very strange time."

Silence.

"Are you there?"

"You're not coming home, are you?" Janey's voice sounded resigned. "You're in love with her."

Ellen laughed. "Don't be ridiculous."

"Well, you may as well be. You ran off with her, didn't you?"

Ellen explained, "I know I'm being selfish but this is right, me being here. This morning I saw it, looking down from the Empire State Building, all those dark canyons stretching into infinity. I've got to follow my own dark canyon."

"What's that supposed to mean?" Janey asked bitterly.

"Just that life is beckoning me, even though it hurts."

"Audrey wants you to call her."

"Sure, I'll call her. I'm sorry I left so suddenly, Janey, but I just had to catch Jumper. Did you get the car?"

"Yes, we did...How long are you going to stay?"

"I don't know. We haven't even *left* yet, Janey. This afternoon we'll ride the Staten Island Ferry. It's a gorgeous day here, very clear. This morning I could almost see clear up to Bowles."

A pause. "The painters are here today. Did you happen to see *them?*"

"Oh, sure. Gee, yes, I forgot. How's it going?"

Silence.

"Oh, Janey, I just can't help you from this distance. I wish I could help you, sweetheart."

"Yeah, sure." And Janey hung up.

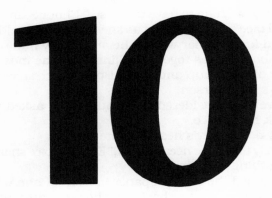

10

"Do you ever take a child in your lap, Miss Kowalski?"

"No, never," Janey answered quickly.

"Or touch a child in any way?"

"No." She flushed.

"Still," her interrogator turned to a fellow member of Friends of the Library, "the parents may well worry."

"I'm always very careful," Janey assured the four women and two men who sat with her at one of the wooden reading tables in the otherwise empty library. Six weeks to the day after Ellen had left, Janey had been invited to this evening meeting to discuss "certain issues." The impetus had come from the newest member of Friends of the Library, Boy Walker, a follower of the Rev. William Wilson. Balding and taut-bodied, Boy sat aggressively at the head of the table firing his questions at her.

By now Janey felt broken. She sat looking down at her hands—her guilty hands—feeling ashamed. It was hard to remember that she'd ever chanted at the gay rights march. It was hard to remember that she'd been moved to tears by Audrey and Ellen's pleas at the town meeting. All her attempts to reassure herself were failing. Being a lesbian was shameful. Even being in love with Ellen had turned out as badly as possible, worse than she could ever have imagined. People were probably laughing about it.

"Janey, we hate to have to pry so." Elinor Samuelson's worn old face looked worried as she twisted her gold watch back and forth on her wrist. She and Janey had run half a dozen book drives together. Elinor was the most active member of the group and, until Boy Walker arrived, had been its spokesperson.

"Have you considered resignation?" he asked now in his quick hard voice.

"Oh, no." Janey's heart plummeted.

"Surely there's no need for that!" Elinor's voice sharpened. "Why, nothing's happened!"

He tapped the sheet of paper in front of him with two fingers. "You saw my chart." It showed patronage had declined slightly since the family lesson. He had continued his downward-sloping line until no one at all came to the library.

"Perhaps a retraction letter!" Marilyn Bradstraw, the sixth-grade teacher, put in brightly. She wore dark red lipstick and earrings that were little pianos. "Janey really isn't what people think, we all know that. Why, we've known Janey for years. She's not, you know, perverted." She shook her head in tiny motions as if batting the idea away. "That's nonsense. Would you be willing to write a retraction letter, Janey?"

"Yes," she said doubtfully. Retract what? Did they mean retract the family lesson, or retract being a lesbian? "But what should it say?"

Marilyn looked to Boy.

" 'What should it say!' The truth, obviously!"

"I mean—"

Elinor came to the rescue. "Say that your friend misled you, that you're not really a, uh, lesbane. That you want to be forgiven for trying to help another and getting in deeper than was wise. Something of that sort."

"Yes, I see." Janey nodded. Her throat ached with held-back tears. She doubted if anyone would believe the letter but maybe it didn't matter. Its purpose was not to tell the truth but to reassure. The letter was to say, "Don't worry. This business is closed and will never again be heard about in Bowles."

"Make clear it was not your fault, what happened," Marilyn advised. "If you bring it to me at the school tomorrow," she added, "I'll show it to the others and then take it over to the newspaper office. It can go out as an open letter to the citizens of Bowles. We can still make Saturday's *Clarion.*"

"If it speaks of true repentance and is not merely an empty gesture, perhaps the town will open its arms to you again." Boy's hard voice softened. "The spirit of public forgiveness is strong."

Janey nodded. What would have struck her as ludicrous and insulting any other time now seemed vaguely hopeful. "I'll draft a letter tonight," she agreed.

They looked temporarily relieved, but Marilyn took a breath and went on, "There's another thing, Janey. About your new boarder. You really must do something about her. It doesn't look right. One day she's wearing a long, filmy dress and the next she's in boots, with chains dangling over her shoulders. No one knows what to make of her."

"Cynthia? Yes, well, she'll be leaving soon. She just needed a place to stay for a few days."

"There goes your soft heart again." Marilyn, the teacher, shook her index finger at Janey. "Now, promise me you'll leave these queer girls to fend for themselves. First that Ellen Harmon woman and now this!"

Janey did not like having a finger shaken in her face. She did not like hearing Ellen and Cynthia maligned. She felt if this meeting went on much longer she'd start to scream uncontrollably.

"I'm sorry to have caused so much trouble," she said. "But I'll do as you suggest. Tomorrow I'll bring that letter to you, Marilyn. And I'll speak to Cynthia," she added.

The members of the group murmured and nodded. Boy regarded her paternally. "You're a nice girl, I can see that," he told her.

Rage rose suddenly in Janey. She could not look at him and nod and smile, as she tried to do. Something in her prevented it.

On the way home, in the warm Indian summer darkness, she reproached herself: *You can't afford the luxury of getting angry. You should have smiled. Done whatever was necessary to keep your job.*

But something in her could not submit.

When she reached home, both Ida and Cynthia were standing at the window waiting for her, their dark forms outlined against the light. Cynthia's head of curly hair seemed as large and confused as a tumbleweed.

As Janey entered the living room, she wanted to cry. Even here, in her own home, things had become unfamiliar and foreign. The place smelled of Cynthia's favorite spice tea. Ida was wearing a new red kerchief tied around her black furry neck. "Look, Cynthia, Ida doesn't like—"

Cynthia interrupted. "Janey, the coincidence is manifest. I told you it was meant to be. It happened just as I said. She heard my plea across the miles, picked up the phone, and dialed." Cynthia's ethereal, high-cheekboned face, a silver star glued to her forehead, beamed.

"Do you mean—"

"She called."

Janey's heart beat faster. "Ellen!" For all the trouble Ellen had caused, Janey still wanted nothing more than to hear her voice again.

"That's the lady." Cynthia looked as pleased as if Ellen had been *her* long-lost lover. Cynthia's rangy body was decked out in a white, see-through Indian shirt, a long, blue calico skirt with ruffled, uneven hem, and a denim jacket with metal studs. She leaned against the back of the couch and twisted one leg around the other.

"Did she leave a number?" Janey asked eagerly.

"*Unfortunatement, non,*" Cynthia said in French. "But she said to tell you she'll call again. Ellen is living life a capella." She touched the star on her forehead. "I must tell you, Janey, that I learned some things about her. Why didn't you tell me she was a narcissist!"

"Oh, Cynthia, you don't even know her." Janey had told herself she was over Ellen, but she'd been wrong. She felt like her elation might lift her straight into the air and all the way to California. Let them take their precious job! She was not going to grovel for it. "Did she say when she'd call back?"

"No," Cynthia answered. "But Janey, I need to tell you some things about Ellen. They explain everything. Not that anything's wrong, you were definitely made for each other, but you have to realize—she's only in love with herself. Most people are."

"Yes, but is there any of that casserole left?" Janey asked as she headed into the kitchen. She'd been too nervous to eat much before the meeting. Now she felt ravenous.

"I kept some warm for you." Cynthia trailed after her, lifted the lid of the white enamel double boiler and peered in. "You see, Ellen has to be the center of attention. Narcissus stared at himself in a pool, but it was not for love exactly. Ellen doesn't know she's self-centered. She thinks she's a good person, no doubt. Witness her coming out at the school. But if she'd thought of you she wouldn't have done it. She doesn't have long-range judgment. Which is one of your strong points, actually. But people are different. You were the cause, Janey. She wanted to impress you. She's always been on the dead side of life, you're of the living. That's what was going on. She was begging to be among the alive. Probably her mother didn't pick her up when she cried."

As she held out a plate for Cynthia's lentil and walnut surprise, Janey listened with a certain hunger to this garbled analysis. She had met Cynthia at Rhea and Sally's just after Ellen left. When Cynthia turned up on her doorstep a few days later needing a place to stay until her mail-order teepee arrived, Janey had invited her in for the night.

A month later she was still there, the first person Janey had known who lived on the edge of society, with no home of her own and no regular job. In Bowles she'd found odd jobs, cleaning houses and weeding gardens. Regularly she confided to Janey her secret attractions to the various women of the town. "It's a shame they're wasted on men," she said wistfully. But although Cynthia talked a lot, she was not a complainer. There was something accepting about her that soothed the pain of Ellen's leaving. And at first Cynthia's non-stop analysis and kitchen clatter had been comforting; it broke the unbearable silence of Ellen's being gone.

"Did you tell her when I'd be back?"

"I said around nine."

Janey glanced at her watch: eight-forty. "I don't like to think of her as a narcissist," she ventured. She was wolfing down her food; Cynthia was a wonderful cook.

"Oh, no, she might look like a narcissist, but she's the very opposite." Cynthia never minded contradicting herself. "She has no sense of herself at all. I think she was hoping for Bowles to define her. She was begging. That's why she looks so pale in her pictures. Inside, she feels like nothing."

At that moment Janey became aware of the faint word "lesbian" ringing in the air. Alarmed, she listened harder. From upstairs came the sound of someone singing, with musical accompaniment, the word "lesbian" over and over again.

"What's that song?" she interrupted. "Why's your record player on?"

"Oh, I meant to tell you. I invited Ruthie and her girlfriend over to listen to my records. They needed a place to be alone."

"Those high school girls?"

"Yes, I met—"

"You don't mean to tell me those teenage girls are upstairs in a room with a bed in it!" Janey hurried back through the living room to the stairs.

Behind her, Cynthia hastened to explain. "Janey, these girls are in love and they have nowhere to go. They told me they really admire you and Ellen, and I thought they'd have a safe place here. They're badly in need of some sister-hood."

Janey took the stairs two at a time. She had come to know the girls at the library. Ruthie was a high school senior, the daughter of Hattie Carter who worked at the dry cleaner's and lived on the road to the dump. A year before, Janey would have labelled the girl a withdrawn loner who lived life through the fat novels she was constantly checking out from the library. Lately, though, all that had changed. Now Ruthie seemed to smile a lot, could be seen mooning over slim poetry books and running around town at all hours with her new friend Donna, the youngest daughter of the mayor. Janey had seen them together in the drugstore, stealing bites of each other's hot fudge sundaes, or walking through town arguing, or sitting down by the creek looking into the water, their shoulders touching. Janey liked them and could not help rejoicing at their friendship, but the last thing she wanted was for these two girls to be introduced to lesbianism in her house.

"They need *some* place to go, Janey."

"What, are you crazy?"

The door to Ellen's old room was ajar. Ruthie, tall, taut, dark-haired, and Donna, also tall, muscular, healthy-looking, blond, looked as if they'd just jumped up from the bed. They were straightening their clothes and smoothing their hair down, while Alix Dobkin sang on: "Les-be-in no man's land. Lesbian, lesbian, any woman can be a lesbian—"

Janey gave them a moment, then pushed the door wide open. "I'm sorry but you two girls shouldn't be in this house. Cynthia, would you please turn that thing off?"

The radiant look on the young women's faces dimmed. "Cynthia said—" Ruthie offered in her low voice.

"Well, Cynthia shouldn't have said..."

The song stopped abruptly as Cynthia lifted the needle.

"You shouldn't even be *seen* near this house," Janey went on. She was agitated but not sure what to say to these two rosy, excited young women. At the same time that she wanted to sternly lecture them on the gravity of what they were doing, she had an urge to congratulate and hug them. "I'm sorry to be so brisk, but this town is very un-understanding about these things. To say the least. You saw what happened to Ellen Harmon."

"We were just listening to records," Donna assured her, smoothing the wrinkles out of the bedspread and picking up her bookbag in one graceful motion.

"If you want, we'll leave right away. We don't want to get you in trouble too," Ruthie added quickly. She was aglow with sexual energy.

The girls collected their things and hurried down the stairs after Janey. She led them into the kitchen, peered out the window into the dark back yard. "You can cross through the Cutters' garden—they're not home—and sneak from the Marshes' down to the drugstore. Do you need a flashlight?"

"Ruthie can see in the dark," Donna said. She looked at her friend admiringly.

"Like a cat," Ruthie almost purred. She and Donna giggled.

Cynthia handed them each an oatmeal cookie drizzled with chocolate.

Donna stuck one arm in her jacket. "Thank you both for letting us use your place. It was the first time we could really relax together."

At this the two girls gave a sudden delighted laugh, then glanced apologetically at Janey.

Janey could not help smiling, but she stared harder into the night. "I think it's safe," she said.

The phone startled them all. "Go," Janey hissed and shooed them into the dark, struggling into their jackets. She hurried to pick up the receiver, thinking *Ellen!*

"Janey, this is the mayor. Is your boarder there?" He had a smooth, commanding voice.

Janey caught her breath. "Yes, Cynthia's here."

"Will you put her on?"

"Just a minute."

At her name, Cynthia had looked up expectantly, chewed her cookie fast, gulped, and reached out her hand for the receiver, but Janey held on to it and shook her head. Now that she thought of it, putting Cynthia on did not seem a good idea. "I'm sorry. I thought she was here but I can't find her. Something I can help you with?"

"I'm looking for Donna."

"Oh. Is she missing?" Janey put on a worried tone.

"Not exactly. But she was seen earlier with that friend of hers Ruthie Carter and your boarder. I want her home."

"Well, Cynthia was here half an hour ago. I haven't seen your daughter. Don't worry. I imagine she's fine. You know how teenagers are." Janey glanced at her watch. "Do you want Cynthia to call you if she has any information?"

"Yes..." The mayor seemed about to add something.

"Anything else?"

"Janey, do you know this Ruthie Carter?"

"Not really."

"Girls like that prey on the innocent, if you know what I mean."

"No, actually I don't. She's very well-read, I know that."

"Yes, but what kind of reading?"

"Mayor, I'm sorry but I really have to go," Janey said. "I'll have Cynthia call you if she knows anything."

She stopped herself from banging down the phone and hung up carefully. "Asshole," she said, but her hands were trembling. "Oh, yes, your daughter was here. With Ruthie Carter, listening to lesbian songs in the bedroom." Janey gave Cynthia a dark look, sank down in the breakfast nook, and covered her face with her hands.

She sensed Cynthia sit down across from her. "He might have understood—"

Janey uttered a yelp of outrage.

"Except that he's a Scorpio Rising," Cynthia added quickly. She adjusted the star on her forehead, moving it slightly to the left. "Janey, I appreciate your taking my place with the mayor. I would have been pleased to talk to him but my planets are in the wrong place."

Janey did not disagree. "Cynthia, I hate to say this but I'm getting in worse and worse trouble at work, and it would help a lot if you, well—have you checked about your teepee recently?"

"They say it's on the way. It should be here any day now," Cynthia said worriedly. Her pale fingers fluttered over her star. She seemed to have lost all her usual optimism. "My teepee will be my heart space. Perhaps, until then, I could sleep in the park. Like Ellen is in California."

Janey sat up. "Ellen is sleeping in the park?"

"Yes, and she's out of funds."

"Is that why she called? To ask for money?"

"No, she said she'd just gotten a job counting cars. She stands by the side of the road and counts cars. Near some bridge in San Francisco."

Janey looked at the time: nine-thirty. She leapt up, paced around the kitchen worriedly, stopped to lift the phone to check the dial tone.

"That sounds dangerous. Why doesn't she call?" She checked her watch again. "Doesn't she know it's getting late here? But she doesn't care—" She looked at Cynthia. "She took a job?"

Cynthia started to reply

but Janey went on agitatedly, "So she's planning to stay for a while. And she doesn't even have the decency to call and tell me about it!"

"She did call," Cynthia pointed out. She was cleaning off the salt shaker on her skirt. "She can't live without you. She needs your egg-ness. But, now that I think about it, I guess she won't call back right away. She's an Aries, so you'll have to be patient. They're very jealous. They'd sooner their mate died than that they turned to someone else. Even just a boarder like me." She smiled and seemed to glow again, back in stride. "I'm sorry, Janey. I always said, never choose an Aries unless you want to live dangerously. They're hot-headed. Being a Cancer, you're more adaptable. I knew a couple—"

"Please be quiet, Cynthia," Janey asked.

"I'll tape my mouth closed," Cynthia promised. A moment later she added, "I'll move out tomorrow or the day after. I'm sure that my teepee will arrive by then."

Janey nodded tiredly, thinking, *May God speed your teepee to this house.*

It was midnight and Ellen still had not called. Janey sat down at her old dressing-table-turned-desk and wrote two letters in angry succession:

Dear Ellen,

I cannot believe your thoughtlessness. Don't you ever think of anyone but yourself?

This is to notify you that I don't wish to see or hear from you ever again. I mean it.

Janey

To my fellow citizens:

I hope you all know me as a friendly member of our community. I've enjoyed serving as your librarian and I hope you feel well-served by me. Recent events make it necessary to convey some information to you and to ask for your understanding and compassion. Over the past year I was influenced by another to claim membership in a group with whom I have nothing in common. I have never been, nor am I now, a lesbian. I trust this will put an end to rumor and I can once more be simply your librarian.

Janey Kowalski

Janey sat staring at this letter. The sentence "I have never been, nor am I now, a lesbian" leapt out at her. "I have always been and am now a lesbian," she said in a low voice. She closed her eyes and rubbed her forehead. "I have never been, nor am I now, a lesbian. I have always been and am now a lesbian. I have never been, nor am I now, a lesbian. I have always been but am no longer a lesbian. I have never been but am now and will always be a lesbian."

There came a knock on the door. "Janey, are you okay? Do you want me to fix you some warm milk?"

"Go to sleep, Cynthia," Janey called. "I'm just talking to myself." She turned off the light and went to curl up in the window seat and look out into the darkness. The moon had come out and was shining on the fir tree. There were wispy clouds slowly moving across the sky. Ellen might be seeing the same sky, lying in some park; probably not a city park, as Janey had first imagined, but a park where people camped, a state or national park. During the day, Ellen stood on some city street and counted cars. What kind of a job was that for a naive person like Ellen! California was full of lunatics. All it took was one, driving by. Janey clasped her hands together. "Whoever and wherever You are, keep her safe," she whispered.

She would not submit the retraction letter, she thought. Ellen would have wildly objected to it. "Are you going to be dictated to by some pinhead?" Janey could imagine her asking.

"Do you mean *you*?" Janey whispered fiercely back. It seemed she could almost feel Ellen in the room with her, that special indescribable feeling of Ellen, just being there.

In the morning, practical considerations seemed more important than noble thoughts concocted by the light of the moon. She stopped by the school at recess time and found Marilyn in her classroom, writing words in large, looping letters on the blackboard: "antidisestablishmentarianism," the longest English word, and "a," one of the shortest, Marilyn pointed out. She brushed the chalk off her hands to read the retraction letter, nodded, then frowned. "This is just what I envisioned, Janey. However, this word, 'l-l-lesbian,' doesn't it stand out too much? It's not a calming word. Isn't there some other word we could use?"

"Homosexual."

"Let's try that." Marilyn moved a box of American Dairy Association pamphlets on good nutrition from her desk, laid the letter down, crossed out "lesbian" and wrote in "homosexual." "Oh, no, that's worse." She crossed out "homosexual" and put "stet" next to "lesbian." "Isn't there some other word?"

"Pervert," Janey suggested. "Deviant. Gay. How about 'gay'?"

"Oh, no. People here might resent using that word to mean...you know. That's an old English word."

Janey stood waiting. Through the window half a dozen children hung and teetered on the jungle gym. She recognized two girls from the family lesson doing a particularly complicated maneuver, their brows furrowed, their lower lips caught in their teeth.

"Well, I'll try 'gay.' " Marilyn crossed out "stet," and wrote in "gay." "No, people won't know what that means." She crossed out "gay" and wrote in "androdyne." "Isn't that a word?"

"Androgyne."

Marilyn corrected her spelling. "Is that okay? 'I have never been and am not now an androgyne.' "

"Fine," Janey said, staring at a large, black plastic map of the United States, each state outlined in white but not named.

"It sounds rather elegant," Marilyn said, pleased with herself.

Later that day she called Janey at the library. "Boy refuses to approve the letter unless you say either 'l-lesbian' or 'homosexual.' He doesn't like 'androgyne.' Perhaps he's right."

"How about 'lesbian'?"

"All right. But it's certainly not calming."

Janey pushed her pencil lead into the order form she was completing until the point broke with a satisfying crunch. "They should be able to stand reading the word at least once," she said dryly.

Marilyn laughed. "Let's hope this is the end of it."

Ellen didn't call back and Janey grew more and more depressed. When her retraction letter appeared in the *Clarion* three days later, she lost her appetite. There seemed some connection between the letter and Ellen's silence. It didn't help to tell herself that master politicians made false statements like hers all the time, that it was a tactic of modern life, redirecting public opinion. Every time she thought of the letter her stomach fell. Audrey called and Janey was immediately defensive.

"I know you don't approve, but you're not in danger of losing your job, Audrey."

"Janey, I'm sure you had your reasons. Look at what happened to Ellen despite all our work. I understand completely."

"I don't feel good about it. I didn't think it would bother me. But reading it..."

What especially bothered Janey about the letter was imagining Ruthie and Donna's reaction to it. *They're just young girls, what do they know of life?* she told herself. Neither of them had come to the library that week...it was just as well, she thought.

As for the rest of the world, Cynthia was disturbed momentarily but explained it all as a function of Janey's essential nature. Bert didn't mention the retraction letter, just referred to the *Clarion* as full of "rubbish." Library use went up slightly and even though Janey thought that had more to do with the weather—people read more in a cold spell—the Friends of the Library group seemed satisfied.

Slowly her depression lifted. She decided to set up a special shelf at the library. At first, she conceived of it as holding books about women in general, but almost all she found were written by men. She altered her plan: the shelf would be entitled "Interesting Books by Women." Elinor, who helped her set up the shelf, remarked, "It would be much easier, given our holdings, to come up with something called 'Uninteresting Books by Men'." They laughed together, Janey's troubles with Friends of the Library temporarily forgotten. They agreed on a dozen books and Janey supplemented them with most of Ellen's feminist collection.

Ruthie and Donna came in after school one day, examined the new shelf, and turned to Janey, clearly pleased. Ruthie made a suggestion: *The Dialectic of Sex*, by Shulamith Firestone, belonged on the shelf and should be ordered. As the young women made their choices—Ruth Herschberger's 1948 classic, *Adam's Rib*, and Robin Morgan's 1970 ground-breaking anthology, *Sisterhood is Powerful*—Janey beamed. She felt a particular pleasure, handing the two young women these revolutionary books.

Shortly afterward she had a dream. She was in the arena of a huge stadium and all the seats were filled. She and four other women were dressed alike in pinafores and they were attempting to dance a square dance. None of them was particularly attractive and their dancing was awkward. The audience was restless, uninterested. Janey was mortally embarrassed. She felt, "I am not like these women I dance with. They are pathetic. By being with them, I too become pathetic."

Then something changed. She felt a kinship with them. She felt she belonged with them. She cared for them. She cared more for them than she cared for the audience.

A letter from California arrived, but not in Ellen's handwriting. Janey tore it open, standing in front of the mailbox in the cold. Her breath was steamy. Around her the air was crackly and a cold wind stirred the bare branches of the maple in her front yard and the elms by the garage so they rubbed against each other and whined.

Oct. 10, 1975

Dear Janey,

In case Ellen hasn't written to tell you, she has been down in the dumps since calling Bowles. She imagines you are with someone else although I think that's unlikely. She obviously still loves you. I thought you should know. She has a post office box: P.O. Box 2992, Fairfax, California.

I guess it's starting to get cold where you are. Here the skies are clear and sunny every day.

I'm taking off for Oregon for three months. Ellen will be staying in California.

Hope you're fine.

Sincerely,
Jumper

Oct. 20, 1975

Dear Ellen,

I swore I wasn't going to write until you called back. But Jumper wrote to me and said you were worried I was in love with Cynthia. Ellen, this is very far from the truth. You are so volatile, it's like having a relationship with a firecracker.

Are we having a relationship? For all I know, you've found someone else in California. Although I guess Jumper would have told me if you had. She seems to care more about you and me staying together than you do.

Cynthia said you took some kind of job there. I hope it's just temporary.

I need to hear from you, Ellen. PLEASE WRITE OR PHONE.

Love,
Janey
P.S. Ida sends her love

Dear Janey,

Just because I haven't written or called doesn't mean I haven't been thinking about you a lot lately and wondering what you're doing. It's true: after talking to your new roommate I got this idea in my head you two were together. She seemed to have a lot of insight into you. (A few things she said stuck in my mind—that you didn't know yourself very well, nor how power-ful you could be, and that you were the epitome of earth energy.) Anyway, even though she told me she was only staying there temporarily, I didn't believe it. I went into a jealous funk and stayed there till your letter came.

I don't blame you if you're still really mad at me. I came into your life and turned it upside down, all the time preaching at you in a way. I notice out here that the women who are most impressed with my account of the family lesson are the younger ones, the ones the others call naive. I hate to think of myself as naive, but I guess I was and both of us have suffered from it. I'm sorry, Janey, really I am.

Part of the reason I didn't call or write was that things hadn't been going very well for me until yesterday. I had this idea if I found a good job and a place to live I could get you to move out here, so I looked for a teaching job. But nobody'd hire me after the family lesson—that letter you for-warded to me from the state Teachers' Certification Board should have been a warning: the patriarchy all across the continent was furious at me for saying the word lesbian aloud! I finally ended up with a low-paying job counting cars for Jumper's genius cousin Roger. He's a computer programmer who's working on some programs to control traffic.

Roger may be a genius—I guess he is—but you could also call him an idiot savant. He's lousy at almost everything in life except a certain kind of logical thinking. I could see his project was never going to get off the ground. Talking to him, I got more and more interested in working on it myself. Yesterday I got up my nerve to ask if I could get some programming training and become his assistant. He agreed and I'm scheduled to start a three-week computer course next week, paid for by his backer.

Now, I know this probably sounds like I'm going off in some cockeyed direction and need you to calm me down, but another good thing just happened which makes me hopeful that everything may work out for us. The big apartment below Roger's is going to be free in mid-November and the manager said I can have it. It's got four rooms and a yard out back and they don't mind pets. (Ida, are you listening?) The place I'm in now is fun in some ways. I share with three lesbians and we're constantly talking politics. But Althea, who's only twenty-one, is developing a crush on me, I think. She's always mooning around my room these days. You'd think I'd like this but it only makes me uncomfortable. I miss *you.*

How is Ida? I miss her, too. Sometimes, when I let my imagination go, I see us living together in that big apartment under Roger's. I imagine us walking out in our shirt sleeves on some warm, sunny January day, jumping into our car, and whipping off to the gorgeous beach (only twenty minutes away) where I often see dogs having the time of their lives.

Janey, if this is a possibility, I will be so happy. The other chance for us to be together, me returning to Bowles, I have trouble imagining. I wish I could be different and sacrifice everything to be with you. I wish I were stronger and more courageous about returning to forge a life again in Bowles.

Rereading this letter, I see that things haven't changed, that I am still trying to get you to do what I want. If only, if only, there was a chance you wanted the same things...

     I love you,
     Ellen

Janey sat at her dressing table, rubbing lotion nervously into the dry spots on her heels and rereading Ellen's letter. She did not know what to make of it. Her heart popped with excitement: Ellen loved her, they would be together again. Then she grew depressed. "She doesn't love us enough to come back," she told Ida sadly. "Still," she went on, "don't be too upset. She still loves us. We may see her again. But you wouldn't like California, would you?" Ida looked like she would.

"No, you wouldn't," Janey told her. "First it's real dry and then it rains all the time. Besides, this is our home." Janey looked around at the walls papered in cream-colored flowers, the dark green drapes, and shining furniture. "This is where we belong." She bent over the dressing table, resting her head on her folded arms. Ida came and laid her head on Janey's knee in commiseration. Janey could smell Ida's fresh, wild, doggy fur and the almond lotion on her own hands. From downstairs she could hear banging in the kitchen where Cynthia was rearranging the shelves: her teepee had not yet arrived. "At least, this room is our home," Janey muttered to Ida. "I don't know about the house or the town any more."

The mayor was seated behind a large, carved desk in his study. "I asked you to come over tonight, Janey," he began, "because my daughter insisted. The situation is this: she has entered a phase that I understand is not unusual for an adolescent girl—a crush on another female. They have not only exchanged love letters," he indicated a piece of lettered stationary in front of him, "but have engaged in some..." He waved again and frowned. "This is not unnatural. Not unnatural. But it cannot, I repeat, *cannot* continue. It has gone on too long as it is."

Janey wished she could vanish. The mayor's voice was controlled, but his aristocratic face was flushed and a muscle in his cheek twitched. Donna sat nearby in a large, dark leather chair, her eyes red, her hands nervous. Beside her, Janey was perched in her own mammoth chair. The well-appointed study was so emotionally charged it was hard to breathe.

"I told him," Donna fixed her eyes on Janey's face hopefully, "that you would tell him how important loving another woman is. That it can't just be stopped."

"Well—" Janey began uncertainly.

"I'd hardly call that Carter girl a woman." The mayor laughed shortly. With studied patience, his cheek twitching, he turned his attention to Janey. "But I promised Donna I'd hear you out. Go ahead."

"Well," Janey began again. What did they want from her, this mad pair? It was almost ten—she'd been getting ready for bed—when the mayor's command phone call had arrived: would she come to his house immediately? The study with its giant furniture was close and stuffy, the drapes were pulled. The mayor in his silver hair and charcoal-grey sweater sat metal-like in front of her; Donna was a pink and green patch of anxiety to her left. Janey was confused. Her sympathies were not very clear: wasn't it more sensible, as the mayor thought, to separate the two girls? They were too young to be so serious. They'd bounce back. At the same time she felt him the enemy: an intolerant, arrogant man trying to stamp out soft and tender things.

"I—" she began again. "I'd like to help but I really don't see how."

"Aha! Yes." The mayor failed to control a triumphant snort; he turned to his daughter. "Just as I predicted. You're barking up the wrong tree. Your champion's a smart woman. She renounced the whole sticky business in the *Clarion*, called it a mistake. Just as you should do."

"Not a mistake exactly," Janey put in.

"In so many words. You washed your hands of it."

"Yes, but—" Janey shifted uncomfortably in the leather chair, pulled herself forward to its edge to plant her feet solidly on the tan carpet. "I think you'd call that letter a tactical statement. I was trying to reassure the town."

The mayor eyed her warningly. "Then don't un-reassure us. This business hasn't been good for Bowles. Ellen Harmon's outburst unsettled many good peoples' lives, you know. Including my daughter's and my own."

"Jesus Christ's outbursts unsettled many good peoples' lives too," Janey pointed out.

He snorted. "Not exactly the same."

She hesitated. "They both talked about love," she ventured. It was strange. Janey did not exactly want to be saying what she was saying. She did not think her words were wise; part of her felt quite in danger. But she hated

117

his putting down Ellen, she hated his once-happy daughter's red eyes and nervous hands, she despised the scribbled notes on his desk about private schools strewn over Ruthie's careful script: the love poem he'd intercepted.

He laughed disparagingly.

"You're right to laugh." Janey was angry. "I shouldn't put them in the same category. Christians have killed millions to get their way. Homosexuals never hurt anyone."

"That's right," Donna said excitedly. "She's right, Dad."

"My daughter is not a homosexual!" he said tightly.

"I am too, and I'm proud of it." Donna darted a triumphant glance at Janey.

Janey quailed and then set herself for a fight. It was as if she had walked on stage, Ruthie and Donna had thrown a dramatic purple robe over her and she was now Queen of Homosexuals, whether she liked it or not. "Homosexuality's nothing to be ashamed of. You should be proud of her."

"Donna, leave the room."

"I won't." Her hands grabbed the arms of the leather chair.

"Don't be difficult. I need to talk to Miss Kowalski alone."

"I won't leave. I can hear anything."

"Then I'm afraid this discussion must come to a close." He stood up.

Donna shot him a bitter look. "Okay, okay, I'll leave." As she obeyed him, her eyes sent out a long swell of appeal to Janey.

He lowered himself into his swivel chair to stare at Janey. "A few months ago I had a decision to make, just as you do now. A number of interested parties wanted your resignation. Bill Rice's daughter is a librarian in Boston, as you probably know. What you may not know is she'd move back to Bowles in a minute if your job were available."

Janey's heart pounded. "No, I didn't know." Bill Rice was the mayor's fishing buddy. His daughter Amy was young and smart and well-liked.

"I wasn't ready to lose a perfectly good worker like you unless it was really necessary. I stood by you, Janey, in that difficult hour."

Janey nodded warily. "I appreciate that."

"I want you to stand by me now. Don't feed Donna this idealistic nonsense you people use to rationalize your problem. Let her know instead how that Harmon girl misled you, exposed you, and betrayed you. Just as this Carter girl has misled her. This isn't love between them— it's some adolescent sickness." He leaned toward her, spoke to her directly, man-to-man. "Help Donna see that."

"In fact," Janey said, "I can't help her see that since I don't believe it. I imagine they love each other just as any two young people do. More, perhaps, since society's against them."

The mayor sat back angrily.

Janey persisted, "Theirs could turn out to be a very strong relationship."

His cheek twitched. "I imagine if either of us is an authority on strong relationships, I have the better claim. My wife and I have been together twenty years. What's more, there's never been a harsh word between us."

Janey flinched inwardly but set her shoulders. "Really," she said. His affair with a woman in the next town was common knowledge. Yet everyone agreed his wife adored him.

His face softened in a practiced way. "I often say to her, 'A man provides the strength and decisiveness, a woman the compassion and understanding. I am the rock. You are the rose.' "

Janey had heard this embarrassing passage before; it was part of the mayor's campaign speech. He went on, "I can come home out-of-sorts and she always knows exactly what to do to calm me down. Exactly. Now, *there's* a strong relationship. That's what I want for Donna."

He was sincere, Janey could see that, but her compassion was not aroused. "Your daughter's had years to observe your marriage. I guess if she wants one like it, she can find one," she said flatly.

His face hardened. "Yes, that's what I intend. But I see I can count on no help from you."

"You can count on the whole world for help," Janey said. "She can only count on people like me."

He stood up, as did Janey. She knew he wanted her to go, but she hesitated. He loomed over her, a tall confident man, momentarily upset over his daughter but assured of his power in the world.

In that moment she seemed to see her future in Bowles: retraction letter after retraction letter. "No, she was not a lesbian," "No, she had not meant to anger the mayor," "No, she was not an advocate of teenage sex," "Yes, she would do what everyone wanted," "No, she would not argue again," "Yes, she would apologize," "Yes, she would stand on her head to keep her job out of Amy Rice's hands."

Janey and the mayor regarded each other across the wide desk. His eyes were impatient, held no sympathy. Nor did hers. For his part, she saw, she was no longer of use to him; for her part, she hardly thought him human.

"I believe I'll submit my resignation," she said.

He frowned. "There's no need to be hasty," he reproached her. "I'm sure we all count on you."

"Don't worry. I'll give proper notice."

She turned to leave. A curious floating feeling had come over her. She picked up her brown purse, her green wool coat; the little woolly hairs on it gleamed.

"I won't consider this final," the mayor said as he followed her down the carpeted hall to the door. "A decision made at the height of emotion. Let me help you with your coat."

Janey hardly heard him. She stepped away from him, out into the cold night. There were thousands of stars in the black sky. They seemed mysteriously reassuring.

12

Moments later, as she started up her car, she was startled by Ruthie slipping out of the shrubbery to tap on the passenger window. The tall, dark-haired girl was tense, cracking her knuckles. She wore a thin jacket and her features were pinched from the cold. Janey leaned across the seat to roll down the window.

"Is he sending her away to school?" Ruthie asked.

"Maybe, yes. He didn't say. But he'd been making some calls."

A car turned onto the street, its headlights in their eyes for a minute. Janey motioned Ruthie to join her in the car but the young woman shook her head.

"I'll go to the same school," Ruthie said desperately. "I have good grades. I could get a job at night. Could you train me to be a librarian or something?"

Janey nodded reassuringly. "But for now why don't you get in. I'll give you a lift home. You look like you're freezing."

"I don't want to go home until later, when they're asleep."

Janey got out of the car and took off her green coat. "Take this then—it's okay, take it." She opened the trunk and rummaged there. "Here's a hat and some gloves. You can return them tomorrow."

"But you need—"

"Take them. I'm not at all cold." It was true. Quitting had thrown her into a kind of trance. Her hands trembled slightly, the world seemed extraordinarily clear, and Ruthie seemed not herself but a character in a poignant tragedy. "He has chopped us all down," Janey reflected, still holding her feelings at bay, as if the mayor was a power-mad dictator destroying a beautiful forest in some distant land.

Driving slowly away, she watched Ruthie shrug into the coat and vanish again into the darkness. Janey headed home, driving carefully and concentrating on turning corners with grace. Fears were beginning to knock at the doors of her mind but she stopped herself from feeling. Freedom—that's what she should focus on. She was free.

Cynthia would be waiting at home, curious to know what had happened. Cynthia would seize hold of Janey's quitting, mix some air and sugar into it, and fill the house with frothy theories that would threaten to engulf Janey. But no, Cynthia was not downstairs but upstairs taking a bath, a ribbon of light showing under the bathroom door, water splashing noisily into the tub. Janey and Ida slipped into the bedroom. Janey lay down on the bed and Ida sat with her chin resting on the cream-colored bedspread. They looked at each other. "Whatever happens, I'll always be with you." Her throat tightened, her face crumpled. The idea of herself and Ida alone in the world finally brought the streams of tears.

She lay there crying silently into the pillow. Sometimes she'd drift into a daze again, smile, and feel calm, as if she were in some other world where it was not necessary to talk to people and make a living; then reality would strike and her breath catch, her heart seize up.

Once she thought, "I don't really have to quit. After all, he's not my real boss. The county administrators are." But she knew how influential he was. Once, she struggled up and rushed to the dressing table, jotted down figures: the mortgage payments, utilities, fees, groceries, her savings.

At some point came a knock on the bedroom door. "Janey? Are you there?"

Janey tried to control her voice. "Yes, I'm here. Just going to bed."

There was a pause. "I won't bother you then. I'll lock up."

"Thanks. Good night."

"Night."

Janey stood up and started to pace. Ellen! Ellen's blue eyes, warm breath, Ellen laughing. "But of course, that's the best news in the world. Good for you, taking a stand! You don't know how happy you're making me, coming to California. I love you so much. I want to be with you so much."

But Ellen hardly ever said strong loving things like this, Janey thought. She might write them, but in person or on the phone, no, she didn't say them. She might not even feel them, for all Janey knew. She raised her hands to cover her face.

Downstairs the phone rang once, twice, stopped. A moment later footsteps came up the stairs, there was a tap on the door. "Janey?"

"What is it?" She opened the door.

Cynthia wore an old quilted bed jacket over her long nightie and bunny slippers. Her frothy head of hair was still moist from her bath. "It's Ruthie on the phone. She wants Ellen's address. I told her it was just a post office box but she wanted it anyway."

"What is she calling at this hour for? Where's she calling from?"

Janey followed Cynthia down to the kitchen, but when they got there the line was dead.

"You look terrible," Cynthia said. "I'll make you some hot tea especially for sleeping. What's the trouble?"

"Nothing. And thanks, but don't bother about the tea."

Cynthia ignored her and put water on to boil. "It's something to do with your job, isn't it?"

"No." Cynthia was like a bloodhound tonight. Janey asked anxiously, "Where was Ruthie calling from? Do you have any idea?"

"Probably down at that phone outside the drugstore. I thought I heard a car drive by. Oh, and she said your coat was hidden in the bushes where you left it. She sounded in a hurry."

Alarmed, Janey thought *running away*, but she didn't say anything. "Please don't bother with the tea. I'm going to bed," she said as she headed for the stairs again.

"I'll bring it up."

Back in her room, Janey lay on her back on the bed with her arm over her eyes. Running away! Hitchhiking probably. She lay there for a few minutes, then jumped up and ran downstairs, almost crashing into Cynthia who was carrying up a little tray holding a piece of toast and a mug of tea.

"I think the girls are running away. Do you want to come look for them?" Janey twisted her hands together as Cynthia ran upstairs and came down again, still in her night clothes with a jacket, wool pants, socks, and boots in her arms.

"I can change in the car," Cynthia said.

There was no one on the road. It was almost midnight. They drove down to the drugstore, Cynthia struggling into her clothes. Only a few streetlights in the center of town were on; the houses and shops were dark. The city lay asleep on this autumn night under a sky full of crisp, cold stars. Janey turned and left town, heading south toward the freeway. Her chest was filled with anxiety. "They could be home in their beds," she said, trying to reassure herself.

"Or maybe only Ruthie went," she added. There was no sign of anyone, hardly a car, just the dark hills and the stars spread out around them.

Cynthia was unusually quiet.

"I should call their folks," Janey said. "Just in case. God, I hate to do that. They'll raise an alarm. They'll call the sheriff, he'll call the highway patrol, the whole eastern seaboard will be involved." She shook her head, glanced at her watch: twelve-thirty. "It'll be like a manhunt. I'll do it when we get back. I can't do it now," she explained to Cynthia. "There're no phones here. We'll keep looking. Maybe I'll turn around at the freeway. Maybe the toll-taker'll remember something."

Cynthia murmured agreement. They drove on into the silent night.

At the same instant, twelve miles southeast of Bowles, Janey and Cynthia saw two figures trudging toward them in the distance, one about fifteen feet behind the other. "It's got to be them. They've turned back." Janey peered intently. The headlights picked out shiny down jackets, dark hats, dark pants.

As the car approached, both figures stopped, still apart, watching. "Ruthie!" Janey pulled to the side of the road, unrolled the window. "God, I'm glad to see you."

"What are you doing here?" Ruthie asked, coming across the tarmac. "Hey, it's Janey and Cynthia," she called back to Donna.

"I can see that, can't I?" Donna called back irritably. And then, coming up, in a friendlier tone, "Am I glad to see you, Miz Kowalski."

Janey smiled with relief. "Get in, you two."

They came to opposite sides of the back seat, got in separately.

"Did you get your coat?" Ruthie asked, as Janey turned the car around.

"Not yet, but thanks for the message. Actually, that was the least of my worries."

"Were you two running away to California?" Cynthia turned from the front seat to gaze at them.

They were silent. Finally, Donna said, "That was the idea."

"We still might go but we need our own car." In the mirror, Janey saw Ruthie smooth her dark hair down with one hand.

"We had some trouble with a man who picked us up," Donna began calmly, but then her voice changed and she turned to Ruthie accusingly. "I still don't see why I had to be the one to sit next to him. Why didn't you sit next to him?"

"If she'd just said he was pawing her, we could have gotten out five miles earlier!" Ruthie explained in an upset voice.

"Oh, sure, what am I supposed to say, 'This guy's got his hand on my leg'?"

"Well, why not?" Ruthie argued.

"You can't say that. I told you in so many words. I told you with my eyes."

"Jeez, I'm sorry. For the ninety-fifth time, like I said, I couldn't see your eyes in the dark. I would have killed the guy if I'd known."

"Oh, sure."

Silence fell.

"It sounds like a terrible experience," Janey said.

"He was just a creep," Donna said tiredly. "He seemed okay at first."

"Yeah," Ruthie agreed. "He said he was going all the way to New York."

"Awful," Janey murmured.

"Yeah...Did you just happen to be driving by?" Ruthie asked politely.

"No." Janey shook her head. "No, we were looking for you."

"Does everyone know?" She sounded alarmed.

"No. At least, not that I know of."

"Hey, it's nice of you to come looking for us. I mean, just on the chance we'd turn back," Donna said.

"How long have you been walking?"

"About six miles, I guess. I'm beat."

"It's another twelve back to Bowles."

"You said it was only eight," Donna reproached Ruthie.

"Yeah, well, I figured we might get a ride."

"I told you, I'm never hitchhiking again."

They were silent again. Janey had turned on the heater and the little car was snug. Outside, the trees and starry sky rushed by.

"Damn," Ruthie said, "I really wanted to make it to California."

"Me too, bunny." Donna had a catch in her voice. There was the crinkle of down jackets in the back seat and in the mirror Janey saw the two move closer together. "I would have killed that guy," Ruthie muttered.

"If you say you would have killed that guy one more time I'm going to puke," Donna told her.

They giggled.

Janey drove into Bowles quietly, dropped the young women off in a shaded part of a back street not far from Donna's house. "Can you get back in?" Janey whispered worriedly.

"Sure, no problem."

They slipped out, murmured thanks. She watched as they cut between two houses and disappeared into the darkness.

Janey sat unmoving, looking after them.

"You got fired, didn't you?" Cynthia asked.

"No, I didn't get fired. I quit."

"I knew it. When I consulted the I Ching this morning I—"

"I don't want to know, Cynthia. I don't want you telling me all about my life. I have to think it out for myself."

The night before she moved to California, Janey woke from a dream in a sweat. In the dream, she had arrived in San Francisco and was living with Ellen in a small room that looked onto a blank, white wall. There was city noise—traffic, jackhammers, music—so loud she couldn't hear Ellen's voice. She kept asking Ellen to speak louder, but as often as Ellen repeated herself Janey couldn't hear. Then she was sitting not with Ellen, but with a stranger. Some other people came into the room and the stranger went off with them, leaving her alone.

Waking from this dream, Janey sat up in bed and pulled her flannel pajama top away from her sticky breasts. She turned on the light and blinked around at her once-cozy bedroom, sad now with its bare walls and bare floor and pile of packing boxes.

The first time she'd seen this room she'd had trouble keeping the frown on her face that announced to the realtor: this place is ready to fall apart, you'll have to lower your price. She'd rattled the windows, old, wavery glass, touched the rotting frames, gingerly lifted one window seat on its creaky, rusted hinges. "It needs some work," the realtor had agreed, but he must have seen she loved the place.

She'd been twenty-five then, with a five-thousand-dollar inheritance from her grandmother, a new job as Bowles' librarian, and an eye on Angie Noojin, the young officer at the bank who smiled so hard whenever Janey came in to cash a check.

"I'm buying that old house down on Lowell Road. Going to fix it up," Janey had told Angie confidently as Angie made out the cashier's check for the down payment. Angie had smiled at her in such a swimmingly warm way, the moment was still clear and fine in Janey's mind: the sunlight flooding in through the windows of the bank, the sound of a calculator, the murmur of voices, Angie's blue eyes. It was as if she'd known then that Angie would be kissing her in front of the dusty brick fireplace in that broken-floored living room, eating with her in the tableless breakfast nook, and making passionate love on the floor of the bedroom between the two dilapidated window seats. Holding out her hand for the check, touching Angie's small, firm, manicured fingers, Janey felt two-ways blessed: Angie and the new house, like gifts from heaven, beckoning to her, "Here I am, do what you will with me. Love me, I'm yours."

Dust. Tons of dust. Disintegrating wood, rusted pipes, layers of old linoleum, a yard shot through with stones: Angie had helped and so occasionally had Angie's brother Fred with his pickup. The house had been like an old beaten-down soldier they'd raised from the dead and fallen in love with. How could Ellen ever know how Janey felt leaving it?

"I know you love it, but after all, in the last analysis, it's just a house," Ellen had written.

"And after all, in the last analysis, you're just a person," Janey had shouted back, throwing down the letter.

Her thumb moved back and forth over her heart. It was 4 a.m. Today the movers would come. This room and all the rest would be stripped bare by men who'd fit everything into a huge truck and take it to California. She reached a hand out to touch the cream-colored wallpaper, imagining the old yellow paper under that, the original plaster, the wood slats, and, at the center, the heart of the house. Her fingers stroked the paper as gently as a lover. The roof creaked in its familiar way.

The next morning she oversaw the packing, watching as the moving men, their large arms bare and hairy in the sharp frosty air, carried out the living room couch, the mahogany bed, the big desk. Inside the yawning truck these pieces shrank to nothing and soon disappeared behind smaller pieces of furniture and the hundred-plus cardboard cartons she had packed. By mid-morning the truck was half full, the house empty. Janey stroked Ida briskly, her face set in a half-smile, as she watched the moving men maneuver back down the street. She turned back into the bare rooms, swept the floors quickly, not looking around.

She was early for an eleven-thirty appointment at the realty office. There were final papers to sign transferring the house to the new owner, ironically the young male fourth-grade teacher who had replaced Ellen. His wife had listened earnestly the week before as Janey explained about the care of each of the plants in the garden, many of them hidden now under six inches of wet snow. The young couple had not paid her asking price: the house needed new plumbing and wiring, the man had declared. She believed the plumbing and wiring were fine, but the realtor had urged her to accept the offer. She had. She could not stand to argue about her house, nor hear it maligned in any way.

Most of her good-byes were done. Cynthia's teepee had arrived two weeks earlier and she had left for her plot of land on horseback, having arranged with the horse's owner to deliver the horse to the owner's brother near Hutchins' Bridge. Cynthia had trotted off not across the mountains and through the forests, as she'd dreamed, but along Route 25 North, leaving before dawn on an icy day, a big wool muffler streaming behind her. Janey had never seen such a lonely sight, yet Cynthia called back happily, "I left you casseroles in the fridge!"

Shortly after Cynthia left, Audrey gave Janey a farewell party to which half the town turned out; Janey was stunned at how many people came up to shake her hand. Each face she recognized: they were the faces she'd been seeing for years as they handed their library books to her, or returned her change in a store, or stopped to pet Ida in the street.

"Why are you leaving us?" Martha Baker, who lived across from the library, had cried.

After a moment of confusion, Janey told her, "I'm going to seek my fortune in California."

"But your roots are here!" Martha exclaimed. "Your roots are here!"

Audrey had stepped in as Janey had stood silent. "She'll come pay us a visit, won't you?" she said and Janey had dumbly nodded.

She'd seen Bert for the last time yesterday. He had pressed her hand between his wrinkled, liver-spotted ones and wished her luck. Her replacement, Amy Rice, the engaging woman who had arrived in Bowles as promptly as the mayor had promised, had been with them a week, learning their procedures. She had made it clear that one change in policy she would make was a seven-day limit on new books.

"But our older people can't get here every seven days," Bert and Janey had argued.

"Oh, yes, well," Amy had said, but they could tell the seven-day book was to be her watchword.

"Don't you worry," Bert had reassured Janey yesterday. "I'll waive those fines."

Janey walked past the library quickly; looking at it was painful: the old, weathered walk up to the marble steps, the handsome, white wooden door with the window into the vestibule, the big maples, leafless now, stretching their bare branches like big fishnets into the grey sky.

In California it was green; flowers were blooming. Curious. All wrong. *All wrong*, Janey thought.

But it was done. She was moving, right or wrong. Tonight she and Ellen would sleep together, Ellen warm and excited in her arms, their breath on each other's faces. Janey set her shoulders, hurried back home, her nose feeling sharp and pointed with the cold. Ellen had said on the phone last week that she'd sat on the beach in California wearing a tank top, whatever that was.

Janey came down the hill, spotting her house in the distance. The sight of it, with the orange berries of bittersweet still clustered around the living room windows but the windows empty, like blind eyes, stabbed her heart. It was gone, put down, put away, abandoned. Already the couple who'd stolen Ellen's job might be tearing out pipes and wires and destroying the place. But no, there was no car, and there was Ida now come to look out the window, her paws on the windowsill, just like always. Janey waved.

In half an hour Audrey would arrive to take Janey and Ida the sixty miles to the Windsor Locks airport. A week ago Janey had sold Ellen's car and yesterday Rhea and Sally had taken Janey's, driving it off with a great, awful grinding of gears. Once she stepped on the plane that afternoon, there'd be nothing left of Janey Kowalski in Bowles.

An hour before the plane was to touch down at the San Francisco airport, she stood in the tiny lavatory arranging the combs in her hair, then adjusting her blue and white sweater and brushing her teeth.

The hours had passed rapidly. She'd been seated between a man and a woman in their late sixties, married to each other; they'd let her know they always sat one seat apart. Whoever sat between them they pounced on: who was she, where was she going, why?

Who was she, where was she going, why? "I'm moving out to San Francisco to live with a girlfriend," Janey had told them.

"How wonderful," they'd exclaimed, but in the course of the trip, as if they sensed her fear and couldn't help themselves, they'd recalled one story after another of disappointment: jilted lovers, sudden illness, jealousy, divorce.

Janey smiled at herself encouragingly in the mirror as she toweled her hands dry. Earlier she'd listened to the country music station on the headphones and Patsy Cline's yearning love song "Crazy" kept going through her mind.

She returned to her seat; the older couple were dozing now and she had to wake the husband briefly to pass. She, too, sat with her head back, wondering about Ida in the hold, about Ellen in San Francisco.

From up here in the sky, Ellen seemed so volatile; all Janey's images of her ran together: Ellen's soft-eyed face close to hers, Ellen confident and on stage, Ellen fearful, Ellen leaving, that false smile on her face. That snapshot Janey loved of Ellen laughing as she threw leaves over her head. Ellen in bed panting and slick with sweat, Ellen excited over some new cause, Ellen tussling with Ida, Ellen earnest and naive, smart, tough, trembling with determination. Ellen's big rust-colored skirt, her being unable to lie, her stupidity about people, the little chipped place on her bottom tooth.

That same morning, in San Francisco, Ellen had woken up happy. For an instant she didn't know why; then she thought, *Janey's coming.* She lay on her back on her foam mattress in one of the two inner rooms of the railroad flat, listening to the honk and throb of Fifteenth Street, Roger moving around in his place directly above, a garbage truck grinding away down the block. The city was a huge animal waking up and Ellen liked being part of it.

"Some people can't handle San Francisco," a woman had told Ellen and Jumper that early September afternoon when they'd first arrived in the city. This doomsayer was a confident-looking woman with tousled hair who had been stapling fliers at the offices of Daughters of Bilitis, the lesbian social organization. "This city's too free for them," the woman had said and Ellen had thought, "Not for me."

A few minutes later she wasn't so sure. The only letter waiting for her at the city's main American Express office had been a businesslike note from Janey enclosing a letter from the Massachusetts Commission on Teacher Credentialing. The Commission wanted to make an "informed decision" about her accreditation and needed a "description of the events that led up to" her termination at Bowles.

"The events that led up to your termination?" Jumper had scoffed as they'd left the travel office and headed down Market Street under sunny skies. "First, one numskull was appointed to the school board. Second, another numskull was appointed to the school board. Third, a third numskull was appointed to the school board. And so forth."

Ellen had laughed but, numskulls or not, the school board had made enough of an impression on the state commission to cause a hold to be placed on Ellen's certification. As she'd soon found out, their doubts about her effectively wrecked her chances for a teaching job in California. She might as well have been a felon, tracked by the certification boards through the FBI. "If I were you," advised the friendly gay man with whom she'd managed to obtain her one teaching interview, "and I wanted to stay in the Bay Area, I'd look for some other kind of work, at least temporarily."

Stunned, she'd made her way back that afternoon to Samuel P. Taylor State Park, where she and Jumper were staying. Later, as they sat at their damp campsite, the rough, brown bark of the tall redwoods around them had reminded her of turds.

"Can you believe it?" Ellen had asked Jumper for the dozenth time. "They can just ruin your life because you say you're gay? Even here in California?"

"How about that job with Roger?" Jumper asked, also for the dozenth time. Blond and wispy-haired, thick-shouldered, she was wearing gloves with the fingers cut out as she tried to trim the wick of their kerosene lantern.

Roger was no less unusual than his cousin Jumper. The two women had visited him after Jumper's mother had written to remind her daughter that "the genius who built a radio at age six" was "still unmarried," and was "sure to want to show them the sights of the city where he's lived for fifteen years."

"Just what a dyke wants to do," Jumper had said. "Marry her genius male cousin and have retarded babies."

But despite their misgivings, and because Jumper remembered liking Roger as a kid, she'd arranged to visit. The two women had driven into the city one morning and made their way to his place in the Mission District. Fifteenth Street, where he lived, was lined with a mixture of stucco apartment buildings and old, colorful Victorians, some of them with their paint flaking off. A telephone company repairman was just coming out of Roger's building. As they climbed the steps, he held the door open for them, then hopped into his double-parked truck and zoomed off.

Inside, the hallway was wide, bare, and painted grey. They climbed the stairs to the second floor, found a door with a metallic "2" on it. Jumper knocked.

In a moment, the door opened. A man appeared who looked something like Jumper: blond, straggly hair, amused eyes, and a heavy build. He wore oversized pants and a frayed, yellow flannel shirt with grease stains. Behind him, piles of computer equipment, manuals, and paper were everywhere.

Jumper and he exchanged greetings, she introduced Ellen, and he led them back through the long apartment to the kitchen. Ellen glimpsed more computer gadgetry and paper in the rooms they passed, but the kitchen was uncluttered and seemed normal, with four chairs drawn up to a plain, white table.

Roger had made strong coffee and they sat around the table, awkwardly trying to make conversation and looking into their mugs. It wasn't until Jumper asked Roger about his work that he'd started talking. He was a computer programmer and had invented something new. It either was a simulator, or involved a simulator, whatever that was. He'd fetched a pad and pencil and drawn many blocks and arrows, which he showed them with obvious enthusiasm.

At some point during his excited description, Ellen became interested. He was writing a program that would imitate cars moving through streets, stopping at street lights, accelerating onto ramps and freeways—this was his traffic simulator. She'd found herself caught up in his diagram. "What are these?" She'd pointed to some arrows that looped around.

"Flat tires. They re-enter the system again here."

"And this?" Nearby lines passed through a kind of gate.

"The delay caused by rubbernecking."

"Neat." They smiled at each other. Ellen had felt very cheerful suddenly.

The phone had rung and he answered it. "Yes, I'm the one. I need four or five. Four dollars an hour. Sure, come on over." He'd sat down again.

"Who's coming over?" Jumper had asked.

"I'm hiring some car counters."

After that, Jumper had begun urging Ellen to take a temporary job with Roger counting cars.

"But I'm a professional," Ellen had argued. She had not wanted to count cars. Still, she felt an affinity for Roger and his project and had borrowed the most elementary book he had on the theory of computer simulation. The notion of a computer representing real life fascinated her. The ideas in the book reminded her of those that used to excite her in mathematics. Sometimes, while Jumper was asleep in the tent, Ellen had sat up late at the picnic table in her down jacket, studying Roger's book by the light of the kerosene lamp.

Now, as she lay in bed, thinking back, there came a thud from upstairs. That would be Roger, absently knocking a book off the table with his elbow as he studied some technical article. Ellen was almost embarrassed at the fondness she'd developed for him. She still was enraged at men, read books by feminist women, and loved railing at injustice with her new radical acquaintances...but she liked Roger.

When she'd finally decided to take the car counting job, he'd seemed delighted, or as delighted as someone so equable could be. He'd said she could start immediately and the next day she'd left the cold, foggy campsite before seven in the morning with Jumper.

By eight she was ready to count cars. Roger gave her varied assignments over the phone. Howard and First from eight-ten to eight-fifty, Howard and Second from nine-ten to ten-thirty, and so forth. In a hardware store at lunch she found hand-held counters that she could click in increments of one, five, or ten. One counter added up cars, the other, people in them. She was also to verify Roger's verbal description of the traffic controls: stoplights, stop signs, crosswalks. As the days passed, she figured out forms for her work, charging Roger for the photocopying. She bought an official-looking cap and khaki shirt to signify her role to passers-by. For all these innovations, Roger was grateful and paid willingly. His two other car counters quit. When another turned up, he had Ellen train her.

As she counted cars and people, she'd often entered a kind of daze. Sometimes her eyes went out of focus and she got confused. At other times, her mind ranged wide and her counting went on automatically. She counted thousands of cars. It was as if she counted all of modern California. Occasionally someone hovered nearby wanting to ask a question, but she just shook her head as she counted and they walked off. She was in a kind of automaton hell; the work held her in suspension and dropped her tired at the end of the day.

When she imagined telling Janey about her new job, she thought she'd present it in a comical way, but deep down she felt humiliated. Was this why she'd run away to California?

It had been late September by then: fine, clear days. In November, she'd known, it would start to rain. Ellen counted cars during the day and at night sat at the picnic table in the dark campsite wrapped in her sleeping bag. By the light of the kerosene lamp, she continued to read books and journals borrowed from Roger on simulators and artificial intelligence. Most of it was beyond her; she was not sure why she kept on with it. "Maybe to prove I'm as smart as your genius cousin," she said to Jumper.

By this time, his disheveled appearance and lack of social graces had ceased to dismay her. She'd begun to find these qualities endearing. He was remarkably intelligent in his line of work and he was often willing to take time answering her questions. Occasionally, after twenty minutes in conversation with him, she felt again like the excited, exceptional math student she'd once been. He had a regular computer programming job with the city, having worked for a dozen years there maintaining the programs that produced payroll checks, W-2 forms, and a host of associated reports. He went to work very seldom; he seemed to collect a paycheck solely on the basis of being available at home in the middle of the night to answer questions from other staff. The simulator project was his alone. His current ambition was to simulate San Francisco traffic, coming up with traffic light settings that would minimize congestion and delay.

"You'll present it to the city then," Ellen asked, "for them to use?"

"That depends on Arthur."

"Who's Arthur?"

"There are those who think there are millions to be made in data processing. They invest in projects like mine hoping to hit the jackpot. Arthur's one of those."

"He supplies the money then, to pay me and the others?"

"Correct."

"He thinks the simulator might be worth a lot?"

"Correct. But what does he know?" It appeared that satisfying his backer was not of any particular interest to Roger. Nor was making money or impressing anyone. Every few days Ellen saw him to turn over her data and collect a check. The first time he was excited; he had found a perhaps insoluble logic error in his design. The second time, he looked tired and wild-eyed; the logic error had involved changing everything, but he thought he had a better idea. The third time he didn't come to the door; later on the phone, he admitted he'd been so involved he didn't hear the bell.

The forms the car counters filled out were stacking up in one corner of his kitchen. "How are you going to feed all this stuff into your program?" Ellen asked him.

"Each intersection will be a block." He outlined how the information would be organized. "All these need punching."

She found a key punch place, prepared the forms and took them in. The key punch place charged twenty dollars for fifty forms.

"You're becoming Roger's gal Friday," Jumper had told her that night as they walked up a dark hill not far from their campsite. The moon lit their path and shone on slivers of black ocean in the distance.

"Yeah, he has the fun and I do the work," Ellen remarked.

"Tell him you want to be a programmer like him."

"I don't know, Jumper, that takes years. Plus I don't know if I want to spend my days like he does, staring at a little screen with green letters. Besides...maybe he'd say I wasn't smart enough for his kind of work."

"Why don't you ask, anyway?"

"I don't know...yes, I do. I couldn't stand to be rejected one more time."

A few nights after that conversation, on their way back from the city to the park in the pickup, Jumper had some news. "I got an offer to do a job up in Oregon with this guy."

Ellen had swallowed this with difficulty. Jumper leaving? "You mean, for a while?"

"Three months. It's wiring some housing development up there."

"Do you have to go, Jumper? Can't you get something here?"

"I could, but I'd like to see Oregon. We can't stay in the park much longer anyway. You want to come?"

Ellen had stared out the pickup's window into the darkness. Until then she hadn't realized how much she counted on Jumper being around. She'd never thought that Jumper might up and leave California just as she'd left Massachusetts, for her own reasons.

"Oh. Well, of course, you should go. If you want."

"You're welcome to come."

"Yeah. Well, maybe tomorrow I'll call Janey," Ellen had said. That pitch-black night in the tent, she'd felt frightened. She'd seen doors closing on her right and left. The car counting seemed endless and terrible. Her bones ached from sleeping on the ground. Soon, she'd thought, Jumper would be gone and Ellen would not have that slow, sleepy breathing to keep her company. She'd be alone in the wild, black, California night woods.

Now, remembering how cold it had been, she snuggled down into her warm bed, looked hopefully at the print of a pale blue glacier she'd tacked up yesterday in preparation for Janey's coming.

How stupid and selfish she'd been about Janey, not calling for so long and then, when she did, calling at a time when she was so down and jumping to the conclusion, without any real evidence, that Janey and Cynthia were in love. After that, she'd been afraid to call back; she'd felt too unhitched to anything, too vaporous to withstand what she dreaded Janey might be like: cheerful, newly in love, friendly, and solicitous. If it hadn't been for Jumper writing Janey...

Ellen smiled at the glacier print. It was wonderful to think that Janey still loved her and wanted to be with her.

She heard the mailman in the outer entryway of the building: eight o'clock already and she wanted to buy some plants for Janey, straighten up, and put in a few hours with Roger before her programming class and the airport. She lunged off her mattress and hurriedly pulled on jeans, a blue work shirt and turquoise wool sweater. It was cold in the apartment, much colder than in any house back East. She reminded herself to leave the thermostat up and the electric heater on all day so Janey wouldn't be chilly that night.

She unlocked the apartment door and, walking a few steps through the empty hall to the heavy front door of the building, held it open with her foot as she unlocked her mailbox and pulled out some junk mail, a phone bill, and a letter from Buffalo.

Her heart thumped anxiously at her mother's familiar handwriting. A letter from her family, although she was always eager to read it, generally left her feeling like a scorned eight-year-old. If she were smart, she'd throw this one away immediately.

Three weeks before, the first one had come. Ellen still remembered the subtly patronizing tone and her own stilted reply.

Nov. 27, 1975

Dear Ellen,

Your father and I were just saying how good it will be to see you at Christmas, seeing how we missed being in touch at Thanksgiving—I know it's a trip but we will pay your way, dear.

Your trouble at your Bowles job took us aback, I must say. (I would have preferred hearing the news from you, dear, rather than through an old friend of your father's, but I understand facing us with such news would have been difficult—you like so to please us, Ellen, and this, of course, was not pleasing news.)

Still, whatever you may be or do, you are our daughter and we love you. I am sending this to your address in Bowles although we don't know just where you are now. I trust this will reach you. Please send us your new address so we can send you a check for your fare home for the holidays.

Eric has won yet another art prize and, of course, he, Mike, Patsy, and Tom will be here, too, for our Christmas get-together. Jack Kelsey, of course, won't be coming. Your father and I were shocked to find out that the accusations against him were not fabrications, after all. Jack *was* behaving very badly, even toward your sister Patsy, I was horrified to learn. Why she never told us I have no idea. What secrets we all harbor, dear.

Please write promptly, Ellen. We do so want to hear how you are. We worry about you.

Love,
Mom and Dad

Ellen had written back with the abrupt honesty with which she'd defended herself as an anxious child:

Dear Mom and Dad,

Thank you for all your understanding. I
should have written but just didn't have the
heart for it. As for your invitation to fly me
home for Christmas, unfortunately, I already
have plans, very important ones, since my
lover, Janey, is moving West around that time.
She is a wonderful person and I'm sure you
would both like her.
I am happy. I am learning computer
programming and making a permanent switch
into that field. You remember how I always
liked math but we thought I wouldn't be able to
find a job in mathematics, so I followed in the
family footsteps and became a teacher.
I am increasingly involved in the women's
liberation movement out here. It is appalling
how badly women have been treated over the
centuries.

Love,
Ellen

Now, today, came her mother's reply. Ellen paused,
girding herself, before tearing open the envelope.

Dec. 11, 1975
Dear Ellen,

We are disappointed you won't be here for
Christmas. Your nephews are only young once,
Ellen. It's a shame to miss them, but if that's
your decision...
Perhaps you will be happier in computer
programming than you were in teaching. We
occasionally wondered if you were a natural-
born teacher, Ellen, or if you'd just gone into
the field to please us. Heaven knows it was
hard bringing up a girl as sensitive as you, who
took any suggestion of ours as something
engraved in stone, either to be obeyed or
fought against.

Your women's movement activities smell of the latter, dear, if I may say so. I doubt these groups are ever very constructive. But your father and I are pleased at your interest in computers. I think you may have finally found your niche in life.

Love,
Mom and Dad

As she went back inside, Ellen ripped this letter up, then pieced it together again to show Janey. Back in the bedroom, she looked at the glacier print doubtfully: maybe Janey wouldn't like it. She hurried down the hall to the kitchen and breathed a sigh of relief at its large, pleasant sunniness. As soon as she'd put plants in the garden, just visible through the thin bars on the windows, it would be almost like Bowles.

As long as there had been any doubt that Janey would move to California, Ellen had been sure it was the obvious thing to do. Of course this was the place for two lesbians to be. The city was beautiful, the weather was great, and the women were like-minded. Ellen and Janey could be themselves. Women organized here over every issue. They marched for lesbian rights, spoke out on rape and street harassment, and wrote stirring articles on discrimination.

But since those two calls of Janey's, the first to say she'd quit her job—under pressure, it had sounded like—and the second to say she'd sold her house, Ellen had been beset by doubt. Janey's putting her life in Ellen's hands was too real. Ellen felt as empty as she had those weeks after she'd been fired. She tried in vain to rise up, to puff herself up to be worth Janey's move. It seemed as if they were doomed, that their life together would be a farce somehow and that Janey would fade away with disappointment. It seemed that this dark apartment, this gusty wind, these streets crowded with men in jeans holding hands, this arid computer work—all would be nothing to what Janey had lost: her house, her garden, her job, a town that knew her, Audrey, Bert, the beds of violets, the luscious roses, the soft winter snow on the firs.

Ellen swallowed and looked at her watch. She had to get going.

"I'm not moving out there just to be with you," Janey had said on the phone. "I'm interested in California, too, you know." They had both gone on in this formal vein.

"I'm glad you want to come," Ellen had said. "I think you'll like California," and from Janey, a little later: "I want to look around Berkeley," as if admitting that they counted so much on each other would put a jinx on their future.

That evening, Ellen drove the twenty minutes to the airport in a daze. Occasionally a smile would flit across her face and her body would tremble slightly in anticipation. As she paced at the gate, her hands deep in the pockets of her windbreaker, she squared her shoulders. A proud thought crossed her mind: a woman was moving clear across country to be with her. Could the passers-by sense the significance of this meeting? She winced, catching herself in this self-centered thought.

There was movement at the gate, the plane came into sight, wheeling into place. The crowd's energy went up a notch. Ellen stood, trying to look attractive, watching for Janey's face. Here came the strangers, weary-looking and excited.

Suddenly, Janey stood before Ellen, as sturdy as a burro, her red-brown hair in waves to her shoulders, her pretty mouth quivering, her legs beneath her pleated skirt tanned and round.

Janey's arms came around her; Janey's lips kissed her cheek. She smelled Janey, mouth mints and her own special smell. She felt a familiar sizzle as Janey's hand touched hers.

"Where do we pick up Ida, do you know? I won't be able to relax until I see her," Janey said in her familiar, husky voice.

She stood back and looked at Ellen. "Are you crying?"

"I'm so glad you came," Ellen blurted, laughing in her tears.

"Well, so am I," Janey agreed. "I expect to have a wonderful time, thank you very much."

Ellen hugged her again. "Janey, I don't have much for you. The apartment's so *dark!*"

Janey propelled her along in search of Ida. "Does it look out on a blank, white wall?" she asked.

"Not exactly." Ellen sniffled. "I put some flowers out in the garden."

"Flowers!" Janey sounded pleased.

"The place is big. And I can work right upstairs. And so can you, if you want to work for Roger too. We need someone to help test the simulator."

Janey laughed. "Let me catch my breath first."

"I got all kinds of fruit and vegetables and salad stuff. Or we could go out, if you'd rather do that. And I got dog food for Ida."

"I'd love a good salad. The food was awful." Janey frowned at the signs. "They said to pick her up at the freight office. Do you know where that is?"

"I'll find out." Ellen wiped her eyes. It was good having Janey back. She'd almost forgotten how wonderful it was to be with her, that comfortable familiarity spiced with sexiness. Ellen looked around, spotted an agent. How nice to find out he knew the way, to be able to return victorious to her own wonderful Janey with the deep-set eyes and take her straightaway, without mistake or delay, to her dog.

14

Even though Janey thought, *I forgot that she was so nervous,* and Ellen thought, *She sure wears old-fashioned clothes,* their old connection, and the pleasure at feeling in love with someone they thought they knew, had them hanging on each other's words, laughing at anything the slightest bit clever, and walking so close together they kept bumping into each other. In the borrowed car going back to the city, Janey sat right up next to Ellen. ("We can be as close as we want in San Francisco," Ellen had assured her.)

Janey moved her finger tips lightly over the back of Ellen's neck, tickling the hair there.

"Oh my God," Ellen muttered excitedly, but when Janey stopped, Ellen said, "No, don't stop." As the car hurtled toward the city on the lighted freeway, they sat close, not bothering to talk, feeling a delicious excitement. Janey stared out the window smiling, trying to take everything in. The night sky billowed with clouds; it had rained earlier and the pavement and tops of cars in the parking lots glistened. Her eyes took in the dark industrial and office buildings, the Christmas lights twinkling over the rows of look-alike houses, the shining body of black water. The bay? Ellen wasn't sure.

"It's beautiful," Janey said. "And the sky is so grand!"

"Oh, no, this is nothing, Janey."

Janey stared at her lover as she brought her fingers around to caress her ear and her cheek. "You've gotten a little tan, haven't you?" She loved Ellen's long eyelashes, the way Ellen's lips parted when she was excited.

Ellen glanced at her with dark, tender eyes. "Have I?"

"Yes, and your throat..." Janey trailed her fingers down over the skin on Ellen's neck and throat.

"Wait a minute." Ellen took the next exit and found a place to park near a building under construction. Nearby, a steam shovel sat beside a truck loaded with earth, pale in the darkness. Ellen and Janey kissed, a soft, wet, titillating kiss that left them aching. When Janey started to unbutton Ellen's shirt, Ellen stopped her. "Janey, Janey. Not here."

Janey toyed with Ellen's hand. "No?"

"No." Ellen laughed between kisses. "It's not *that* free yet."

Nevertheless, Janey felt that it might be possible to do anything in California. Even the sight of Ellen's treeless street and very plain apartment building didn't dampen her enthusiasm. "It feels so 'real' here," she assured Ellen, as they left the car parked illegally and hurried into the stucco building.

As soon as they were in, they reached for each other eagerly. Janey pressed Ellen to her, feeling all the ache of those months apart vanish in the tender pleasure of holding Ellen tight again. Ellen led them, passionate and hot and half-dressed, to a foam pad in a dim room. There, Janey gave herself over to sex, dove into its greedy, luscious center. In that hot, bright center of the earth, nothing else mattered. She grabbed at pleasure, embraced it, and forgot everything else.

"It's funny," Ellen said at one point, as they lay catching their breath, "that you, Janey, out of all the millions of people on earth, should be so special that just seeing you makes me feel so—I don't know—so safe and warm on the one hand and so excited on the other."

"So why did you leave me?" Janey whispered.

Ellen stiffened. She stroked a damp tendril of hair from Janey's pink cheek. "I must have been crazy."

"I guess so." They continued to look at each other intently, Ellen's hand quiet, cupping Janey's face. But something new had come into their eyes: a wariness, a sadness.

After a minute, Ellen looked away. "Ida, come on over!" she called and the dog, who'd chewed up the huge Milkbone Ellen had left for her, bounded onto the foam mattress, her dog claws digging into Ellen's legs as she clambered over her. They laughed and snuggled with her, happily familiar again.

"Remember that first day, when Ida ate the deviled eggs?" Ellen asked, as she propped herself up against a pillow.

Janey settled Ida down between them. "I was so nervous that day."

"*You* were nervous. I about lost my voice."

"Remember how we used to pet her when we couldn't touch each other?" Janey asked.

They laughed and Ellen went on, "Remember how smart she was, learning to jump in the window at the school?"

"Yes!" But Janey's smile faded as she remembered the occasion of that jump, the family lesson.

"I want to *see* this place," she said brightly, jumping up. Her white blouse was still fastened at one wrist and hung off her arm. The rest of her—full breasts, rounded stomach, strong legs—was naked and flushed pink. She peered into the room where they'd dropped her suitcases; the shades were down.

"I like this square room," she called back to Ellen as she pulled on fresh jeans and buttoned up her blouse. The room was very plain and featureless. Just a box, really. Janey couldn't think of anything other than its squareness to comment on. She pulled up the shade at one of the windows. Through grey metal bars, she saw three young men walk by a few feet away, talking loudly, close enough so she could see each shiny black hair on their heads. She stepped back in alarm. A car sped by, honking its horn.

"Come look at the kitchen and the garden. That's the best part of the place," Ellen urged from the doorway.

Janey lowered the shade and followed Ellen through the hall to the back of the long apartment. Here it was quieter. The kitchen was large with a dark red linoleum floor. To the right was a shiny white table and four art deco, metal chairs with light blue plastic seats and back pads. The Formica counters were edged with blue and white Dutch tiles. There was a gas stove, a new refrigerator, and two tall windows on either side of the back door. Janey smiled. "I love those old painted cabinets."

"Yes, and look at this..." Ellen unlocked two locks into the yard, switched on the outside light. A few dozen flowering plants sat in their pots on a square of neglected earth; the flowers looked fiery and alive and hungry. Around the plot was a new board fence, bleak and unadorned.

"I didn't know how to arrange them."

"They're wonderful, Ellen." Janey stepped among the festive plants, knelt, and scratched at the earth, damp on the surface but hard and claylike underneath. Ida sniffed around and peed in one corner of the yard on a pile of dead weeds.

"I thought *you'd* like to plant them," Ellen told her.

Janey laughed. "I can see you have my work cut out for me."

"Well, I'll help. So, you like it okay?"

"Sure. For a city apartment? And to be able to have Ida here?"

"I'm so glad. I was so scared that, compared to Bowles, this would seem like nothing."

"Oh, no." Janey glanced around. Dozens of houses and apartment buildings surrounded them. Hundreds of people could see the garden from their windows. "Not 'nothing,' " she reassured Ellen.

"I've got to return that car I borrowed. Want to come?" Ellen asked, but Janey said no, she wanted to stay and look around.

Once Ellen was gone, Janey and Ida walked through the apartment, Ida sniffing in the corners. "What do you think of it?" Janey asked as she looked doubtfully around at the yellow-grey walls.

Ida looked up and wagged her tail.

"Oh, you like anything."

Overhead came the faint sound of footsteps; out on the street someone shouted in Spanish and a car revved its engine.

"Remember Bowles? Were we really there this morning?" Janey hadn't intended to feel nostalgic, but saying the name aloud brought the memory of Bowles in all its sweetness sweeping over her. "Remember the living room?

Remember the window seat? Remember coming down the walk? Remember walking to the library?" At each memory, her loss felt more poignant. She sank down against the wall and put her hands over her face. Ida came to stand close by, attentive. They stayed like that, Janey very still, Ida staring. When Janey took her hands down, Ida was only a few inches away, looking concerned.

"Oh, Ida. Did I make a terrible mistake?"

Ida rolled over and bared her speckled stomach.

Janey petted her anxiously, eyeing the front room. She imagined various decorative touches: wooden valances over the windows, carved wooden shelves on curved supports, trim where the ceiling met the walls.

She was starting to feel hopeful when a truck went by noisily; a faint smell of exhaust leaked in around the wooden windows and through the shades.

"Oh God!" Janey leapt up. "We may as well be living in the middle of a freeway! Come on, Ida. Maybe the kitchen..." And Janey fled to the back of her graceless new home, Ida padding cheerfully after her.

As soon as Ellen came back, Janey felt better. Ellen held out a deep red rose, barely open, clear drops of water clinging to its velvet petals.

"This is so little," Ellen said, "but I was thinking of the enormity of what you've given up. I just hope..." She stood awkwardly, presenting the flower.

Janey took it happily, breathed in its peaceful fragrance.

"Tomorrow," Ellen suggested, "I want us to go over to Marin County and I'll show you how beautiful it really is around here."

"Yes, I'd like that." Janey found a knife and glass, trimmed the rose, and set it in water. Graceful and alone, it sat in the center of the table.

"And I want you to meet Roger."

Janey nodded. "Ellen, I was thinking. Could we paint this place before my furniture comes?"

"Paint it?" Ellen looked around. "Does it need it?"

"It'd look much lighter with a fresh coat of paint."

Ellen laughed. "I bet you're right." She came around behind Janey, embraced her, and kissed her ear. "Janey, you're so smart. I'm so glad you're here."

Janey turned in Ellen's arms, so they looked into each other's eyes. "Are you really?" Janey asked seriously.

"Yes, I am."

Janey felt a swell of loving happiness. "Then we'll make a home here, Ellen. I know we will."

"I feel so taken care of with you here. Oh, Janey." Ellen surprised Janey by sinking down to her knees on the old red linoleum, holding Janey tight, burying her face in Janey's stomach.

"Honey, what is it?"

Ellen said something in a muffled voice, then started to tremble and cry.

Janey couldn't move, afraid they'd fall over. She patted Ellen's head tenderly, reassuringly. "It's okay, honey. Come on, get up."

"I'm sorry I ruined your life," Ellen suddenly blurted out. Her voice was hoarse and anguished. Her words hung in the air like the strange cry of a wounded bird. She had pulled her head back to speak, but now she buried it again in Janey's stomach.

"Oh, honey, it's not ruined." Janey stroked Ellen's hair as Ellen continued to sob. "We're starting over, aren't we? In a better place. Maybe it's all for the best, what happened. We're here now, we'll get to know lots of other women. We'll do things with them, have a community. Maybe we can have parties. It's okay, Ellen...Come on, stand up, honey."

Ellen struggled up. Her eyes were red. She was sniffling and small sobs made her catch her breath. She smiled through her tears at Janey.

"You'll see," Janey assured her. "We'll have a wonderful home together, we'll be happy. We're starting over, aren't we?"

Ellen nodded, still jerking a little.

"Things'll work out, you'll see."

"You don't hate me?"

"Of *course* not, Ellen." Janey smoothed the tears off her lover's cheeks. "Of course not. I love you."

As Janey reassured her, Ellen quieted. The two women stood close, their arms around each other. "Of course I love you," Janey whispered. She kissed Ellen's neck tenderly.

"And I love you, Janey."

In the distance Janey heard the sound of a siren. Horns blared for a minute and then it was quiet again.

"You know," Ellen said, pulling back to look at Janey, "maybe you're right." She wiped her eyes and ventured a smile.

"Of course I'm right." Janey laughed.

"Maybe it will be for the best. Maybe," Ellen said hopefully, "there'll come a day when you'll even *thank* me for the family lesson."

Janey felt a shiver of irritation, but she said good-naturedly, "Maybe."

"Maybe," Ellen went on, encouraged by Janey's smile, "you'll even thank me for running out on you. Like—"

"I doubt that I'll ever thank you for *that,*" Janey interrupted. She leaned back to regard Ellen worriedly. "You know it hurt terribly, your leaving like that. Terribly. It feels better to at least know you're sorry."

"Of course I'm sorry."

"Good." But Janey couldn't calm her rising agitation. She disengaged herself from Ellen to pace around the kitchen. "Not only leaving like that, but then not calling. Why didn't you call?"

Ellen looked at her helplessly. "I don't know, Janey."

"It wouldn't have taken much time."

"I know, but I just wasn't ready somehow. I was—"

"Not ready!" Janey set her jaw and went to stand at the window, looking out through the bars at the flowers, bright under the outside light. "You weren't ready."

"No."

"You made me a pariah in my own town, then you vanished one day with one damned hour's notice." Janey controlled her voice. "And you weren't *ready* to call?"

"That's the truth," Ellen said. "But I can see why you're mad at me."

Janey turned around angrily. "You're damned right I'm mad at you. Your leaving like that? I couldn't believe it! I couldn't believe you'd do such a thing!"

"It was just a necessity." Ellen bit her lip.

"A necessity, was it?" Janey looked balefully at her lover. "Like the family lesson was a necessity? Your necessity is my downfall. Your necessity is a monster. It has me out here, *dependent* on you! What can I do? I'm supposed to turn this, this army barracks, into a comfortable, attractive home. I'm supposed to turn that square of dirt out there," she flung a hand toward the back yard, "into a garden. I'm supplying all the furniture, I assume, and the money I get from the sale of my house, I assume, is to be used for our other expenses. Am I wrong?"

Ellen stood flushed, stubborn and defensive. "Yes, you're dead wrong. I don't give a damn for your furniture or your money—I could care less. I thought you'd *want* to work on the garden. As for the apartment, I like it fine the way it is. I'll help you paint it, since you want to, but, as far as I'm concerned, it's perfectly okay as is."

"This dump, okay?" Janey turned to kick at the dusty radiator. "Look at this place!"

"Okay, so it doesn't have any maple furniture or wallpaper. But it's in the heart of a beautiful, exciting city where you can do what you want, where you can make things happen, where you don't have to stay home, frightened, with the shades drawn, not offending anyone."

"What do you mean, calling me frightened! Who ran away? Who fled with her tail between her legs? Do you know what Audrey said about you?"

Ellen looked at her lover guardedly. "What?"

"That you were 'immature.' "

"So who cares what Audrey says."

"You do."

Ellen stood, holding onto the back of the blue metal kitchen chair, glowering silently. "What does she know?" she muttered.

"And who was that young woman Althea?" Janey asked.

Ellen shrugged and glanced at her lover. "Another immature person, I guess. I told you I never encouraged her," she said bitterly.

"I had to pack all your damned stuff. I had to sell your car—if you don't think that was hard."

"Yeah, I appreciate it, Janey."

"You act like I can manage all this—being left alone, made to feel ashamed, forced to give up my job and at the same time handle all the practical matters of the house and money and everything."

"No, I don't think that."

"Well, sometimes you act like it."

"No, I'll take responsibility, Janey. Didn't I find us this place? And a job? I even found a job for you, if you want it."

"I don't know that I want to work with you. At *computers*."

"Don't say it like that. What's wrong with computers?"

Janey sighed. Tiredness had just hit her hard. It was past midnight back in Bowles. She sank down in a kitchen chair and put her head in her hands. She felt numb. "I don't know. They're not human."

Ellen didn't respond. She stood at the window looking out, her shoulders set. "Do you want supper?" she finally asked.

"I'm not hungry."

"Maybe you should have a rest."

"You think I could sleep? Are you crazy?"

"I thought you might feel better."

"I don't know how you could possibly think that I could sleep before the two of us are back together again. How could you think that, Ellen?" Janey was not angry now but exasperated. "I mean, don't you think this is horrible, us fighting like this our first night?"

"It's awful," Ellen agreed.

They regarded each other, half-wary, half-friendly.

Janey tapped with her fingers on the table. Ida went from one to the other of them, looking worried.

"It's okay, Ida," Janey said.

"So maybe we should eat?" Ellen asked again.

"I guess so."

"Grilled cheese?"

"What about I make a salad?"

And they proceeded to make dinner together, at first politely and warily, then teasingly and lovingly, in their new home.

Ellen sat motionless at her terminal in Roger's middle room as Janey peered over her shoulder. "Look," Ellen said excitedly, "it's working again."

They both stared at the screen with its changing numbers representing the number of cars between various intersections near the Bay Bridge.

"You fixed it so fast? How did you know how to do that?" Janey was still not used to Ellen's speedy cadenzas on the computer keys.

These mild, California winter days, while she looked for library work in the afternoons, Janey spent her mornings upstairs with Ellen and Roger. Like Ellen, she had caught on fast to the basics of the computer, but there the similarity ended. Ellen seemed positively in love with their dry, mental work on the traffic simulator.

"You know," she had said recently over dinner, "the pleasures of the mind are every bit as wonderful as the pleasures of the body. I'm talking about real happiness."

"You mean the satisfaction in getting the right answer?" Janey had asked.

"Well, there's that, but there're other kinds of pleasure too, sharper pleasures." Ellen thought for a minute before she went on. "Say Roger gives me a problem to solve and I don't have the foggiest. I'm in the dark. I turn this way and that way and all I do is bang into things. Then I think, hey, how about going up? I lift my foot and there's a stair. I lift my other foot and there's another stair.

"That's what it's like when I first see the answer. Pretty soon I'm racing up into the light. That's real happiness."

Ellen's eyes as she spoke had been full of sparks, as if she were as passionate about this new pursuit as she'd ever been about feminism. Every morning she trotted upstairs, worked hard all day, came down late to help fix dinner, and then spent any spare time jotting down notes and numbers. Even the relatively mundane testing they were doing now seemed to please her. They'd already been at it for three hours this morning and she showed no signs of wanting to stop.

Janey heard footsteps coming up the stairs and raised her arms to tuck stray hairs into her combs. "Ellen, honey. Arthur's here."

He strode in, the project's backer, a big, dazzling man in a white shirt and dark expensive suit. After greeting them all formally, he waved the three of them ahead of him into the sunny kitchen. They sat down around the white table, which was kept immaculately clean for such occasions. Roger, in his usual baggy pants and raggedy flannel shirt, folded his hands and looked directly at Arthur, but Janey could see his mind was somewhere else.

Arthur crossed his trousered legs. "As you know," he began, "I've been engaged in talks with certain city officials for over a month now. Yesterday, two of these gentlemen finally acknowledged an interest in our traffic simulator."

Janey saw Ellen sit up straighter and glance excitedly at Roger. His expression hardly changed; he was definitely in another world. "Roger, did you hear that?"

Roger nodded.

"That's terrific," Ellen said to Arthur.

"I agree." Arthur turned his easy smile upon her. "Terrific is the right word. These chaps have been less than eager up to now, as you know." He scratched the tip of his nose with one manicured finger. "What I need to know from you people is where exactly are we? What kind of product can we show them?" He looked at Roger encouragingly.

"Ellen's taking care of all that," Roger answered.

Arthur turned to Ellen. "Where would you say we are?"

She answered in definite terms, and she and Arthur proceeded to discuss the status of the simulator. Ellen referred to it as "quite robust." Arthur described the nature of the men they were dealing with as "old guard but not averse to trying something new if it'll make their job easier." The two of them proposed various schedules.

"I want you to take full responsibility for this," Arthur declared at one point.

Janey saw Ellen's breath catch in surprise, but she nodded calmly.

Arthur continued, "You can ask Roger technical questions. Organizational, personnel matters you may feel free to bring to me. I have every faith in you." He turned his smile on Janey. "You and your very intelligent helpmate."

Janey smiled back. "Will she get a raise?"

"I should have said, 'very intelligent and perceptive helpmate,' " Arthur said. "Yes, of course. Ellen must be paid considerably more in this new role." He took from his inside jacket pocket a small leather notebook and leafed through it. "Shall we say another five hundred a month?"

Ellen and Janey's first party was in full swing. Ellen had asked all the women she'd met in the last six months and they had asked their friends. Over thirty women had shown up so far and more were still arriving. Walking into the living room with a plate of hot cheese squares, Janey was immediately surrounded. By the time the plate was empty, she had smiled into so many friendly eyes and received knowing looks from so many sultry ones, she felt intoxicated.

"Ellen, where the hell have you been?" she heard and turned to see a brown-haired, fresh-faced woman in a black T-shirt smiling eagerly at Ellen. "We missed you last few meetings."

"I keep meaning to come again but I've just been too damned busy." Ellen, in her new, faded denim jacket, jeans, and Frye boots, reached out to draw Janey to her. "Sandy, this is my lover, Janey. Janey, this is Sandy from the Anti-Rape Group I told you about."

Janey smiled warmly and said hello. She knew from what Ellen had said that this group was very idealistic and ambitious. Its members wanted to provide a hotline for rape victims, accompany them to police stations and hospitals, compile a pamphlet of resource lists and advice, and—although this was apparently a subject of tense discussion—even implement some of the bolder members' terrifying suggestions for revenge on rapists. Ellen had attended a few months' worth of meetings and almost participated in a plan to photograph a rapist and plaster his photo on phone poles around the neighborhood. Fortunately (at least from Janey's point of view), she'd gotten cold feet.

"So what's she been up to?" Sandy asked Janey. "You two been painting the town red?"

Janey smiled. "No such luck. She's been working."

"I'm heading up a computer project." Although she spoke nonchalantly, Ellen's enthusiasm and pride shone in her eyes. "We've written a set of programs that imitate cars driving down streets and stopping at lights. We're trying to get the city's commute traffic moving faster."

"Hey, neat." But Sandy frowned. "Commute traffic, huh?" She smiled at Janey. "Listen, I got out of that patriarchal rat race five years ago. I don't take a job I can't walk to."

"Really?" Nearby, a woman with a fluffy curl falling artfully over her forehead spoke up. "I don't take a job, period."

The others around them laughed. Ellen smiled politely but was unstoppable. "I think I told you before, I work with this guy Roger, upstairs? He's some sort of computer genius."

"According to men, they're all geniuses." Sandy spoke seriously. "Have some respect for your own genius, Ellen, and forget about theirs. Every man I know says he's a genius."

"Roger doesn't say he's a genius. He just is," Janey put in loyally.

"He's not macho at all," Ellen explained. "He's more like someone from another planet."

"Don't tell me this is the traffic plan for evacuating the city in case of nuclear war." A woman in a khaki shirt and black pants had just walked up. Everything about her— snapping eyes, confident voice, solid stance—conveyed *I know what I'm talking about* and the others looked at Ellen doubtfully.

"No, this is to save commuters time," Ellen explained.

Janey had fully expected Ellen's friends to "Oh" and "Ah" and compliment her on the importance of her work, but only one friendly woman with grey bangs said anything nice and her appreciative remark was overshadowed by the reaction of the others.

"Personally and politically, I don't like computers," the woman with the snapping eyes declared. She stood with one foot up on the seat of a chair Janey had refinished and helped herself to handfuls of peanuts.

There was a murmur of agreement. Janey learned that the woman was a journalist named Carolyn Blake.

"Male technology is responsible for the environmental mess we're in," someone offered.

"I have a friend who lost a good clerical job when her company went to computers," another said. "You know what they offered her instead? Key punching. Now, *there's* a deadly job. She needed glasses after two months. After six months she went bonkers and quit. Those old key punch machines are noisy!"

"I'm sure nuclear weapons and nuclear plants couldn't have happened without computers," Sandy put in.

Ellen fell increasingly silent.

"They dehumanize anyone who works with them," Carolyn concluded. She emptied the dish of nuts into her hand, at which point Janey couldn't contain herself.

"Our society's deep into computers," she burst out. "They're part of modern life, whether you like it or not. I don't know why you're acting like this. Ellen and I are giving this party, you know. You're eating peanuts computer work paid for."

"Hear, hear!" Denise, a large, dramatic-looking woman in a batik print robe, smiled at Janey.

"Oh, hey, don't take it personally," Carolyn responded, putting the dish down and taking her foot off the chair. "We were just letting off steam." She smiled apologetically at Ellen and Janey and shortly moved down the hall toward the kitchen, trailed by Sandy and half a dozen others. The woman with grey bangs moved forward to draw Ellen's story out. Janey stood listening, her face flushed from her outburst, as Ellen described the traffic simulator to the three or four women left around her.

"Well and proudly said," Denise muttered to Janey. "I liked that, your speaking up for her. But let me ask you something. Society uses computers. But who says society is on the right path?"

"I didn't say it was on the right path, I said it was on the path it's on."

"Spoken like a realist. But, you see, we're here to turn you into an idealist! Come on, I want you to give that loudmouth Carolyn Blake a chance." Denise steered Janey down the hall to the kitchen where Carolyn had launched into an indictment of society.

She was sentencing men, militarism, Christianity, democracy, patriarchy, corporate America, and technology to the bowels of hell. Denise offered her commentary, nodding at parts, scoffing at others. After some initial resistance, Janey found herself listening carefully. Once, she saw Ellen standing alone in the hall and thought, "I should go to her," but by that time she was too caught up in what she was hearing.

Janey's practical side found most of Carolyn Blake's ideas too radical to accept. Still, the fiery words made her heart race. To throw everything out and start over—there was something deeply satisfying about a clean sweep, realistic or not. To build a world based on women's gentle ways and life-affirming views, to stop deadening male technology in its tracks. At this point, all the women in the kitchen quieted and smiled seriously at one another, as if they'd each touched the same ancient, long-lost source of hope.

"Listening to Carolyn, I wonder if everything I grew up believing isn't bullshit," Janey said to Denise later. She had put out more food and drinks and was now going around the apartment collecting dirty glasses. Denise had offered to follow along collecting trash. The conversation was still lively around them.

"Want to hear my take on it?" Denise asked as they made their way down the hall.

"Sure."

"First, the powers that be are giant insects...Yeah, hi, guys, talk to you later," she said to someone they passed.

Janey snorted, turned to look back at her.

"Metaphorically, of course. Through the media, mainly TV, they exude a sticky, gooey mess over us all, things like 'Men are better than women,' 'The government knows best,' 'A growing girl needs plenty of red meat,' that sort of thing. We can't move with this stuff all over us, we can't see through it, we're sluggish. Maybe we vaguely think something's wrong, but it takes a lot of energy to struggle out from underneath and see what's really going on."

"It's easier to stay under the covers," Janey suggested. "It's easier to keep believing what everyone else does."

"Right." Denise nodded to someone else she knew and exchanged a few words.

Janey waited a minute, then moved on into the living room. She liked Denise and was pleased when a moment later her new friend reappeared. Janey told her, "I've been a librarian for years and I can vouch that libraries are full of that goo you talked about." She reached here and there collecting glasses as she told Denise about setting up the women's shelf at the Bowles library. "You should have seen the stuff they had on the nature of women! To hear them tell it, our time is divided between worrying that we don't have a penis, doing painstakingly detailed work, which we love, and having hysterical nervous attacks."

Denise laughed. "The more I get to know you the more excited I get." She was ignoring the wadded-up, guacamole-stained napkins and cigarette butts around her; her bag seemed empty. "What would you say if I told you that a few of us are starting a women's bookstore and all we need to make it a success is a librarian from the East?"

Janey stopped in midstep. She felt a zinging feeling, like she would never forget this moment. She put the glass she'd been picking up back down. "A women's bookstore?"

"Four of us have been talking about it for a year. We just started meeting seriously. A couple of the others should show up any minute. I'll introduce you."

Janey broke into a huge smile. "A women's bookstore!" She tried to stay calm but Denise's words had called up a picture she'd never had before: rows and rows of books written by women, with women on the covers in strong poses, women characters, women salespeople, histories of women, analyses by women, anthologies of women.

Her heart raced. Gone was the resigned, so-what-did-I-expect feeling she had when she contemplated her computer work with Ellen and Roger or the corporate library jobs she'd been half-heartedly applying for. Gone was her usual caution at new things. She beamed her smile on Denise.

Of course she was interested. Tonight, in those exhilarating moments in the kitchen, she'd glimpsed the movement's power to touch something profound. That glow, the excitement of talking to Denise, the gathering sense of energy and ferment in the voices around her—this was the beginning of a new world, she thought, if not eventually for everyone on earth, at least here on Fifteenth Street for Janey Kowalski.

It was 3 a.m. Janey sat cross-legged on the mahogany bed, talking away to Ellen, who lay on her back, her hands behind her head. "And I'm going to meet seriously with Denise and the others in three days."

"That's great, sweetheart," but Ellen's voice was flat. "I just hope it'll work out. These women have grand ideas, you know, but whether they can actually make a go of it..."

Janey fought irritation. "Why do you let these things get to you? A few women spout some anti-technology rhetoric and you're ready to dump on the whole movement? I'm sorry they were so down on computers, but can't you just let it go?"

"I didn't expect them to love them, but to be so narrow-minded?"

"They're radicals, Ellen. They can't afford to discriminate between good and bad uses of things. Their points have to be clear and sharp." Denise had suggested this analysis to Janey.

"It makes me wonder about feminism, this crazy dismissal of something without even knowing much about it."

Janey sighed. "They like you, Ellen. They were all glad to see you. Can't you be happy about that? Do they have to think everything you do is wonderful?"

"Yes," Ellen pouted.

"Oh, silly." Janey leaned over and, looking into Ellen's eyes, rubbed noses with her. "Now cheer up. It was a great party. Everyone said so."

Ellen grumbled. Janey tickled her under the arms.

"Don't," Ellen cried, but she began to chuckle.

16

Midnight a few weeks later, Janey plodded up the stairs to Roger's place, her housecoat wrapped around her. Roger and Ellen were sitting working at their terminals.

"Ellen?"

Ellen didn't reply. She was intent on her screen.

"Ellen," Janey repeated. "It's past midnight."

"I'm coming," Ellen said absentmindedly.

"You can do that tomorrow," Janey said. "Why don't you stop now and get some sleep?"

"I'll be there in a few minutes," Ellen said, still in that same faraway tone. "I just want to finish this."

Janey took Ellen's shoulders in her hands, dug her thumbs into the muscles there, massaged them. Ellen protested with a moan and sat up straighter. "Yeah, I'm coming, sweetheart."

Janey plodded downstairs again. "They're like two ghouls," she said to Ida as she heated milk for cocoa. "She's getting as bad as him."

When the milk was hot, she took a broom and banged it hard three times against the ceiling overhead. She heard Ellen stand, move around. "Good. At last."

"This is crazy, working this hard, Ellen," Janey said as they sat at the kitchen table drinking cocoa.

Ellen's eyes were tired and over-bright. She stirred the creamy chocolate in her mug nervously.

"Hire another programmer," Janey urged.

"No. I'm the only one who—"

"You're the only one. *You're* the only one."

"I'm the only one who—"

"Ellen, the Great, is the only one who knows anything." Ellen gave her a hurt look. "That's not fair."

"Another programmer isn't going to take away your importance. You can tell them what to do just like you tell me."

"It doesn't have anything to do with importance," Ellen said. "There's just not time enough to introduce a new person to the project."

"But you've thrown yourself into this so completely! What about us? I know it's a big project and it's been dumped on you, but isn't there some other way to go about it? Some more organized way? I bet Arthur isn't losing sleep over this."

Ellen rubbed her tired-looking eyes. "You're right. I should have asked for more time. I just didn't realize it would take so long." After a pause, she took a deep breath. "Anyway, there's not that much more. We only have twenty more intersections to do. If we can get ten done tomorrow and finish up the day after, we can—"

"Tomorrow's Saturday," Janey put in. "We were going to look for a car. And I have to work on that loan application for the bookstore."

"Oh." Ellen looked worried. "Could you look without me? I trust your judgment completely."

"Dammit, Ellen." Janey's temper flared.

"I'm sorry, I just have to do this right." Ellen's voice rose too.

They glared at each other. Eventually, Janey said, "All right. But as soon as this city test is over next month, we get back together, right?"

"Right."

"You take weekends off, we talk, we have fun, go for hikes," Janey persisted.

"Right."

Janey nodded. Ellen might be sitting here talking to her, but already her mind was back inside the simulator. "We split up, I move back to Bowles, you kill yourself programming, right?" she asked.

"Right," Ellen answered mechanically. Then she said, "Don't say things like that, Janey," and, a moment later, "Maybe, if I get an early start I could get fifteen done tomorrow."

"Right," Janey agreed resignedly.

The morning she was to deliver her input to the city, Ellen found a small but crucial error in her program. She was working upstairs with Janey and Roger when it happened. At first, when she realized her mistake, she felt a fear and despair so great she could hardly contain it. All the blood must have drained from her face because when she called Janey over in a hoarse whisper, Janey's face was shocked. "Are you all right?"

"I made a mistake, Janey."

"Everyone makes mistakes. Is it a big mistake?"

Ellen swallowed. She tried to concentrate on Janey's question. All seemed lost. She nodded. "It means testing everything again."

"That's not so bad," Janey said. "It's not as if the whole thing doesn't work."

"I'll have to tell Arthur."

"How about Roger?"

Ellen confessed to Roger, who seemed untouched. "Either let it go or call the city and tell them you'll be a few weeks late," he said.

"I can't let it go, Roger. How can you even suggest that? It might cause terrible accidents. But I don't need more than a week. If we work really hard..."

"May as well ask for enough time," he advised her.

She returned to her terminal, her hands trembling, called Arthur, who wasn't in, and left a message with his secretary that she had made a mistake and was delaying the project two weeks. Then she called the city's head traffic engineer. He was a gruff, intelligent man who, in their earlier meetings, had freely described his department's current method of setting traffic light timings: a blend of tradition, hunches, and elementary arithmetic. At the end of the week, Ellen was scheduled to give him the new simulator timings for some ninety intersections in the area around San Francisco's end of the Bay Bridge. If he approved, the control boxes for each of these ninety intersections would be reset the following Saturday night. The new timings would be in effect for ten days or until traffic jams and/or calls from the public indicated the changes were a bust.

"Too bad," he said when he heard about the delay. "Traffic Maintenance's set up for this weekend."

"I know," Ellen said. She apologized profusely.

"That's okay. I'll let them know. You're sure you'll be ready in two weeks?"

"Yes, that should be plenty of time."

"All right. As long as when we get it, it's right."

"It will be," she said humbly.

With the extra days, Ellen had time to check and re-check her work. No matter how late she stayed up, a sharp, burning sensation in her chest woke her early every morning around four. She lay in bed worrying, going over and over the details of the simulator. Nothing seemed so important as avoiding failure. Success wasn't necessary. All she wanted was to avoid disaster. It terrified her that after only a couple of demonstrations of the simulator the city was ready to actually change its traffic lights; that they counted on her, Ellen's, one small mind (for Roger had turned everything over to her) to catch errors that might stall traffic for hours or, worse, end a tradition of lawful driving in America and start people dashing through red lights, crashing, and killing pedestrians.

Before Janey woke up each morning, Ellen snuck out of the bedroom and upstairs to her terminal to check her work yet another time.

Occasionally, she remembered the days when she'd been a teacher; they seemed altogether different: brighter, easier, younger. "Please, God, let it go okay," she prayed. When Janey asked her about plans for the week after the test, she shrugged her off. "I don't know. Wait and see if I sink or swim." If she sank, she imagined never rising again, never smiling, never going to the beach again, never kissing Janey again. Occasionally, she dreamt of glory; at these times it would seem her due. She imagined a certain exalted state; it was what she'd always longed for.

"It's not the end of the world if the timings don't work out," Janey reminded her.

"Yes, it is," Ellen groaned.

She delivered the simulator timings, as agreed, two weeks late. The traffic engineer looked them over. "Why the ninety-second red at Brannan and Fifth?" he asked.

With this sort of method, she explained, she couldn't answer that question. All she could say was under the simulator, traffic moved most efficiently with those timings. Maybe it had to do with the interface to the lights outside the test area.

He cut her off impatiently. "We usually know why we're making a setting," he said. "That's a long red."

Ellen floundered.

"Traffic Maintenance will be changing the settings Saturday night," he said. "My people will be driving around on Sunday, but we won't really know much until rush hour Monday."

"Good luck," Ellen told him.

"Good luck to you, Miss."

All day Saturday, Ellen ran to the bathroom, peeing as nervously as a small dog in dangerous territory. She could not sit still. For dinner Janey made spaghetti, her personal way to ward off unforeseen catastrophe; Ellen gorged on it, then felt sick, took an Alka-Seltzer and lay down.

The men were to start work at midnight. At quarter of, Ellen and Janey drove toward the Bay Bridge. Whenever a light turned from red to green or green to yellow or yellow to red, Ellen felt relief. Occasionally, they saw a city truck stopped at an intersection, a man in work clothes and an eerily gleaming vest opening a control box under a light, beaming a flashlight in, playing it over the clock and switches there, and reaching in.

Once, driving down Harrison in the dark, the two women were forced to stop at every light. "This isn't right," Ellen cried. She felt frantic. "This isn't right!" They circled around, tried again. This time they only had to stop twice. Ellen's breathing slowed. "Maybe it's okay."

"They seem fine, Ellen," Janey said.

Ellen looked around at the dark night, the empty parking lots, the cavernous buildings. As far as they could see down Harrison Street, it was empty. "It's crazy that nobody's out here. Wouldn't you think that for something this important they'd have some government officials out here trying it? The mayor or someone?"

"Probably not the mayor." Janey laughed.

"We shouldn't have had to stop on Harrison. Try it again." But by now it was 2 a.m. and all the lights on Harrison had been switched to yellow blinkers.

Monday morning rush hour, in an effort to find out what a commuter coming into San Francisco would find, Janey and Ellen drove across the bay to Oakland, turned around, and crawled back to the always-crowded toll plaza, Ellen tapping her fingers on the steering wheel, tailgating the truck in front of her. The bridge traffic moved well, but she might have supported it all on the tension in her shoulders alone. Ellen came off the bridge, off the freeway, down Harrison. Harrison was moving well. When they got home, Ellen dashed upstairs, asked Roger, "Any news?"

He started to tell her about his latest breakthrough, something about wave lengths.

"No, the city, the traffic lights, the *simulator*, Roger," she cried.

"Yes, of course. No news. I assume it's fine."

"You don't know how worried I've been."

"I've got a puzzle for you. Three men are—"

"Let me call the city first, Roger."

"Yes," the traffic engineer said. "Traffic seems to be moving okay. No big snarls. But it's the evening rush hour that separates the men from the boys. Nine thousand cars go over that bridge every hour."

Ellen drank cup after cup of coffee. The puzzle Roger had given her was impossible; she could no more concentrate on it than fly. Five o'clock came and no word from the city; six o'clock, nothing. She finally called. There was no answer. Were they all out trying to untangle the worst traffic crisis in the history of San Francisco? Ellen and Janey drove with trepidation to the Bay Bridge. Traffic seemed to move as usual, perhaps slightly slower, but there was a stall in the rightmost lane. They had the radio on and the traffic news mentioned a change in the lights.

"Commuters will see if the computerized traffic lights set up by a whiz kid in his Mission District apartment can fix what ails this city. Right, Bob?"

"Right, Sue. If you think traffic moves faster tonight, give us a call at 988-8888."

As the two women came off the bridge into Oakland, the station was broadcasting a call. *Yes, Joseph Riley had reached home ten minutes earlier than usual.*

Ellen hollered with pleasure; Janey beat a tune on the dashboard.

Another call came in. *University car pool to San Francisco. Five minutes earlier.*

More calls, summarized by Sue: "We've had a dozen early commutes. Congrats to the whiz kid. Did you get his name, Bob?"

"No, but you can be sure he's smiling tonight."

Ellen hooted at the radio. "What about the whiz kid's helper? *She's* the one who's smiling. The whiz kid isn't even paying attention!"

"And what about the whiz kid's helper's helper?" Janey joined in. "Don't you know *women* were the ones to bring this about?"

But Bob and Sue had moved on. Janey and Ellen didn't know what to do with themselves. "Who can we tell? Who can we tell?" They couldn't think of a soul. To most of the women they knew, moving cars around in a hurry was not a cause for celebration.

"Lord Arthur must be pleased," Ellen finally cried.

"But do we really want to talk to him?" Janey asked and they agreed no, the idea of talking to such a patriarch, with his faint British accent and royal bearing, was unappealing. They wanted a community of friends to toast them warmly, they wanted squeezes of the hand, pats on the back, a warm kitchen, and open arms. They wanted to be rocked safely to sleep with the murmur of voices. As they drove back to San Francisco, their excitement died and tiredness set in. When they got home, they lay down close together on the mahogany bed, spoon-style, and slept.

Janey woke up the next morning with a sense of anticlimax. Her friends might be right about technology, she thought, for what would the simulator really do but encourage more people to drive cars, use gas, get places early, rush, and generally adhere to the frenzy of modern urban life. The whole city beat like an anxious heart. Janey could see that Ellen, when she woke, was buzzing with this same pervasive, anxious, exalted state of hurry and importance.

"How about we take the day off and go to the beach?" Janey suggested as they stood in the kitchen eating their breakfast of English muffins and peanut butter. She knew before she said it there was no chance.

"How about tonight?" Ellen replied. "We'll catch the sunset."

"Well, *I'm* taking the day off, anyway." Janey sat down at the kitchen table and leaned back, chewing slowly.

"Okay, sweetheart."

"Have a good time," Ellen said a minute later as she left for Roger's. "'Bye, Ida."

"Ellen," Janey called with her mouth full, wanting to arrange when they'd meet again, but Ellen was already out of earshot. "Ghoul heaven," Janey remarked to Ida, tossing her head in the direction of Roger's place upstairs.

On the kitchen table were two letters from Bowles that had arrived the day before and been forgotten in the excitement. Janey tore the first one open as she waited for the kettle to boil.

It was from Ruthie. She no longer wrote in the careful, elegant script of her love poems to Donna; this letter was typed single-space and signed with a flourish.

Ruthie had seen Donna over Christmas a few times; Donna had a boyfriend, but just for form's sake; Ruthie had gotten her driver's license and was saving for a car; she'd gotten a job as a checker at Top Foods after school; she thought life was "fierce."

The second letter was from Audrey. She said that three of them from the defunct women's group had had supper together and talked about having a "Family Lesson" booth for Family Day the following year. They planned to put on skits about non-traditional families. Did Janey or Ellen have any ideas for a lesbian skit?

"How about a witch burning?" Janey asked Ida cynically but, looking at the Bowles postmark, she felt the sharp pain of nostalgia. She wondered how her old house was. It seemed just yesterday she'd arrived in Bowles to start her job as librarian, found that sweet old house with the honeysuckle, and fallen in love with Angie. And it seemed just yesterday Ellen had arrived like a hurricane and Janey had left it all behind.

Sitting there, the kettle boiling on the stove, Janey felt the energy drain out of her. She stared at the bars on the kitchen windows.

Ida requested with her dark eyes that they please go to the beach.

Janey rubbed her temples with her palms, shook herself a little. "Okay, it's no good sitting here." She stood up, turned off the gas under the steaming water. "You realize I should work on the income projections," she told the dog.

Longingly, Ida continued to plead.

"You're right." Janey stood up briskly and fetched her jacket. "The need to accomplish something efficiently is the obsession of the patriarchy and I will not be caught by it," she proclaimed.

Ida, in agreement, ran out the door ahead of her.

Within the month, Arthur was engaged in negotiations for sale of the simulator, presumably to the city although the words "state" and "federal" were also mentioned. "Aside from documenting it, don't worry about it further," he told Ellen and Janey. "Roger, I believe you have already begun educating Ellen on your 'Human Face' project?"

"I believe you're right," Roger said.

Janey recognized Roger's difficult mood. Whenever the backer made the mistake of sounding authoritative, Roger became very reflective. Turns of phrase seemed to interest him inordinately.

"Good. How is it coming, if I may ask?"

As Roger pulled a piece of paper toward him, the backer added warningly, "Generally, I mean. In one or two English sentences, if possible."

"*English* sentences," Roger reflected. "Not in French." He seemed lost in thought.

"The main idea is to digitize a distributed associative memory," Ellen explained. "We're modeling a holistic system."

Janey sympathized with the backer's puzzled look. She knew the project was to enable a computer to recognize a human face.

Arthur, never at a loss for words, plunged on, "Is this a new approach?"

"The Finns have had some success," Roger put in.

"Pardon?"

"The Finns. In Finland. They've had some success."

"Do you need more equipment, Roger?"

Roger considered. "Perhaps a plotter. A 3950. They're available in knocked-down versions."

After the backer left, Roger and Ellen continued to discuss equipment. Arthur had suggested that they move to bona fide offices, but Roger liked things as they were. The wiring to the house was constantly being upgraded; a powerful air-conditioner roared in Roger's dining/printer room; a new security system had been installed.

Janey glanced at Ellen in awe. Phrases like "distributed associative memory" and "techniques for normalization" tripped easily off her tongue. She seemed to know as well as Roger what they meant. Often, as the three of them sat down to talk, Janey felt as if they were like three horses at the gate. At the shot, the other two galloped off in a cloud of words and dust. She trotted after them for a while, then gave up and munched some grass by the side of the track.

Although she counted on the computer work for her small paychecks, the bookstore collective was her real love. She and the others had finally finished their application for a small-business loan and sent it off. Not that there was much hope: up to now, women had not been considered "minorities" by the Small Business Administration. The bookstore needed a loan from somewhere. Two fund-raising events requiring hours of work had hardly brought in enough to pay the rent for a month and, although Janey and Denise had each put in some of their own money, the collective wisdom discouraged any heavy investment by its members.

In searching for ways to finance the bookstore, Janey had considered everyone she knew who had money, including Arthur. He seemed to have endless funds. She had asked Ellen, "Where does all his money come from?"

"He's an entrepreneur," Ellen said.

"Do you think he's with some government agency?"

"Ask him, if you're interested," Ellen suggested.

When asked, Arthur said he had friends in the government interested in energy conservation. But no, he was not a salaried employee; he was independent. Would he be interested in helping to finance a women's bookstore, she asked cautiously? After a moment's consideration, he answered yes, he could donate a thousand dollars. She should call his office and arrange it with his secretary.

Janey was so pleased with this donation she wanted to kiss Arthur, but he was too tall, too suave, too immaculate to kiss, so she just shook his hand. No matter what she learned later about him, she always retained a soft spot for him because he'd made the first sizable statement of faith in Womanbooks.

Denise's call caught Janey at lunch one day that spring. "Come right over, Janey. It's good news," she said, in her dramatic way.

"Can't you tell me over the phone?"

"Of course I can. I just wanted to see you. We got an anonymous donation of eight thousand dollars! A cashier's check. It just came!"

"Eight thousand dollars! But who—?"

"A wonderful rich dyke, what do you bet? I'm calling a meeting of the collective tonight. Can you come early? I want to discuss things with you."

"What time?"

"I'll tell the others eight. Come at seven."

That evening, as she and Ellen gobbled stir fry and salad, Janey asked, "Do you think Arthur had anything to do with this donation? He must know other rich people."

"I doubt it. He's not *that* nice." Ellen stuffed a dangling leaf of lettuce into her mouth. "Does this mean you won't be working with us anymore?"

"It could."

Ellen sighed. "It's been so much fun working together."

Janey, although she was no longer unhappy in her work with Ellen and Roger, still would not have described it as "fun." But she nodded.

"How much is Denise going to pay you?"

"Ellen, the bookstore is a collective. It's not Denise's."

"Oh, yeah." Ellen considered. "So none of you are going to make much."

"I've got the money from the house."

"Oh, no, you shouldn't eat into that. You're going to buy another house with that some day. No, I'll help out, I make enough."

Janey was touched. Assuming she'd work full time at the store, she'd try to get along on whatever she got paid, but still...

"That's really nice of you," she said formally. "I might need to borrow."

"You don't have to borrow. I like the idea of being the breadwinner. Besides, if I help you out, it's a contribution to the movement. This way I won't have to feel bad about not photographing rapists. I won't have to defend computers or sit in planning meetings for hours. And when you bug me about working too hard, I can just say, 'I'm doing it for you.' "

Janey arrived at Denise's large, messy place off Mission Street just after seven. Three mongrel dogs and two cats with scruffy fur and watery eyes were ensconced on cushions in the living room: Denise took in stray pets. Over her large body, Denise wore a large, bright green caftan that she'd found at Thrift Village. Her family had plenty of money, but she preferred living frugally. What money she'd been given or inherited she passed on to the women's movement.

Over herb tea in the kitchen, she confided, "I want you to manage the bookstore, Janey. I figure you should have a starting salary of seven hundred and fifty a month. Can you manage on that?"

Janey nodded. "Probably. But doesn't the collective have to decide? And wouldn't *you* want to manage it?"

"No, I'm no manager. Look at this place, it's a mess." Denise waved a hand in the direction of the cat and dog dishes and piles of papers strewn around. "No, you're the professional. You've met a budget, you've managed a department, you've dealt with the public. As for the others, I think some part-time arrangement would work out.

Eventually we'd have one other full-time job and three part-timers. They can draw straws for the jobs. How does that sound?"

"Fine. I'm delighted. But—"

"But what?"

"What about the others? Won't they want—"

Denise pretended to tear out handfuls of her light brown, curly hair. "What a pain in the whazoosis this collective business is! Can't they see we need a professional? Are they so idealistic they think that any ignoramus can walk in and manage a business as problematic as this one? Are they—" She was interrupted by the doorbell. "Don't worry, I'll handle it," she said.

By the end of their lively meeting, it was decided. Janey would be employed full time, three of the five others a third of the time each. Janey, to be known as a "cooperative manager," would be paid at a rate considerably higher than the others, in view of her experience. The collective would continue meeting once a week. The following weekend they would begin their search for a suitable location, preferably in the low-priced and popular Mission District where they all lived. It was a testimony to Denise, Janey thought, that none of them ever had a sense she was directing things. She seemed more prescient than manipulative.

Afterward, they bounced out of her apartment and over to the recently opened Full Moon Coffeehouse, where a dozen or so women sat drinking tea, eating muffins, murmuring together, and glancing at one another. Paintings by women softened the white walls of the large, airy space. In a small room off the main one were a dozen shelves of women's books and periodicals for sale: a miniature version of what Janey and the others hoped to build.

Denise conferred with a staff member, was introduced to the room at large, and told everyone present the good news. Immediately came cries of congratulation, hugs, and tears. Janey was glad that the coffeehouse staff, who might have resented the competition, instead offered to help their fledgling sister business in any way they could and started by handing out free muffins.

In the midst of the celebration, Rita, the most exuberant and graceful member of the bookstore collective, dragged a chair to the end of the room, jumped up on it and, dark eyes shining, big Afro gleaming, body radiating energy, told the others, "A book is a message from one woman's heart to another woman's heart, from one woman's mind to another woman's mind, from one woman's soul to another woman's soul. We're going to help those messages flow freely. Right on, sisters!"

Janey, Denise, Rita, and the other collective members threw themselves into an often intoxicating, sometimes depressing, flurry of activity for the bookstore: squinting over the small print of ads and rental listings, checking out dingy storefronts, and meeting with potential landlords and wary building managers. Every night they were on the phone with each other: was the street they'd visited too forbidding? Could they afford the rent? Were the proportions of the rooms pleasing? ("Do we really care?" Denise asked, but the rest said yes.)

Before long a large, pleasant store on a semi-residential block of Eighteenth Street came free. "Too expensive," they agreed, but called each other at dawn the next day: wouldn't the additional number of women who could visit such a central location make up for the extra rent?

They signed the lease the following week. Janey was as excited as she'd been when she found her Bowles house. From everywhere, women popped up to help: carpenters, wood finishers, painters, haulers. Ellen showed up almost nightly, tired-eyed but eager, to sand shelves.

Meanwhile, the collective pored over book lists from publishers and distributors and sent out their first orders. Two hundred women appeared at the opening. That day Womanbooks took in fifteen hundred dollars.

During the next months, Janey learned more terrible things than she could ever have imagined about the crimes perpetrated against women through the centuries. Any doubt in her mind that the world was a patriarchal place was washed away by the scores of books, magazines, and newspapers that came through the store exposing the rape, clitorectomy, wife beating, foot binding, witch burning, chastity belts, purdah, and all the other atrocities that made up women's history. Modern America still paid a woman fifty-seven cents for every dollar a man made, refused to acknowledge rape within marriage, and praised films such as *Snuff*, which presented the dismemberment and murder of a woman as sexual entertainment.

This was the awful reality. But women had stopped accepting it. They'd been divorcing, shouting, marching, lobbying, running for office—and writing. Lesbians, feminists, witches, philosophers, artists, mothers, victims of discrimination and violence, and thousands of others— all told their stories. Every oppression was analyzed, matriarchy was discussed, and God the Father dismissed. Women's presses published lesbian novels with happy endings and women distributors sent them out to women's bookstores. Wives read of wives walking out on their husbands; secretaries read of secretaries talking back to their bosses. "I refuse to accept your authority. I have my own now," these books said. Inspirational biographies, thought-provoking analyses, lesbian sex manuals, resource lists, angry poems, and books about new ways of loving flooded the store.

It seemed that everyone stopped by that first year, or at least phoned in. "Do you have a book on incest?" "Where can a lesbian go to meet someone?" "Do you sponsor consciousness-raising groups?" "Does anyone know anything about the statistics for women going bald?"

One late afternoon, while she and Rita staffed the store and a dozen women browsed the shelves, Rita looked up from the newspaper she had spread out on the counter. "Hey, how about this? The American Psychiatric Association has just declared male chauvinism a certifiable psychiatric illness!"

Janey was ringing up a sale.

"Does that mean I can get my husband locked up?" the customer asked, laughing.

Two women in their twenties who often visited the store came in excitedly, carrying a tape recorder. "You'll never believe this," they told the three women at the counter. "You know, we started this group working to stop street harassment?"

Janey and Rita nodded; they'd heard about it.

"Well, we got this idea to interview men on the street who came on to us. Go right to the source. So what do you suppose happened with the second guy we tried this on?"

"What?" Janey loved these women's pizzazz.

"Can I play this here if I keep it low?"

Janey nodded. The recorder was switched on and the others bent to listen.

There were sounds of traffic and then a woman's voice, "Excuse me, but you just spoke to us. I think you said, 'Hey, baby'?"

There was a male mutter.

"We'd like to know what made you do that? What did you expect? Did you think we'd really answer you?"

More traffic noise. The sound of the machine being clicked off.

"That one walked off. We were too much for him. But wait, it's the next guy who's a trip."

Her voice, thinner and higher on tape, came from the machine. There were different background noises now, the sounds of children playing. "Did I understand you correctly? Did you say, 'Want to fuck?' to us?"

"Yes, yes, I did," a rather worried male voice said.

"We're doing a survey on men who speak to women in the street. We want to know—do you do this often?"

"That's strange," the man said. "I just came from my psychiatrist and we were talking about it. I probably say it to women four or five times a day."

There was a pause. "And, uh—" The second woman's voice took over. "What happens? Does anyone ever respond?"

"No, they're mostly annoyed. Some of them say, 'Fuck off,' or something. I've been saying it for, let's see...since... well, I can't remember, but a long time. Sometimes I say, 'Want to suck my cock?' instead."

The first woman spoke sharply. "That's harassment. It's extremely annoying and demeaning to women."

"I know," he agreed. "My psychiatrist says I need a healthy relationship. It started when I was a boy, say eleven or twelve, maybe thirteen. Are you girls really interested in this?"

"Yes," one of them said, but she sounded doubtful.

"My psychiatrist says I didn't develop the correct boundaries. What happened was—"

"And he went on like that, with us standing there nodding—this jerk had us reverted to two nice girls! He would have continued all day if we hadn't finally stopped him." The woman flipped off the recorder. "Can you beat that?"

"More than anyone ever wanted to know about street harassment," the second woman added. "As we were leaving, he asked if one of us would like to go out on a date. Either one of us would be fine, he said." She smiled wryly, shaking her head.

"You've got to get tougher, girl," Rita said fondly.

Half a dozen customers had gathered around by then and the tape was played again. The phone kept ringing: a woman checking to see if the textbooks for her class had come in, a distributor with a delay, and someone who wanted to know if they allowed men in the store. Janey said yes. Meanwhile, Rita rang up sales and made notes on the inventory sheet.

Janey and Rita moved easily around each other but each of them sometimes tripped over Ida, who was popular at the store and liked spending her days underfoot behind the counter. Now she nudged Janey's leg and looked at her meaningfully: she needed to go out.

They made their way toward the door through the women, Ida gathering pats and smiles. Another member of the collective, who was just coming in, asked if Janey wanted to speak at a Women in Business workshop. Yes, she guessed so, Janey said, as she stepped out onto the sidewalk. She strolled back and forth in front of the store, turning her face to the hot, autumn sun. Ida sniffed around at the ends of burritos, dog shit, crumpled bags, and other intriguing objects that littered the concrete.

"Ida, no. No, Ida. Will you leave that stuff alone?" Janey made a mental note to call the city again about the lack of street cleaning in the neighborhood.

"Faggot!" a guy shouted from a big, flashy car going by. She looked around; the insult seemed to have been directed at her. From across the street, the jeweler who had just stepped out of his store to smoke a cigar, waved to her, pointed to the departing car, and shrugged his shoulders: don't pay any attention, he seemed to say. She waved back at him.

The shout had shaken her, but only a little. She considered what she might say about the bookstore's operations if she spoke at the Women in Business workshop. She looked around at the now-familiar shops: the jeweler's and the corner grocery, the garage and the taco place. There was broken glass on the street and down the block two people were shouting back and forth. A weary Chicana woman came down the street lugging her groceries in a shopping cart; they smiled. They'd often complained to each other about the city's neglect of the block. One day, Janey hoped, the woman would venture into the bookstore.

This life was not at all like Bowles. Still, with the faint sounds of the women's talk and laughter coming from inside, with Ida trotting around sniffing for signs of other dogs that might have passed that way, with the sunlight blooming and the feeling of life going on all around her, Janey had a moment of transcendent happiness.

"You know, Melody's really smart, it turns out," Ellen said one night around ten; she and Janey had both worked late. Melody was the fashionable young woman Arthur had found to replace Janey.

"Most women turn out to be smarter than we think, don't they? Rita dreamed up a women's bookstore before she'd even heard of one." Janey wet the sponge and wiped up some crumbs left over from breakfast.

"Sure, well, that's intuitive. But Melody's really got a head for figures. Most women don't."

"That statement doesn't sound very feminist."

"But it's true."

Janey paused, studied her lover who was pouring hot chocolate into mugs. "You were such a feminist when I met you."

"I am a feminist. I was just making an observation."

"Still, generalizing like that...You make it happen by predicting it."

Janey buttered toast and the two of them sat down at the kitchen table. They smiled at each other tiredly. Janey said, "You know, don't you, that some women have set up a meeting Friday to discuss this guy Briggs who's out to get gay teachers?"

Ellen sighed. "Yeah, of course I have to go. Are you going?"

"You want me to?"

"Not necessarily."

Janey nodded. She'd arranged to go with Denise to a planning meeting for a fund-raising concert Friday, but she might have canceled that if Ellen had wanted company. Janey liked imagining Ellen speaking out with her old political fire and conviction. These days Ellen often begged off women's events. "Too busy," she said, or "too tired," but Janey wondered. She thought Ellen had lost her enthusiasm for the movement not only because of her devotion to work, but because the radical women she at heart so admired had refused to allow her to shine.

In early 1978, Arthur succeeded in selling the traffic simulator to the federal government. The energy crisis was a fact of life; reduced time at traffic lights would reduce gas consumption, the government decreed. Use of the simulator was recommended to states dependent on federal funds for highways. Ellen received offers from as far away as Alaska to install and maintain it.

She pinned these flattering letters to the kitchen bulletin board. "None of them interest me," she told Janey airily. But she enjoyed rereading them. "Cordially, Harvey Waters, City Manager, City of New Orleans," she read and "Sincerely, Andrew Sarsi, Director of Streets and Roads, State of Oregon."

She and Roger and Melody continued work on the Human Face. Unlike the simulator, which had so early and easily proved a success, programming a computer to recognize a human face seemed more difficult every day. The problem was this: a woman might befriend someone at a party one year, lose track of her, and five years later easily recognize her in a crowd. She recognized her despite the intervening years, despite anguish, hat, glasses, or wrinkles. How did she do it? Did the human mind, like a digital computer, register all the dimensions and colors of each face in the crowd, say, "That woman's eyes are exactly one eye-length apart. Her nose is exactly two inches long. Her complexion is the shade registered as Number 7648590. When she smiles, her second molar is visible if you are at an angle of sixty degrees from her exact center..." and so forth, breaking down the range of human physiognomy, style, and expression into thousands of precise lengths and proportions? Did it then take each of these mammoth conglomerations of numbers and compare them to lengthy catalogs of equally mammoth conglomerations representing human faces known to the viewer? After all this comparing, did it finally decide, "No, I don't know that one," and go on to the next lengthy calculation, finally perhaps reaching a match: "Yes, that must be my friend Sue." To a human, recognizing a human face had none of this turgid quality; a known face was immediately familiar. The name and circumstances might need searching for, but the face was immediately known.

This was the problem Roger and Ellen and others like them were working on. An assumption that the human mind did, in fact, work in this long-winded way through unconscious rules and volumes of precise measurements had pervaded the field of artificial intelligence since its beginnings in 1965. It had been predicted then that within twenty years a computer would be able to do anything a human could do. Nothing of the sort was happening. Computers remained sophisticated tools; they took on no life of their own. As Janey once asked, "Why should a computer be able to think like a human when a human can't think like a computer?"

By the time Roger began in the field, a few researchers had turned their attention to a different conception of how the brain operated. They were studying holograms, those mysterious interactions of light waves that could not only reproduce a three-dimensional image of an object, but, more importantly, recognize similarity. If a hologram were taken of the letter R, if a second hologram were made of a page of print, if then the two holograms were superimposed— eureka! All the Rs on the page would be immediately recognized and highlighted. Perhaps, these researchers thought, some similar holistic system existed in the mind: when the outer crowd of new faces was compared with the inner crowd of known faces, the known faces in the outer crowd were immediately recognized. Roger, Ellen, and Melody were working hard, through mathematics, to simulate a holographic system on a conventional computer.

As the months passed, Arthur sometimes betrayed impatience. "Do you need more people?" he'd ask. "More training? Decent offices?"

"No, no, no," Roger would assure him absently. Where Ellen and Melody were defensive or apologetic, Roger was calm. Where Ellen and Melody were obliging and helpful, Roger was resistant. As the backer's wing-tipped shoes clicked down the steps, Ellen would ask, "Roger, couldn't you tell he was accusing us of laziness, of padding our hours?"

"Was that what he was doing? He talks so politely I never know."

"Oh, *Roger!*" Ellen laughed. She had learned that Roger regarded human beings as if from a great distance. His own acts of kindness—spontaneous presents he might buy for his parents or herself or Melody—seemed to be prompted by whimsy. Roger was never wracked with emotion; the closing of his favorite Chinese restaurant, the success of their traffic simulator, Melody's orange and blue hair, the death of his father—all, to hear him describe them, seemed to have little effect on him. Humans ate, wrote programs, dyed their hair, and died—the human condition, he seemed to say. He occasionally told Ellen stories of his life. They had a certain poignancy: a lonely man going about his lonely life. Yet Roger did not seem unhappy. He skated around the fringes of the world and felt himself the center of it.

"If you're a genius, does that mean I'm one too?" she asked him once.

"Yes, it does," he assured her.

"Do you know Roger thinks I'm a genius?" she told Janey that night.

"I guess you are," Janey agreed. She had gotten over thinking it strange that Ellen, who, while intelligent and interesting, had never seemed phenomenally smart to Janey, should have been reborn in California as a whiz-bang computer wizard.

18

Early in the morning of March 28, 1979, on Ellen's thirty-fifth birthday, the nuclear reactor at Three Mile Island in Pennsylvania lost its cooling water, quickly overheated, and came within half an hour of a catastrophic meltdown. More than a hundred thousand people fled the surrounding area. That evening, as the TV coverage assured the public that technicians were successfully bringing the reactor under control, the guests at Ellen's birthday party eyed the TV skeptically. The remains of a chocolate cake sat on the coffee table. Yellow candles with little burnt wicks and rings of fudge icing lay on a saucer nearby. Ida was staring at the last piece of cake intently as the women talked and watched the TV screen.

"I bet some heads are going to roll on this one," Denise said. "Safe, clean nuclear power—sure!" She was sprawled in an easy chair, her curly hair, which had started out the evening in a bun, now escaped from its barrettes and returned to its natural, electric state.

Nearby on the couch, two women in clinging silk blouses and pants sat close against each other, one's hand resting casually on the other's thigh. Marie was a painter who worked as a typist; her lover was a body therapist. When Ellen and Janey found time to go hiking or dancing or out to dinner, they always called Marie and Jean.

"I doubt if women would ever have come up with nuclear power," Marie said. "I mean, smashing the atom isn't the sort of thing to appeal to us in the first place."

"That's for sure," Denise agreed.

"Unfortunately, you can't stop the human brain," Ellen put in as she squatted in front of the TV trying to improve the color. "Once it gets an idea, it wants to try it out." Her cheeks were pink with excitement from being the center of attention all day.

"Oh, but Ellen..." Janey had just come in from the kitchen with cold bottles of wine and sparkling cider. "No matter if millions of people may eventually be killed? No matter if the earth may be destroyed?"

"I don't think it's the human brain, Ellen, I think it's the male ego." Rita, in a scoop-necked yellow blouse, a gold chain shining against her dark brown skin, sat cross-legged on the rug, her back against the couch. "Women give birth so we have a corner on life. Men are jealous. They want something big to control and what's left? Death. So they grab that. And run with it."

Ellen's shy friend Dolly, a fellow computer analyst, looked uncomfortable, as if she feared that at any minute she might be called upon to argue Ellen's case. She chewed a thumbnail and smiled at Janey nervously.

Ellen was back in her easy chair. "Maybe you're right. Maybe the ego and the mind are the same thing," she answered Rita. "But I picture these guys getting this idea to smash the atom and unleash all this power. Then they try to think how—it's a challenge. They come up with an idea—blast the atom with a laser beam or whatever. Try an element that's unstable. They do all the calculations. Will it work? Will it work big? Will a chain reaction start? Will the world be blown up? They have to know. They're not thinking about people at this point. They're in the grip of their need to know."

"But why do they need to know?" Janey cried. She stood looking concerned, one bottle in each hand.

"To see if they understood it right. To see if the idea is good."

"I could have told them right off that the idea of smashing the primary particle of the universe was not *good.*"

"Do you mean you think it was okay to build the atom bomb?" Marie asked Ellen.

"Well," Ellen hesitated. "I don't know about 'okay.' I just—"

"Ellen, you know you're against all that," Janey interrupted.

Ellen glanced up, saw the alarmed look in Janey's eyes. "Of course I'm against it. I was just explaining how these guys think." She pulled the cake plate closer, took a last piece for herself, and put the plate on the rug for Ida. "Of course I don't condone building the atomic bomb, what do you take me for?"

Marie nodded and Denise sank back in her chair.

"I think there is something in women that would stop us from building a bomb," Janey concluded. "Now who wants something more to drink?"

Later, after the guests had gone and they'd cleaned up, Janey and Ellen lay watching TV together on the couch. They'd turned the sound down, but it was obvious from the excited, urgent faces on the screen that the disaster was not over.

Ellen held Janey close with one arm. Now that they were alone, what was happening in Pennsylvania made her heart pound. Human life was so vulnerable. Even she and Janey seemed in danger. The smell of Janey's familiar shampoo and the smooth touch of her hair seemed very precious. "I'd feel so awful if anything ever happened to you."

"I know, honey."

"I couldn't stand it." Ellen kissed her sweet-smelling hair.

"Nothing's going to happen to me."

"Good." Ellen pulled her closer still.

Their attention was caught by a fresh image: a diagram with moving arrows. Janey extricated herself to turn the sound up, then sank back onto the narrow strip of couch into Ellen's arms, her head touching Ellen's cheek.

The diagram was a simplified plan of the nuclear plant. A flashing box highlighted a crucial valve that had stuck open for two hours without any of the technicians being alerted.

"What do you bet the system was programmed to say the valve was closed before it actually issued the instruction to close it?" Ellen said. "So some indicator said it was closed when it wasn't."

Janey thought there were probably a million reasons for the failure—the primary one being that the plant should never have been built at all—but she was impressed that Ellen had come up with an intelligent-sounding technical explanation already.

"Imagine being responsible for *that* programming error," Janey said.

Ellen groaned. "I don't even want to think about it."

The newscast, which was called "Meltdown USA," returned to one of the three experts they'd heard from earlier. "Let's turn it off," Janey suggested. She wore soft, green velvet slacks that hiked up as she eased farther down the couch and stretched out one strong, bare leg toward the TV.

"As far as can be determined from the facts at hand—" the expert began tiredly.

Janey poised her big toe in front of the power button and moved her foot carefully forward. The set clicked off.

She crept up again into Ellen's arms. They lay facing each other, their legs interwoven, settling together.

"Thank you for my present. I love it." Ellen wore the bright red rayon blouse Janey had given her that morning. Through it, she could feel the pressure of Janey's large breasts. "And thank you for the party."

"You're welcome."

"How do Marie and Jean manage to look so great all the time?" Ellen mused.

"Which one do you think is sexier?" Janey asked mischievously.

"Of course, neither of them is as sexy as you."

"Of course."

"But there's something sizzling about Marie."

"And Jean?"

"You're attracted to Jean?" Ellen asked.

"I like her and I like her smile."

"Oh, her and her smile. Sure. You don't care about her beautiful, bouncing breasts and that silk draped over her curvy legs. Just her and her smile."

They exchanged a warm, loving, challenging look. Janey adjusted her arm, which had started to fall asleep.

"You and I don't see enough of each other," Ellen said. "Day after day passes and I don't even give a thought to how lucky I am to be with you."

"I was thinking about that first march we went to in New York four years ago. Remember? You wore a red shirt that day, too. You looked really good." Janey drew a finger down Ellen's cheek. "But your eyes were different then. Restless eyes."

"Not bloodshot anyway."

"No, they're happier now. Calmer anyway. And that mouth," Janey said. "Your mouth looked so juicy to me. Right from the start."

Ellen pursed her lips and then laughed. "Juicy?"

"Yes." Janey traced her lover's lips with a finger. "I knew they'd feel just this way—sort of firm and pushable on the outside and then a little smoother inside..." She ran her finger along the inside of Ellen's lower lip.

Ellen felt a thrill run from her mouth straight down her body. She nibbled Janey's finger. Her hand moved to the back of Janey's neck and up into her fine, silky hair. She tightened the muscles of her legs around Janey's and felt Janey's hand come up under the red blouse to touch her breast delicately, knowingly. For one minute Ellen pictured Marie's small perfect face with its parted lips, but then the fantasy vanished.

"Janey," she murmured. She wanted to eat Janey up, absorb her right into her and keep her there forever.

"I love you." Janey's husky voice was low and tender.

"Promise me we'll always be together."

"We'll always be together."

"Even after we die."

"Yes, honey."

Tears came to Ellen's eyes. She was swept with longing for Janey, whom she was so used to and yet hardly really saw anymore. She was about to say more, but Janey was touching her breasts in that special way she had so that it was impossible to do anything other than follow her into the delicious, fiery, irresistible world of sex.

19

Her name was Christine. She arrived one Monday night in August 1984 for the regular open meeting of the bookstore collective. She was strikingly dark-haired, low-voiced, full of energy, restless, and charismatic. She seemed fierce, more suited for leading a demonstration than waiting on customers at a bookstore. Janey expected that, like others who had come to the collective looking for radical action and left soon in disgust at the mountain of paperwork, Christine would not show up the following week.

But she did. What's more, she made some suggestions: the bookstore should modernize its music, bring in some street sounds, mix in some punk and new-wave with the women's folk songs. T-shirts were where the money was these days, T-shirts and greeting cards; why not carry some? Even if that wasn't their primary business, the income from it could buy more books. Finally, she said, the bookstore should sponsor a series of debates on women's topics—abortion, rape, sadomasochism—show both sides, even have some men in to argue their side of things. It was a great store, but why not bring it up to date?

After these offerings, delivered in her compellingly low voice, Christine leaned her chair back, hooked her thumbs in her jeans pockets, and waited.

The collective was as stirred up as if an aviatrix had just landed in its midst. The younger members' faces brightened; they seemed to buzz.

Janey and Denise glanced at each other. They and easy-going Dorothy were the only members of the original collective left.

"If you need some guy to speak, I know a professor who'd argue that rape is a symbol of 'man's need to communicate.' " Pat laughed dryly. Twenty and still at City College, she sat with her thin legs apart, her thumbs hooked, like Christine's, into her jeans.

There were sounds of dismay.

"Are you suggesting we invite a man like that to speak here at the bookstore?" Teresa asked Christine. "Are you crazy?" Teresa was small, dark-eyed, and well-muscled. A crack roller-skater in Golden Gate Park on Sundays, she sometimes skated to the bookstore for her Saturday shift. She'd come flying up to the door that night, spun around, and skated in, cheeks flushed, dark hair flying.

Christine continued to balance on the back legs of her chair. "I was thinking more along the lines of Margaret Terry."

"Margaret Terry!" They all knew who she was: an Englishwoman currently in New York, author of a recent bestseller called *Grain of Truth*. In it she acknowledged, in snazzy, articulate terms, that there was some truth to the patriarchal myths other feminists hated: "All a woman needs is a good fuck," "Women ask for rape," "Women are irrational," "Abortion is murder," and "A woman's place is in the home." Janey had hoped the book would not do well at the store, but she'd been disappointed. Controversy always helped sales.

Denise spoke with her usual authority. "No, thanks. She's not in our league. She's Masonic Auditorium."

"She might come here. She owes me a favor," Christine said.

Janey shook her head; her hair was short and tinged with grey now. "She purports to be a feminist, and maybe she is, but she couldn't do worse for the movement. The male press love her. I wouldn't want to ask her here."

"But what Christine was suggesting was we'd set it up as a debate," Pat explained, rummaging in her bookbag for a paper and pencil. "We wouldn't be endorsing her. I've got a friend who's pro-choice who'd love to have a go at Margaret Terry. I'll give you her name," she said to Christine.

Denise said tiredly, "This debate idea is not okay by me."

"Oh, but I saw Margaret Terry on TV and she does have something to say." Cool, shy Anna, who produced beautiful designs at her layout desk, had left her husband four months ago on a Wednesday and shown up to volunteer at the bookstore Thursday after work. "Not that I agree with her, of course."

Janey thought quickly. "You know what I think you should do?" she said to Christine. "If you're interested in this woman, call her agent and see if she's scheduled to come out here. Mention your debate idea. Maybe they'll like it. Once you get something lined up, come back and talk to us then."

Christine frowned. "So you want me to get this going?"

"It's your baby," Denise said. "But don't use the bookstore name. That would be misrepresentation. We have a collective system here. We all have to agree."

Christine smiled and looked around the room. "Funny. I wouldn't have picked this for a collective."

"Well, it is," Denise informed her.

"Why doesn't it seem like one?" Teresa frowned.

"Janey and Denise act like they own this place. Is that how it's set up?"

There was a confused jumble of sound.

"That seems a bit strong." Jennifer, who was coordinating the meeting, frowned at the interloper. Jennifer wore a T-shirt saying, "My body's bigger than yours," and five thin gold rings in her right ear, which she fingered nervously.

"I do own the store," Denise announced. "That's common knowledge."

"She owns it," Janey explained, "but only on paper. It's in trust for the women's community. If we make any money, it goes back into the store. All our policy decisions are by consensus."

"Everyone has an equal voice?"

"Not only that, we have to agree."

"But before you have to agree, there's some discussion." Janey nodded.

"Then I'd like to hear more discussion on my suggestions."

There was silence. Christine tilted her chair back again, one booted foot crossed over her knee.

"I don't think it's fair to pick on Janey and Denise."
Helen was a warm and energetic woman from Taiwan who
had started the store's Asian-American section. "Without
them, we wouldn't have the store at all."

The others murmured assent.

"But still," Anna said tentatively, "coming from outside,
Christine may see something we don't. I think it's important
to discuss this. I know I sometimes don't bother suggesting
something because I know Janey and Denise won't like it."

Janey looked at her in surprise. "But, Anna, what
don't you suggest?"

Anna shrugged. "Oh, about redoing the catalog and..."
She considered. "Changing our sign. Things that you'd say
we couldn't afford."

"Even though they might bring the store new customers,"
Christine pointed out.

"I do the same as you." Teresa reached across Jennifer
to touch Anna's knee through her flowered skirt. "I have
an idea and then I think, no, I shouldn't waste time talking
about my idea because Janey and Denise won't like it
anyway."

"Well, it's a shame you feel that way, there's no need,
but you're still new," Janey told them. "It makes sense that
when you first join you're feeling your way but then later
it's, uh..." Her voice trailed off as she looked at the others.
"No? Am I wrong? Kirsten?"

Kirsten had been with the bookstore for almost two
years. Her large hands were always stained with paint and
glue from the collages she made. She looked at Janey and
picked nervously at a spot of glue. "It's a manner you
have," she said, "as if you've been through everything
already. It's patronizing. Denise kids around or dozes off.
You're so focused, trying to get us all to approve whatever
you want to do for the store. It's easier just to agree."

Janey was stunned. "But we spend hours discussing
things!"

"But you don't really listen to our ideas."

"Yes, I do. What ideas haven't I listened to?"

"Discounts for poor women," Teresa reminded her.

Janey flushed. "We can't afford it and we could never
administer it fairly. You know that, Teresa," she appealed.

"I think women are able to do anything they want to
do," Teresa said feelingly, her dark eyes earnest, her small,

strong body poised on the edge of her chair. "All that's required is hard work."

Denise leaned forward, her hands on her thighs, and looked meaningfully at Janey.

"Even with hard work, some things aren't possible." Janey meant to speak persuasively but she cringed hearing her own voice: oily, somehow, and righteous.

A truck rumbled by the front of the store. "Another thing you didn't listen to was selling crafts." Kirsten fidgeted.

"I did but—"

Denise fluffed up her large mass of hair and shifted her weight. "This is a bookstore and we sell books. That's why we exist: books. We don't have room for crafts."

Pat adjusted her body so her breasts were apparent through her cotton shirt. "I've been thinking. Books are really pretty male when you get down to it. Who controls the publishing industry, after all? Crafts are things you can use, things made by real women." She glanced at Christine.

"Right on," Christine said.

"Books are precious things," Janey protested. "They're not male. What are you doing here if you don't care about books, Pat?"

"I just meant—"

Jennifer raised her voice. "I'm having a severe case of *deja vu* at the moment. We've been through these discussions."

Janey frowned, pushed her glasses up on her nose. The back room where they sat smelled vaguely of Lysol. "I don't know what's going on here. All this dissatisfaction is news to me." She was beginning to feel scared. She knew Denise had had misgivings about the current collective. Every combination of women had its own character and this one had already shown signs of impulsiveness, of "refusing to listen to their elders," as Denise called it.

"I think we need to schedule a gripe session."

"That's one way of avoiding the issue," Christine said.

"Will you kindly keep your mouth shut for one minute?" Denise tapped her large foot angrily. "This is delicate business."

"How do we feel about a gripe session?" Jennifer asked.

"I wanted to say one more thing. I don't know if this is the time, but I've been wondering if Janey is always going to have one of the full-time jobs," Anna said in her high, clear voice. "I know she—" She looked at Janey. "You are very good at it, but others of us deserve a chance."

Janey swallowed. For a minute she thought she'd lost her voice. Then it came out high and panicky. "This is my job you're talking about, Anna. You can't just—"

"How about Sunday at seven?" Denise interrupted, looking pointedly at Jennifer.

"Yes, let's have some input on that," Jennifer flicked her earrings and steered them to safety. "Denise has suggested Sunday at seven for the gripe session. Any objections?"

Ellen's voice came excitedly from the kitchen as Janey walked in, something about the Human Face. When Janey didn't answer, Ellen came down the hall into the half-lit living room and peered at her lover. "What's wrong, sweetheart?"

"They're turning against me at the bookstore," Janey said in a dead voice.

"That's ridiculous. You *are* the bookstore."

"Apparently not."

"Oh, sweetheart." Ellen tried to take Janey in her arms, but Janey didn't respond. From out on the sidewalk and behind the peach-colored drapes a woman's laugh got louder, then faded away as she passed. "Those snots," Ellen said, stepping back a little, her hands on Janey's arms. Ellen's pale face was lined and tired, and she now wore glasses from her years of computer work.

"I thought you were one big happy family."

"I did too."

"Denise didn't—"

"Not Denise." Janey told her what had happened.

"Is Christine the one who makes collages out of pubic hair?"

"That's Kirsten and it's not pubic hair!" Janey said irritably, impatient at Ellen's inability to get the details of the bookstore clear when she had no problem with her infinite numbers, formulas, coefficients, and differentials. "Christine's the new one. I told you."

"Those snots."

"They're not snots. They're just young and want to see their ideas implemented. Can't you understand?"

198

Ellen's mouth twitched, but she responded sympathetically, "Anyway, Denise owns the store."

"It's not that simple." Janey's voice rose. "Women don't necessarily value that kind of ownership these days. It's a male construct."

Ellen sighed and raised her arms to rub the back of her neck under her dark, curly hair. She wore a faded blue workman's shirt and jeans stained with ink from one of Roger's old daisy wheel printers. "Still, I assume she does own it," she said tiredly.

Janey led the way down the hall into the kitchen. "That sly Anna practically asked me to resign and hand over my job to her."

There was a plate of Janey's favorite black-bottom cupcakes on the blue Formica table, the empty bag from the store still beside it. Ellen held out the plate but Janey frowned and shook her head. Ellen took a cupcake. "I thought you liked each other."

"Oh, I'm sure she'd say she likes me." Janey imitated Anna. " 'And I just wonder whether Janey's always going to have her job.' Ellen, you shouldn't eat so much sugar," she added.

"What a snake in the grass."

"She was one that was pushing this stupid idea of Christine's for a debate." Janey told Ellen about Margaret Terry.

"She can't be that famous, I never heard of her."

"You've never heard of anybody anymore." Janey rubbed her forehead anxiously. "I can't stand this debate idea. It conflicts with everything I believe in."

Ellen murmured sympathetically, finishing off her cupcake.

"And I thought they were my friends!" At the word "friends," Janey's eyes teared up. She remembered having dinner a month before with the others from the collective. They'd laughed over the teenage waiter's "You girls—gals—women want something to drink?" Anna confiding she'd been attracted to a woman, the others soft-eyed, delighted for her, Janey happy in the midst of all their intimate, female energy. The precise feeling: central, respected, loving, loved.

"Damn!" She fended off her tears by slamming the breakfast dishes from the counter into the sink, starting to wash them furiously. "You were supposed to do the dishes, not run out for cupcakes."

"Don't take it out on me," Ellen protested.

"They don't know how to run a store. Who's going to pay the invoices? Who knows how to order? It's all idealism." An orange mug knocked against the dish drainer and crashed onto the red linoleum, breaking. "Oh!" Janey covered her face with her wet hands.

This time she leaned into Ellen when Ellen moved to embrace her. Her body softened. "There, there." Ellen stroked Janey's back. "It'll be okay."

"They said I was 'patronizing,' " Janey sobbed.

"I'm sure that's the 'in' word these days. Anyone who knows anything is called 'patronizing.' "

"They said I don't listen to their ideas." Ellen started to respond, but Janey disengaged herself to take a cupcake and bite into it. "That's so wrong. We spend hours discussing their ideas!"

"I know, sweetheart."

"Denise warned me about this group."

"Too young," Ellen suggested.

"No, it's that relative to us...I don't know." She was silent.

A minute later she suddenly burst out, "It is my store, after all. It's practically my whole life."

"I know."

"I don't know what I'm going to do. It's so scary, Ellen."

"Sweetheart, this'll pass."

"No, they don't like me," Janey said hopelessly. "I'm like a parent or a teacher who won't let them do anything they want. You know, when some woman says, 'I'm my daughter's best friend,' and you know that can't be true? I'm like that deluded mother."

"Janey, Janey," Ellen soothed her. "You're going off the deep end with this. They probably just needed to let off steam. Tomorrow everything'll be fine."

"No." Janey shook her head against Ellen's shoulder. "This happened at the co-op and the switchboard. It's happening all over to collectives." Ellen held Janey around the waist, Janey leaned back and stroked a pale ink stain on Ellen's shirt with her chocolate fingers. "It signals something terrible for the movement," she said tearily.

"You're engaged in a grand experiment. Of course there'll be setbacks. There always are. We've had setbacks all along in my work, you know that."

Janey didn't like hearing the two worlds compared, but she nodded. "Maybe our premises are all wrong. Maybe collectives can't work," she said.

"Maybe not," Ellen echoed.

"You don't think so?"

"Janey, I don't know."

Janey slumped at the table. "I know. This isn't your thing." She sniffled. "I shouldn't unload it all on you."

Ida lay her chin on Janey's knee and looked up soulfully. Janey patted her black head. "Your mommy may be out of a job again," she told the dog mournfully.

Ellen corrected her. "Don't listen to that nonsense. The only way she'll be out of a job is if she gives it up. Which is a financial possibility," Ellen added, "considering what happened today."

Janey looked up. She saw now that Ellen had a different air about her. She wasn't biting her nails, for one thing. And she'd been unusually sympathetic, now that Janey thought about it, not distracted and touchy as she often was. "I forgot. You were excited about something when I came in."

"I don't want to go into my thing until we've finished yours. Are you sure you're okay?"

Janey nodded tiredly, although "okay" seemed eons away.

Ellen's excitement broke through. She grabbed the back of one of the kitchen chairs, her eyes gleamed, and her voice sped up. "The most amazing thing! We changed one of the routines today and Albert suddenly started recognizing us like mad—we're not even completely sure why! The Human Face is going to be a big success!"

Janey wrenched her attention onto Ellen. "Gee, that's great!" She knew that Albert was the name they'd given their invention. The idea that he was "recognizing them like mad" sounded ominous, like a scene from science fiction where the monster suddenly comes to life and destroys the laboratory. Somehow, despite nearly eight years of work, she had assumed Albert would never live and breathe. "Gee, honey, that's great," she repeated, pretending enthusiasm.

"Even Roger jumped up and down a bit. You remember I told you about the normalization routine? Aside from that and the exit module, we're done. I called Arthur and told him he could start to look for buyers. He's pleased as punch."

"Wow! Well, congratulations," Janey said, but she couldn't really rejoice. She dutifully sat and ate another cupcake and drank tea with Ellen, but it was a strange celebration: Ellen periodically remembering to look sympathetically at Janey, Janey feeling worse and worse. In bed, with Ellen sleepily holding her, she dreamt fitfully of Albert rising from his laboratory table, of herself struggling against him, of Teresa and Pat and Kirsten and Anna watching motionless from the sidelines as she grew smaller and smaller in his grasp.

Janey walked into the store warily the next morning. Anna was already there, arranging red and pink gladioluses in a tall, light green vase.

"Those are lovely," Janey said brightly.

"Yes, I love glads." Their eyes met and they smiled awkwardly.

Janey checked the cash drawer; they would open in ten minutes. She made a few phone calls: a theater group wanting to perform at the bookstore, the landlord about a rent hike, one of their distributors who was changing procedure. These were all business matters the collective hadn't gotten to the night before. She left messages that she'd call again in a week.

The morning was slow as usual. At one point Janey was sorting mail into piles and Anna said, "Maybe I could do that."

"Oh!...Sure!"

Janey explained: these were bills to be paid right away because the creditor was important to the store; these could wait; this stuff was plain old junk mail; this should be glanced at since a wealthy woman who had once sent a donation to the store was on the board of this organization; these were business letters to be handled by Dorothy. The rest—catalog orders and personal requests—Janey usually looked at. They worked together, Anna doing what she could, Janey the rest.

At noon, Teresa joined them to go over the "returns": books to be returned to the publisher because they hadn't sold fast enough. The three women sat at a battered kitchen table in the back room, going over their lists and eating egg salad sandwiches Teresa had picked up on her way over. Dollops of salad plunked onto the waxed paper. Teresa said she couldn't bear to return several of the books she particularly liked.

"We'll sell them eventually," she said. "It just takes time."

Janey warned, "We have this same discussion every time. If we don't return them now, we won't get credit. We've got to treat these like any other books. We can't play favorites. Having a firm returns policy is why this store has stayed in business." She tried to control the rising note of frustration in her voice.

"But have we tried another kind of policy?" Teresa asked.

"Yes, at first, and we got in trouble."

"You've tried it but the rest of us haven't," Teresa pointed out. She brightened. "Maybe we can feature these slow-moving books more, call people's attention to them."

"We tried that."

Teresa and Anna were silent. They seemed downcast.

"Believe me," Janey said.

"We know, you've told us," Teresa said glumly.

"If you want to try again, let's keep back that one then," Janey suggested, pointing to the book in Teresa's hand.

"All right." They smiled.

"If we're keeping that one, we should keep this one too." Anna picked up another.

"Okay. We'll see how they do. They can be test cases," Janey agreed, although privately she wrote them off as a loss.

"Hey, I'm going to push these books," Teresa vowed. "Get them out where customers can see them. Do a poster or something. Just wait and see."

Two nights later Janey called Denise. "I have an idea."

"What?"

"We show our good faith by transferring ownership to the collective. Then we come up with some terms—no one stays more than five years. After five years, no matter who you are or how valuable you feel, you leave."

"No way."

Janey was silent.

"The store'll go down the drain."

"Not necessarily."

"You're suggesting you and Dorothy and I voluntarily bow out and turn it over to that motley crew? You're crazy."

"We don't exactly bow out."

"Aha!"

"The three of us stay one more year. Enough to train the others and find work."

Denise was silent. "I hope this is just a temporary attack of nobility."

"Power corrupts."

"Oh, please," Denise groaned. "Spare me."

"There's something about that jazzed-up, my-time-is-so-important feeling I'm starting to suspect. Other people can do what we do, Denise."

"Don't I wish. You've taken flak before. This'll pass."

"No one's ever suggested I give up my job before."

"We'll give Anna some more hours. How about Thursday nights?"

"Won't you think about this?"

"Janey, this is one hour, one night, out of eight years!"

"You know it's happening all over, collectives are breaking up. We've just been lucky."

"I don't think it'll work. They've no business sense. They don't know how to order. They don't *want* to know how to order. They want to follow every idealistic or selfish whim. This debate idea—that Terry woman would make mincemeat of any radical that bunch'll come up with. All Pat can think of, what do you bet, is 'What's Christine like in bed?' Kirsten wants to sell her collages—that's why she's so big on crafts. Anna wants a taste of power. And Teresa! She'd have us bankrupt in no time flat."

Janey laughed tiredly. "Listen to what you're saying. That's why they don't want us around. We're constantly dismissing them."

"Jennifer and Helen are fine."

"Think about it."

"You know what you need? A vacation. Why don't you get Ellen to take a week off? Go up to the country. Think about all this. Come to your senses."

"I'm going to bring this up on Sunday, Denise."

"I'm not going along with it. You're going to make me the bad guy?"

Janey winced. "I don't want to do that."

"Then keep it under your hat for now. If you're still feeling the same way in a month, I'll go along with you."

"You will?" Janey's heart turned over. "Honestly?"

"Yeah. But I think you'll come to your senses."

Janey twisted the phone cord. She was sitting at the kitchen table. In front of her lay some photos: pictures of the store, the women of the first collective cheering as the sign "Womanbooks" went up, Rita delivering a speech to the Women's Foundation, Janey and Denise cutting the huge, coffee-colored, one-year birthday cake. Janey asked, "How do we handle things on Sunday then?"

"Calm, cool, and collected," Denise said. "We'll try to do better. The consensus method is worth fighting for. Women together can do anything. And so forth."

Janey rubbed the place over her heart. She looked at the birthday cake picture. Denise had looked softer then; so had she. They appeared to have tears in their eyes. "Remember how idealistic we used to be?"

"Were we? I thought you and I always had our feet pretty much on the ground."

Denise attempted to manage the gripe session in her old quick-thinking, throw-your-weight-around style, but she and Janey emerged shaken. No one was intentionally cruel. The words "racist," "hierarchical," "ageist," and "condescending" were spoken in earnest tones. The general thrust was that everyone should have a chance to set policy and it was pointed out that even the presidency of the United States was limited to eight years. The main gripe was not against Denise but Janey, who, as one of the two full-time workers (Helen was the other), was seen as controlling the store by virtue of her years of experience, conscientiousness, and conservatism. Anna, Kirsten, Teresa, and Pat did not like feeling Janey was their boss. Given more responsibility, they made clear, they would do things differently. Throughout the discussion, Jennifer, Dorothy, and Helen murmured support for Janey, but only Denise spoke eloquently on her behalf and Denise's words no longer seemed to count for much.

Janey had her turn to gripe but she hardly spoke. The ground was falling from under her. Once, when Anna called her "elitist," she felt furious—her eyes blazed, her body trembled—but Denise silenced her with a warning glance and all Janey did was nod, her lips tight.

"If we persevere through this, take it easy, and try not to hurt each other, I suspect we're going to reap some real benefits," Denise concluded finally, managing to sound as if this strained situation was just exactly what was needed.

Everyone nodded, stood up, and hugged each other. Try as she would, Janey could not trust the friendly look in anyone's eyes.

The next few days she felt muted and careful, helping the others, answering questions. Anything spontaneous in her was in hiding. The store was no longer a safe and comfortable place. At the Monday night open meeting, Christine was back with her charismatic energy and disruptive remarks. Janey spoke very little; Denise alone couldn't carry the day. Plans proceeded for the Margaret Terry debate.

Afterward, on the sidewalk outside the store, Denise told Janey, "You can't let them get to you like this!"

"Anything I say, they pounce on."

"Not true." Denise frowned. "Did you ask Ellen about taking some time off?"

"No. But she's too busy anyway."

"Go off by yourself then."

A couple of men were approaching. Janey and Denise both watched them with steely looks as they passed under the streetlight.

"It'd be even harder coming back after a vacation, with everything changed."

"Maybe. Maybe not."

"I'll think about it," and Janey turned to trudge home down Eighteenth Street.

It was talking on the phone to Jumper in the country that convinced Janey to take Denise's advice. Jumper sounded so calm, talking about her pear crop, and so matter-of-fact, inviting Janey to come up and stay as long as she liked, that Janey felt her shoulders loosen. She imagined standing on a ladder, picking spotted yellow pears; she imagined sitting on Jumper's deck, looking out at the wooded hills.

Ida perked her ears up at the word "Willits," a place where she'd gone various times for vacation.

"Okay, we'll go. Even though it may be a terrible mistake."

Ellen, when she heard about Janey's plan to visit Jumper, seemed enthusiastic. "It'll do you good. I wish I could spend the week there too. I'll miss you a lot," she claimed, but Janey suspected Ellen was sick of hearing about the bookstore and wanted to devote herself to the Human Face.

Denise, who'd orchestrated all this, was pleased. "Those trees and birds always cheer you up."

"You're still up for the five-year plan if I still like it in three weeks?"

Denise paused. "Yes. I said I'd go along with you and I will."

"Good."

"It's a terrible idea, though."

"It's not a terrible idea. It's a terribly sad idea."

"That, too."

20

Ellen drove up to Willits with Janey the following weekend. She planned to stay over one night with Jumper and then return to San Francisco with the car, coming back for Janey a week later. As she drove, Ellen chattered on excitedly about her project. "And Arthur's got a man from the Department of Energy *very* interested."

Janey frowned. "The DOE? Oh, no, Ellen, they're the bad guys."

"What do you mean, 'the bad guys'?"

"They're the old AEC."

"The AEC?" Ellen asked.

"The Atomic Energy Commission, Ellen. The ones who build nuclear plants and nuclear weapons."

Ellen was driving and she sped up. "Oh, well, no, Janey. I mean, they're the ones who bought the traffic simulator." She shook her head. "You and Denise are so into politics you see bad guys everywhere."

"I'm telling you, they're gung-ho nuclear energy and nuclear bombs."

Ellen shot a dark glance out the window. "Well, the Human Face isn't nuclear," she said and then accusingly, "Why didn't you say anything when they bought the traffic simulator? Why do you wait to say something *now*, just when everything's turning out so well?"

Janey shrugged. "I'm sorry," she said. "I know you don't want to hear it."

"You're right, I don't," Ellen said sharply. "Anyway," she went on, "plenty of institutions do things we don't approve of. One can't be too purist. Just because they build nuclear plants. How could they use the Human Face at a nuclear plant, for God's sake?"

"I don't know. But don't start thinking about it or you'll probably find a way."

Ellen sighed. "I'd never compromise my standards like that."

Janey reached over and squeezed Ellen's leg. "Good."

"Of *course* I wouldn't work on nuclear stuff. Not in a million years. You know me better than that."

"Not knowingly you wouldn't, Ellen."

"Not *any* way. You're blowing this all up, Janey. The Human Face is not part of any nuclear anything." Ellen tugged with her teeth at a hangnail. "I don't know how many times I have to say it."

"Okay, as long as you're aware of the DOE thing." Janey glanced at her lover. "Stop biting your nails."

"I'm not. It's just some skin."

Ida nuzzled Janey's neck from behind and she reached back to pet her.

"I know you're down about the bookstore. It probably makes everything look bleak," Ellen suggested.

"Sometimes I feel so awful. I wonder if it's really the right thing to do, going away when I'm feeling so bad. I know I'll miss you."

"If you want to come home any time, just call me and I'll drive up, sweetheart."

"Yes, okay." Janey stared at the dry hills. "It'll probably be okay."

"It's probably just what you need."

It was too quiet in the country, too quiet and too hot, Ellen thought, as she made her way down the dirt path to the privy. All you could feel was the dry, hot, hay-smelling air wrapped close around you; all you could hear was the faint drone of insects. Ida was asleep in the shade, her paws stuck full of small burrs. Janey and Jumper were studying seed catalogs in Jumper's house; they talked endlessly about vegetables.

Maybe she'd leave early and get back to the city. It used to be she enjoyed the silence and the slow pace for a change but today she couldn't slow down. And this afternoon, with Janey and Jumper, she'd felt like they were the couple and she was the odd man out. "Yes, but peas need shade," one would say and then they'd spend what seemed like hours discussing this fact. Jumper seemed to cheer Janey up in a way Ellen wasn't able to.

"Watch out for snakes," Jumper had reminded her as she slipped out the door.

Of course she'd watch out for snakes. Hadn't she been watching out for snakes for years now? She'd jumped at every clever design in the leaves, every rustle of a bird, every curved stick in her path. She'd seen only a dozen snakes in the wild in her entire life but that was enough. Seeing one was like feeling it crawl right into your armpit.

The privy, which Jumper had built years before, was a little shed-like structure. It had no door; instead, one side stood permanently open to a few delicate manzanita bushes. The floor was a foot or so off the ground and the wood siding beneath it was flush with the dry, reddish earth. In the early days one squatted, balancing carefully, over a hole in the floor. Nowadays a toilet-like box could be pulled over the hole. Ellen sat gingerly upon it, breathing through her mouth, reached around and found a roll of toilet paper under a tin can.

She and Roger had only six weeks left before the demonstration for the DOE man. There was still a lot to do. She should be working right now.

Why had Janey had to bring that up, about the DOE? Ellen bit her lip, squirmed, started shredding the wad of toilet paper. She noticed her dirty nails, put the wad in her lap and cleaned each nail with another.

To hear Janey talk, the DOE was some evil agency. Janey ignored that they must do plenty of things other than nuclear. Ellen would have to look them up at the library. Get Janey to help her research them. No, maybe not. She picked at a hangnail, frowning. Janey didn't know what she was talking about.

But Janey always knew what she was talking about! Janey had gotten so smart, so up on everything, it was rare Ellen could tell her anything she didn't know.

Why had Janey had to say that Ellen should be able to think of a way to use the Human Face in a weapon? It was obvious. If you'd read anything at all about that defense plan of Reagan's called "Star Wars," you could easily see that something like the Human Face would be necessary to sort out objects in space before opening fire. Roger and she had even talked about it once. It was a relatively simple matter compared to the Human Face, they'd agreed. Not trivial. Nothing in the field of automated perception was trivial. But surely it must be the Pentagon or the Department of Defense, not the Department of Energy, who was worrying about that.

Ellen folded and refolded the toilet paper. A turd was stuck halfway in, halfway out of her—what a frustrating, helpless feeling. She pushed her toes down in her sandals: "pinch your toes," her mother had said. God, she felt anxious, her heart beating a mile a minute.

Soft, coiled around in itself, brown and tan as the leaves around it, its diamond-shaped head lying on its body, its eye open and on her, its rattle visible in the coils, motionless, huge as hell, small enough to fit in a frying pan, a rattlesnake lay under the manzanita bush six feet away.

"Christ," she whispered. Her insides suddenly went to mush.

At that moment the world of leaves and pattern dissolved and the snake lifted its head, thrust it forward in short, jerky movements like something mechanical, then oozed slowly out from under the bush onto the path in front of the privy. The sinuous ribbon of brown muscle moved toward her. Its black, forked tongue flickered, tasting the air.

"Go away," she cried. She stamped the wood floor of the privy.

The snake slithered quickly out of sight. But not away from her, not back under the bush, but toward her, under her, either at the very base of the privy where she could not see or beneath it. Hurriedly, in a panic, she wiped her bottom, threw the messy toilet paper into the hole. It might be anywhere, ready to spring into sight. For a moment, she crouched, immobilized, trembling, then with a cry leapt as far as she could from the privy, stumbled, caught herself with her eyes closed, and flew back to the house.

In a few minutes Janey and Jumper returned with her. They had closed Ida in the house. At Ellen's insistence, the three women scanned the ground conscientiously, bent over like crones. Jumper went first, carrying a spade. She banged on the back wall of the privy with the end of it. Nothing.

They followed the path to the side wall. Again Jumper banged.

"Careful," Ellen whispered, as Jumper stealthily craned her blond head around the corner. "Do you see anything?"

"No," Jumper said in her normal voice. She moved forward, tapping at the privy with her spade.

"Look, it could have gone through there." Ellen pointed to a crack at the base of the wood.

"No, it's long gone by now."

"It was lying right there." Ellen pointed under the manzanita.

"Probably the same one I saw there last week." Jumper raised and lowered her heavy, rounded shoulders. "This means I have to get off my butt and do something."

"I killed a snake once in Bowles," Janey offered.

"Couldn't you—I don't know—get indoor plumbing?" Ellen smiled wanly.

She hung around for dinner but was so jumpy there seemed no point in staying. "Look, I'm going to head back," she told them.

"But, hon, you said you'd stay the night. Tomorrow we'll go swimming," Janey urged.

"No, no. I'll be back in a week. We can swim then."

Janey walked with her out to the car.

"Listen, be careful of that snake," Ellen told her. "Be sure to make a lot of noise when you go to the privy. Tell Jumper she should get someone to get rid of it."

"I will." They embraced. "And try to find out what the DOE wants with the Human Face, okay?"

Ellen nodded. "I will. And have a good time. Don't worry about the bookstore. You'll see, they'll be wild to have you back again."

"Remember to put the trash out on Tuesday."

"I'll call you mid-week."

Ellen hugged her, said good-bye to Ida, and got in the car. "Bye then."

"Bye, hon."

She turned the car around in the dark driveway, hesitated. Janey stood smiling, her eyes dark and in shadow, her hand half-raised to wave good-bye. Jumper stood in the lighted doorway nearby, smiling too. All around them was night sky and dark hills and trees and the quiet of the country.

Ellen waved good-bye. She felt a pang leaving them, a pain she couldn't identify. Once Jumper's place had been so special; now Ellen fled from it. Her mind anxiously turned from this thought to the exit module. By the time she reached San Francisco she had the details all worked out.

"I should get rid of that snake before Ellen gets back here," Jumper said as she and Janey cleaned up the dishes from dinner.

"Kill it, you mean?" Now Ellen was gone, Janey felt a little awkward with Jumper; they had never spent much time alone together. She had imagined telling Jumper all her problems but now, faced with the real Jumper and her particular kind of reserve, that didn't seem right.

"No, move it." Jumper placed a plate in the dish drainer. Her wispy, blond hair was bleached almost white from the California sun. Otherwise her appearance had hardly changed since Bowles; looking at her still made Janey smile. "I'd need some help." Jumper glanced at Janey.

"You're asking me? I don't know. I might panic." Janey carried a picture in her mind of the snake she'd killed long ago: a sudden, brown, thick creature who'd strayed into the middle of her rock garden. She'd come down hard on his neck with a forked stick, then cut him in half with a hoe, the parts squirming long after he was dead. As soon as she'd hit him, she'd been sorry.

"You strike me as someone with your feet on the ground."

Janey shook her head at this echo of Denise's remark. "Thanks," she said, "but I'm so wrapped up in my own problems right now, Jumper—you know, what with the bookstore and things with Ellen—it's hard to imagine doing anything brave."

"I can probably get someone else."

"Let me think about it, okay?"

They continued doing dishes in silence.

"Damn," Jumper said. "I forgot to show Ellen that letter from Mary Sue and Roy. We met them on our way out West. They're the ones that got that nuclear plant shut down." Jumper dried her hands and went over to a shelf, where she hunted through some papers. "Here, have a look."

The letter was typed on a plain piece of paper with a decal stuck on it: "Nuclear Power Kills."

"Dear Jumper," it read,

> Thank you for your nice letter. Roy and I are sorry it took so long to answer it. Your place sounds really nice.
>
> Things have been moving finally at the plant. We heard Colorado Light and Power is definitely going to shut it down this year! Not that anyone would tell us officially, but we still have some friends at the plant. A lot of people who we thought were our friends hardly speak to us now. They think our going to Washington and testifying about my illness and the baby was some sort of betrayal. They act like, if the plant closes, it will be Roy's and my fault. As if my little testimony mattered when there were so many other problems. (I am enclosing a flyer about the terrible safety violations that are being found in nuclear plants all over the country. Roy and I urge you to write your Senator and Congressman about them.)
>
> Would you be upset if you came to your door one day and there we were? Not to stay, of course, just to visit. Roy said the other night that meeting you and Ellen on your way out West many years ago was a sign. That is the direction that the pioneers and outlaws always headed throughout history. I never thought I'd think of us like that. I would be sorry to lose

my friends here but things are not the same as they used to be.

I am going to try having an injection of healthy "T-cells," as certain of the immune cells are called. Apparently some people react very well to these—one woman we heard about was totally cured!

When you have the time, send us another letter. Give our love to Ellen, too. (We wrote but since we never received an answer, we thought maybe we'd gotten the address wrong. Or maybe she's kept too busy with her computer work—it sounds very important.)

Hope you're fine, Jumper. Roy and I always think of you girls fondly.

Love,
Roy and Mary Sue

"They sound brave," Janey said. "What happened to her baby?"

"Born deformed. Died at two."

"Oh." Janey sat down tiredly at the old painted blue table. She put her head down on her arms, tried to forget everything and let her mind blank out. After a minute she felt Jumper pat her shoulder.

"I shouldn't have shown you that."

"Oh, Jumper." Janey looked up and wiped her eyes. "Everything just seems terrible these days, you know?"

Jumper sat down nearby in her wooden rocker with its worn cushions. Her presence seemed reassuring. "You're in the thick of it." She shook her head sympathetically, her rocker creaking. After a minute, she ventured, "What a change from Bowles, huh?"

Bowles came back to Janey, sweet piece by sweet piece: her garden, waking up in that quiet bedroom with the shades drawn, sitting with Ellen on the library stoop watching the sugar maples drop their fiery leaves. "I don't think back much anymore." She frowned. "I was pretty ignorant then."

"When I met you, you were wearing a navy blue blouse with a white collar and looking hard for a job for Ellen. You didn't seem that ignorant to me."

Janey smiled. "Maybe that's because you were ignorant, too."

Jumper chuckled. "Could be." She pushed the toe of her dirty sneaker against the rung of one of the straight-back chairs. "Do you want some tea?"

"Maybe later." Janey folded up the letter in front of her, put it back in its envelope. "You know what I'd like? To see some stars. Would you like to go out with me and Ida?"

Jumper nodded and stood up. She was tall, with a strong chest and firm, substantial body. "Living up here, I don't think of it."

"But you're so lucky to be here." The prospect of their walk cheered Janey. "When I was in Bowles, I was the same though. I hardly ever saw the sunrise or sunset even though I knew they were gorgeous." She talked on as she opened the door and Ida bounded out. "Look at that sky full of stars. Isn't it magnificent!"

It took Janey a while to stop talking animatedly. Once she did, it was uncannily quiet. There was just a rustling now and then in the brush and, ahead of them in the darkness, Ida's nails clicking occasionally on a stone in the dirt road.

The next morning Janey woke to the sound of hammering. She skittered her sleeping bag over to the window of the loft and kneeled there, looking out. It was an unusually mild, tender sort of morning. The air was still soft and the sky a gauzy pale blue. Janey breathed in the fresh air and the quiet. A few birds were hopping about in the sparse, straw-colored grass looking for seeds. Jumper's fat cat, Siren, sat on the roof of the nearby shed, her tail twitching.

"Hey, you're up. Hope I didn't wake you." Jumper, in denim overalls and a white T-shirt, came into view lugging a large wood-framed box with densely-screened sides and a latched top. "For the snake," she called up to Janey.

"Where'd you get that?"

"Made it."

Janey whistled in admiration. "That was fast."

Jumper nodded, disappeared around the cabin, and came back with a forked stick and a broom handle. "I was thinking about asking this dude down the road to help. He's the rattler expert around here."

Janey nodded.

"Course he's into killing them," Jumper went on. She was putting grass into the box, arranging it nicely. She glanced up at Janey and continued, "Yeah, he's gun-happy, all right. Kind of a macho cowboy."

When Janey still didn't say anything, Jumper glanced up again. "Nothing he likes better than killing something on the first shot. He's really more than I need since I'm going to catch it. I just need someone for back-up and to go for help, if I need it."

Janey considered. "What exactly would you want me to do?"

"I'll show you."

After breakfast, they practiced capturing a piece of clothesline and Janey agreed, yes, she could do it. It took her mind off the bookstore. From a trunk in the loft, Jumper dug out some hard, snakeproof clothes: leather, dense wool, plastic, rubber. Janey practiced driving the pickup on the rutted road in case she had to go for help. Periodically, they checked the bushes near the privy. "We're ready, Snake," Jumper told the blank space under the manzanita. "Where are you?"

Until the snake arrived, they did what Jumper called her "chores." Janey was strong from heaving boxes of books around the store. Still, she hadn't worked so hard since she'd fixed up the house in Bowles. They picked five lugs of pears, dug a shallow irrigation ditch, patched a leak in the roof, and chopped dozens of logs into kindling. Every few hours, Janey excused herself to catch her breath and look for the snake, but it was never there.

"I try not to plan too much for one day," Jumper said as Janey sprawled exhausted on the raggedy, green couch that evening. "But maybe I overdid it."

"No, that's okay," Janey said. "I've forgotten all my troubles. Exercise is good for me." A little later she woke up to the smell of dinner cooking. "Did I doze off? Sorry."

As long as Jumper was around to distract her, Janey was fine. But the next day Jumper left to wire a neighboring cabin and Janey was left alone to face her tumultuous feelings.

In mid-afternoon she found herself among the pear trees with her hands thrust into her hair, pulling at it like a madwoman. Her chest felt like it would explode and she wanted to scream but couldn't. Just making it from one minute to the next seemed more than she could do.

Hot rage overwhelmed her. She imagined how she'd demolish the bookstore women, swatting them furiously with the back of her hand and kicking them hard when they were down.

In the midst of this angry fantasy, a butterfly landed on a nearby leaf. She glowered at it and scuffed at the pale, dry earth and greyish grass. The butterfly flew off.

Janey paced around the orchard, glaring at the pears, most of which were spotted with worm holes. A crow cawed loudly and she yelled back at it at the top of her lungs, swearing. Ida, who'd been sleeping in some shade near the house, came running over. Janey grudgingly crouched to pet her and looked for a while into Ida's faded, black eyes in her greying face.

Shortly after that the light seemed to change: the pears grew healthier, the leaves greener, the earth redder, the grass more golden. The fire in Janey's chest eased and her fists unclenched. A glass of Jumper's iced tea flashed into her mind: she felt thirsty.

This is how I felt after Angie left, she thought, and again when Ellen took off. It was hard then, too, to imagine things would ever feel better, but they did.

An idea came into her head: she would surprise Jumper by cutting down the dry grass around the house with clippers. Jumper was always worrying about fire.

"I've come to a decision," Janey told her that night. "I won't suggest the five-year plan since Denise doesn't like it. Instead I'll step down as they request—that's the mature thing to do—and work part time, teaching them everything I know. With the other half of my time, I'll start a travelling women's bookstore and take it all over the Northwest, bringing books to women in small towns."

Jumper agreed this was the honorable thing to do.

The next night, Janey informed Jumper, "I've been thinking. I'm seriously afraid the bookstore will fail without me in charge. The other women don't know their ass from their elbow about managing a business. It's my duty to our customers to stop them from wrecking the store. I'll join with Denise in her plan to give Anna more hours and power, so she won't want ours."

"Very clever," said Jumper.

Wednesday night Janey called home.

No one was there, but Ellen called early the next morning. "I got to working late. How're you doing, all relaxed?"

"Yes. It's great here. Jumper's a good hostess." Janey smiled brightly at Jumper.

"Did she get that snake killed?"

"Not yet, it hasn't been back. Did anyone from the bookstore call?"

"No..."

Janey's heart sank. After a pause, she asked glumly, "Did you talk to Arthur yet?"

"No, I'll see him today."

"Okay. Well, I'll see you Saturday."

"Sure, hon. Give my love to Jumper."

"I will. 'Bye."

"'Bye."

After this conversation, Janey felt dissatisfied. "We never really talk anymore, Ellen and I," she said to Jumper, but Jumper just looked at her, smiled, and acted like she hadn't heard.

Janey called Denise: not home. She dialed the bookstore number.

"Womanbooks," Jennifer's cheerful voice came on.

"Jennifer, it's Janey. What are you doing there today?"

"Anna didn't come in. She's sick."

Janey was secretly pleased; things were falling apart. "Maybe I should cut my vacation short."

"Oh, no. We're managing fine. You have a good rest."

"Did...uh...the trash get out?"

"Oh, yes. Don't worry."

"Anything new?"

"We're planning a mobile—pictures of women in the community." Jennifer sounded pleased.

"What a good idea!" Janey forced enthusiasm.

Jumper appeared just then at the door. "Snake's back."

"Listen, I have to go. I'll see you next week."

"'Bye, Janey. Hang in there."

Janey hung up quickly, breathed deep. The bookstore paled beside the reality of the snake. She looked at Jumper anxiously.

"Come on, we can do it," Jumper urged her. "We must have caught that piece of clothesline a dozen times by now."

Janey nodded. They began pulling on the thick clothes Jumper had found for them.

"Okay." Jumper rehearsed them. "First thing a snake does when it senses danger."

Janey focused. "It stays very still."

"Second thing."

"Tries to escape."

"Third thing."

"Into a striking coil, an S shape, with lots of leverage. Takes it a minute to get into that position. Then you hear the rattle and a hissing sound, like water escaping from a pipe." Janey pulled on her boots.

"And?"

"It may or may not strike. If it does, it hits whatever is closest, normally your leg." Janey quoted the passages they'd memorized. "It can't get through heavy leather and its fangs may get hung up in clothing."

" 'Fangs may get hung up in clothing.' Great." Jumper pulled on a tall pair of leather riding boots.

"Hopefully we won't get to that point," Janey said.

The women looked at each other. "You should have your pants outside your boots," Jumper told Janey. "Let's go do it. I feel like a kid in a new snowsuit in these clothes."

Quietly, carrying the box between them, Jumper with the forked stick, Janey with the broomstick, they crept to the privy. As they rounded the corner, Jumper stopped and motioned.

At first Janey couldn't see the snake. Then suddenly the leaves swelled, curved, grew ominously plump: there she was, dozing or watching, her eyes eternally open.

They retreated a step and set down the box silently. Janey opened the lid slowly, left it hanging, and moved into place so she could close it with her foot. Jumper nodded at her, edged toward the snake, carrying both sticks. Janey saw Jumper's blue workshirt sticking to her back, incongruous white gloves stretched over her strong forearms. She could no longer see the snake. Jumper's body was in the way.

Suddenly there was a rustling noise, Jumper leaned forward. All was silent again. Jumper held the stick down at an angle. Janey bit her lip. She felt hot all over and prickly in the still, bright, scorching air.

"All right now." Jumper was talking to the snake. "There, there, girl." She stood up again. A three-foot brown rattlesnake with light and dark markings hung docilely from the broomstick. Jumper took two steps toward the screened box and lowered the snake in. It slid under the grass and weeds she'd placed there. She pulled out the stick and Janey slammed the case shut with her foot. The latch caught.

"Hallelujah!" Jumper rubbed her brow with her forearm. Sweat was pouring down her face.

"You made that look easy."

Jumper was all smiles. "A piece of cake," she joked.

The snake had emerged from the grass and was exploring its cage now, trying to escape. Jumper inserted the broomstick through the two rope handles, each woman took one end, and they went up the path to the pickup. Their captive kept slithering up and down the sides of her swaying, bumping cage. Janey arched her body as far away as she could.

"Don't worry," she told the snake. "It's going to be fine." The snake seemed to glare at her.

"She doesn't believe me," Janey told Jumper. "She's giving me the evil eye."

They loaded the box into the pickup carefully, drove the ten miles the snake books recommended, and made their way with the cage downhill through the dry, rustling brush. Once Janey tripped and barely caught herself; she pictured the cage springing open, the angry snake attacking them. "It's for your own good," Janey kept reassuring her. "I hope you didn't have any children waiting for you at home." But the snake had given up exploring and lay silent and resentful under the grass in the cage.

"I was down here last spring," Jumper said. "It looked like a good place, from a snake's point of view. Lots of rocks and holes."

Janey looked around. "There's a nice spot, with lots of tiny caves and a flat rock to sun on. Or that one, over there. Let's put her there." They tipped the box on its side and Jumper pulled out the pole. The snake was moving around nervously.

"I'll open it." Janey found a stick and poked at the clasp. After a few tries it came open but the lid stuck. She pried at it; it suddenly fell onto the ground. She stepped back in surprise, felt Jumper pull her back. The snake slithered over the door, inches from her foot, and disappeared into the brush.

Janey leaned back against Jumper; Jumper's arms held her. They laughed weakly, relieved.

"We better get going before she turns around and comes gunning for us." Janey straightened up.

They took off their snakeproof clothes, stuck them in the box, reinserted the pole, and, making a wide berth around the bushes the snake had dashed into, began the trudge back uphill. Here and there, in the silences between their observations on the trees and plants they passed, Janey remembered the fine, reassuring feeling of Jumper's body holding hers.

"...And so," Janey told Jumper as they stood next to each other that night doing the dinner dishes, "I saw what I really need to do is confront Christine. Stand up to her and fight it out 'like a man.' Let her see how furious I am."

"Good idea."

Janey considered her friend. "Every idea I have you think is good."

Jumper flushed as she rinsed off a soapy glass.

"Don't you have your own thoughts on what I should do?"

"I guess you'll come to the right decision."

"But what would you do, in my shoes?"

"I think you got a raw deal. I'd probably yell at someone and make things worse."

Janey patted her friend's shoulder.

Jumper said, "It's hard to imagine anyone getting mad at you, you're such a good person." She sluiced soapy water over a plate. "I've been thinking about it, your being a librarian and then working at the bookstore. Your choosing books for the rest of us—it's a real generous thing."

Janey took the plate from Jumper's hand and dried it. She flushed. "That's nice of you to say."

"I mean it. I always thought Ellen was lucky."

"Really!" For a moment, this remark pleased Janey inordinately. Jumper's strong body seemed like a ship in the night. Jumper's kind eyes seemed to beckon her closer. Janey longed to be comforted with kisses. Jumper would take care of her, they would fall in love, and live here in the country with their dog and cat. The bookstore, Christine and Denise, Ellen and the Department of Energy— all left behind, a clean sweep. Wonderful Jumper, standing with her strong, scarred hands in the soapy water, hands that could handle snakes and electricity. Kind and loving Jumper: blushing, awkward, lonesome.

Janey moved to touch Jumper's arm but Jumper must have misunderstood. She handed Janey a wet glass.

Janey took it, dried it carefully, and the moment passed.

22

"Our presentation for the Department of Energy man is going to be at Lawrence Livermore Lab," Ellen told Janey the following Sunday. They were sitting on Jumper's deck waiting for her to get back from the wiring job she was finishing up.

Ellen added quickly, "But it doesn't mean anything, it's just where he's visiting." The Livermore Lab was well known as one of the two major weapons labs in the United States.

Janey paled. "What do you mean, it doesn't mean anything? The Department of Energy, the Livermore Lab... That's where the money is these days, you know—in weapons."

"Arthur said the Department of Energy is interested in it as a pure research project. It could have all kinds of uses."

"I know," Janey said sarcastically. "Recognizing someone when they take money out of the bank. I don't know why the Department of Energy would care about that."

Ellen slumped down further in her lounge chair. "I don't know either." It was hard at the moment to remember that yesterday something marvelous had happened—the others had chosen *her* to do the presentation rather than Melody. Sometimes Melody seemed to have been imposed on Ellen as the modern-day equivalent of her perfect sister Patsy. When Arthur had confirmed that Ellen should present, she had felt an enormous relief and pride. She tried to recapture the feeling.

"Ellen?" Janey pleaded. The wooded hills spread out peacefully before them. "You know things look suspicious. Wouldn't it be awful to find the Human Face is part of some weapon? You know, you could easily get another job."

Ellen closed her eyes against this advice. "I know."

Janey sat up to face Ellen. "I know you like working with Roger but I'm sure you can find something else you'd like just as well."

"I could not," Ellen argued. "Do you tell yourself that you can leave the bookstore and be just as content?"

"Yes, I do," Janey lied. "Wait a minute." She leapt up, leafed through Jumper's papers, and came back with a flyer. "This came in the mail yesterday. There's an anti-nuclear demonstration outside Lawrence Livermore Lab next month on the 16th. Terrible things go on—"

"October 16th?"

"Yes. And you know what this—"

"October 16th is the day of my presentation!" Ellen wailed. She leapt up and pounded the side of the house with her flat palm. "I can't stand it." She felt a surge of hatred for Janey and the whole righteous anti-nuclear movement.

"Can't Melody do the presentation?" Janey asked.

Ellen looked at her in a rage. " 'Can't Melody do the presentation?' " she imitated in a strained babyish voice. "I've been working on this for eight years! I helped Roger make the breakthrough. I know the Human Face backwards and forwards. There was a chance Melody, because she's so damned pretty and charming, would get to do the presentation but yesterday, just *yesterday*, I learned it would be *me*." Her voice was loud and angry. "How can you take that away from me? How *can* you? 'Can't Melody do the presentation!' "

Janey nodded and fell silent.

Ellen stormed off the deck.

Later, on the drive home, she said, "I've decided that if there's any sign the Human Face is going to be used as part of a weapon, I'll quit."

"I should think there were signs already," Janey said mildly.

"Don't bug me about it. This is the best I can do."

As soon as she was at her terminal, Ellen forgot all these wider questions and became concerned with how far she could push the normalization routine. It was a huge, lovely thing that made it possible for the computer to rotate a person's face, or make it bigger or smaller as necessary to match the other faces in memory. The hours passed, and she was startled when the buzzer rang and it was Arthur come to take her out for a look at Livermore. With him was the taciturn technician who was responsible for hooking up the camera and voicebox to the lab's super computer. Running Albert on a super computer would make him sound fifty times more intelligent; it would no longer take him a long, dense minute to recognize someone.

They sped along in Arthur's grey Mercedes, past Oakland, Hayward, and into the brown hills.

"I wish this Department of Energy man had thought to see things some place other than Lawrence Livermore Lab," Ellen said. "That place is *persona non grata* these days, you know. There's going to be an anti-nuclear demonstration out there on the same day we're giving the presentation."

Arthur nodded, frowning. When he spoke, it was not about the Department of Energy man, nor the Livermore Lab, but about the anti-nuclear forces. "The passion and earnestness of young people is terribly moving, isn't it?"

"Very," Ellen agreed. His words reassured her. They brought to mind something naive and childlike about people who thought they could go against the history of mankind. She herself hated to be thought naive. "But wars will continue to be fought, scientific discoveries continue to be made, no matter how loud the protests," she said.

"I think you're right. Still, where would we be without that purity of feeling?" Arthur mused. "That same purity of feeling that crops up all over the world and is such a mystery to an old jade like me. The purity of feeling you and Roger bring to your work, for instance."

Ellen was diverted by this compliment. She thought, yes, there was an honesty, an integrity about her love for her work that was as pure as any idealist's. "Didn't somebody once say, 'Mere enthusiasm is the all in all'?"

"Exactly...and yet not exactly, for you have more than mere enthusiasm, Ellen. Your powers of concentration are combined with a gift for public speaking and a patience for simple teaching. I've often thought that without you, Roger and Associates would never produce. It would be a mass of scribbled paper tumbling in the wind."

Ellen thanked him. His praise warmed her, he opened the world and gave her a place in it, a rightful place, a throne at a proper height. She looked down tenderly upon the anti-nuclear forces yelling like pure, powerless children; she looked down tenderly upon the bomb makers, in love with their toy computers; she looked down tenderly at the people of the world, watching their little blue televisions. "It would be a very tragic thing if the human race were ever to disappear," she said, a dreamy melancholy feeling coming over her.

"A very tragic thing," Arthur echoed.

The technician was silent. Ellen imagined how sweetly and simply she would conduct the presentation the following month. The car sped on toward the weapons lab.

Janey cranked the microfilm reader as fast as she could, looking for a January 1971 article on a case involving Arthur Raines. Finding it, she read that at that time, he and three other men were suspected of bribing a public official in a local development scheme. But the case never had been heard, apparently, or she'd have found a record of it in the civil court records. And Arthur's very gracious secretary certainly hadn't mentioned it on the phone. Janey printed a copy of the page, rewound the reel of film and loaded another in her stack of reels, a 1945 city directory for Boston, where Arthur had grown up. Not in England after all. His father's profession was listed as "antique dealer." At age nine, in 1945, Arthur had two older sisters, one in college at Radcliffe. Janey added to her notes.

Although she'd been awed by the variety of terminals with unfamiliar instructions that had appeared on the library scene, she was finding her research skills still alive and well. Arthur was a Republican who had contributed to Reagan's presidential campaigns. He had majored in economics at Harvard, where he'd earned the nickname "Mr. Smooth" (and where he'd adopted his English accent? she wondered), and upon graduation, married Elizabeth Summers, of Summers Electronics, earning a mention in the Boston society column. They had had no children. His wife was an artist; they were often separated by her need for quiet, his for business. He was described in Who's Who in Business and Finance as a major stockholder in Rockport Oil, a small offshore oil drilling company. While he had been active in fighting drilling off the coast of Northern California (where his wife lived and he summered), he had encouraged it elsewhere. He had always generously supported the arts, in honor of his wife.

Janey got up and paced around. She'd spent the past few nights in this detective work and had turned up nothing that had the slightest effect on Ellen. Ellen kept saying, "But it sounds like he loves his wife," and "It's good of him to support the arts!"

"Napoleon was good to his wife. Hitler supported the arts."

At the moment, Janey's own problem with the bookstore seemed minor compared to her unfolding suspicions about Ellen's work. Denise had prevailed on Janey to wait another month before suggesting the five-year plan. Denise was still against it; Janey, although she professed to be for it, was undecided. It was hard finding the others capable of doing things she'd thought only she could do. Anna had learned enough about the store's creditors and cash flow to handle the mail and most of the bill-paying; Teresa had introduced a "specials" table to push slow-selling books at a slight discount; and Jennifer had taken over all dealings with the landlord. Janey was no longer central; there'd been a few evenings when she walked home feeling completely insignificant. Once she'd forgotten her new role and said something spontaneous— she was not sure just what—and Teresa had stormed out of the store angrily. They were in danger of losing Dorothy, who'd taught herself to keep the books. She liked the old order better, she'd told Denise, not because of the new jumble of paper she received with everyone now taking part in the ordering and invoicing—Dorothy could handle disarray—but because of a certain strain in the air that she said reminded her of a wind chime that never let up.

That straining sound, Janey thought, might have come from her own indecision. She could not bring herself to give up the store nor could she do what was necessary to help Denise hold on to it. She marked time, watching the others take hold, watching the store slip slightly into debt. "What is debt?" Christine asked in her provocative, dismissive way, to which Janey and Denise were relieved to hear Jennifer answer, "Debt is when you owe people money. Too much of it and we'll lose this store."

Janey had spent some time on the phone with women from other collectives in trouble. It struck her that almost everyone on both sides of any dispute worked hard, that earnestness was part of the problem. As long as she focused on the store, she worried about it; whenever she was more concerned with Ellen, the store came into perspective: a functioning group with some problems, none of which came close to Ellen's. Janey had come across a chilling sentence in an article on Silicon Valley: "Virtually all the really interesting work going on in computers these days is funded by the defense industry." In her mind, "defense," like "energy," was just another name for "war."

It was past nine. She collected her notes and the reels of microfilm and made her way back to the reference desk where a calm-faced woman was leafing through a book and giving information to a bearded man in glasses. A second woman in a back office was talking animatedly on the phone, a pencil stuck behind her ear. There was a terminal with a note "Broken. Service requested" taped on it. Three patrons waited for help, one frowning, one resigned, one reading.

If she tried to get a job here, would they hire her after all these years away? And if they did, could she stand working for someone else again?

"How do I look?" It was October 16, the day of the presentation. Ellen turned around in the kitchen for Janey's approval.

"All right." Janey buttered a piece of toast and leaned against the counter eating it.

"Sweetheart, don't be like that. Give me a hug. I need it today. This is my Big Day," Ellen cajoled her. "Come on."

Janey allowed Ellen to hug her. "Watch out, I've butter on my fingers."

Outside, the birds were twittering in the garden. Ida chewed eagerly at a rawhide bone.

"Here." Janey wiped her fingers on a dish towel, adjusted Ellen's suit jacket and smoothed it. "You *do* look very handsome in that suit." It was maroon wool over a creamy silk blouse open at the neck. "Do you want my pearls?"

"I'd love your pearls."

Janey fetched them and fastened them while Ellen held her dark hair off her neck.

"There, that's fine." Janey stood back.

They smiled awkwardly at each other. "Wish me luck?" Ellen asked.

Janey's face set, her chin trembled, and she shook her head no. She turned to the sink and started running the water.

Ellen stood watching Janey's stiff back for a minute. She wanted to cry herself, to run down the hall, fling open the door, march upstairs to the waiting group, and, with Janey listening, extend her apologies: she could not do the presentation, she offered her resignation. Janey would turn to her smiling, her eyes relieved, they would embrace lovingly...Ellen glanced at her watch: past time, they'd be waiting for her.

"Why don't you *go* then to your damned presentation," Janey said bitterly.

Ellen picked up her briefcase and left.

Upstairs, the technician was disassembling the camera and voice box, ready to take them out and reassemble them at Livermore. Roger wore a navy blue suit, circa 1910. His hair was cut properly and he was shaved; still, he clung to his scruffiness and was eating a jelly doughnut carelessly, as if hoping it might spill down his white shirt front and paisley tie.

Melody looked more subdued and even prettier than usual. Her hair was a reddish blond and her dress matched it. She clicked around expertly in black high heels, assembling the technical material they might need. The three tapes the computer center had sent over, which contained the set of Human Face programs that ran on the super computer, were stored carefully in a sturdy carrying case.

Ellen collected the notes for her talk. They had decided the Human Face would be the only technology on view: no foils, slides or film.

Arthur arrived shortly. Since he always dressed in an elegant suit, he looked no different than usual. His only sign of nervousness was a slight tapping of fingers against the wooden desk while Roger searched for a journal article on gene mapping.

"What is gene mapping?" Arthur asked.

Ellen replied, "The initial step in creating a computer that can learn like a human child."

She and Arthur exchanged an excited look that said: so that's where we're going next.

Despite Janey's bitter good-bye, Ellen was in good spirits. This was her family, she thought: this boy genius, high-heeled beauty, and dignified moneyman. "How do I look?" she asked them, turning around.

"Elegant, intelligent, and vital," Arthur said.

"Smashing," Melody pronounced. She had acted not at all bitter about being left out of the presentation.

"Like a tall redwinged blackbird," Roger pronounced. He had finished his doughnut safely and found his article.

"Shall we be off?" Arthur asked, with a flourish of his arm.

On the drive out Roger regaled them with stories of his clever chess companions, who were also members of a Suicide Club that left sneakers and outrageously-worded suicide notes on bridges and near open windows. Ellen grew more nervous as they approached the lab. The presentation was not scheduled for two more hours. They planned to arrive early because the camera and voice box needed to be set up and the presentation rehearsed. Meanwhile, Arthur had told them, the Department of Energy man would be attending other top-secret presentations. Ellen's would be the last in a busy round of morning meetings. She took long, slow breaths as she ticked over in her mind the operating procedure she and Melody had set up. She glanced gratefully at the technician: he was highly competent and would do his part effectively. Hopefully Roger would not want to discuss anything but would simply sit in a corner and read his scientific journal.

She heard the demonstrators before she saw them. They lined both sides of the road ahead, waving signs:

MAKE LOVE NOT WAR and DUMP RONALD RAY-GUN and NUCLEAR WAR IS UNTHINKABLE. Ellen swallowed, smiled as if she were part of them, then saw their faces staring hungrily into the car. Their mouths were open: they were yelling for the car to stop, for those in it to get out. Ellen smoothed the skirt of her suit down nervously and looked straight ahead. Arthur drove carefully as the monitors with green armbands and a few uniformed police tried to keep the demonstrators off the road.

"JOIN US. JOIN US. DON'T GO IN THERE!" and "BOMB MAKERS!"

She could see them out of the corner of her eye. They were like angry dragons, these large, willful people with righteousness in their voices. She bent slightly away from the window. She had visions of their blocking the car, swarming over it, dragging her out, and trampling her. She closed her eyes.

"Hey, Ellen! JOIN US!"

At her name she turned. Her eyes opened right into Jumper's. Jumper's face was big and wild through the glass. Ellen smiled tentatively.

"Come on, Ellen, you can do it," Jumper urged. "Hey, where's my cousin, Roger? JOIN US. JOIN US!"

"HEY, ELLEN, ROGER, JOIN US, JOIN US!" The crowd took up the chant.

Roger, interested, craned his head from the other side of the car. "Hello, Jumper!" He waved.

"Kindly don't encourage them, Roger," Arthur said. Ahead was the entrance of the lab where they must debark to procure their security badges.

"ELLEN, ROGER, JOIN US, JOIN US!"

"GIVE 'EM HELL, ELL-EN. DODGE 'EM, ROG-ER!"

Ellen, her hand nervously at her mouth, looked back and suddenly caught sight of Janey beside Jumper. Ellen's mouth fell open and she felt a wave of despair. Janey, too, had her hand at her mouth. She was biting her lip and staring right at Ellen, stricken. She held a sign saying DYKES AGAINST NUKES.

The car moved slowly forward. Ellen's eyes lost Janey.

"JOIN US! JOIN US!"

"GIVE 'EM HELL, ELL-EN! DODGE 'EM, ROG-ER!"

"BOMB MAKERS!"

Ellen sat, twisting her hands, staring at nothing. Janey!

"Bomb makers indeed." Arthur shook his well-groomed head. "We're too old to be bomb makers. Bomb makers are young, eager chaps in their twenties."

The car left the demonstrators behind; police guarded the entrance area to the Livermore complex. Arthur parked and they all climbed out to be examined and given badges. Twenty-five feet away the demonstrators surged and yelled, a sea of roiling, colorful, angry life. Inside a barbed wire fence, the buildings of the lab were low and grey, the grass was grey and sodden, and there was no one about.

When asked, Ellen numbly gave her birthplace, handed over her driver's license. The lab made a quick FBI check on each visitor. In ten minutes they stepped out and into the car again; the crowd of demonstrators was still yelling, this time at another car that had driven up.

Their new green badges were pinned to their lapels. Now they must pass by the guard's kiosk. An older, tired man, he touched each of the badges lightly; his wrinkled fingers settled on her badge, withdrew. Touching it herself, over her heart, she remembered Janey's habit when she was upset, her thumb rubbing her chest just there. Ellen fought off the ache in her throat; she must get hold of herself. Arthur was driving on, past the barbed wire and the gate, past one building after another. The cries of the demonstrators grew fainter, disappeared.

"Ellen, you're the boss at this point," Arthur said, as they unloaded the car in the parking lot outside the conference building.

She straightened her shoulders. Her voice felt unsteady but when she spoke, it immediately hardened into place. Her mind cleared. She saw what had to be done. "Melody, the tapes go to the machine room. Rod, will you show Melody where that is? Rod, ask for Ernie, have him back them up first. Don't let them out of your sight. We'll be there shortly. All the rest of this stuff comes into the conference room." She moved forward, her suit skirt swinging against her stockinged legs. She felt Janey's pearls sway against her throat. I'll talk to her tonight, she thought coolly. Then she turned her complete attention to the presentation.

23

Two hours later, Ellen, trying to appear calm as her stomach churned, smiled a welcome at the four men and one woman who appeared at the conference room door. They were a bland Livermore executive who was acting as host to the DOE man, the hearty DOE man himself, the DOE man's two polite technical assistants, and a smiling, weary-looking female Livermore secretary who would take notes. Two intense young men in short-sleeved shirts also arrived; they were Livermore researchers busy arguing over some point. They paid little attention to anybody, talking heatedly together in the back of the room. A second, rangy, Livermore administrator came in on their heels and with him a slight older man with a squint and a warm handshake: a journalist writing a book on the Livermore Lab.

Ellen surveyed this group as they chose their chairs. In front of each was a fresh yellow pad and a sharp yellow pencil. A tray with glasses and a pitcher of ice water, the ice still visible, sat in the middle of the rectangular conference table. Ellen busied herself checking over her notes, smiled at the tired-looking secretary, who smiled back, then smiled at the balding, jowly DOE man, who also smiled back. Ellen imagined herself living up to Arthur's description: "elegant, intelligent, and vital." She looked inquiringly at

Arthur, who stood up and quietly closed the door. It was time to begin.

"As you know, the path toward a computer with human intelligence has been a thorny one," Ellen began. She had a slow, clear speaking voice with a certain authority. "One by one researchers have let their projects fade away with a parting: 'Much work remains to be done.' "

The DOE man laughed and his assistants followed suit.

"On this project—that of programming a computer to recognize a human face—we, too, have had our moments of doubt. Three years ago, we threw everything out and started over. Two years ago we did the same thing. But I'm pleased to tell you that today we have a success on our hands. One day a month ago we introduced seventy people to the computer. The following day the same seventy people returned. The computer recognized over sixty of them and called them by name."

Ellen paused a moment to let this fact sink in. "Not many of us could do as well."

The audience murmured its agreement.

"Let me introduce each of us before we go on. I'm Ellen Harmon, senior programmer on the project. Roger Grapling is our systems analyst, the brains behind the Human Face. Melody Martin is not only a programmer but our test director. Arthur Raines keeps us in food and shelter—he's our backer." She held out her hand to each one and, as they smiled self-consciously, felt a touch of pride and tenderness for them.

"And now for the fifth member of our team..."

She pressed a button on a control panel under the table and the back wall folded accordion-style along its track to reveal an almost empty room. The left wall of this room was a blank white screen. Facing it was a camera mounted on a five-foot-tall tripod. A bright red necktie was looped around the top of the tripod so the camera poked above it like a black and silver head. Like a long braid, a cable hung down the back of this head to join other cables and wires snaking across the floor. Ellen walked past the conference table to stand beside this contraption. "Meet Albert, named for Albert Einstein." She stood with her hand on the red necktie as if she were holding Albert's shoulder.

"He's a one-eyed fellow. He's got a movable ear...with an on/off switch..." She picked up a microphone on a long cord that lay on a small stand nearby. "Please keep it turned off except when you're speaking to him. He himself speaks from here..." She pointed to a speaker set up at the foot of the camera.

"At the moment Albert knows no one. We've cleared his memory. He doesn't recognize me or any of the rest of us. He's waiting for someone to step into this four-by-ten box we've outlined in chalk on the floor. As soon as he sees someone, he'll ask for your name. Please don't confuse him by saying anything other than your name. I'll show you what I mean."

Ellen, microphone in hand, stepped into the box. She had practiced this an hour before; still, things could go wrong, power could go down, the unforeseen could happen...

The camera began to click. Albert was photographing her, saving version after version of her ever-changing face. He was deciding if he knew her.

Immediately he spoke. "Kindly give me your name," he said in the voice that was uniquely his—Melody's slowed down to a male register.

She flipped the microphone on. "Ellen," she said. She flipped it off. Albert would instantly connect her name with his constantly expanding image of her.

She stepped out of the chalked box, out of Albert's sight. The room was quiet. She walked around the camera, entered the box from the other side, stood in profile.

Albert had never seen her in profile. He clicked at her. Then he said, "Hello, Ellen."

She let out a pleased laugh. The audience, too, exclaimed with pleasure, as if a dog had suddenly sat up and recited the Gettysburg Address.

"Marvelous, isn't it? But, you're probably already thinking, perhaps Albert calls everyone 'Ellen.' Can I have a volunteer?"

One of the young Livermore scientists stepped into the box and raised his hand in greeting to the camera.

"Kindly give me your name," came Albert's voice.

Ellen smiled and handed over the microphone. As the scientist introduced himself, as Albert recognized him, as more of the men joined in the experiment, she felt a comforting, floating feeling come over her. It was as if she loomed larger than anyone in the room, as if Albert's success—for such it was during the next half hour—had crowned her queen. Below her the men played like children, moving in and out of the chalk box, trying to get the better of Albert. One of the administrators cracked his knuckles in excitement. Upon being identified by name, the DOE man slapped his thigh and said, "Damned if it doesn't curdle your blood." The men mobilized their stiff faces trying to fool Albert. They pursed their lips, bared their teeth, scrunched up their noses, and crossed their eyes.

From her commanding place in the heavens, Ellen orchestrated this play. When Albert was successful, she praised his talents. The few times he failed, she guessed why. All the time she kept one eye on the DOE man and Arthur. At a certain point, she and Arthur exchanged a nod: time to bring things to a close. "Let's wind down now," she said firmly.

"What about the other uses of this?" the DOE man asked as they settled back in their seats. He looked flushed and pleased. "The same program could recognize enemy missiles, decoys, that sort of thing, couldn't it?"

Ellen stopped short. "This is really geared to the human face," she reminded him.

Arthur spoke up in his careful, modulated voice. "But theoretically the method could be modified to recognize anything, couldn't it, Ellen?"

Ellen was silent, she looked here, looked there. "Yes, it could," she finally agreed. "But it's really geared to the human face."

The DOE man nodded and conferred with his assistant. A moment later, he said, "Well, I want to thank you, Miss. This may or may not have been the most exciting thing I've seen this morning—I'm not at liberty to say—but it's certainly been the most entertaining. It may prove very useful."

Ellen smiled automatically. She was no longer floating but falling in space. The likable DOE man wanted to send Albert to war.

He stood and the others with him. The Livermore experimenters were deep in conversation with Roger. Arthur brought the journalist up. He asked her questions about herself, she answered politely, hearing her voice as if from a great distance.

"I assume you didn't work on this project as part of any weapons development," he asked her.

"Oh, no. I hate that sort of thing," she told him earnestly.

He smiled and thanked her. Shortly after that the room cleared. Arthur had walked out with the DOE man. Ellen went up to the camera.

"Hello, Ellen," it greeted her.

"Hello, Albert," she said sadly. She undid the red necktie and clicked off the camera.

Albert's innocent eye went dead.

"The Department of Energy is tentatively interested," Arthur told them as they drove away from the lab through a rear exit. He reproached Ellen. "Ellen, I found you a trifle hostile to his questions at the close of the presentation."

Ellen felt accused. "But I *was* hostile," she said. "You know I don't want anything to do with weapons."

Arthur flashed an annoyed look at her. "We all have our personal opinions," he said, "but we don't inject them into our professional lives."

"You wouldn't sell the Human Face to the Department of Energy if it was going to be used in a weapon, would you?" Ellen asked, with a sinking feeling.

"I don't see anything wrong with defensive weaponry. This would be only a small part of a larger defensive structure. A good defense can stop a war before it starts."

Ellen turned to Roger. "Roger, you wouldn't want this, would you?"

"What's that?" Roger asked.

"The Human Face used to recognize missiles in a war."

Roger considered. "We'd have to perform a number of transformations."

Melody spoke up. "My feeling is, if they're determined to use some program like ours, why not ours? It's the best. At least it wouldn't make mistakes and lead us to blow up something by accident. All the Human Face can do is recognize something. It's not a bomb. I'd never work on a bomb."

"Of course not," Arthur said.

Ellen rubbed her forehead. "Defensive weapons are still weapons."

"Ellen, look at this," Roger said. He had jotted down a diagram on a yellow pad.

She glanced at it.

"The transformations necessary," he explained.

"Oh, Roger," she cried. "Don't be thinking about it."

Roger looked bemused. "'Don't be thinking about it,'" he repeated. "A curious request."

She glanced again, looked away. "Take it away. I don't want to look at it."

The car sped along.

"Aside from those last moments, I want to commend you for a splendid job, Ellen," Arthur said then.

"Thank you." Although she was still upset, Arthur's good opinion always reassured her.

"Truly, an excellent job, Ellen," he pressed on. "Couldn't have been better."

"You looked so cool up there," Melody agreed. "Everyone was so excited and you kept us all in order somehow. I bet it was the best presentation they've had out there in the boonies in eons."

Ellen thanked them again. She tried to imagine telling Janey what had happened.

Perhaps the conversion from a human face to a missile wouldn't be technically possible. Ellen leaned back and thought about the diagram of Roger's she'd just glanced at. Her mind dove into the innards of the Human Face and played around with the scraps of Roger's transformations. Part of it would work, that was clear, but the normalization?

She looked over Roger's shoulder at his scribblings.

"What about the normalization?" she asked.

"The normalization." He reflected, scribbled some more.

"That might work. But how about this?" She took the pad and wrote something herself.

"Too narrow, but—" He added another variable. "For the speed."

"What about reflection on metal?"

Together, they bent over the pad, crossing out and rewriting.

"Good, it's impossible," Ellen said at one point.

"But how about—" and Roger flipped to a fresh page and started a new diagram.

When Ellen got home, it was already dark. Janey was not back yet. Ida came to the door wagging her tail. In these October days of Ida's late middle age the rest of her moved more slowly than it used to, but her tail still carried the same eagerness. Ellen undressed and pulled on jeans and a turtleneck.

She started dinner, cutting up zucchini and eggplant, onions and peppers for Janey's favorite ratatouille and measuring water for rice. While she waited for Janey, she sat swigging at a cold mineral water and staring at the news on the small kitchen TV: there was a minute of coverage on the demonstration but neither Janey nor Jumper were visible; nor was Arthur's car, thank God. Ida sat close by; Ellen played gently with the dog's black, floppy ear.

An hour passed. Janey must be coming home or she'd have called, wouldn't she?

At that moment came the sound of the outer door opening. Ellen stood up nervously, turned off the TV, and paced back and forth across the kitchen linoleum. She heard the apartment door open and Janey greet Ida.

Ellen went to the door of the kitchen. "Hi."

"Hi." They looked at each other down the long hall. Janey took off her jacket and hung it on its hook.

"I'll do dinner," Ellen said. She turned to the stove to switch the burner on under the rice water.

Janey came into the kitchen; she straightened the salt and pepper shakers on the table. Neither of them said anything. Ellen clicked on the roaring fan over the stove.

"How'd it go?" Janey asked then.

"Fine. Thank you for the pearls. They're on your dresser."

"Oh." Janey looked around.

"I—" Ellen began, at the same time Janey said, "I—"

"What?" Janey asked.

"What were you going to say?"

"Nothing. Just that I wanted to change my clothes."

"Okay. Yes, better change." Ellen turned the fan off, then on again.

Janey vanished toward the front of the apartment and her room.

Ellen eyed Ida, who was sitting watching her. "Why are you looking at me like that?" she asked the dog. "I'll tell her, don't worry."

The rice water started boiling, and she measured the brown grains and turned the burner down.

"How was the Department of Energy man?" Janey asked when she returned.

"He was nice."

"Really?" Janey raised her eyebrows. "I pictured him with horns."

They smiled together.

"As a matter of fact," Ellen said, "he does have a set of horns." She felt shaky, wanted to throw herself into Janey's arms and have Janey make everything okay. But she said calmly, "He wants to convert Albert to recognize enemy missiles. It would be used as part of a defensive weapon, a defensive structure actually."

"Oh, no." Janey looked like she'd been shot.

Ellen felt her stomach turn over. "I don't think a defensive weapon is anywhere near as bad as an offensive one. A good defense might even stop a war before it gets started," she said.

Janey shook her head sadly. "Oh, Ellen, Ellen."

"It's not that bad."

Janey didn't reply. She looked miserable.

"I know you think I should quit. But I like this job. Roger and I worked out some transformations this afternoon—it's exciting working with someone like him. Why should I give up what I like just to please you?"

"To please *me*, Ellen!"

"To save humanity then. What has humanity ever done for me?"

Janey put her palm to her forehead, closed her eyes.

"All right. I didn't mean that," Ellen conceded. "But look what they're doing to you in the bookstore. And look what they did to me in Bowles."

"Right. That makes a lot of sense. You do some idealistic, off-the-wall thing and get fired. In return you destroy the whole human race as well as possibly the planet Earth. Fair's fair."

"I'm not destroying anything. You're being melodramatic."

"You're being opportunistic and selfish."

They eyed each other angrily.

"I can't stand your holier-than-thou attitude," Ellen raged. "I'm always having to worry, 'What would Janey think?' "

"You never give a damn what I think. You do exactly what you want. Damn the torpedoes, full speed ahead."

"What do you mean? You're always trying to tell me what to do," Ellen said bitterly.

"When have I told you what to do?"

"What about yesterday when we were shopping and you wouldn't let me get any more cookies?"

"You eat too much junk food."

Ellen stormed to the cupboard, took out the cookies and began stuffing them in her mouth. "And I'll continue to," she said through a mouthful of chocolate chips and cookie crumbs, staring at Janey.

"You're disgusting!" Janey told her.

"Yes, I am." Ellen continued to chew with a full mouth. She ate as disgustingly as possible, staring at Janey, whose face was set in anger.

Ida whimpered. "It's okay, Ida," Ellen said. The sweetness of the cookies started to pale. She set the bag on the counter. "They *are* awfully sweet," she conceded.

The women softened their stances slightly at this first concession.

Janey grudgingly offered, "I guess you should be able to eat what you want."

They smiled briefly at each other.

"Wasn't it awful this morning," Ellen said, "seeing each other out there?"

Now they really looked at each other, exchanged a long, painful glance.

"Awful," Janey whispered. Her arms reached out and Ellen came into them. "I kept thinking how bad you must feel."

"I thought you must be so ashamed of me," Ellen cried. She had started to feel an ache in her throat as soon as she felt Janey's arms.

They held each other tightly. "It's not that easy, Janey, quitting. I know you're right, I should do it. But it's not that easy."

"I know, honey," Janey said tenderly. "You're good at your work and you like it. It's hard to quit something like that for an idea."

Ellen moved her head around and their lips came together, clung together in a heartfelt kiss. *I want to make you happy,* Ellen thought as she fell into the place where she and Janey spoke not with words but yearning, yielding touch. *I love you, Janey, so much, but sometimes, I don't know...*

They drew back to look at each other. Janey's deep-set eyes were soft. "Sometimes," Janey said, "I feel like I've lost you to them..."

"Oh, no, sweetheart."

"Let's make love, honey."

"But the rice..." Ellen felt too keyed up to make love.

"Turn it off. Come to bed."

Ellen hesitated.

Janey embraced her again, softly. "We'll just lie together then." Ellen let herself be led away into love.

The next day Ellen marched purposefully up to Roger's place. She and Janey had had a long night of love and reunion that was somehow grounded on Ellen's quitting.

"Ellen!" Melody greeted her. Melody's dark eyes were sparkling. "*Newsweek* wants to do a spread on us!"

"You're kidding."

"Arthur just called."

"You're kidding." Ellen smiled broadly. "Roger! What do you think?"

Roger looked up. "About what?"

"*Newsweek*, Roger."

"Hot dog," Roger said and returned to his work.

"It'll be in the December 17 issue. They're calling it 'Artificial Intelligence—Risen from the Grave.' " Melody did a tap-dance step.

"*Newsweek!*" Ellen laughed, dialed Janey first at home, then at the bookstore. "Janey! *Newsweek* is going to do a spread on us...I know, but...No...Listen, Janey, *Newsweek!* How often does a person get a chance to be in *Newsweek*?... All right...Mmmm..." She hung up. "Party pooper," she said to the phone.

"They're sending someone out tomorrow to take pictures and start the interviews," Melody said

"This might mean someone else will buy the Human Face!" Ellen exclaimed.

"Sure! What are you going to wear?"

"Just a sec." Ellen dialed Janey back. "Janey, having an article in *Newsweek* might mean someone else will buy the Human Face!...Yes...Why not? Someone good...Well, at least I want to wait and see...Okay, 'bye." She hung up smiling. Janey sounded mollified. "What I wore for the presentation?" she asked Melody.

"In this office?" Melody smiled at her as they looked at the familiar shambles.

24

Janey and Jumper slogged through the rain. They were carrying parts of a small generator Jumper had offered to loan to a new neighbor. The red mud of the road spattered on their black rubber boots, the rain streamed down their yellow rain hats and suits.

"So she's a big success," Jumper said.

"It's just what she's always wanted. Some women's computer group has her up for a 'Distinguished Woman of the Year' award. Her father was very impressed with the *Newsweek* article—he wrote a letter complimenting her."

"Seems as if asking her to quit at this point is like asking a carrot to jump out of a stew. If the man's world opens its arms to you, it must be hard to say, 'No thanks.'"

Janey avoided stepping on a beetle that was making its way across the puddled road. Ellen seemed to float away on Jumper's words. Lately Ellen had hardly been home, rushing here and there, not eating right, but glowing, burning with excitement. Last Wednesday she'd grabbed Janey and squeezed her so tight it hurt, had showered her with love words, then run to the kitchen for a bag of cookies and sat in bed dropping crumbs all over and talking a mile a minute about nothing at all. Janey had tried to soothe her, calm her down, but Ellen had said, "No, I'm high, high, high, Janey. Janey, sweetheart, I love you, I love you. I'm

riding high. Oh, I'm blessed. Everything's going my way."
She'd stood up on the bed and belted out the song, "Oh,
What a Beautiful Morning," her arms spread wide, her
gestures exaggerated and wild.

"Too bad we can't stick Ellen in a box and take her away
like we did that snake," Janey said. "Somewhere quiet, with
no computers. She has this wonderful, buzzing feeling a lot,
she says. And a floating feeling, like she's above everybody.
She hardly ever listens any more, at least to me."

Jumper's nearby face seemed bigger than usual and
soft. "I'm sure she still, you know, loves you, Janey."

Janey sighed. "I don't much care these days."

They walked along without talking, listening to the
sounds of the rain. Janey was aware of Jumper's solid,
always-there sort of quality. It was why she'd come: to get
away from her feeling in San Francisco that nothing could
be counted on. It was not only Ellen. Denise had once
again waffled over the five-year plan, Janey had argued
for it more strongly than she really felt, and they had
finally, somewhat at odds, brought it before the other
women. At first they were far from consensus. Helen and
Jennifer didn't like it because it would force Janey to leave
and they counted on her; Anna didn't like it because she
hoped for a career at the store and didn't want to leave
after five years herself; and Christine didn't like it because
it wasn't her idea. Kirsten, Pat, and Teresa were enthusiastic.
Easy-going Dorothy was willing to go along with the others,
even though it meant she, too, might have to leave.

"Being willing to throw yourself into something, knowing
you'll have to give it up in five years, is risky, I know,"
Janey had said. "But we women are trying to create a new
world, aren't we?"

There was disagreement. The feminine need for
continuity and stability had to be taken into account.

"Let me try again. We're part of a grand experiment."

Objection. Experiments were too scientific and patriarchal. The movement was seeking some deep, underlying
truth of human relations.

Janey had thrown up her hands. "We want to keep
the store going and this might work. We can't be sure but
it's worth a try."

Christine, at this point, had said the plan might be
okay. After another hour of discussion, Jennifer and Helen

had agreed that it had merit. Anna, however, held firm. She set her jaw and valiantly parried all argument: she did not want to work there knowing she'd have to leave, it was too sad. It was like marrying some one, knowing you'd divorce in five years.

Janey had continued to present her case, using the presidency as an example, but her words sounded lame; she knew exactly what Anna meant.

Now she stared at the wet sprouts of green by the side of the road, she sensed all around them the fresh, green-leafed winter oaks and the taller, darker pines.

After another quarter mile, Jumper turned down a steep, rutted drive to a wet, wooden cabin almost hidden in the trees. A light was on and when Jumper knocked, Andrea, a long-faced smiling woman wearing a red and blue woven shawl, came right away to the door.

Immediately, upon seeing the way Andrea's eyes went to Jumper's face and the way Jumper shifted her shoulders, Janey knew that something had either already happened or was about to happen between them. Jumper seemed tongue-tied. Andrea went on about how good they were to come, how stupid she herself was about things mechanical, how there was a leak in the bathroom and she didn't know what to do.

If Janey had been alone, she would have immediately wanted to help, but as it was she felt stubbornly resistant. Why had Andrea bought a house in the country if she didn't know a thing about basic repairs? Why did she have to sound so seductive talking about toilets? Why did Jumper have to act strong and accompany the noise of her wrenches as she set up the generator with all those manly phrases: "We'll fix you up" and "No trouble at all" and "I'll take a look at that leak"?

Andrea expressed dismay and astonishment: while she'd been away the week before, someone had come into the house and stolen a valuable Oriental carpet, some wool sweaters, a down sleeping bag, and some money.

Jumper seemed truly sympathetic. Janey pretended to be but wasn't. The woman's innocence reminded her of Ellen and enraged her. Plus, she finally admitted, she was jealous: all of Jumper's attention had suddenly shifted to this friendly, sensual, impractical woman.

Jealousy. As if Jumper were hers somehow. Janey felt ashamed and became doubly nice, exclaiming over the house furnishings, the black currant tea, the mugs it was served in, Andrea's shawl. While Jumper hooked up Andrea's new electric saw to the generator and busily began cutting bookshelves, sending sawdust over everything, Janey helped Andrea mop up the bathroom floor. The two of them exclaimed all the while about how handy Jumper was, how smart, how good, how fine, what a good neighbor, and yes, how lucky to live near her. When she'd run out of superlatives, Janey spotted a photograph of a sweet-faced dog on the wall opposite the woman's toilet and they were soon lamenting its death a few months before. Over the noise of the saw, Janey spoke of Ida. Jumper cut the power and her words hung in the air, "...can't stand the thought of her ever dying."

"So hard." Andrea looked at Janey with heartfelt feeling and took her hand gently. Janey forgave her all at that moment.

Janey and Jumper ended up staying most of Saturday and returning Sunday. With more tools from Jumper's they wrenched the ancient bathroom pipes apart, cleaned them up, drove to town to replace a damaged fixture, and fixed the leak. They bought a chain and combination lock for the little shed in back of the house: tools and valuables could be stored there. They sanded and polyurethaned the pine shelves and stopped Andrea from putting books on top of them while they were still tacky.

Once, as the three of them strained to push a pipe into place, Janey met Jumper's eyes. A thrill went through her, something romantic, melancholy, and lovely. She and Jumper, alike somehow, might have fallen in love, might have lived happily together, might have known peace and real happiness...the pipe had almost reached its mate. Janey strained and pushed and held her breath. Andrea, who was only inches away, was red in the face with pushing and the clear skin of her forehead was streaked with grease. The pipe moved another eighth of an inch. "Hold it," Jumper breathed as she struggled to pull the connecting fixture. The three of them were jammed practically on top of one another in the small spaces to either side of the toilet. "I've got it!" Jumper said. Janey felt Andrea's breath against her cheek and the pressure of Jumper's breasts against her arm. Her heart beat faster, as if she were making love with the other two. The sounds of their labored breathing mingled as Jumper slowly tightened the fixture. Finally, the pipes were restored as they should be. The three of them worked their way out of their contorted positions, smiled happily, and stood up to congratulate one another.

"Stay for dinner?" Andrea asked them in a glow of good feeling.

"I'd love to but I should be starting back," Janey said. When she hugged Jumper good-bye, she felt sad. It was as if she were turning Jumper over to Andrea, when really she felt as if the three of them belonged together after this weekend; Jumper and Andrea had pulled her into their own new, hot feelings for each other.

"You'll come again soon?" They made her promise.

"When?" she asked.

In early January, Arthur arranged a meeting at Fifteenth Street to announce that the Department of Energy had bought the Human Face. They were going to modify it to recognize missiles and other objects in space. It would be part of the Strategic Defense Initiative (or "Star Wars" project, as it was publicly known), which aimed to put defensive battle stations into space. The Department of Energy wanted to hire any or all of the employees of Roger and Associates, pending clearances, to work with them on the modifications. Did anyone want to take advantage of this opportunity?

"But what about the grapefruit company?" Ellen asked. They were sitting in Roger's kitchen, where all their meetings were held. She clicked a spoon nervously against the table.

"Union problems," Arthur replied. "In any case, the Department of Energy is our most obvious client."

"How much are they paying?" Melody asked.

"Three million."

She whistled. "What kind of salaries are they offering?"

"Similar to what you're earning here. More benefits, less freedom."

"I'm quitting," Ellen said.

Arthur frowned at her. "Ellen, don't be premature."

"You can't quit," Melody said feelingly. "Who'll answer all my questions?"

"What about gene mapping?" Roger sounded truly surprised that Ellen could think of leaving such an interesting project.

"Roger counts on you, Ellen," Arthur put in.

Ellen sighed. "You know how I feel about weapons. What about gene mapping? That sounds pretty sinister when you think about it. Maybe that too will turn out to be a weapon. A killer robot or something."

"Robots are mechanical," Roger said. "This is biological."

"Mechanical, biological, I don't care, Roger."

"I'm disappointed in you, Ellen," Arthur said. "Bill Cole particularly asked for you to come out to Washington. He needs someone to turn over the Human Face to his technical staff. He described your presentation as 'excellent' and thought you would be the perfect one to do the turnover."

"Not in a million years," Ellen said.

"That's what I told him," Arthur said. "I told him weapons work was against your principles and that I would send both Roger and Melody in your place."

"Smashing," Melody said.

Ellen sat staring grumpily at the tabletop.

"So," Arthur said, "with that in mind, will you reconsider staying on with Roger and Associates?"

Ellen felt angry but she was not sure at what. She stood up. "I don't know, I have to think about it all." She left the apartment, ran down the stairs, and walked for blocks through the Mission, kicking telephone poles.

That afternoon she heard Roger in the next room with Melody, trying to explain the basic theory of the Human Face. At first it seemed impossible; Melody didn't seem to understand anything. But then she asked a key question. Roger answered. Melody asked another good question. Ellen squirmed in her chair.

After a few minutes, she stood up and went next door. "I've been thinking about it," she said, "and I guess I could go to Washington, after all."

Melody looked disappointed but Roger sighed with relief and stood up.

"Roger, don't you hate all this weapons stuff too?" Ellen said, following him back to his office.

"Hate it? No, I can't say I hate anything," Roger said.

"Not hate millions of people being killed in a nuclear war? The earth being destroyed? Life as we know it ended?"

Roger slid into his familiar seat at the terminal. "The cockroach might live on," he said thoughtfully.

That night, Janey sat at the kitchen table, updating her resume. A friend had called about an opening as producer of community events for the library system at large: was Janey interested? The friend had pointed out that library programs might reach a lot more women than bookstore programs, that whoever got the job would be working with three friendly dykes, and that the pay wasn't bad.

Janey had agreed to apply. Discussions at the bookstore were still going on about the five-year plan. Whether or not the collective adopted it, Janey planned to leave the store. A few weeks before, she had had a dream. She was on a cliff, holding a rope to which the bookstore was attached. It dangled below her over jagged rocks. Her shoulders ached with straining to hold it.

Suddenly, the rope slipped from her hands and she watched the store plummet down. But instead of crashing, it landed intact between rocks. At first, when she'd thought over the dream, she'd imagined it meant she must hold on to the store, not let it slip through her fingers. But when she'd told Ellen about it, Ellen pointed out that the store had ended up okay. The more Janey thought about it the more she'd had to agree: the dream was saying not only that she had to let the store go, but that she'd feel a relief when she did.

Now she debated whether to include the terms "collective" and "consensus" in her resume. They had gentle enough meanings but would a personnel office consider them fighting words?

She heard the front door open and close, and a minute later Ellen banged in. "I am so angry!" Ellen said.

"What happened?"

"Arthur went and did it. He sold the Human Face to the Department of Energy. I have to go to Washington and turn it over."

"But you said the grapefruit company..."

"I was so hoping for that, Janey. I don't know why it didn't work out. 'Union problems,' he said."

Janey tried to look into Ellen's eyes. Ellen was pacing around the kitchen, not settling anywhere. "I tried to quit but they wouldn't let me."

"I see." Janey stared unseeingly at the papers in front of her. She was not really surprised. There was no point arguing with Ellen. It was as if they had been marching steadily toward this moment for months. "So you're a weapons designer. That's the truth of it."

"Don't say that!" Ellen looked righteously at her. "I just—"

Janey covered her ears. "I don't want to hear it." She held up a hand. "Let's just take a break from each other for a while. I'll eat out tonight and then I have a meeting. I need some time to think about this." She took her papers and her purse out to the hall, then thought to go back and fetch Ida. Ellen looked up with a guilty, hangdog expression. "Janey, I—"

"Come on, Ida." Janey walked with Ida to the front door and closed it on Ellen's voice.

25

The next week was a strain for both of them. Ellen was busy preparing for her trip to Washington. By the time she got home each night, Janey had already been back from the store, eaten, picked up Ida, and left again. She and the dog did not return till late, after Ellen was in bed.

Always Ellen waked to a moment of panic; for ten years Janey had been there to snuggle with and talk to. Now there was no one; Janey slept alone in the mahogany bed while Ellen was relegated to the second bedroom. Twice that week Ellen determined to quit work—but each time it seemed that Janey was forcing her. Nobody could tell her what to do! She steered her own course.

Her feeling of success in the world continued. Those interested in the Human Face invariably ended up talking to her. To the public, she was the Human Face. A handsome attorney, a lesbian she had met through Arthur, came by for coffee, flirted with her green eyes; Ellen was thrilled.

By the time the week was over, she was thinking that the relationship with Janey was over. In the cab to the airport, she told herself jauntily, "I can find someone better." At the thought, a strong pang in her stomach bent her almost in half. She was alarmed that her connection to Janey went that deep.

Waiting for the plane she took from her briefcase a letter, much worn from folding and refolding.

Dear Ellen,

Thank you for sending us the copy of *Newsweek*. As we told you on the telephone, we had already seen the article—Patsy was the one who spotted it and called us up.

Ellen, your mother and I are both very proud of you. We've received many calls from neighbors and friends about the article. You always had a gift for mathematics. I remember as a girl how you would show us your neat little papers with your times tables written out painstakingly.

As an educator, the question of how a child learns has always been of great interest to me. This idea of the brain as a holistic device— could this not explain the phenomenon of the gifted child who knows more than he's been taught? He is simply more adept at recognizing similarity in situations. He...

Here Ellen skipped a few paragraphs to the end.

I'd like hearing your views on the above ideas.

This she reread a few times. She could see her father's face before her: distinguished, male, clean-shaven. His eyes would watch her directly, waiting for her reply. She drank in this image, these words—they filled her with well-being. Her breathing slowed. He had never before wanted her opinion on his thoughts.

Love,
Dad

She refolded the letter and sat back waiting for the plane to be announced.

The night of her third day in Washington, Ellen let herself into her hotel room. Richly decorated with pale pink drapes, a thick, milky blue quilted bedspread, and four lamps with elegant cream-colored shades, the room looked fresh and spotless. Through the window she could see a streetlight, roofs, city lights, the night sky, a crescent moon. She kicked off her shoes and plopped down on the bed, lay there for a few seconds, then got up again, went to the window, and stood frowning out.

On one of the Department of Energy office doors she had passed that morning, two pictures had been Scotch taped up the night before. One was a colorful map of Russia, the water in blue, the tundra in white, the forests in green. The caption was "Before Proudy." The second was a photograph of the surface of the moon, pitted, grey, and desolate. The caption was "After Proudy."

She hunted the night sky for a way to explain these pictures away. Proudy was one of the men she was turning the Human Face over to. On the surface he was quiet, intelligent, and easy-going.

Did he like the story those pictures told? Did he eat them for breakfast? Did they make him strong and fit?

Had he once been a baby wearing diapers? Had his mother held him close, kissed the tips of his baby fingers? Was he a father himself? Did he play ball with his son on a dusty field bursting with the shouts of men and boys?

She rubbed her forehead. The pictures had obviously been a sick joke. People in this kind of work needed some relief; it didn't mean they were hungry for war and devastation. She was tired; today her confidence had flagged. One of the DOE technicians had found a weak point in Ellen's understanding of the mathematics involved in the transformations; he kept badgering her. The more insistent he became, the fuzzier her mind. She had felt panic and dizziness at one point and had had to excuse herself. When she'd returned to the room, she'd overheard him saying, "...the real brains behind it," and known he meant Roger. She had often referred to Roger in the same way; still, the comment unnerved her.

That speck in the dark sky might some day be Albert: floating, slowly turning end over end, watching and waiting.

Once he was transformed by the Department of Energy, Albert would be powerful and deadly. He'd have nuclear missiles under his wings. Surveyor of the world, king of all he surveyed. Like Ellen standing on the curb counting cars so long ago, except Albert would watch meteors, airplanes, rockets to the moon, shuttles, satellites. He would watch stars and planets; he would see the sun rise in the morning and the moon at night. And if he saw something wrong, Albert, protector of the earth, innocent Human Face Albert, would have the power to start a nuclear war.

She was there, she was Albert, she was alone in space. Nobody knew where she was exactly. They were miles away, filling her mind with images of war. They'd planted bombs along her sides; they'd said, "If you see anything wrong, detonate your missiles."

She had not wanted to realize this. When the men today had talked about how the response to an attack must be instantaneous and how no human could possibly handle the complexities quickly enough to make such a decision, she had protested, "But surely, no government is going to let a computer start a nuclear war!"

Proudy had raised his eyebrows. "It must. We must intercept in the boost phase and boost-phase intercept requires a computer decision."

Albert would unleash the missiles, they would speed toward their targets in space, they would collide, explode. Vast amounts of energy would escape in blazes of light and heat and furious sound; humans would look up and know this was the beginning of the end. Panicked men with set, stern faces would order something to be done; submarines would detonate missiles from the depths of the ocean; they would fly up out of the restraining arms of the seas, the water rising in foamy protest around them. All over the land, giant concealed doors would slowly groan open and missiles rise from the bowels of the earth, straining up, up, their tails blazing, into the atmosphere, aimed at each other—unknowing, innocent missiles, the stuff of the earth turned against itself.

Ellen shook her head and reached for the phone. Her hand was trembling.

"Yes?" A clear, unknowing voice came from the unknowing world.

Ellen gave her home number.

"Just a minute, please."

She heard the operator dial, the phone ring, and ring again. Five, six rings. "I'm sorry. No answer," the clear voice said.

Janey wasn't there.

Ellen went to the dresser, opened her briefcase, took out her papers on the Human Face and twisted them, trying to rip them. The paper resisted. The formulas, the words, the knowledge lived on. Lived on in her mind, in Roger's mind, on computer tapes already turned over to the Department of Energy, on annotated listings, on disks, on back-up cartridges in vaults in San Francisco. Would one day live in reality: Albert in the sky alone, having to decide alone...It was too late to change any of it.

"Careful, careful, Ellen." She sat down on the edge of the bed and rubbed her shaking hands together. "It's okay, it's okay."

"Please, God." She got down on her knees, held her hands in prayer position, and stared up. She saw the white ceiling, the circle of soft light from the lamp. "Help me, help me," she pleaded.

But nothing happened. Waves of panic enveloped her. It was as if her insides were being evaporated over and over again. The sky, Albert, Proudy, the explosion, the light, people looking up, the terror...

They were looking at her, judging her. Nay...nay...nay.

"What can I do? What can I do? I must get out of this."

The phone rang.

Janey! Ellen scrambled to pick it up.

"Ellen, this is Arthur."

"Oh, Arthur. I—"

"How are you?"

"I...what is it, Arthur?"

"Ellen, we've had a request from the Washington people to send Roger on out. Some of the finer points they want covered. I'm sure you're perfectly capable but we must humor these chaps. Roger will be arriving on the four-ten plane tomorrow afternoon. Perhaps you can arrange to meet him."

"Oh...yes. I'm sorry, Arthur." She tried to keep her voice steady. Roger coming meant Ellen had not performed well enough.

"Nothing to be sorry for. You're doing the best you can, I'm confident of that. As I said, it's wise to humor these chaps."

"Yes, Arthur."

"How's the weather there?"

"It's a..." She could not think. "Cold...Arthur?"

"Yes?"

"I'm not doing too well. I'm a little shaky. Do you know they're giving Albert the capability to start a war all on his own?"

"Who told you that?"

"These men I'm working with."

"Ellen, those are technical men. They don't have a complete picture. They live in science-fiction worlds of their own imagining. You should have realized by now that one can't pay attention to the ideas of technical men where power is involved. I want you to ignore what they say. They don't know what they're talking about."

"But—"

"Trust me." Arthur's voice was reassuring. "You'll meet Roger tomorrow then?"

After she'd said good-bye to Arthur, Ellen sat unmoving, the tones of his smooth voice still ringing in her ears.

A strange and terrible thing had transpired. A few moments before she had been half-crazy with panic about her part in starting a nuclear war. Now all that had vanished. Everything Arthur had said about power and technicians had vanished with it. All that was left was the knowledge that Roger had been called in, meaning Ellen had failed, was judged again and found wanting.

A few moments before, she would have gladly retracted everything she'd taught the DOE men; now she flayed herself for having disappointed them.

If only she'd studied the retrograde transformation... how could she have been so stupid...Arthur must now see how truly worthless she was—so went her thoughts. Crazily, obsessively, painfully she hated herself: not for building weapons but for failing Arthur.

But do you want to help start a nuclear war?

The voice came to her as if from outside. She sat up and stared into the distance. The voice had authority, the ring of importance.

"Of course not," she whispered, near tears, trembling, trying to hold on to that solid voice. "Of course not," she repeated.

She struggled to understand. Something had brought her to this point where she could prefer nuclear war to personal failure. And this something was not Arthur or Roger or the people of Bowles, but something in herself. She tried to see.

She saw a skinny, innocent, ignorant, ambitious girl. No, no, "skinny" had nothing to do with it, that was a mother-word, a culture-word, used to make her despise herself. An innocent, ignorant, ambitious girl.

Ellen nodded, crying. She wrapped her arms around herself.

Had not this innocent, ignorant, ambitious girl helped Roger with the transformations, ignored Janey's warnings and the writing on the wall, even volunteered to come to Washington? Hadn't she all the time known the Human Face could be used as a weapon? Hadn't she years ago read an article about the need for a missile-recognition system and thought about the Human Face, even discussed the possibility with Roger?

She shrank from these questions, quavered, tried to drown herself in self-pity. But the voice kept on.

Hadn't she?

"Yes," she whispered.

Why?

"Because I so desperately want to be a success," she moaned. Yes, yes, that was it. She had always hungered for glory, for her rightful place. Her sister had come and taken it.

So badly she wanted it, a special place in the world. She'd give anything for it, build bombs, anything...

"Albert, Albert, I'm so sorry." She wept into the pillow. "I'm so terribly, terribly sorry."

She lay there sobbing, her body jerking on the bed, her throat aching with remorse.

She saw Janey in her mind's eye and felt a wave of love and gratitude. Janey was large of heart and infinitely patient. But no, not infinitely, nobody could be infinitely patient. Lately Janey had hardly spoken to her. Weekends Janey spent with Jumper in the country. Her eyes when she looked at Ellen were hurt and hard.

Did Janey still care about Ellen at all? Had Ellen killed the Janey who loved her?

She stood up and looked wildly around. The Human Face papers lay in a wad on the floor. She grabbed them, took them into the bathroom, and set fire to them, one by one, so as not to set off the smoke alarm. She watched the ashes run down the drain in a cold trickle of water.

Even such a small act of disobedience made her heart beat hard, her lungs feel raw with anxiety. The mirror showed a pair of desperate eyes in a white, white face.

She would not go to the Department of Energy tomorrow morning; she would not meet Roger at the airport. She'd be on the next flight to San Francisco. If Janey were only there, she would throw herself into her arms and beg forgiveness. Janey would help her decide what to do next.

Ellen stood up. A fire, part frantic, part fierce, burned in her eyes. She pulled her suitcase out and, with trembling hands, started packing.

26

That same night, Janey sat at the kitchen table at Fifteenth Street, leafing through some attractive sample catalog pages Anna had laid out. She'd attached a note:

Dear Janey,

I know you don't think we need a redesign of the bookstore catalog but aren't these nice? I'm hoping you won't be able to resist.

As far as the infamous five-year plan goes, I've had a change of heart. In five years I'll probably need a push to get me on to something else. And I can see what you all mean about giving other women a chance. I certainly appreciate your being willing to give me one. It's clear from your eyes when you talk about the store how much you care about it.

So at our next meeting I plan to concur with the others so we will have consensus on the five-year plan. I know I, for one, will miss you when you're gone. I have learned a lot from you.

Fondly,
Anna

Janey smiled faintly. She knew she should feel this was good news. Somewhere inside her she was relieved, but it was hard sorting out her feelings at the moment.

Ida lay on the dark red linoleum, her chin flat on the floor, her eyes watching Janey. They were both tired, having driven eight hours that day, four of them in the rain. A lot near Jumper's had come up for sale and Janey had taken the day off from the store to dash up to see it. The lot was mainly steep and wooded but had a flat building site already cleared within a circle of small, fairy-tale trees. The money left over from the sale of the Bowles house could cover its cost plus that of a small cabin.

Striding around the lot picturing the future, Janey had seen herself living up there alone, driving a school bus, and starting a mobile women's library. She'd had an excited, I-can-do-anything sort of feeling. She'd felt free as the hawks that circled and swooped over the woods. She had flirted with Jumper, looking at her with hot, hungry eyes; Jumper had hardly mentioned Andrea except to say that she was home visiting her family.

But now, home again, she could not hold onto anything to do with the bookstore or Jumper. It was Ellen, Ellen, Ellen. These last weeks, missing Ellen, sleeping apart, staying apart, Janey's feelings had ranged all over. At first she'd been furious. She could think of nothing but that Ellen was a bomb maker. This fact was so powerful, so painful, so incisive that it seemed certain to split them apart for all time. Janey's fists would clench, her throat ache with anger. "It's not as if you couldn't easily get another job!" she'd rant at the Ellen in her mind. "I'm willing to give up mine. Why can't you give up yours?"

Then she'd think, "But she's still Ellen, my Ellen, not a bad person." Memories of their years together would seem very precious. She'd feel as heartbroken as if Ellen were dying.

"I've got to stop thinking about her," she told Ida. "What is there left between us but criticism? Before she comes back I should move out." Janey stalked to the phone, started to dial Jumper's number, then stopped and hung up. What about that library job that might come through? What about the store? She couldn't leave too abruptly.

In last Sunday's *Examiner* there'd been an advertisement for a one-bedroom apartment on Guerrero that allowed dogs. Janey found the paper, started to dial, and put the phone down again, sighing.

"I must want to stay with her," she told Ida sadly. "Crazy, huh?"

Ida roused herself to scratch her ear.

"Maybe tomorrow I can get up the strength to do something."

Shortly, the lights off, the heat down, Janey crawled between the cold sheets.

She had trouble falling asleep, slept restlessly, and woke as if at a noise. There was nothing but the faint patter of rain and an occasional car going by. She lay there listening, staring into the darkness. Uneasy, she climbed out of bed and tiptoed around the apartment, turning on lights abruptly, looking into each closet and behind every door: no one. In the front room, from outside the front windows, she heard a sniffle. She flicked off the light. "Is there someone out there?" She patted Ida's head nervously, stood in the darkness waiting.

Nothing happened. After a minute, she went to the front shade, moved it ever so slightly to peer out. "Everything's okay," she told Ida, scanning the street. Suddenly, she jumped back. There was a person with a suitcase huddled on the stoop.

Janey elbowed herself under the shade, unlocked and raised the window, hissed, "Ellen, what are you doing out there?"

The figure started. "Janey!"

"What are you doing out there in the rain? God, Ellen, someone could mug you!" Janey hurried back through the apartment out into the hall, opened the front door to the building. "You're soaked. Why didn't you come in?"

"I couldn't find my keys. I didn't want to wake you."

Janey maneuvered Ellen back into the apartment and closed the door. Ellen seemed unaware of her surroundings. She peered at Janey intently. "What is it?" Janey asked. She wanted to get Ellen's wet clothes off but Ellen seemed oblivious to the fact that she was cold and dripping.

"I've done something very wrong, Janey. Very wrong." Ellen's voice was full of dread.

Janey felt her heart clutch. "What is it?"

"The Human Face!"

"Oh, the Human Face. I thought you'd killed someone."

"But I have, I have." Ellen's eyes were burning.

Frightened, Janey wished she could hold and soothe Ellen, but there was something wild and untouchable in her. She was like a gull whose wings were drowned in oil. Janey fixed her fear on Ellen's wet clothes. "You must get out of those wet things. Look, you're shivering."

Ellen got down on her knees, looked up at Janey longingly. "Can you forgive me?"

Janey tried to pull her up but Ellen continued looking at her imploringly. "Of course I can forgive you. Now, come on, get up."

Ida looked anxiously back and forth between them.

Ellen smiled, her chin trembling. Her wet hands fumbled for Janey's and held on tight. Dark strands of hair were plastered to her forehead; water dripped from her clothes to the wood floor. "You've always been so good to me...Oh, God." Ellen seemed about to crumple and Janey knelt down, took her in her arms, and stroked her lover's wet hair. Ellen let her pull off her damp jacket, her blouse and skirt, then help her up and into an old bathrobe.

"Come, I'll run you a bath," Janey said. "Do you want some tea?"

"I'll get it. You shouldn't...don't you have to go to work in the morning?" Ellen looked at Janey in consternation.

"Yes, but—"

"You should get your sleep. Let me make *you* some tea." Ellen hurried to the kitchen to put water on to boil. Janey and Ida followed, Janey sitting down tentatively at the kitchen table, Ida taking up her post between the two women, watching first one, then the other.

"Aren't you supposed to still be in Washington?" Janey asked cautiously.

"Oh, it's so hard to tell you, Janey. I feel so ashamed." Ellen shook her head. Tears rolled down her cheeks as she made the tea, pouring the boiling water into the pot, shakily carrying it to the table. "You don't take sugar, do you? No, of course you don't," she said anxiously, then went on, "I just left, Janey. Packed my bag and left. I don't know what Arthur will say." Ellen twisted her hands together. "I'm not going to think about it."

"You really left in the middle?"

"I'm here, aren't I?" Ellen asked doubtfully. They glanced at the clock. It was 5 a.m., which meant 8 a.m. in

Washington. "I'm supposed to be walking into the Department of Energy conference room right now." Her face crumpled. "I saw some awful pictures, Janey."

"Your nightmares?" Ellen had been bothered by nightmares for the past few months.

"No, real pictures." Ellen worriedly described the Proudy "before" and "after" pictures and the vision of Albert in the sky. "I burned all my papers."

"You destroyed the Human Face?" Janey asked excitedly.

"No, no. It's far too late for that." Ellen sank her head in her hands.

Janey felt agitated, stood up and paced around the kitchen. "I don't know how you could have gone on so long with it, Ellen, let it go so far."

Ellen lay her head on her arms. Her shoulders shook. "I don't know either," she whimpered, but after a minute she cried, "No, I do know. I've been too goddamned proud."

"But this is a fine time to see it, when the damage is already done."

"I know." Ellen sounded miserable. "I'll never be able to make it up."

Outside, the rain continued falling against the building and running down the dark windows.

"So Arthur doesn't know about your leaving?" Janey asked.

Ellen looked up. "No, not yet." She paused. "Janey, you don't have to stay with me."

"I can go in late."

"No, no. I mean, why would you love me?" Ellen's voice was filled with despair. "I don't want you to stay with me out of pity."

"Oh, Ellen." Janey sighed. "Don't worry about that."

"No, no, I'll understand. I had an idea maybe Jumper really likes you and you two might..." Tears began to roll down her cheeks again. "Oh, Janey, I know I haven't been good to you. I haven't listened to you when I should. I just thought you'd always be there. I'm not worth your loving me, Janey..."

Janey's throat was tight. "Yes, you are, honey."

"I want to be worthy of you. I do, Janey."

Janey saw despair in her lover's eyes, glimmers of hope, and fear. She felt that old protective feeling, born the first time they'd seen each other back in Bowles. "Why don't you come to bed with me and we'll lie down together?" she asked.

"Oh, Janey." Ellen stumbled up and then knelt beside Janey, burying her face in Janey's lap, wrapping her arms around her.

Ida tried to get her head in Janey's lap, too.

"Come on," Janey said, half-laughing at the dog. The two women stood up and held on to each other. "You've done a good thing," Janey said.

"But too late."

At eight that morning, Ellen, sleepless and wired, called Arthur at home.

"Arthur?"

"Speaking."

"It's Ellen."

"Yes, Ellen. How are you this morning? A remarkably clear connection. You sound like you're next door."

"I'm home. I decided to quit after all."

"To quit?"

"Yes. I flew back last night. The Department of Energy people are probably wondering where I am."

Silence. Arthur's voice was tight. "Am I to understand that you simply left this project in midstream?"

Ellen swallowed. "Yes. I always told you I didn't want to work on weapons."

Another silence. "What a child you are."

"I don't think so." Ellen's voice wavered.

"This 'decision' of yours will be irrevocable, I assume you understand that."

"Yes."

"The remainder of your materials for the turnover—where will Roger find them?"

"I burned them."

Again, silence. A sigh. "I'm very disappointed in you."

"Good-bye, Arthur."

Ellen hung up the phone. She and Janey burst out in excited cheers and jumped around in their nightgowns with Ida, shouting, "Free, free, free!" Ellen smiled, they grinned together, Ellen's chin quivered.

Janey pulled her close. "It's okay. I promise. It's going to be okay."

Janey called Jumper from the bookstore that afternoon and told her what had happened.

"So she came back." Jumper sounded resigned.

"I'm so relieved. I can hardly believe it."

Jumper muttered agreement and was silent.

After a pause, Janey said, "Ellen and I have been
together for ten years."

"I know that."

Janey sighed. "Sometimes...lately...I've been acting
like I'd forgotten it myself. I'm really sorry, Jumper."

"Well, she damned well better stay reformed, that's all
I can say."

"She wants to talk to you. Can she call you tonight?"

"Oh sure. I'd like to talk to her. How is she?"

"Shaky. Full of plans one minute, frightened the next.
She's like an alcoholic coming off the stuff."

"Are you okay?"

"I'm fine. She's letting me in. I'm fine."

"Probably you won't be wanting the lot we saw."

"I don't know. I don't know what we'll do. We'll probably
move away from Fifteenth Street anyway."

"Well, I hope you get what you want," Jumper said briskly.
"I better be getting off now. I've got some," she cleared her
throat, "chores."

"All right. I'm sorry."

"I'm glad she's back," Jumper said unconvincingly.
"Have her call me."

"Thanks."

" 'Bye, Janey."

"It wouldn't have worked with us anyway, you and
me," Janey blurted out. "We're both too nice."

"It would have worked great," Jumper said firmly,
"but, as the man said, 'it ain't to be.' "

Sometime during that night Janey heard Ellen whispering, "Are you awake?"

"Yes."

"Can I put on the light?"

"Sure."

271

Ellen's face was excited. Her energy was high, her cheeks flushed. She said a curious thing, not at all in her usual language. "Janey, nobody gives a good goddamn whether I'm a success or not, do they?"

Janey blinked. "Of course we want—"

"No, no. I mean, people who care about me want me to be happy but they, for themselves, they don't care if I'm a success." Ellen spoke excitedly.

"Well, I suppose not. Maybe your parents..."

"Of course, of course, my parents." Ellen's eyes were ablaze. "Of course, them. But you, and Jumper, and our neighbors, and Marie and Jean—they don't care."

"No, I don't suppose so."

"That's not why you like me."

"Oh, no, Ellen."

Ellen put her hands together palm to palm. Her eyes were distant. "I'm seeing something I never saw before, Janey." Her voice became slow and careful and deliberate. "It's as if all of you are out there," she motioned away from herself, "and I am here." She put her hands on her heart.

"Of course, honey."

Ellen lifted her face, pressed her hands against her breast. "God help me." Her eyes were tearing but alight with whatever was happening. "And we're equal. In some basic sense, some human way, we're equal, all of us."

"Yes, honey."

Ellen sat quiet, tears streaming down her cheeks, while Janey watched. When they embraced, Janey felt herself held as tenderly and lovingly as a new baby.

Ann MacLeod grew up in Connecticut and studied mathematics and English at Cornell University. In the early '70s, she was an activist in the New York City women's movement, working with the Women's Center and the Women's Anti-Rape Group under the name Ann Filer. For twenty-five years she has made her living as a computer programmer. Currently, she lives in San Francisco and works at a local university.

spinsters book company

Spinsters Book Company was founded in 1978 to produce vital books for diverse women's communities. In 1986 we merged with Aunt Lute Books to become Spinsters/Aunt Lute. In 1990, the Aunt Lute Foundation became an independent non-profit publishing program.

Spinsters is committed to publishing works outside the scope of mainstream commercial publishers: books that not only name crucial issues in women's lives, but more importantly encourage change and growth; books that help to make the best in our lives more possible. We sponsor an annual Lesbian Fiction Contest for the best lesbian novel each year. And we are particularly interested in creative works by lesbians.

If you would like to know about other books we produce, or our Fiction Contest, write or phone us for a free catalogue. You can buy books directly from us. We can also supply you with the name of a bookstore closest to you that stocks our books. We accept phone orders with Visa or Mastercard.

Spinsters Book Company
P.O. Box 410687
San Francisco, CA 94141
415-558-9586

OTHER TITLES AVAILABLE FROM
SPINSTERS BOOK COMPANY

All The Muscle You Need, *Diana McRae* $8.95

Bittersweet, *Nevada Barr* $9.95

Cancer in Two Voices, *Butler & Rosenblum* $12.95

Child Of Her People, *Anne Cameron* $8.95

Considering Parenthood, *Cheri Pies* $9.50

Coz, *Mary Pjerrou* $9.95

Desert Years, *Cynthia Rich* $7.95

Elise, *Claire Kensington* $7.95

Final Session, *Mary Morell* $9.95

High and Outside, *Linnea A. Due* $8.95

The Journey, *Anne Cameron* $9.95

The Lesbian Erotic Dance, *JoAnn Loulan* $12.95

Lesbian Passion, *JoAnn Loulan* $11.95

Lesbian Sex, *JoAnn Loulan* $12.95

Lesbians at Midlife, *ed. by Sang, Warshow & Smith* . $12.95

Look Me in the Eye, *Macdonald and Rich* $6.50

Love and Memory, *Amy Oleson* $9.95

Modern Daughters and the Outlaw West,
    Melissa Kwasny $9.95

Prisons That Could Not Hold, *Barbara Deming* $7.95

Thirteen Steps, *Bonita L. Swan* $8.95

We Say We Love Each Other, *Minnie Bruce Pratt* $5.95

Why Can't Sharon Kowalski Come Home?
    Thompson & Andrzejewski $10.95

Spinsters titles are available at your local booksellers, or by mail order through Spinsters Book Company (415) 558-9586. A free catalogue is available upon request.

Please include $1.50 for the first title ordered, and $ .50 for every title thereafter. California residents, please add 8.25% sales tax. Visa and Mastercard accepted.